The Emerald Queen

J.W. Webb

Acknowledgement for:
John Jarrold, for editing
Susan Bentley, for copy-editing
Roger Garland, for the illustrations
Ravven, for cover design
Jason & Marina of Polgarus Studio, for book design and formatting.
Elizabeth Jones for map design

*Dedicated to the memory of Roger Garland the Tolkien artist.
A wonderful man I was lucky enough to know, and whose
sketches like the ship below feature throughout this series.*

Get a free eBook from the series.

Introducing Corin an Fol.

Raiders stole his childhood. It's time he made them pay.

Gray Wolf is an action-packed tale of vengeance, passion, war, and loss. The first in a series featuring Corin an Fol, a man chosen by the gods to walk a dark path.

Join the J.W. Webb VIP Lounge and get your free copy of this exciting tale. You'll find more details and a sample at the back of this book.

Contents

Part One

Strange Roads

Chapter 1 | Ariane

A sudden gust of wind parted the curtains, killing the lantern's glow and extinguishing the sconces on the walls. The drapes were flung wide, and darkness filled the room.

Ariane stirred, blinked, and rolled free of the sheets. Outside her window, she glimpsed the faint hint of stars—a sprinkle of dust in the blackness beyond. She rose, her lean body shaking slightly and her mood edgy, irritable. And scared. There was little Queen Ariane of Kelwyn feared these days, but total darkness was one. The empty void—the realm where the Gods once dwelt.

The young queen fumbled for the nearest lantern, blew on the fuse, cussing and fiddling until the lamp lit, slowly filling her chamber with faint yellow light. A fragile bastion against the night, allowing her to glimpse the crystal decanter half full of brandy on the table close by. She shuffled across, her night clothes shimmering gold in the lantern glow. Normally the queen drank tea but tonight she needed something stronger.

Ariane sipped, wincing slightly as the strong liquid found an exposed nerve in her tooth. She tried again, allowing the fiery warmth fuel her inside. A third sip and she felt strong enough to reach the drapes and tie them back in orderly fashion. Once that was done she was ready to face the awful silent dark.

A knock on her door.

"My Queen?"

Ariane heard her consort's worried tones. They slept apart these days because of her frequent nightmares. Ruling a country came with a price. "Is all as it should be?" Lord Raule of Calprissa sounded weary, resigned. "Can I—?"

"It's not locked." Ariane heard the latch turn behind her and soft urgent footsteps approach. She turned slowly, seeing her husband standing there, his sandy, thinning hair disheveled, and that once-handsome face lined with worry.

"I heard noises."

"Just the wind." Ariane poured a second glass and offered it to her husband. He seized it in trembling hands and downed the contents quickly.

"Are you sure? The night seemed calm." Raule looked uncomfortable, as though a worm chewed at him from within. "The Watch should have reported this sudden storm."

"And that's what we're reduced to?" Ariane said angrily, then finished her brandy and slammed the glass on the table. "A storm in the night can shake our resolve? We who once led armies against the foul usurper in Kelthaine— outnumbered twenty to one. Have you forgotten, Raule?"

"I haven't, of course. It's just—"

"We valiant Kelwynians, trampled underdogs who freed our cousins up north from the sorcerer. We who witnessed the Gods fighting in the sky around this very city." Ariane felt the anger rising. "We were strong then, Raule, but now we're afraid of our own shadows."

"For good reason," Raule said. "Assassins strike in the dark."

"I have no fear of footpads," Ariane said. "I sleep with a knife— remember."

Seven years since the war and the queen's famous temper hadn't improved. Ariane glared at her husband. Raule looked exhausted, but then he never slept much these days. "Seven fucking years," Ariane said under her breath, and poured another glass. She caught the ghost of a smile on the consort's face. "What?"

"You haven't changed, Ariane." Raule took a seat by the table and rubbed his eyes. "You're still that feisty foul-mouthed lass I met and fell in love with."

"You forget your place, Sir—I was a queen then too, and you were . . .what? A general?"

"A lowly captain until you promoted me, Your Highness."

Ariane sipped her brandy and curled a slight smile, her nerves calmed by the liquid. "A generous promotion. I wonder what came over me."

"We were short staffed, as I recall."

"Desperate, even." Ariane flashed him a wry grin and turned her head towards the window. Down in the city a bell tolled three times. Calm outside, no wind—just faint starlight glinting and the yellow glow beside them. Ariane sighed and pulled up a chair beside her husband.

"You look awful," she said, rearranging a stray lock on his forehead. "Go back to sleep."

"I'm worried about you."

The irritation again. "No need," said Ariane. "Bad dreams and sudden wind are hardly worth the mention."

"Bad dreams—it's more than that, isn't it?" Ariane didn't respond so Raule grabbed her arm, his eyes huge in the lamplight. "Not your usual nightmares from the past—they don't affect the weather."

"What are you saying?"

"The Royal Dreaming—has it returned?" Raule's gaze was intense, anxious. "Did you cause that wind Ariane?"

"Now you are being foolish."

"It would explain the sudden gust," Raule said. "The Goddess waking inside you."

"The Goddess is dead, Raule," Ariane snapped, angry again. "The Dreaming died with her. That's all gone, barely a crust remains of the magic I once felt."

"Then why did you send that poor fool east to find your hopeless cousin?" Raule's expression withdrew to weary patience; this was old territory for them. "You said *that* was the Dreaming, Ariane. Why everyone listened. Why Garland went."

"Well, perhaps some of it remains." Ariane waved a dismissive hand. "I *did* dream of the seeress Ysaren at the Lake of Stones—saw her clearly, know she can help us." Ariane sighed. "Dream or vision, or maybe female intuition, I know not which," she said. "Doesn't matter—the oracle was real enough."

"Two months ago."

"What?"

"Captain Garland and his seven volunteers left over two months ago." Raule reached for the decanter again. "We've heard nothing, Ariane."

"It's remote out there."

"He took birds aplenty, could have got in touch anytime."

"You think Garland's dead too—is that it?" Ariane snatched the glass from her husband and downed the liquid, furious now. "Lord Tamersane, his Rorshai lady, and now the brave Captain and company I send to find them—all dead at my foolish bidding."

"Ariane, I didn't mean that."

But she wasn't angry with him. It was not Raule's fault her crazed cousin had abandoned court on some wild venture east, after news of another war brewing between their countries.

Tamersane, cousin, the trouble you've caused.

"I'm sorry love," Ariane stroked his face with a pale finger. "Not much company lately, heh?"

"I married a queen," Raule said, smiling wearily. "Ariane of the Swords they once called you. Even the Crystal King loved you they say."

"We were friends," Ariane felt the hint of moisture dampen her eye. "I miss him, and the others. Miss those days when it was us few rebels against the monster." She smiled again. "You were part of that too, husband."

"At the end, a small contribution," Raule said.

"You helped me win at Calprissa, hence your title," she said. "Without that victory neither of us would be here. The first time anyone stood up to Caswallon and the evil he reawakened."

"A turning point in the war," Raule nodded, and then raised a brow. "We've finished the brandy, and you not a drinker. Shall I send for more?"

"No," Ariane said. "Go and get some rest—I have pondering to do. I have need to clear my head for court." Ariane stood and turned to face the window again; the darkness beyond showed a slight pink glow. Far away she saw the silver glimmer of Lake Wynais a few miles outside her city. Morning coming soon, and in its bustle a brief escape from the void that drained her soul.

She heard an awkward shuffle of feet. Ariane turned back and stared hard at her consort's face. "You're still here."

"Going now." Reluctantly, Raule turned to leave.

"Wait," Ariane's voice stopped him in his tracks. "Do you think we've lost them forever, Raule? That I *was* wrong to chase after shadows in the dark. False hopes?"

"I do not, My Queen," Raule said. "But . . ."

"Say it."

Raule chewed his mustache. "Perhaps there are some who are

7

better off dead." He awarded her a knowing look, and then turned again and vacated the queen's bed chamber. Ariane watched him go, the trace of an angry tear staining her cheek. Then a thought struck her like lightning from a cloudless sky. *What if?*

Ariane shook slightly with the possibility of hope renewed. *Dare I believe?* She stood for long minutes, her sharp mind racing with sudden unexpected excitement.

Raule was right—how could she dream the Dreaming if her Goddess was dead?

Something has changed.

And for the first time in seven years Ariane felt like she was no longer alone. She kneeled by the bed, dark eyes streaming, and hurriedly spoke the words she hadn't uttered for so long, and as she spilled them out in urgent whispers the wind returned and blew out the sconces and lanterns again. Ariane no longer cared. She knew another dance had begun.

***

Lord Calprissa refused his Queen's advice and summoned more brandy. The servant returning with a fresh decanter found the queen's consort hard at study, a large map sprawled across his table, the lantern hanging above.

Raule hardly noticed the man as he placed the decanter on the table beside his lord. Raule nodded thanks and dismissed the servant with a wave of his hand.

His tired eyes strained over the map, studying each land as if for the first time, memorizing cities, rivers, and old battleground markings—what he did these days to help him sleep.

Raule recited the Four Kingdoms in his head as his fingers lightly brushed over the parchment: Morwella in the north with its new naval port; below that Mighty Kelthaine where the high king—or

Crystal King as most people still called him—ruled supreme; Raleen, the arid land to their south. And finally, Kelwyn, his queen's beloved nation, named after the first king, Kell's son Wynna, as Kelthaine had been named after the other twin boy, Thanik.

The four ancient kingdoms had almost been obliterated in the war with the sorcerer Caswallon and the madness that had followed, leaving mankind in tatters—the Gods falling from the sky that dark wintery day seven years ago.

Raule sipped his brandy slowly and let his aching eyes wander over painted mountains and blue-sketched winding rivers, probing eastwards on the map, past the horse country ruled by their allies in fierce Rorshai, across the wide endless steppes and beyond. To what?

Ptarni. And the mysterious realms rumored beyond. Raule's map didn't show those as no-one had ever ventured so far, but rumors spoke of strange alien places. Hostile lands ruled by the mad emperor Callanz who'd recently seized his ailing father's throne. As dangerous and volatile a ruler as could be imagined. Raule's fingers hovered over the mad emperor's city. Caranaxis, the City in the Clouds—the place to which Ariane's cousin Tamersane was rumored to have fled.

Good riddance.

Raule had struggled to be sympathetic. Lord Tamersane was a hero of the wars, once the most loved man in Wynais City, perhaps even in all of Kelwyn. And a personal friend of the High King himself. More importantly, he was loved by Queen Ariane as a dearest cousin.

But it had all gone so wrong for Tamersane after the incident with his treacherous brother. A bad business, but strong men move forward. Instead, Lord Tamersane had stewed and drunk himself into a mess of misery and hopelessness, almost bringing his queen down with him.

Then he'd departed without word and turned up briefly in

Rorshai—his wife's country. But word had come from there that they'd left that land too, faring east across the steppes, leaving Ariane fretting that her favorite cousin was bound for Ptarni with what could only be described as a death wish.

It was depressing. They'd come so far since that terrible day seven years ago. Alone, the Gods having deserted them. The country was fragile, exhausted. And now it seemed another war was looming. And Ariane's troublesome cousin was in the midst as before.

Raule wiped his eyes. Not constructive, dwelling on such nonsense. Ariane was strong, but she'd been through so much and wasn't impervious to worry and pain. And the queen looked older than her thirty-two years.

Hopefully, sooner or later they'd receive word of Lord Tamersane murdered in a gutter, and they could all move on with their lives. A sad necessity. Raule placed the brandy glass on the table and closed his eyes. The room was spinning slightly. He really did need to get some sleep.

A few rooms away, Ariane stared at the distant water as morning light showed green fields and smoky mist-veiled hills, and the shadow of the mountains behind her city. She breathed in the scented air— Kelwyn, her beloved green land.

She dressed plainly, and bid her maids leave her be. Once ready, and armed with fresh tea, Ariane skipped breakfast and instead walked briskly through the palace, nodding to the odd retainer alarmed to see her at this hour. Ariane allowed one guard to escort her from the palace, the deep hood hiding her face as she walked in brisk strides toward the ancient temple. Deserted, as it had been for years. Why worship when the Gods were dead?

But Ariane was no longer so sure. She bid the guard wait outside the huge doors after entering. She paused and took a deep breath as memories surged back. She took in the wide hall, the tall stone effigies—some still standing, most broken and ruined—and clouded dust coating the flagstones.

She approached the nearest effigy and gazed up at the serene face of her goddess—Elanion. Ariane felt the fresh rush of tears dampen her cheeks as emotion almost choked her. She sank to her knees, clasped her hands together, and for the second time in seven lonely years mouthed the words to a silent prayer.

Give me a sign that not all is lost, an echo, whisper, or even hint that we are not alone in this universe and you haven't abandoned us forever . . .

Silence.

Ariane struggled to her knees, and then almost fell as an explosion of light erupted all around her. Green light, darting and stabbing-bright, causing her fall back and lose her balance. She heard a shout, and half-glimpsed the guard rushing toward her, ducking as stones and rubble exploded into motion, the whole temple shaking around her.

"Earthquake!" The guard reached down and heaved her up, his tough features stained with grime and fear. "We must flee, My Queen." But Ariane smiled at him. She knew she'd been answered.

Later that day she stood on her wide balcony overlooking the Silver City, as visitors always called Wynais. The lake was gleaming—a blue reflection of that fine spring day. Lord Calprissa approached looking worse than earlier. And very angry.

"You went to the temple—alone?"

"Not entirely."

"You could have been killed," he said.

"The tremor occurred throughout the city, Raule. Everyone was at threat, and, as I was informed, few were even hurt."

"We were lucky—but what possessed you to go to the temple?

No one goes there."

For an answer Ariane walked over to her bureau and picked up a small green object, secreted in a drawer. She held it up to the light.

"It's stamped on our memories, Raule," Ariane said eventually, her eyes still on the tiny object she held. "You and I—everyone in this city. The Goddess rising above, defending us . . . and then, Him." Ariane's lips quivered slightly. "Then He came, that tower of hatred clad in white, and tore Her apart before our eyes."

"I remember," Raule said, his voice quieter than before.

"And yet down there in the temple for the first time I felt . . . *something*. A shifting . . ."

"It was an earthquake," Raule said. "That was to be expected."

"No, I meant from within." Ariane walked across to where her husband stood like a man frozen in indecision. She opened her palm revealing the small green stone. A gem in the shape of a hooded, stooping woman. "Recognize this?"

"The Emerald Queen," Raule said, his lips trembling. "I thought it lost?"

Ariane smiled at the alarm on her husband's face when the gem pulsed sudden green light. "It's starting again," Ariane said. "A new dance—as He called it. Nothing is ever forgotten."

Chapter 2 | The Drinker

The Gods were dead, and Tam had seen them die. Seven years ago, in a distant land – his home, back then. So long ago it seemed— almost a dream. A time of hope and light in a world far away from these sultry dirty days and lightning-lashed nights that framed his life in this alien dangerous city.

Hope and light seemed a life-time away from the teeming sprawl spilling out beneath his window ledge, the dirt and squalor, the ragged children and wailing paupers at the gates. Tam glanced that way. He scowled, witnessing a dismal column of scarlet-robed priests chanting their dirges as they faded off into the deeper dark surrounding rooftop and walls. Tam leaned back in his chair, spilling wine as he laughed at the priests, their chants fading as their hooded shapes were lost around a corner. "They're dead, you fools," Tam said. "They are not listening."

Midnight in the City of the Clouds. From his villa, Tam could see the torches winking above the mad emperor's palace, where the priests were heading with their beads, their eager faces, and their false hope. He glimpsed the oval, fluted towers of worship, and the high battle-flagged crenellations and walls surrounding the emperor's pleasure gardens and mile-long bordello—all winking under the yellow light of torches and brands. The inner city was a different place entirely.

Fuck the lot of them.

Tam drained his glass and chuckled again. So ironic—the Gods were dead, and yet more people were turning to worship in these dark and squalid times. Tam's mirth slid from his lips when a shadow blocked the light beside him. She was there—Teret. His wife, her black hair disheveled and blue eyes tired with worry.

"Did you call me?" Her voice was husky and her tired face strained. She looked older than her thirty years. His fault. Teret wore that short shift he'd always loved. A silk gown cut square above her knees, perfect for this climate. It showed off her strong tanned legs and hinted at the curves he knew so well. But Tam wasn't in the mood—hadn't been for days.

"Go to sleep," Tam waved his wife leave him be.

Teret's eyes narrowed but she nodded. "I'm in need of it, but doubt I'll get any. Sleep doesn't come easy in this city." Teret's cool blue gaze unsettled Tam and a sudden pang of guilt cramped deep inside his belly. *This is all my fault.* Tam leaned sideways in the wicker chair so he could see her better. Silently she watched him, her face pensive and drawn. *What have I done to you?*

"You worry too much, my love. Everything will be fine—quit fretting so." Tam's glib words coated veneer over the lie, and the ghost of a grimace curled his upper lip. "You'll end up like those stupid priests. Dried up turds, chanting and worshipping the night away." Teret said nothing, just pursed her lips in resignation. "Go, then," Tam said, his mood shifting as the bitterness chewed deeper inside. He'd brought Teret down with him—unforgivable, yet he was helpless. Tam despised whom he'd become, how he'd hurt the only women he'd ever loved.

Worse than what I did to you, brother.

Teret stood there looking so beautiful, the city framed behind.

Tam waved a dismissive hand. "Get some rest. I'll be in shortly, when I'm done thinking."

"And drinking," Teret turned away. "That's all you fucking do these days."

"Aye, well it's what keeps me sane, isn't it?" Tam muttered after her, but Teret had already closed the door and left him to the night and its ghosts. Ghosts whose memory came rushing back until Tam's head rattled, and even the wine couldn't hold off the wave of loss and betrayal flushing his veins. Time for something stronger. If Teret knew about Tam's nocturnal habits she never let on. The wine eased his nerves but failed to salve his soul, obliterate the horror of what he had done. Back there, back then. Before the Gods had died. But fortunately, there was something that did.

Why he was here.

Tam tossed the goblet into the night and stood, shaking slightly. He left the balcony and lurched for the door, turned latch, and half stumbled past the bed where his wife lay silent, a vague dusting of smoky-colored hair showing on pillow, her breath soft as snowfall.

"I'm taking a stroll," Tam said. "The shadow's on me tonight, love; I need to walk it off my back." No response, but he knew she wasn't sleeping. "Won't be long," Tam lied. Minutes later he'd left the villa and was crossing the crooked lanes making for the smoky house that held the key to freedom.

Teret opened her eyes the moment her husband left the room. Tamersane was drunk again. Nothing unusual in that. Teret blamed this filthy degenerate city. She hated Caranaxis, the City in the Clouds, named for its elevated position on the southern slopes of the forbidding Urgo Mountains. A dark bulk of craggy slopes, they hemmed the city in an iron embrace, a huge sprawling mass of stone gazing down coldly on the plains and lowlands of western Ptarni.

Living here was Tam's choice. They'd spent long lazy months in this rented villa. For Teret the time was a blur, dragging and fading from one lonely night to the next, as her husband sunk deeper into the shadow of his past. Teret mourned the memory of the man she had once so loved. Back there, back then—how they glossed over those days. Neither could talk about that golden time, before the Gods left them. Before the rot set in.

But it wasn't the Rorshai way to mope. That was Tam's province. Teret wouldn't give up on him yet. She still loved him despite the edges fraying more day on day. It was not Tam's fault his brother had betrayed them, had tried to stab her. Tam's actions had saved the city that night in the dungeon below Wynais, but part of him had died instead.

But what to do? How could she save him from himself? Teret tossed off the sheets, knowing she wouldn't settle until he returned. Nothing to be salvaged by just lying there like a dead thing staring up at the ceiling with its cracks she'd counted one by one. Besides, it was always so hot in this city—even at night.

Teret thought of Rorshai, the chilly breeze coming down from the mountains—those beautiful, distant heights, so unlike the gray ominous slopes flanking Caranaxis. Rorshai, land of horses and valiant men, sweeping rolling folds of green where stallions danced and wild flowers wagged their smiling faces in the sunshine. So far away, both in time and miles. Teret longed to return but knew that to be a forlorn hope. She belonged with her husband, and the demons haunting him were her enemies too. Teret wouldn't forget the man he had been, the sunny, laughing, joking diamond that had lit her soul, filling her life with light and careless laughter.

Back then.

Teret wrapped the silk shift around her lean body and took seat by the table, pouring a large glass of port from the crystal decanter.

At least money wasn't a problem—her brother had seen to that. Thanks to the Kaan they could while away their days in idle comfort, Tam steeped in drink and worse—of course she knew his night-time habits—and Teret lost to her memories of how it should have been. She raised the glass and sipped slowly letting the warm liquid wash away some of her own demons. Why were they here? She knew the answer but mouthed the question all the same.

A shift of curtain, the sound of floorboards creaking somewhere outside. Too soon for her husband's return. An intruder? Teret slipped into a side room where her day garments lay neatly folded on a chair. Quickly she dressed in trousers and loose linen shirt. Silence. It was nothing, maybe a cat? There were many cats in Caranaxis.

Teret rubbed her tired damp eyes, the kohl had melted and stung them making her blink. She was getting edgy, nervy—too much time to think. A soft sound turned her head. Teret saw the door creasing open slowly, allowing a line of light to creep in from the passageway beyond. Carefully, slowly, Teret reached into her leather bag resting on the table to her right. She slid the dagger free and spun on her toes, lightning swift, her balance perfect, and the slim weapon poised to strike.

Laughter. A shadow watched her from the corner. Others loomed into view. Three? Maybe four? Teret stabbed out at them, cutting, slicing flesh, her long angry scream reaching the night outside.

And so, her nightmare began.

**

Tam eased his long bones into the deep sedan and sucked hard on the pipe. The room was a haze of lamplight, ceiling fans turned by blank-eyed slaves, dripping candles and smoke swirls. He sighed, feeling the release rush through him, freeing him from the acid worm growing inside his belly.

The need had been bad tonight. Tam had prowled the lanes like a thief in the dark, focusing solely on reaching this place and filling his lungs with opium. As in recent nights, Tam spent a few hours seeking oblivion, smoking, drinking, watching the girls. These flitted half-naked between the hunched silent shapes of their customers, the room surrounding them shrouded in silence and smoke, a small fire burning low in the hallway.

Occasionally a client would stagger to his feet and the girls would lead him upstairs. Tam had no interest in that particular diversion. And he doubted he could partake even if he'd wanted to. That part of him had faded with the rest. All that remained was a shadow, yet another ghost.

Besides, he loved Teret and would never hurt her with betrayal. He'd sunk low but not that low. Tam would stay loyal to his Rorshai girl, even though she'd most likely be better off without him. He knew he was a broken shell of the man he had been before he killed his brother, and before he'd seen the Gods tear each other apart above the walls of the Silver City in distant beloved Kelwyn, Tam's sweet green homeland where his beloved, brave cousin Ariane still ruled as queen. What would Ariane make of him now? She who never suffered fools. The thought sent a shiver through Tam's spine. Some places you just don't go.

Tam spoke to no one on these visits, kept himself closed. This was a perilous place in a violent city where secrets spilled led to severed throats. A sly whisper here; a cold knife in a dark alley later. Metal on moonlight and the warm spill of crimson on stone. A dangerous house deep in the slums of a volatile, changing city. But Tam had no fear of anyone in Caranaxis. He was past fear—drained dry of emotion and numb at the edges. He'd seen so much and lost more, despite their victory seven years past. If victory was the word for it. "Survival" was perhaps a better one.

Besides, the fragile thread dividing breath from oblivion kept him sharp, even in this altered state. The grubbier, dingier, and deadlier the environment—the happier he was. Tam needed the danger, lived for it these days. Tension kept his mind working, though more slowly than it had once. Tam left the smoking house just before the first pale glimmer of dawn promised another steamy cruel day in Ptarni's greatest city.

Tam strolled the streets, his mind lost in dreams and hardly noticing the early folk already starting their work day. He passed drays, maids delivering goods, errand boys running for their masters, cutthroats and thieves scurrying back from their busy nights. The honest poor rose early in the City of the Clouds, unlike its criminals who retired late. The rich slept without worry ignoring both, their thick drapes and walls hiding such dross. Tam wondered what class he belonged to. Once he'd been a nobleman, but now he'd sit more comfortably with the beggars and thieves. They were his kind of people these days—the company he deserved. No matter.

Tam stopped outside the villa, seeing the door slightly ajar. He frowned, mind clearing slowly. Something awry here. Teret usually took a bath at this hour. Not for her the filthy streets at daybreak. He entered, his dreamy state shifting to cold realization that things were amiss. The worry worm coiled inside and Tam stumbled into the doorway. The lock was broken. They'd been robbed.

"Teret!" Tam bolted up the stairs, tripping, slipping, and cursing his fucking numb legs. He crashed into the solar, wild of eye and purpose, saw nothing, then rushed through to their bedroom where last he'd seen her.

Teret was gone, but the room wasn't empty. Two men sprawled lifeless, their blood soaked deep into the priceless Shen rug. Tam froze, the shiver rattling his teeth. He was aware of dampness in his mouth and realized his lip was bleeding.

Teret . . .

Tam seized the jug at the table close by and drained the contents, once done he hurled it at the wall smashing it into a hundred shards, the red staining the tapestry in a hue much like the blood crimsoning the rugs at his feet.

Sharp shock. Tam needed his wits back, and fast. They'd taken his wife. Who—slavers? Robbers seeking ransom? Tam rummaged the cupboard finding another bottle. He tugged at the stopper with his teeth and glugged down hard. His instinct told him this was no botched robbery and panicked fight. Someone had a grudge. But they knew few folks in this city and had been careful not to court suspicion. So why were they here if not by chance?

Must remain calm.

Tam placed the bottle on the table. He looked at it, focusing his vision and willing his hand not to shake. He'd been a warrior once—a professional.

I've still got it in me.

Enough. Tam was sober now. Sober as the corpses on the carpet. He could hold a sword steady and plunge its steel hard into flesh. That would suffice. Tam turned, suddenly noticing a note pinned by a knife to the wall behind the stiffening corpses.

Tam stepped over the dead and ripped the parchment free. He studied the words, his eyes lost to the madness of rage and failure. They'd taken his Teret!

This is just the start.
I know how to hurt you.
Send greetings to Rol Sharn.

The words were a spider crawl, a sprawled mess hard to decipher. Who had written this and why? Tam had made damn certain all his enemies were dead. Another failure on his part. Tam felt his back crash against the wall. He slid down, his legs fading, and his eyes filling with tears as the last threads holding his world together were cut with razors into ribbons. Tam sobbed and spewed as the drink and drugs waged war inside him. He tried to stand but his knees buckled, and Tam's head struck the corner of the table. He lost consciousness.

When Tam woke, the afternoon storms were well underway. How long had he lain there? Dumb and numb while she . . . Tam spat bloody phlegm at the wall. He felt sick and empty, but sober at least. He stood, wobbly, his legs shaking until the room stopped spinning. Rol Sharn the merchant was his ally. Tam had to warn him. If he saved his hide, Sharn would help him find his wife. Rol Sharn was a reasonable man; they'd shared a past of shady dealings in this city. Tam had the goods on Rol Sharn and could rely on the merchant for aid and counsel.

Tam suspected whomever had Teret wouldn't harm her yet, at least until they'd showed their hand. He'd pray to the Gods but they were dead. This was down to him. Time to move.

He found bread and cheese in the pantry and crammed a wedge of both in his mouth. He wasn't hungry but the stomach needed filling. Tam opened the door to his study, saw his old battle leathers and mail, and the broadsword scabbarded beside them. He swapped gear quickly, pulling on long boots and struggling to buckle the broad belt supporting his sword and dagger. Lastly Tam tossed a woolen cloak over his shoulder despite the heat. It would keep him dry—and more importantly help hide his weapons to avoid unwelcome interest.

He found the street outside empty as the driving rain puddled and streamed into clogged steaming gutters, the stench of stale shit mixing with water, and the odd dead rat damming the stream. Tam walked, his face torn—a pale mask scraped into an expression of self-loathing and bitter determination.

I'm coming Teret!

Two miles through a sweltering tangle and crisscross of streets, steepening up as he reached the merchants' quarter where Rol Sharn kept sumptuous residence. Tam didn't trust Sharn—but he didn't trust anyone and he had to start somewhere. Two guards blocked his entrance through the gates leading to Sharn's manse.

"I need to speak with your master." Tam eyed the guards coldly but they didn't budge. "Today." Tam slipped a hand under his cloak and the guards frowned seeing the sword there.

"Are you a madman?" The oldest and shorter of the two glared at Tam. "Coming here, bearing steel?"

"Clearly a fool," the younger one smiled. That smile fled his face when Tam's dagger pricked the skin under his neck. Tam was still quick when need was upon him.

Tam grinned. "You were looking at the sword; didn't notice the dagger, hey?" The younger guard blanched, and his companion stepped forward, spear leveled at Tam's chest. Tam smiled. "I'll take that spear off you and shove it up your ass, and then slit this gormless lad's throat unless you get Rol Sharn now." The older guard stared at Tam for a moment and then nodded. He looked afraid.

"Don't hurt the lad, I'll be back shortly." He strode briskly off, a crunch of purposeful steel on stone. Tam pulled the other guard toward him so any onlooker would think they were deep in discussion. Twenty minutes later, a red-faced portly man in a russet robe led the guard and six companions down to the gates.

"Oh—it's you," Rol Sharn relaxed his gaze. He smiled, mainly for his guards' benefit. "Leave us! I know this man." The guards obeyed, stepping back; Tam sheathed his dagger and kicked the young guard forward.

"Go play with your mates," Tam told him, and the guard scrambled to join the others, his face still white with terror.

"I said go!" Rol Sharn snapped at his guards, who saluted and crunched back out of earshot. He turned back to Tam. "This is unfortunate. I don't often conduct business at my front gates. People have eyes and ears, Tamersane of Kelwyn." Tam shoved the screwed-up note into Rol Sharn's fist and the merchant squinted at the words.

"Atrocious writing," he said breezily as Tam watched him. If Rol Sharn was nervous he didn't show it. But he was a player like so many in Caranaxis. "We can't discuss this here. We need somewhere neutral and discreet."

"The usual place then."

"Aye, give me some time to ask around—I'll be there in a few hours." Tam nodded and left Rol Sharn at his gates, taking his way back down the street. If anyone could glean who'd taken Teret, it was that wily merchant. And Rol Sharn's name being on the note ensured his diligence in catching them.

Tam would let Rol Sharn settle in their meeting place for a while before he joined him. That way he could study any movement in the vicinity. He needed a plan, and that meant mobility, a horse, supplies. Time to fight back. Tam cursed his growling stomach and shaky limbs—he needed to be sharp today.

I'll work on that too.

At least he had money back at their lodgings—thanks to Teret, another reason to love her. Tam bit his lip thinking of her, alone, scared, at the mercy of some conniving cutpurse, or worse—someone with a debt to pay. But for what? Time would tell, and Tam needed to focus on doing, not thinking. Too much thought could kill a man.

Two hours later, Tam led a fine destrier through the streets to the far side of the city, the shadow of mountain frowning over. He'd returned to the villa, scooped up what coin he'd found in the hidden recess only he and Teret knew about, and then sought out the markets, purchasing horse, saddle, bridle, blankets, and travel gear. He might not need them. But chances were . . .

The rain ceased and the skies cleared slowly. It stayed muggy, and Tam felt weighed down by his gear and the great horse stomping behind him. He led the beast through more corkscrew lanes, at last reaching the only safe house he knew in this treacherous city.

Flies buzzed Tam's face and vendors yanked his sleeves as he pushed on through. Somewhere close, Tam could hear priests yelling the Emperor's words. Callanz was the new god here. Tam would have preferred any of the old ones. They said Emperor Callanz was insane with ambition. Certainly, he was corrupt, and cruel as winter. King Akanates had been a shrewd though sickly ruler. His son was neither.

Scant time to dwell on that. Not his business. The inn was close, and Tam was ready for whatever cheap crappy wine they had to offer—just to quench his thirst and help him work the problem. Men fall sometimes; the important thing was to realize it and get back on your feet. He'd let both Teret and himself down—past time to address the issue.

Tam's face streamed sweat and grime as he trudged along that last street. Ptarni in summer offered little mercy. A gap in buildings revealed a hill where people clustered like ants spilling from nests, listening to yet another dreary priest ranting on about the old Gods' demise, praising the new "god-emperor," and bragging how Ptarni's greatest days were yet to come. And the fools cheered. Tam winced; he didn't share the priests' optimism. But then Emperor Callanz paid his zealots well these days. Almost as well as he rewarded his spies.

A man's face loomed up at him; a greasy hand tapping his shoulder. Tam shoved the grinning trader onto his back and jumped aside. Best to avoid eye contact in this city. In Caranaxis a smiling face could hide a knife held low ready to slice belly or purse. Tam knew the rules here. Don't engage. Keep moving forward. Speak to no one except those chosen few. Trust no one—not even them. Especially them. That way he might just stay alive long enough to rescue his wife.

If they'd hurt her . . .

Tam slammed out that thought. He needed to hold positive. She was alive, and he would find her and kill the bastards that had taken her. *Enough said. Don't fret on how. Focus on when.*

It was dusk by the time Tam found the side alley leading to Red's Tavern, the inn they'd frequented often whilst King Akamates ruled this country. It had served Tam well as a safe house where he and his associates could glean the workings and secrets of this mysterious country. Tam wished he could go back to those days, spying for the Crystal King. The high stakes had given him the edge he needed after the horror of the war with Caswallon. He'd met Teret during that war—a glimmer of excitement amidst the carnage.

Tam had found a kind of peace traveling the steppes with his new wife and her Rorshai kin, who sometimes accompanied them, patching things up after the last war. King Akamates had been a mellow sensible ruler, and thanks to Kaan Olen, Teret's brother, and the man once known as Lord Tamersane, and a few others, a fragile peace had held between Ptarni and the new High King in the west.

That all changed when Akamates died. Murdered, they said: a poison cup of wine, allowing the self-styled god-emperor finally to take his place on the throne after years of subtle scheming.

Callanz was as different to his father Akamates as ocean was to desert. The tenuous peace cracked open like eggs hitting stone, spilling lies, hatred, and suspicion into every corner of this realm.

Another war beckoned as once again Ptarni turned its greedy eyes to the west.

There had been no more envoys or candid meetings in the City of the Clouds. Caranaxis was a melting pot of fear and lies. Ptarni's greatest city was now as corrupt and twisted as its ruler. Tam grinned at the irony. *One thing you can always rely on—man's stupidity. Himself included.*

Not too late—I can fix this.

A boy squinted as Tam approached the shabby red door. He tossed the lad a copper disk and the boy jogged over, grabbing Tam's new mount by its reins. "Nice horse!" The boy grinned rotten teeth.

"And expensive, so feed and water him well," Tam snapped at the boy. "I leave before dawn." It wouldn't hurt telling the stable hand he was staying the night, lest his tongue wagged, which it probably would. The lad nodded, grinned again, and vanished towards the stables hidden behind the inn. Tam loosened the sword at his waist and checked that the two throwing knives he'd purchased were secure in the sheaths hidden up his sleeves. It was a while since last he had been here and this meeting could prove tricky.

Lanterns cast an orange glow as the tall fair-haired westerner stooped inside Red's Tavern and glanced across the room. A few shadowy figures shuffled on stools and watched him enter with wary eyes. Tam feigned indifference, and they soon lost interest, returning to their intrigues and complaints as the tight-faced innkeep—Red himself—replenished their cups with watery wine.

Rol Sharn appeared silently beside him. He'd shuffled in from a shabby corner where drapes hid a room beyond. From there, the soft muffled sound of pipe music drifted through. Eerie and exotic, it left a quiver along Tam's spine. Rol Sharn pulled up a stool. Tam's contact looked edgy, uncomfortable. Tam ignored him and sipped the crappy wine. Rol Sharn sighed and pulled out a pipe.

Tam pretended not to notice. Five more minutes as his ally puffed in mock contentment at the sweet-smelling weed. Rol Sharn had his own way of doing things. Tam's former contact in Caranaxis was an affluent spice dealer originally from eastern Ptarni. Though not from this city, Rol Sharn knew everyone who mattered, and little happened inside its walls that he didn't hear about first.

"They were seen," Rol Sharn mumbled into his pipe. "Leaving by the north gate taking the mountain road. A rider with a slave girl. He had her tied like a sack around his horse, her hands and feet tethered."

"And the guards just let him through?" Tamersane tried to keep his voice neutral despite his urge to shove a knife in someone close.

Rol Sharn shrugged and pulled at his pipe. "This is Ptarni my friend. What did you expect?"

"Who?"

"A Rorshai—gave his name as Sulo when the guards requested it. Said he'd bought this slave in market and was taking her to Rundali where there's a shortage." Rol Sharn's narrow eyes became anxious slits. "You've heard that name before."

"I have—a renegade mad-dog." Tam felt the rage rising up inside him. "My wife's brother banished that slime from Rorshai. I thought he'd died years ago." Tam's mind was racing. He'd met Sulo once and he'd been sick at the time, wounded by his best friend in the arm. His recollection of that meeting was vague. But the memory of what Sulo had done later was clear as daylight. Scorned, Sulo had fallen out with his clan—the Anchai. A former leader, he blamed his misfortunes on Teret's people—the Tcunkai—and had raided their camp, killing the old Kaan, her father, and burning it to the ground. Barely had Tam and Teret survived. The new Kaan and Teret's older brother, Olen, had hunted Sulo down, but then the war reached Rorshai and everything changed. Somehow Sulo slipped away.

"You sure that was the name he gave? It could have been any brigand towing a slave girl."

"Sulo, yes—not a common name. The guards said he seemed proud of it. A savage, murderous looking type—their words not mine. And the Rorshai carry a certain look, even when they disguise themselves in Ptarnian garb. This Sulo is our man, Lord Tamersane. I'm certain of it."

"I no longer use that name or title," Tam hissed. "Why north? Rundal was southeast of here last time I studied a map."

"True enough, but that's not his destination. The mountain passes lead down to the Tseola plains, and once there it's easy to hop on the trade road—the quickest route to Shen. They pay good money for slave girls in Shen. Better even than the Rundal."

Sulo. The past is returning to haunt me again.

Tam gripped his goblet and squeezed. His hand shook and murky wine spotted the table. Tam noticed Rol Sharn watching him with troubled eyes.

"Careful, my friend. Patience. This is not a place to lose one's cool."

Tam nodded. "Don't worry, I'll save my strength. But why would Sulo mention you? How could he know about our dealings in years past? And why threaten you too?"

Rol Sharn looked away, his dark eyes furtive. "He must have been in the city some while asking questions. Even scared tongues loosen for enough coin, and if Sulo's as mad and bitter as you say he is . . ."

"There is more to it than that," Tam said evasively. He didn't trust Rol Sharn a jot but what choice did he have? Tam's friends in this city were few, even before the rise of Callanz. Now they were invisible. But something nagged at him that this dealer knew more than he was letting on. Tam shrugged, forced calm into his veins and slurped his wine. That bastard Sulo had a day on him. No more.

He'd get a map from Sharn and be away before dawn.

Noises reached him from the other room. Someone was singing in a rough voice, drowning out the weird pipe music. Tam heard laughter then shouts, followed by the predictable sound of steel on steel. A man cried out and silence reclaimed the tavern, with the exception of the pipe music that still wafted through.

Another shout. Tam looked up again. A shortish man with curly black hair struggled into the taproom and yelled in Red's ear. "Ale!" The man was clearly drunk. A rough unkempt sort, his face scarred and nose badly broken. Most likely some inebriated horse trader from the wilderness beyond the city. Or maybe a goatherd or yokel who'd taken too much drink. "Ale!" The man pushed the flustered innkeep, Red, with a grubby fist.

"You are not welcome here, Tseole," Red spat the last word out as though it tasted bad. "Go back to your filthy yurt. You nomads are banned from this tavern." He shoved the newcomer backwards and the man toppled to the floor and then struggled to rise, causing wry amusement amongst those seated around the counter where Red held court.

"Clear off, northern scum—go back to Tseola, and whatever three-legged mare you're sleeping with." Red bid two big lads lift the prone drunkard up by his elbows. Together they dragged the unfortunate across the inn, his boots scraping the flags. A helpful fellow opened the door and the two heavies hurled the drunk out into the night. Laughter followed and then dark silence reclaimed its customary seat amongst them.

Rol Sharn looked worried. "You need to leave here, Lord Tamersane. It's not safe for you here. Nowhere is safe anymore. People have memories."

"I'm staying the night." Tam coolly surveyed the thugs at the counter. "That way my horse gets dry rest and I'm ready for tomorrow. And that way I can get drunk enough to forget what I've allowed to happen."

"That wasn't your fault," Rol Sharn said smoothly. "You put too much on yourself, Kelwynian. This Sulo must have seen you enter the city. I suspect he's been lurking here in Ptarni since your Kaan friend chased him out of Rorshai. He probably couldn't believe his luck seeing Teret, the Kaan's beloved sister, in arm's reach."

"That luck's running out. Sulo will be dead soon," Tam said, draining his goblet and hinting to Red for a refill. Tam noticed Rol Sharn's dark eyes locking with one of the men who had tossed out the drunkard. The man nodded slowly to his companion.

"You need to leave!" Rol Sharn hissed in Tam's ear. He seemed agitated, alarmed even. Was Tam missing something? He saw the men watching him slyly from the counter, Red among them.

"Actually, I do need a quiet moment." Tam ignored the hostile glances and shambled toward the door. Outside, the swelter of Ptarni summer night hit him like tossed bath water hard in his face. What a shithole this place was. And why had he returned here? Tam couldn't face that question yet. He'd make it up to Teret, but first he had to find her.

Tam shuffled along the alley making a big show of fumbling with his drawstrings. Instead he lowered a sleeve-hidden dagger into both hands and, turning on his toes, hurled the first one at the man running at him from behind.

That one dropped like a felled tree, Tam's knife in his left eye. The second footpad crashed over his accomplice's body and cursed in disbelief when Tam's other knife sliced into his gut, and he sank groaning to his knees.

Tam stepped forward to reclaim his knives, but a heavy blow on the back of his head sent him sprawling. "I want him alive," Tam heard Rol Sharn's voice command. "The Emperor's man will pay good coin for this impostor."

Chapter 3 | The Prisoner

Teret rubbed her sore grimy hands and took the offered bowl. She sipped the brackish water and somehow kept her cool. Her captor would use any show of weakness against her. Teret determined not to give him that satisfaction.

As though reading her thoughts, Sulo watched her from his horse, his narrow eyes filled with loathing and mistrust. And triumph. Teret knew this was about vengeance, that his warped mind blamed her for all that he'd brought upon himself.

Sulo the rabid wolf. The nightmare had returned. How he'd laughed back at the villa when she'd fought off those three attackers. Rorshai women were skilled with knives, Teret better than most. She'd sliced two of them open and the third had run off to die slowly in the street. But they had hurt her too. Nothing broken, except her pride.

Rage.

Teret glared at the rider looking down at her. Sulo had calmly waited until his hired thugs had brought down his quarry. He'd shown himself after she knifed the third one, leaping out and kicking her in the head. Then he'd wrenched the knife from her hand, lashed her arms behind her back, and laughed at the dying men staining her floor.

They paid dearly for the silver he'd passed their way. But they didn't know Rorshai women. Kicked and beaten, the odd shallow cut, and a badly blackened eye, Teret would mend quickly enough. She'd bide her time and then kill this bastard herself. Old scores.

Neither captive nor captor had spoken since the few curt words he'd thrown her way at dawn. Sulo's silence suited Teret well enough. She drained her water bowl and allowed him to tie her back onto the saddle.

Teret's mind was working fast. She worried most for Tam. Without her to watch over him her husband would destroy himself. Teret knew she was the only rudder qualified to steer him clear of the rocks he'd made. Tam was on the edge, and finding her gone might well push him over.

I won't go there.

Damn him! Tam would have to stay strong; his soul might be crippled but he was no craven. And neither was Teret. She had to remain calm; Sulo would sense any panic or weakness a mile off. Her captor was a mad dog. Unpredictable, deranged, beyond dangerous. He was cunning and vicious, but Teret was clever too. She'd been through a lot. A survivor. There would come a time to slip Sulo's net—or better, slit his throat wide open. But that time wasn't now.

Teret tensed and eased her muscles, lest she cramp. She channeled her thoughts, making her sharp mind work the problem as she let her body relax. Teret had seen thirty winters. Past her prime, perhaps— but still strong. All she had to do was wait until an opportunity arose. Patience leads to providence. She would watch and wait. But that was easier said than done. Sulo was as unpredictable as he was savage.

"Rest," Sulo barked at her as he vaulted into the saddle. He checked her bonds were secure and then awarded Teret a wolf grin. "I need you healthy for the markets, Tcunkai bitch." Sulo spurred the horse to a canter and the mountain road led them up to twisted

33

trees shading deep slopes that fell away to their right. The road hugged the eastern fringe of the Urgo Mountains for several miles before turning north and leading down to the wide sweeping plains of Tseola—a land about which Teret knew little.

As dusk fell, Sulo reined in beside a wood, the wind-ragged oaks awarding cover and shelter. He tied Teret to a stump and boiled some gruel stored in his saddle bags. Neither spoke, and Teret let sleep claim her exhausted body, despite her discomfort and aching limbs.

She woke before dawn. Owls called out to each other and a horned moon slid free from silvered cloud, only to be swallowed again as more clouds circled. Her captor sat on a stone gazing at the road, his shaven head hidden by a deep hood.

The clouds mustered overhead and spots of rain beaded the road just yards to her left. That spotting turned to downpour but still he sat there, motionless as the rock beneath him, watching, a small pipe held to his lips. Lightning lanced a tree somewhere close. The sudden noise made Teret jump but Sulo hardly stirred. When he did it was to mock her.

"You afraid, Tcunkai? Storm scare you?"

Teret didn't give him the satisfaction of a response. "Time to move; I trust you rested well?" Teret said nothing as he lashed her to the saddle, the leather thongs biting into her skin. The pain was nothing; it helped her focus on escape and, even better—revenge.

Sulo caught her defiant stare and slapped her face. Teret spat in his eye and he slapped her again, harder this time. "Bitch."

They rode steadily for two days until a thin line of ash trees hinted a change of direction. "The Great Trade Road," Sulo croaked back at her. "The highway to distant Shen and to your new life servicing the cocks of slavers and silk merchants." Sulo grinned at her as he guided his horse across onto the wide track ribboning east to west beneath the trees. "You had best relax, bitch—it's a good two weeks' ride to the Shen River. Hate for you to suffer discomfort during our sojourn. I want a good price and you're ugly enough already."

"Fuck you," Teret mouthed the words and he smiled again.

They resumed their ride. Sulo ignored her and Teret kept her head together. Looking back throughout that day, Teret saw the grim line of mountains shrink into distance. They were heading east into a world she knew nothing about. Two weeks—a lot could happen in that time.

Later that day, rider and captive entered a steep valley where rough grass sighed and strange shaggy balls on posts lined the road ahead. On closer inspection these were the severed heads of outlaws, spiked and gory. They'd passed many more in the days that followed, lining the road from the city for mile upon mile. Such was the new Emperor's message to those who dared gainsay him. Teret knew little about these border lands, though distant Shen was rumored to be as powerful as Ptarni.

"These are Tseole scum," Sulo told her. "Bandits who ran foul of the emperor; we'll reach the border to that land soon." Teret tightened her lips and visualized Sulo's head on one of the spikes. A fine sight that would make.

Caranaxis was far behind them. Lost behind the mountains. The air was cooler here and a keen wind rose steady and stayed with them. Ahead was open country and wide sweeping hills, the faint hint of pink-gray mountains showing in the far distance.

At dusk, Sulo reined in as was his habit. He untied Teret's hands, allowing her drink and partake in the jerky he'd stowed in his saddle bags. "Your little digits look swollen." Sulo's breath was stale as he leaned over her, pawing at her fingers. "And blisters too; the rope burn cutting into your wrists. I'll rub some salve on those, you'll need nimble digits to please your new masters."

"Fuck you." Teret spat in his eye again and this time Sulo cursed. He stood, kicked her hard in the stomach making her double over.

"That all you can say is it? Well, fuck you too, bitch!" Sulo slipped a curved knife from his saddle bag and crouched beside her. "You give me any trouble, cunt, I'll take an ear, maybe a finger too." He leaned against her, greasy fingers running through her charcoal locks. Sulo caressed Teret's hair and smiled. He rested the tip of his dagger under her right eye. "Such lovely eyes; only Rorshai girls have eyes that blue. Blue as the sky in late summer. One slip and they're gone forever . . ." Sulo chuckled at the horror in Teret's eyes. "But then you'd be worthless to me--they say the Shen prize blue-eyed women more than most."

Sulo flipped the blade through his fingers deftly and slammed it back in its sheath. "Just don't provoke me, my dear. I've a thousand reasons to kill you, Teret. But I can wait and watch you die slowly in the opium dens of Shen. So satisfying, that outcome. But for now— eat. You need your strength."

Sulo awarded her a vicious grin. Teret didn't respond. Instead she chewed hard into the meat as though it were Sulo's throat. "We rest here for the night," he said. "Don't think to run. Every living thing in this country will kill you: man, beast, insect, spirit . . . whatever."

"Tamersane will kill *you*." Teret jerked her chin up toward where Sulo stood hands on hips grinning down at her. "He is coming for you, murderer. You'll be crow-bait soon."

"I've been outlawed in Rorshai for over seven years. Your brother couldn't catch me, Teret, nor his beloved High King up north. We were proud once, and independent. But your Kaan gave our people away. Sold the Rorshai to the westerners, your brother did. The Rorshai wipe western asses now. That bastard with his crystal crown—what does he care about the Rorshai? You were duped. But not Sulo. I'm a survivor, and out here I'm indestructible. There are no rules in this wilderness, Teret. No boundaries for one such as I."

"You're a relic from the past," Teret said. "Primitive and soon to be extinct."

"As for your husband . . ." Sulo chuckled, ignoring her. "I've watched him for weeks—know his habits. He's failing fast is Lord Tam. Decadent and weak like most of those Kelwynians. Ruled by a queen," Sulo spat the last words out with contempt. "You were soft in the head to fall for such a one, Kaan's daughter."

"I'm also Kaan's sister," Teret said, noticing how the rage had slipped form his flat gaze, replaced by an odd expression that hinted sorrow and regret, even affection. Sulo was insane, even more dangerous than she'd thought. Teret dared not provoke him again. Not without a way of following through.

"Olen will hunt you down like the rabid wolf you are, Sulo. He hasn't forgotten you. And there is also Arami, the new Kaan of the Anchai—or have you forgotten your own kin?" She saw the irritation flash in his eyes. *Careful*, Teret told herself. The moment passed and he smiled again.

"Out here a man can breathe." Sulo made a big show of taking in breath and spreading his tanned sinewy arms wide. "In the east a man is truly alive, Teret. Not shackled to rulers and bonds." He changed tack suddenly and took seat on the turf beside her. Teret watched him with hate-heavy eyes.

"It's not personal, Teret." Sulo flashed her a grin more suited to a hyena. "Not entirely. It's how I make my living these days. Selling prisoners for a decent price. Mostly women—though boys too. The Rundali pay well for boys; the Shen sometimes too. It's a grubby trade but a man has to eat. And I eat well, most days."

"It's a long way to Shen." Teret turned her head and closed her eyes for a moment. She was so tired, and more than for herself she fretted about Tam. Always she'd looked after him, ever since that first day they'd set eyes on each other at their camp at Morning Hills, when her brother ordered her clean up the foreigner's hand, after his friend had nearly cut it off. A misunderstanding. Tam had often joked about the incident as he did everything back then. She shut out those thoughts.

I cannot show weakness to this creature.

Three days had pased since her kidnap. Where was Tam and how was he coping? Would she ever see him again? Teret felt a tear trace her lid and blinked it back. *Stay strong!*

But it was so hard. Teret knew without her calming influence her husband would court disaster, vulnerable to any fit of random rage that could prove his undoing, especially in an evil place like Caranaxis had become.

"Shen?" Sulo's grin grew stale. "What about it?"

"That's where you said you're taking me."

"Did I—must have forgotten." He looked vague for a moment and then shrugged. "There are closer places; depends on you really." Sulo waved a hand, brushing a mosquito aside. It was still hot even though the last light had faded from the hills surrounding them. The wind had eased and still night settled deep and silent, broken by the occasional lonely cry of wolves in the distance.

"All eastern slave markets pay good coin for exotic women. And you *are* exotic, Teret. I was only joking about you being ugly. You're old, past your best—but still a prize. Laregoza and Rundali are closer than Shen."

"Those places lie south whereas this road leads northeast." Teret's years spent in Ptarni had earned her a rough knowledge of how the eastern lands were arranged. Laregoza was rumored a swamp, and Rundali and Shen steeped in mystery. Tseola, a vast nothingness of plains and hills split by the odd river, turning into ice in the uttermost north—the realm of endless dark. Tam and Teret had never fared beyond Ptarni, but there were maps and such in Caranaxis showing the outline of such places.

Sulo shrugged, losing interest in the subject. "Time will out. I suggest you sleep while you can; you'll get scant chance once you're sold on the block. Slaves have short lives mostly."

Bored of the game, Sulo left her alone after lashing her hands behind her back. He left her feet unfettered, assuring her she wouldn't get far out here before something ate her. Job done, Sulo ventured up to watch the empty road again, as night closed deeper, a warm moist glove smothering the valley.

Teret closed her eyes. She blamed herself entirely. She'd given her husband too much rope. Since leaving the Silver City, Tam had returned to indolence and drinking, haunted on the hour by his memories. They'd settled in Rorshai, but he'd found small comfort there. Not for Tam the nomadic farming life. He'd always liked the city.

After the harrowing events at the end of the war, Tam had withdrawn into himself. His brother, Yail Tolranna's, death at his own hands, the Gods ripping each other apart in the sky above Wynais, the panic and despair that followed—all factors in changing her husband forever. Gone was the fun-loving joker, the charmer. Replaced by a cynical drinker, who'd not only quarreled with Queen Ariane, but the High King up in Kelthaine as well. Those two rulers had consulted with Teret, and to her lasting regret it had been she who suggested Tamersane head a new spy-ring observing the allies' lands in the east.

Those early trips to Ptarni straightened him up. Tam needed action else he'd fall into self-pity and loathing. It had worked well in those first years after the war. They'd achieved much, warming the relations between Akenates and the High King back west. Then Callanz had murdered his father resulting in the High King severing all diplomatic contact. But despite the danger, Tam insisted on staying in Caranaxis, a decision for which they were now both paying the price. Worn out, Teret's mind drifted back again to when she first met Tam. She smiled briefly at the memory. That helped her sleep for a time.

She woke uneasy. Instinct or premonition—Teret felt wrongness in the air. Tense and wary, she sat up and stretched her limbs as best she could. Something was wrong. Above her stars winked and the moon was swallowed by racing cloud.

A noise to her left.

Teret rolled on instinct, just as Sulo's sword sank into the ground where she'd

lain. "Change of plans." Sulo's rabid eyes glared down at her. "It *is* a long way to Shen, so methinks I'll kill you now!"

Sulo lunged at her again but Teret rolled sideways and ducked under his next swipe. She shuffled clear, found her feet, and sprinted into the trees leading down to a stream and midnight dark beyond. Her hands were tied but at least her legs were free.

Teret heard his curses and crashing as Sulo sped after her. Teret reached the stream and waded across, sinking quickly to above her waist. Something slimy touched her arm. She shuddered but kept moving, making the far bank just as Sulo's shadow slid into the water behind her. Teret distanced herself from the bank and let adrenaline and rage fuel her strong legs.

Chapter 4 | The Tseole

Tam winced as an iron grip raised him to his feet and a rough voice hissed in his ear. "Move and I'll cut your throat, you foreign bastard." Strong hands spun him round until Rol Sharn's grinning face loomed before him.

"You were a fool to come back here, Kelwynian." Rol Sharn's smile broadened showing painted wooden teeth. "I heard how Teret warned you against it. Poor girl, wedded to a fool—doubt there's much left of her now. That Sulo's quite deranged, you know. I don't fancy her chances of keeping the skin on her back. I—" The smile froze when Rol Sharn's mouth filled with blood that sprayed Tam's face, and Tam blinked in disbelief seeing the steel blade protruding from the merchant's gut. Rol Sharn tumbled forward.

Rough hands shoved Tamersane sideways as his erstwhile captor crashed forward yelling, a crooked dagger in his back. Someone kicked him and Tam crashed into a wall. Lamplight hinted shadows, and steel clashed on steel, once, twice, silvery light flickering in the street. Tam heard grunts and groans and the thud of bodies and clatter of steel hitting cobbles.

It happened so fast. Inside a minute, all six men who had accompanied Rol Sharn into the alley lay mangled and twisted, their lifeblood oozing into the gutters.

Tam blinked. Eyes focusing, he saw Red the innkeep hovering at the door, his shaggy ruddy beard thrust out in indignation. Red gripped a knife, pointing it at someone standing behind Tam.

"You'll pay for this, Tseole!" Red's voice was hoarse with rage.

A slow warm chuckle caused Tam to turn and see the shaggy-haired former drunk crouched behind him. The Tseole was wiping his crooked knife on one of his victim's shirts. He winked up at Tam; he looked amused and very sober.

"Reckon you've a chance against me, Red?" The stranger grinned, and Tam thought this must be another madman. The stable boy emerged, saw the mess, and scampered off into the dark at a nod from Red.

"Get your nag, tall fellow," the Tseole said, surveying Red with calm eyes the color of dark ink. "Best we leave soonest."

Red chose that moment to seize the tulwar he'd hidden behind the door and leap into the alley with it swinging. His blow went wild and the stranger's knife tore into Red's throat.

"Guess I'll have to clean the fucking thing again," the Tseole grumbled. He looked at Tam. "You still standing there, Long Legs?" Tam blinked at him.

"I'll explain slowly as you're clearly not the sharpest tool in the box," the Tseole smiled. "Get horses. From stables. Hurry!" The Tseole knelt to clean his knife again.

Tam shook his head, gulped in moist air and staggered across to the stables. Beside his tall horse stood a shaggy ill-tempered looking piebald pony. The pony spat at him as Tam got near it.

"Don't mind Porcha." The Tseole had followed him in and stood cheerfully behind him. "She gets a bit teasy when we're in the city." The stranger whistled a merry tune as he opened his drawstrings and relieved himself on the straw.

"Ahh—that's better. It's the little things in life, hey?" Close by, shouts announced the boy had alerted the city guard. The heavy tread and angry voices were closing fast. "Best we vacate this vicinity—what say you, longshanks?"

"Who are you?" Tam knew he should be grateful but he was still half stunned and wasn't about to trust this savage.

"Apart from saving your scrawny neck, we can call this serendipity, old son. Good timing—so shut up and cheer up. Life's a dream. Come on," he smiled again showing wonky teeth. "Saddle up that expensive nag; let's vacate this charming city before the hordes of Yffarn descend upon us!"

Tamersane stared at the Tseole for a moment, again questioning his sanity, then for want of any better suggestion he nodded. "You're right—time to go." The two men led their horses from the stable-yard, mounting just as the city watch cleared the corner, amid shouts and clashes of steel. Just another night in Caranaxis for them.

They fled the city with the watch yelling curses. With the watch on foot, the two riders soon lost their pursuit. The gatekeepers at the north wall blocked their way, but the Tseole's arrows felled two and sent the rest diving for cover. Tam was impressed by how many weapons his wild-haired companion had stowed beside his saddle. This Tseole rider was a mobile armory.

Guards still hiding, the two riders leapt from their mounts and yanked open the gates, groaning with exertion as the heavy iron-barred oak creaked ajar. Once they'd prized a gap wide enough to get their mounts through, they vaulted back onto their saddles and fled like thieves into the night.

"Name's Stogi," the Tseole horseman said when they slowed to a canter. "I'm wanted in four countries." He sounded proud.

"What are you, a horse thief?"

"Shit, no—I'm a raider, like any decent Tseole. Horse thief

indeed."

"Why did you intervene?" Tam studied the other rider as he urged his beast away from Caranaxis. It was raining again and hard to see more than a few yards in the gloom. At least that would confuse any pursuit. "It wasn't your fight."

Stogi shrugged; it made his earrings jingle. "I like fighting," he said. "And I hate Ptarnians. Good enough reasons both. But that innkeep—Red. He owed me. I've had dealings with that snake before, and the other fellow, the merchant."

"Rol Sharn the Spice Dealer?"

"Rol Sharn the emperor's spy. Right shifty bastard that one—had it coming, so he did."

Tam wasn't convinced. None of this made sense. He studied the other man as best he could while they alternately cantered and trotted along the road, making as much progress as they dared in the cloying wet dark. The road curled up like a sleeping serpent, hugging the mountainside and blurring into a shadow of woods and smothering cloud.

Stogi was short of build but strong, sinewy and athletic. Perhaps forty, he looked tough as wire and his dark eyes flashed feral-cunning in the night. A lined, heavily scarred face paler than the Ptarnians Tam was familiar with; Stogi's hair was a shaggy mess of smoky black streaks speckled with gray. He wore it long and loose, and sported a heavy mustache with close-cropped beard. The earrings were large golden hoops.

The man wore leather trousers and tunic supported by a broad belt with silver studs. A scimitar and three crooked knives hung from the belt, and a horse bow, three short spears, and some weird spiky contraption hung from his saddle belts. For a maniac he appeared congenial enough.

"You're a northerner," Tam said, fighting off exhaustion and leaning into his saddle as their road steepened. "From Tseole?"

"Tseola. Yes, it's in the north. You are observant."

Tam ignored the sarcasm. "And you just happened to be in the City in the Clouds? Passing through, exchanging pleasantries with people you so love."

"Aye," grinned Stogi. "Just like you." Tam chose to ignore that response too. This Stogi, savage or not, was clearly no fool. They reined in ten miles from the city gates as the soft rain soaked the earth by their mounts' feet.

"Best rest up in these woods for a time," said Stogi as he slid from his pony and untied its saddle, removing all the clutter amid grumbles. Tam remained a-horse. "No point us fumbling through the night." Stogi, messing with his saddle, hadn't noticed Tam still seated on his horse.

"Do as you must, but I have a need for urgency."

"Your woman—I know." Stogi awarded Tam a lopsided grin. "Bad business, but breaking your neck on a mountain road won't help either of you."

Tam's hand dropped to his side reaching for his sword. Stogi watched him with cool velvet eyes. The Tseole let his arms drop by his sides feigning indifference, but Tam had seen how quick this killer was.

"What else do you know?" Tam's hand eased from the hilt.

Stogi shrugged. The Tseole showed Tam his back. He hoisted spears and bow across his shoulders and once done with them strolled back to see to his horse. Tam watched him in silence.

"Not much," Stogi said after a moment's fussing his piebald. "There girl, rest up quiet now." Stogi turned and smiled. He folded his bare forearms, and Tam noticed for the first time the intricate tattoos traced from the Tseole's wrists to elbow. "We hunt the same man, Lord Tamersane."

Tam's jaw dropped. "So, you are a spy then. Or an assassin?"

"Merely a brigand with a weighty price on his head. I do have eyes and ears, however, and I'm quick to grasp an opportunity when one presents itself. Your man upset some powerful people in Caranaxis."

"Sulo?"

"Stabbed a notary last week. A well-connected fellow. Favored. The Emperor's put a price on this Sulo's head that makes mine look shamefully pathetic. I get Sulo's bounty and I'm in the clear. Hence, we are united in purpose, Kelwynian." Stogi slid the saddle from his pony and commenced organizing his weaponry with fastidious precision. After a moment he looked up. "You going to sleep on that fucking horse tonight?"

Tam remained seated for a moment then shrugged and slid from his saddle. He was bone weary and Stogi was right, best they rest till dawn and get away again at speed. "So what do you know about me?"

"It's amazing the gossip you can acquire while feigning tipsy in tavern. Master Red and Rol Sharn were quite candid about you, my new friend. Lord Tamersane of Kelwyn—a land I'd never heard of way west across the endless steppes. The queen's favorite cousin living in secret in the City in the Clouds like some dossing dropout. A high-placed enemy noble within their grasp. Sharn's plan was to hand you over to the Emperor, charged with spying. He stood to gain much from your execution."

"But how? And what's the connection between him and Sulo?"

"Money. Rol Sharn knew about Sulo too, doubtless he told him about your lady, knowing you'd seek him out. Once Sulo had served his purpose then Rol Sharn would have had him arrested too, receiving a second sack of gold. Shrewd fellow. I saw them talking at a market stall, just last week. Very casual. I'd been tracking this Rorshai renegade since I heard about the reward. And I knew Rol Sharn's reputation—odd chance, seeing that pair together. Sharn had it all planned, but Sulo proved unreliable."

"How so?"

"He was meant to deliver your wife to the dealer's manse. That way Sharn had you both where he wanted. He sent some men to assist the Rorshai and keep an eye on him. But those men are dead. Sulo played his own game and vanished."

"Where's he making for?"

"East."

"I assumed that much." Tam rubbed his aching eyes. "Rol Sharn hinted at Shen. I don't even know where that is." Tam felt another wash of weariness flood him. He hadn't eaten much, nor had he slept for two days. He tied his destrier's reins to a tree and slumped beside him.

"A long way from here." Stogi pulled a flask from his saddle bag and slurped some cloudy-looking liquid. "You look shattered, mate. Drink this—I'll get a stew going." Tam nodded thanks.

"Fuck but that's rough." The creamy liquid resembled Rorshai fermented yak milk. But this was even worse. "What is it?" Tam said, trying not to choke.

"Cactus juice mixed with cane grubs. Acquired taste, I'll grant you. Drink enough you'll get visions. It's good shit," Stogi told him. Tam gulped it down and struggled to find his breath.

"It's . . . strong."

"Oh yes—and it will give you strength too. Those Rundali know what they are doing. Master brewers, among other things."

"Who are the Rundali?"

"Conniving wizards that live in the far country beyond Rundal Forest. Nobody knows much about them, as sensible folk stay well clear of their country and the woods surrounding it. Weird places. But the Rundali concocted this drink and I acquired a taste for it while traveling out east."

Stogi's inky eyes crossed slightly and he belched enthusiastically. "Rundali cough mixture," he squinted at Tam, his voice croaky. "Clears the head while purging your bowels. Needs a steady hand though. Drink too much and you're hallucinating. Sulo will make for Laregoza, not Shen," Stogi added after a moment's reflection.

"Isn't that in the wrong direction?" Tam regretted not studying the old maps like Teret had. She'd been fascinated by these far flung exotic lands, whereas back then he couldn't have cared less. But he had heard of Laregoza and knew it to be somewhere in the south.

"Yes, but Sulo's not going to ride back through Ptarni and risk capture. They'll be scanning the lands surrounding Caranaxis. Rol Sharn was the Emperor's man after all. Sulo will follow the Great Trade Road for a while and then cut south skirting Rundal Forest—what I would do."

Tam yawned back exhaustion. The foul liquid had soothed his nerves but he felt sleepy now. "I've got to find my wife before that bastard hurts her, Stogi."

"For sure—but you can't do bugger all tonight so quit thinking about it. See to your nag instead, and I'll get a fire going and warm up some stew," Stogi said.

"I pilfered some herbs and spices from the market this morning as I'd an inkling I'd be back on the road again inside a day." Stogi wandered over to set up a fire. Within minutes he had a crackle despite the heavy drizzle. Tam struggled with the big horse's saddle and kit, gave him some water and shivering slightly, reclaimed his seat against the tree.

"You're quite the wilderness expert," Tam yawned. "I'm grateful for your company, Tseole. At first, I thought you'd murder me too. You still might, but I'm too tired to care."

Stogi chuckled. "There's a thought. Roll your handsome head in front of Callanz's golden feet and get pardoned and rewarded all at once, ha! Let me sleep on that, Kelwynian. It's a tempting offer."

The stew was surprisingly good and after several more gulps of ghastly cactus fermentation, Tam had returned to a benign state of numbness. "I wish I'd known about this vile stuff before," he told his companion with a lopsided smile.

Stogi finished his supper and crossed his legs, leaning close to the fire. He produced a small pipe and lit it, sending swirls inches up before the heavy night snatched them away. The Tseole's eyes were half closed but Tam knew he was watching him.

"What are our chances?" Tam straightened, not ready for sleep yet. He had questions, and Stogi's joke about killing him had made him wary again. He didn't know this man. Rol Sharn had duped him, maybe Stogi the Tseole would too.

Stogi shrugged the question away. "So why are you here, Lord Tamersane?"

"Call me Tam. The man you mentioned died seven years ago."

Stogi's eyes narrowed further. "You were there?"

"I was—witnessed the entire . . . happening. Saw them fighting in the sky. It's stained in my memory like an old dead song."

"And I thought it just hearsay, an extravagant lie fed by western propaganda. But I also felt the shadow of them passing, as did many of my kin. The Gods themselves, tossed about like dead dry leaves on a blowy winter's day. We Tseole tasted the fear on the wind and knew something momentous had occurred. But how could such a thing happen—the Gods perish and a man still draw breath?"

"They out-lived their purpose," Tam said. "Failed like all things fail."

"That's not overly optimistic."

"The world changed that day." Tam reached over and took a long chug at the cactus drink. He was starting to enjoy it, which wasn't a good sign.

49

"Perhaps—who knows? Our shamans said the World Weaver appeared and changed the order of the universe, got rid of the old crew."

"Yes, the faceless man—I saw Him too."

"What?" Stogi scratched his nose. Tam didn't respond, so the Tseole continued with his theory. "Well, the shamans are full of shit. They said the Gods quarreled, an outcome of some witchcraft or sorcery that set them against each other. You'd think they'd be smarter."

"You've a simplistic outlook. It was . . . harrowing, complicated. But I wasn't talking about that." Stogi just stared at him so Tam expanded. "Whatever happened back then happened. I have other ghosts to bury."

"Well, do tell," grinned Stogi. "I'm more interested in you, Kelwynian. Why move to Caranaxis of all places?"

Tam stared at the flames for a moment without responding. Finally, he sighed and tugged the fire with a stick. "I killed my brother in the dungeons below Wynais—the Silver City—where my cousin Queen Ariane rules still. Yail had sold out to Caswallon our enemy. We quarreled, and my Teret was hurt in the struggle. I lost it— stabbed him through the heart. Four times. That was the day my soul died, Stogi."

"And you dragged your woman down with you."

That hurt but only because it was true. "I did. I was so selfish—I see that now. But regret is a useless emotion. I had my reasons, pitiful though they were."

"Go on."

"I don't want to discuss it."

"Just you and me and the rain. Good for you to talk about these things. Get them off your chest. That way you can move forward— get your girl back."

Tam shrugged. "Can I?" He poked the fire again and winced, picturing Teret's sleeping face the last time he'd seen her.

"The war ended abruptly and the Crystal King took the throne of Kelthaine, and became overlord of all four kingdoms as his kin had before the usurper, and everyone was filled with hope," Tam said, noting how the Tseole's deep eyes were still watching him shrewdly. "They had survived despite everything. People celebrated. Except me—I had wanted to die in that war. What could a man like me gain from peacetime? When I saw the Gods destroying each other I wanted them to take me too. I was a broken warrior with nothing to fight."

"So, you went east—why?" Stogi puffed at his pipe and folded his tattooed arms behind his head. Tam envied his relaxed state.

"At first we were envoys mending the nets torn between countries. King Akenates was sensible after his defeat, and our High King eager to patch things up. Everyone was exhausted by war. Except me—after Wynais, I needed the diversion of conflict to calm the self-loathing. Teret knew I had to do something, so it was she who suggested we accompany her brother the Kaan of Rorshai to distant Caranaxis and glean what we could, lest war break out again. One trip led to another; I enjoyed that life to a point. Weeks riding—always on your guard for ambush, and then in the city keeping ears pulled back and eyes peeled open. Teret liked it too, in the early days. But then when mad Callanz murdered his father and seized power we had to flee."

"And yet you returned despite the danger?"

"Folly and madness, but I needed the edge. Couldn't live a normal life, been through so much. The war—it raked my soul apart. I was a sunny fellow once." Tam felt tears welling at the edge of his eyes but held them back. "Everyone urged me not to return," he said. "The Kaan, the Crystal King, my beloved cousin the Queen in

Wynais—all of them. Yet return I did and loyal Teret came with me."

"There's more to it than that," Stogi smiled slightly. "Has to be. If you sought extinction why not ride off a cliff?" Stogi puffed and sighed. "A smoke before a nap, can't beat that." He tapped his pipe and winked at Tam.

Tam nodded. "You're observant. I do have a habit but not for plain tobacco. I acquired a taste for certain plant extractions when first I came here," Tam said. "I cannot access them back home— would that I could. I'm half hooked on the bloody stuff. But it drives the demons away."

"And creates new ones," Stogi rolled on his back and yawned. "A one-way journey resulting in ruin. Lucky, I found you. Get some sleep, laddie, you'll need your wits back by dawn." Stogi's lids closed and within seconds he was snoring.

Tam watched him for a moment wondering why he'd spoken of his past to this stranger. He'd worry about that in the morning if Stogi hadn't slit his throat before dawn. Life was a gamble— sometimes you had to trust your hunches.

Chapter 5 | The Queen's Chosen

The Lake of Stones stretched gray and forlorn into the distance. Its calm water hinted at things lurking below, but the inky surface reflected dark shadows of racing clouds from leaden skies above. A bleak cold place on the edge of nowhere.

The banks fell away steep and stony, beyond them the shoreline chimed with the sigh of grainy pebbles washed clean by the ceaseless suck and surge of murky water. Away off to the left, a mile or so out from the shore, an island of twisted rocks suggested a castle, fortress, or some kind of dwelling. But Garland knew they were just rocks piled upon rocks, the home of naught save rook and crow. That said, it was easy to imagine some strange being dwelling within. A sorcerer or magician perhaps.

Garland sighed and rubbed his tired eyes. This entire region sapped a man's soul dry like defeat on a battleground. He glanced back up the bank. Doyle sat his horse in evident discomfort. Cold wind buffeted his ears and the horse looked skittish. Close by his lieutenant's steed, Garland's mare stood motionless, her reins looped around a scraggy thorn. Both horses looked miserable as Lieutenant Doyle.

Loyal Doyle.

Garland recalled when he'd first seen the lad, scarce more than a

boy, flush- faced and shouting on the heights of The High Wall—
the long mountain range that protected Queen Ariane's domain from
the wild lands beyond. Those same wild lands surrounding him.

Poor Doyle—timid lad he'd been. They'd called him Doodle
back then. But Doyle, like everyone else Garland knew, had changed.
To witness what they'd seen you had to change, else your memories
would tear you inside out. But the war of the Gods was over and
those epic times lost to gray emptiness that filled not only his vision,
but his life too.

Even so, Garland hadn't leaped at this opportunity when Lord
Calprissa presented it to him. A wild stab in the dark looking for
someone who most likely didn't want to be found. A fool's errand.
But the Queen's consort was ever persuasive, and Garland had
complied—decent, honorable fool that he was, and more for his love
and respect of Ariane herself, rather than Raule's smooth words—
Raule Calprissa, Lord of Kelwyn's second city who had once been
called Tarello, a common soldier like himself.

Strange choice, but hard to refuse Queen Ariane—those dark
clever eyes, her winning smile. She had a presence beyond regal. Her
father's daughter. You just wanted to please her—everyone did. She'd
saved their country after all. And her Dreaming was legendary. That
had saved them several times. Besides—-Garland wasn't ready to retire
yet, and neither were his men.

And here they were camped outside this lake in a world of winter
and wind. But soldering was his life—his duty. Garland been content
enough in Wynais, though he'd never married—something he
regretted, and at fifty-six winters believed he'd lost his chance.

"Anything?" Doyle's croak reached his ears bringing his mind
back to the present and their task at hand. That lad had no wish to
linger here and Garland could scarce blame him.

"Nothing yet."

"How long do we wait, Captain?" Doyle fiddled in his saddle. He looked exhausted and Garland suspected couldn't grasp what his captain hoped to glean from this visit.

"Long as it takes," Garland growled back at the boy. Seeing Doyle's morose expression, he waved a hand. "But no point us both lingering here. Go back to camp and get a brew on, and make sure the troop's ready to move when I return."

"You going to be all right out here on your own?" Doyle leaned forward in his saddle. He looked relieved but worried too. "What if she doesn't show, or worse puts a curse on you?"

"I'll be fine," Garland waved him off, and Doyle, after checking his captain's mount had enough water, urged his own beast turnabout making for the rudimentary camp where the other six waited. *I hope.*

Garland was aware of his men's dim view of this visit. They had volunteered expecting to go to Caranaxis, to infiltrate the City of Clouds and bring back that wastrel Tamersane. A tough honorable job with high risks—perfect for men like them. Plenty of action. Instead, they had detoured to this remote lake without any explanation from their captain except "The Queen dreamed of this place," a lame reason but all he could offer at the moment.

"First you must stop by the Lake of Stones and consult she who dwells there," Ariane had said. "Ysaren the Seeress will help find him." No other explanation. Laughable command coming from anyone else, but the Queen had smiled that smile and he, fool, had saluted, flush-faced, and strolled out the court, his mind full of purpose.

But here by the lake he was no longer so sure. Garland watched the dust settle as the rider cantered out of sight. He smiled despite the gloom encasing him. Doyle was a good lad to put up with his captain's whims without complaint. The other men had been with

Garland in the Batlle of Darkvale, during the war with Caswallon. They'd witnessed the death of their leader General Belmarius. The first day they'd encountered Ptarnians. That seemed so long ago. Seven years.

Doyle had been spared that horror. The boy was fresh from Calprissa after Queen Ariane's first victory there. He'd joined the Rangers, Ariane's elite bushwhackers who'd successfully led a guerrilla campaign against the sorcerer, and then after the Ranger's leader's untimely death, the new commander, Garland, had taken the lad under his wing. Truth be told he had a soft spot for Lieutenant Doyle.

Movement caught Garland's eye, again breaking his train of thought. Something out there on the water. A ripple, perhaps nothing more. It widened, lapped the shore, then disappeared in the middle distance.

Garland pulled the eye-glass from the pack resting beside him on the pebbled shore. He flicked it open and placed the steel rim to his left eye. He squinted, scanned back and forth, but saw nothing. At last satisfied, Garland sighed again and placed the spy-glass at his side.

A sudden sound of splashing water had the glass back in Garland's hand. Again, he held it to his eye and saw nothing. This time Garland pointed the glass toward the island, but all was as had been.

Sod this.

Garland stood slowly, stretched his stiff muscles, and willed his aching limbs into movement. Perhaps it had been a mistake coming here, but he'd promised the Queen he'd visit this place before risking Caranaxis, where Garland suspected her renegade cousin would be found.

Another splash, this time much nearer. Something *was* out there and Garland had the nasty feeling it was stalking him beneath that inky water. He stowed the spy-glass and pulled his heavy broadsword free of its scabbard.

"Show yourself—spirit! I know you're out there."

Garland wandered back down the bank until his feet were washed by the stale milky water. He shivered at the clammy touch. The Lake of Stones they called this water for obvious reasons. Between the steppes and the arid plains surrounding the Ptarni border. A mass of water in the middle of nowhere, rimmed by shale and rock, with not a tree in sight—just ceaseless wind and slate skies overhead.

Garland shuddered, feeling the water seep through the leather of his boots. There was something unclean about that touch. He turned away from the lake. Doyle was right; they should leave this place— nothing for them here. A shadow flickered past him. Garland froze. Turned again; very slowly, sword leveled in palms.

A woman stood scarce ten feet away, her huge pale-blue eyes watching him as hawk studies sparrow. Her face was pointed, thin, the skin stretched like brittle parchment. The cheekbones and nose were prominent, and yet she was striking. Garland rammed the sword point down into the bank and waited for her to approach him. Ysaren had come just as his Queen foretold. The oracle—the one he'd been sent to seek.

She appeared both ancient and beautiful. Those were his first impressions. Tall and wretchedly thin, with wispy golden hair trailing down her back and blowing around her pale face. Willow-graceful, despite her evident age, the frail features were chiseled and those large eyes intelligent and hypnotic. There was power in that gaze. Enchantment. Danger.

I've a job to do.

Garland removed his gloved hands from his sword and held his arms out wide, palms forward. "I mean you no harm, Lady," he said to the apparition watching him with those uncanny eyes.

"If you did you'd be dead." The voice was soothing yet sinister. A

57

contradiction; it lingered in the air and the sky crackled slightly on the horizon.

"You are the lady Ysaren?" The woman nodded slightly so Garland pushed through with his message. "My Queen sent me to consult a seeress called Ysaren at the Lake of Stones. Said she alone could help find someone she has lost." The woman approached him a slight smile on her lips. Her gossamer shift left little to imagination, and despite his wariness Garland felt a stir in his loins.

"Do I excite you?" The woman—Ysaren—stopped inches from his face. He could feel her hot dry breath. She reached down quickly with thin bony fingers and teased his groin. Garland jumped back in alarm.

"You're not what I expected!"

Ysaren's eyes hinted sorrow and disappointment. "Too old perhaps. Too frail?"

"No—you are beautiful." The woman smiled hearing that.

"I was once," Ysaren told him. "Now I'm just lonely and tired. Stuck in this place." She sighed, took seat on a rock, her slim shoulders hunched and her legs parted just enough to hint at what lay between them. She rested elbows on knees, hands cupped beneath chin, her cool uncanny gaze surveying him in silence.

Garland, feeling increasingly uncomfortable, rubbed his gauntlets together and fidgeted. How to handle this and move on? Job to do. The men would be worried about him. He needed to get back, but first he must do what had to be done. No time for small talk.

"I seek a nobleman. A cousin to my Queen. Missing these last three years. Feared dead."

"Then dead he probably is—that's usually what happens to the missing," Ysaren's laugh was abrupt and crow-rough. "They turn up dead, or not at all." She traced a crooked finger along the inside of her thigh while smiling at his discomfort. "Have you any idea how old I am?"

"Nope." Garland hadn't known what to expect at the Lake of Stones, but it certainly wasn't what he was seeing before him. "But you are very beautiful—I'm not just saying that."

"Three thousand years, seven months, and fifteen days to be precise."

"That's a long time," Garland nodded, having no idea where this was going. "But the years have been kind to you, I'm thinking."

"Have they?" Ysaren rose to her feet expression suddenly brittle, eyes flinting like ice chips. "How the fuck would you know, Mortal? You've scant fallen from your mother's tit. What do even you know about anything?"

"I—"

"You're all the same—human folk." Ysaren's stare raked him. "Shallow. In it for yourselves. Short-lived, selfish, and witless."

"For my Queen," Garland persisted. "Ariane of Kelwyn. She it was who sent me here."

"Then she's as stupid as you are." The woman turned away in irritation, her attention now on something sliming across the surface of the lake. Garland followed her gaze and tensed, seeing a ripple, something gray and coiling, another ripple, and then a sudden plop, and whatever it was had vanished.

"What is that thing out there?" Garland's gloved hands found his sword again.

"My jailer," the woman said, her bottom lip dragging. "Reason why I'm here."

"You're a prisoner?"

"You're not very bright, are you?" The woman glared at Garland. "Yes—prisoner I am. Have been for millennia. Cursed by a relative."

"Well—can I help? My men are close by, maybe will can kill that thing? We have bows." Garland glanced at the water again. All was quiet save the constant chilling breeze that buffeted along the lake shore. The woman chuckled softy.

He turned to look at her. "Did I say something funny?" She was smiling again, but her eyes held an ironic, slightly sad expression as though lost somewhere else.

"Kind of you to offer," Ysaren said. "And forgive my harsh words. I mean you no ill, mortal. I become angry, stuck here alone. Bit frosty around the edges. But you cannot help me, sir. No one can. Besides, I thought you came here to ask for my help?"

"I did—but . . ."

"I was cursed by an enemy who is now dead," Ysaren explained. "Unfortunately, the kraken he created from spell-craft isn't. The bloody thing's programmed to keep me here. If I try to leave this region that rusty bag of coils will rise up and devour me."

"That's a . . . shame," Garland said not knowing the right words. "Well, the offer's there, Lady—maybe we can do something?"

Ysaren slunk back on the rock again, her pale straw-colored hair covering her face. She brushed it back with a dirty finger nail. She looked tired now, defeated. "You are a strange man." She pulled the shift across her shoulders as if suddenly cold. "I wonder . . ."

Garland noticed the sky darkening overhead. "I need to get back to camp; I promised my men we'd be moving out in the morning. They don't like it here. But first I need answers concerning Lord Tamersane—the reason why we dropped by."

"No one likes it here," the woman said. "You think I like it here?" Then she stood with sudden passion and grabbed his arm. "Are you brave, Garland the Ranger? Do you have true metal in that heart?"

"How do you know my name?"

"I know a lot of things—fat good they've done me. Sometimes it's better to be stupid. My race were sorcerers steeped in lore and wisdom, but that didn't stop us from destroying each other, even after our enemies were defeated."

"You're Aralais—the golden folk?" Garland noticed how her hand still gripped his arm. "I thought you all dead?"

"I'm probably the last, trapped here by my foolishness. Except for my sisters of course. Those bitches still endure though I wish they'd rotted years ago." Ysaren's huge eyes were level with his own. Hypnotic and urgent; he couldn't stop staring into them. "Have you heard of the Aralais treasures—the artifacts fashioned millennia ago?"

"Indeed, and our High King in Kelthaine has two of them—the crystal crown called Tekara, and the sword Callanak. Weren't there seven originally?"

"Thirteen. Most were destroyed in the war with our foes, the Urgolais. Three are rumored hidden near Rundal Woods, the Emerald Bow known as Kerasheva among them." Ysaren leaned against him until Garland felt her small breasts resting against his chest. "I need that bow and the arrows accompanying it. I was a huntress once." Her flinty eyes were on the ripples still brimming the lakeshore.

Garland dropped his hands by his sides, torn between desire, confusion, and a need to move on. He was a practical man, not used to such eccentricities. Besides, this Ysaren was clearly on the edge of madness.

"Well, like I said we have bows."

"Can you find Kerasheva for me, Garland the Ranger? Bring it here?" Before he could respond Ysaren kissed his lips, her mouth hungry, eager. "Can you save me?" She pulled away suddenly, and to Garland she appeared as a shy girl for the briefest moment before cunning and guile returned to her face.

"I . . ." She kissed him again. He backed away and wiped dribble from his lips. This was proving an interesting afternoon.

She leaned against him again, her knees rubbing his thigh. "That

61

bow alone has the power to free me, if fired by a man without malice. A Journeyman, such as lived in ancient times. Kerasheva is useless in the hands of evil. It needs an honest heart to pull its strings."

Garland coughed and pushed her back a little. He didn't want to appear rude but he had a bone on and, well, this was business. "I'd love to assist, honestly. But it's not why I'm here. And if our bows won't work . . ."

"The one you seek is going to die." The woman's eyes were crafty now. "And his woman. I see their blood dripping in the water down there." Garland looked but saw nothing. "Free me! Don't be boring! Become my noble Journeyman—Sir Garland—and I might be able to divert their fate. Might. But I can do nothing in this place. My scrying powers are much curtailed here. My color is sapphire yet here I am mere gray."

Garland studied her eyes again. He saw desperation; a savage determination, but the guile had gone, replaced by a wild glimmer of hope. What would Queen Ariane say? He knew the answer—she would bid him do as the woman asked.

Follow your heart, Captain.

"How do I know I can trust you?"

"You don't—and you probably shouldn't." Ysaren brushed gold locks from her face again. "But the young couple you seek will die if you don't. Your queen dreamed of me, didn't she? Why you're here. Ariane has the Dreaming?"

"She does," Garland nodded. "It saved us all from disaster seven years ago." He sighed, rested his gloved hands on her shoulders lightly and stared hard into those huge weird eyes again. "All right, I'm in—you've beguiled me, wench, and I'm caught, fool that I am. Just tell me how long it will take me and where do I start?"

Ysaren sighed, a sound like steam venting from kettle. She crumpled against him, an urgent hand dropping low and deft clever fingers loosening his drawstrings.

"It's been over a millennium," Ysaren breathed. "I really can't wait much longer."

So, Garland obliged—what else could he do?

It was dark before he returned to camp.

***

"Where the fuck is he?" Pash mumbled as he rammed stew into his mouth. "Been gone most the day, so he has." The other five grumbled as Doyle joined them for supper.

"Captain knows what he's doing." Doyle nodded as Pash passed a bowl across. The broth was as uninspiring as the terrain hereabouts, but it least it filled his belly and warmed his bones. "I'm sure he'll be back before dark."

"Next half hour then," long-faced Karlan said. "Night closes fast here."

"And dark things waken," added Coife the Bowyer, who never had much hope at the best of times. "I've heard things crawling around these last few nights."

They ate without further discussion. Doyle watched their faces, studied the expressions. Old Karlan was nearly sixty, and Mullen not much younger with his thick gray beard and drooping mustaches. Both were skilled with ax and sword and both had seen a dozen campaigns. Coife and Tol were younger, though still in their forties, both clever with longbow and horse bow.

Pash used the spear better than any man Doyle knew. He was trouble, Pash—argumentative. Then there was Taylon. He hardly spoke but was a good man to have at your back. Handy with a knife too. They were all so much older than Doyle but they respected him. Knew what he'd been through.

Doyle watched their tired faces. Tough and loyal, but this venture was weighing them down. Garland's troop of volunteers needed action or purpose, or at least the faint notion of what they were up to. They were soldiers. Veterans who had witnessed horror and wonders beyond the ken of most men. They weren't quitters and they'd known Garland for years.

Even so the captain needed to explain why they were here. Garland had been so close. Just said the Queen chose us for this purpose. That had kept them content for the first few weeks; everyone loved Queen Ariane. But even that was wearing thin now. This cold gray plateau was sapping the "chosen's" resolve faster than enemy steel.

Dusk fell—still no captain.

"Maybe I should ride back," Doyle said, then looking up saw Garland riding toward the camp, his face buried beneath his hood and bulk shrouded in gloom. None spoke as Garland vaulted from his horse and demanded Pash get him some stew.

"Well?" Doyle asked after his captain had swallowed a good few mouthfuls. "Did you see anything, Captain, or was it another wasted day?"

Garland looked up sharply. "Aye, I saw something. Quite a lot actually." He looked awkward and the men stared at each other. Coife made a face and Pash's dark eyes narrowed in suspicion. "We ride out at dawn," Garland announced brusquely. "So get some sleep, you're going to need it."

"Ride where—home?" Pash placed his bowl by the fire and folded his arms. "I'm ready for that. Warm cozy inns full of bright-eyed Kelwynian lasses." The other men grinned, and even dour Coife perked up.

"We are not going home," said Garland. "We're going to Shen."

Chapter 6 | The Piper and the Sailor

Teret ran. Rain soaked her skin and clothes, and sweat mingled with rain streamed down her face as she tried to distance herself from her pursuer. Teret could hear Sulo's heavy breathing and curses, knew he was catching up.

It was dark and things reached for her, tendrils, bony stabbing fingers in the night. Branches and roots; she tripped over some and crashed into others. A wood surrounded her, deep and dark. Teret heard Sulo shout. She turned, saw him standing just yards away. A break in the cloud allowing the moon to spill ghostly light on his twisted, hate-filled features.

"I'm going to cut you open," he said brandishing his knife so the tip glinted silver in the moonlight. "There's no escape, bitch."

Teret spat back at him then turned and ran. Faster than before, the trees and scrubs blocking her progress, poking and cutting her flesh, her arms lashed and unable to help her. But Sulo's progress was checked as well. She heard him trip and roll. But cat-lithe, seconds later Sulo was closing on her again. The ground rose steep ahead. Teret forced her shaking legs take her up that ridge.

The rain stopped suddenly, and above the tree line ahead the moon's shadow revealed a woman clad in pale blue seated on a rock, her face ravaged by time and her long hair pale and strewn around her shoulders.

Please—help me!

Teret blinked and the stranger vanished. Just her imagination. Fear surrounded her in this place. Easy to fall prey to terror.

Keep moving girl!

Close behind she heard Sulo's stifled curse—perhaps he saw her too. The strange woman in blue. Hope she scared the bastard.

Teret gained the ridge. She turned, just as Sulo's knife slashed past her ear. Teret kicked out, caught his knee. Sulo cursed and tumbled, but seconds later was on his feet again. Teret sped along the ridge, weaving, hearing his feet crashing through brush behind her, their chase resuming, and him gaining again.

She could see better now and the moonlight hinted a narrow path ahead. Teret forced her way through to the deer track—at last she could make good progress and distance herself from her enemy. She'd always been a good runner and Sulo was overconfident.

Somewhere below Teret heard the sound of water rushing, grinding through rocks. Teret ran full pelt for several minutes then the path fell away suddenly. She hadn't seen the cliff. For terrifying moments Teret was suspended in air. Then she was falling fast and hard, the glimmer of white-washed water rushing up to greet her.

Teret hit the river hard and fast, her grimy body tossed and whirled and stolen away. Rag doll; she was ripped through rapids, the rocks peeping and nodding at her when vision allowed. Teret gasped, gulping air, then plunged under she held her breath as river swallowed her again.

Somehow, she survived that deluge. The water slowed and the rocks slipped behind her. Bruised but not broken, her arms still bound, Teret cut clean strokes with her legs, angling for the nearest bank. But the current was too strong and she was forced downstream, her exhausted limbs barely keeping her afloat.

For a moment Teret thought she glimpsed the small shape of Sulo swimming behind her, but it was impossible to tell. Could have been a log or any kind of flotsam. No point worrying about that now.

I have to survive this.

She'd pray to above begging Sulo had drowned, but the Gods were dead, so unlikely to answer. Strange how the mind works under duress. But Teret was Rorshai. Pride, anger, rage and vengeance—all good reasons to stay alive. And to see her beloved fool husband again.

Don't drown, free your hands, keep moving.

The water carried her down, faster and faster. Rapids came and went, buffeting her into rocks. But Teret stayed afloat, her soaked head above the torrent, her willpower and anger driving her on.

An hour later she crashed into a weedy bank, and limbs torn and bloody, Teret heaved, kneed, and elbowed herself out the water. She had survived—for the moment.

Teret was hurting badly though. Hungry and cold. No matter, she was alive.

Keep moving!

Teret shook her legs into motion. Neither river or enemy would take her tonight. She walked until her legs warmed, then ran until they were lead weights beneath her. Then after a short stop gulping air, Teret commenced walking brisk and sharp until dawn's pink glimmer warmed her tired face.

The forest seemed endless; it surrounded her—a mass of tree, tangle, moss, and rotten leaf, with the occasional glint of blue breaking through from high above like some baleful blinking eye monitoring her progress.

Teret slowed her walk and glanced around. The river must have carried her a good distance because she'd seen no woods barring the odd copse while tied to Sulo's horse. Once they cleared the mountains the lands ahead had been wide and open for many miles.

Strange how this forest hadn't been visible.

Teret stayed close to the river's bank. Keep going downstream. She might find a village or settlement, and providing the people were friendly she could free her hands and eat. If they weren't she could steal a knife and pilfer supplies. It didn't matter which. Survival was all that mattered. Survival and revenge. Then saving Tam before he lost himself.

Focus.

Teret scanned the trees surrounding her and, satisfied, stooped to drink long and hard like a wary deer poised for sudden flight. She was hungry but the water would sustain her. Teret almost jumped hearing sudden sound to her right. A red bird watching her with large golden eyes. Teret blinked at it then lay down for more water.

I wish I had your wings. Teret swallowed gulps. The red bird chirped at her then lifted and vanished into the dense brush surrounding them. At least she'd lost Sulo, and hopefully for good, though the twisted bastard had a talent for surviving better than she did. No point dwelling on that.

Teret walked, eyes scanning as morning filtered into afternoon. She found mushrooms parading a stump and took a chance, tearing at the funges with her teeth. They could poison her but she'd fade before long if she didn't eat something. They looked edible so Teret took the chance. So far luck had been with her. It was an hour later that she came upon the road, the lone white stag watching her in the sunshine.

Teret froze seeing the highway. A clean well-ridden path cutting through trees, the hills split asunder. She'd studied enough maps to know there was no paved way in this desolate region, apart from the Trade Route which ran east to Shen a hundred miles north of Rundal Woods, the only forest marked. Miles from this place wherever it was.

Besides, forests were avoided by sensible folk so no one built roads through them. Too many outlaws. But there it was in plain sight. Wide, paved with cobbles and flags, with no grass splitting its leveled pavers. A smooth highway leading to a distant valley of golden aspens, their leaves shivering and glimmering in the afternoon breeze.

Strange.

Teret felt the small hairs rise up on the back of her neck. There was something astir here. The Gods might be dead but maybe their spirits still wandered these remote lands. She felt eyes probing her back—perhaps the ghostly woman she thought she'd seen last night. There were many stories about the forests in these lands. But she'd thought them further east. Teret pushed such ideas away. Just her exhausted mind playing tricks on her again.

Nothing for it. Keep moving. Teret jumped down onto the road. The white hart watched her some twenty yards away, its large eyes not even curious. It had no fear. Teret turned her back on the beast and forced her battered legs down the road toward the glade of gold where the whispering aspens waited.

Teret slowed her approach seeing a tumble of rocks and what looked to be a rotund figure seated comfortably on the highest. She stopped in alarm. A portly shaven-headed man in a loose yellow robe sat cross-legged, his round face smiling at the sunshine as the aspens nodded high above his head. His toes gripped sandals and he clutched a long silver pipe in his chubby fingers.

"Greetings woman," the man in yellow smiled down at her from his rock. "A beautiful day, are you lost?"

"I am." Teret glanced around looking for others but saw no one. "I need help."

"Just me here I'm afraid," the stranger chuckled. "I live a solitary life."

"Where am I?" Teret wished her hands were free and she still had her knife. That said, this strange man looked harmless enough.

"That's not easily answered," he held the pipe to his lips and played a short merry tune. "You see, this place doesn't belong anywhere in the real sense. A place between places—so to speak."

"I've not time for riddles," Teret said. "Kindly inform me of my location then I'll be on my way. Unless you have some food to spare. I'm very hungry."

"Yes, well, you would be," the enigmatic smile widened. "Been through a lot lately, haven't you, Teret of the Rorshai. You can move your arms should you wish to."

"What?" Teret gasped, seeing her hands hanging free at her side. "How?" Teret's blue eyes narrowed, sensing sorcery here. She rubbed numbness from her fingers and tried to get a hold on what was happening. "Tell me what you want trickster." Teret approached the little man who laughed from his perch on the rocks above and flicked his pipe down at her. She stepped back and glared up at him.

"Why would I want anything?" The Piper smiled. "The sun is shining and the earth spinning round. All appears as it should."

"Everybody always wants something," Teret said. "I suspect you're a relic from the otherworld. A warlock, or sprite who escaped the carnage seven years past, and spends his days creeping out wayfarers in these woods. I don't how you know my name and I don't much care. Just tell me where I am so I can find two men."

"One to kill and one to love." The Piper flicked his pipe again.

"Precisely. Though I hope the first is dead already."

"Sulo? No, he's very much alive and planning all sorts of delights for you," the yellow-clad man chuckled. "Sulo appears quite unhinged. An undesirable fellow. Dangerous too. Oh, but you're safe for now, so don't fret." The Piper nodded, reading her thoughts. He pressed pipe to lips again and played a tumble of chords.

"Yffarn take you, Meddler, I've scant time for your riddles," Teret said. "If you're not going to help me then choke on that pipe." Teret left him to his music and started back down the road. She stopped after a few paces.

What now?

The road had changed. The trees had gone. Vanished from sight. Instead, Teret stood at a bleak crossroads leading off in three directions. An old stone gibbet marked the corner, and something rotted amid the chains hanging down. It was colder than it had been just moments ago, and a chill wind sighed through distant hills.

"What trickery is this?" Teret turned and saw the Piper grinning at her from his station on the rocks. He leaned back, slapping his belly in delight. Back there, the sun was shining and trees still shaded the valley. It was though she had crossed through an invisible door. Teret walked toward him, but the ground shook and the sky above shimmered and shifted, confusing her.

"Too late; you've already crossed over," he called across to her. "You're committed now."

"What is happening here and what do you want from me?" Teret pushed her body forward but she was checked by some barrier she couldn't see. She shivered at the clinging touch that felt like icy spider's webs sticking to her face.

"Three roads. Time to choose!" The fat man in yellow chuckled. "He chose poorly!" The Piper pointed to the shreds of gray flesh clinging to the rusty chains creaking in the wind above her head.

Teret knew there was no point challenging this creature. The Piper wasn't going to help her. Time she moved on. But which path to choose?

"Just tell me what road leads where?"

"That I cannot say."

"You put them there, beguiler." Teret folded her arms and stared across at the Piper.

"I did?" The Piper slapped his belly again. "You exaggerate my accomplishments. I can do some impressive things like free tied hands, but road construction's not one of them. Now you need to get moving girl—you stand in the place between places. Not safe to linger there. So, no dilly dallies. Choose quickly for your own sake, else your friend catches you up. Or worse, you get trapped in limbo. The world fabric is thin here." The yellow Piper sniffed and looked up suddenly as though scenting something in the wind. "Sulo is close—I can feel his hatred scorching the trees."

Teret yelled across. "I don't know who you are or what game this is. But know this, Imp. If we meet again and I have a knife on my person—I shall shove it up your arse!"

"That's good to know!" The laughter again followed by a flurry of random notes drifting from that warmer place. "Maybe I shouldn't have freed your arms."

Teret showed him her back, spinning on her toes and taking short brisk angry steps toward the crossroads. She ignored the creaking gibbet and chose the middle fork. Those mushrooms hadn't killed her so maybe she'd survive this too.

"Good choice—my dear!" Teret heard the Piper's laughter fade as she entered the road. She walked several paces then stone and sky vanished as sudden dark consumed her.

To Teret it seemed she was floating through space, her mind free to wander. She had no sense of time but in the distance spied a faint light. A something in the colorless void encasing her. Without knowing how, Teret steered toward the light. It grew brighter and filled her vision, a lone star throwing darkness and shadows off to her side.

That light surrounded her as though she'd fallen inside a lantern. A waylaid firefly or else a trapped moth in a prism of brightness. Light encased her, dazzling, blinding, painful, and all-consuming. Teret wondered if the mushrooms had got to her after all. The Piper and this glare, all of them just crazy visions brought on by her lunch. But then how had she freed her arms? At least he'd helped her with that, though Teret suspected his reasons were ambiguous rather than kind. She wasn't up for showing gratitude at the moment.

The light dimmed slowly and her eyes adjusted again. Teret could make out hazy shadows in the distance. She saw the road beneath her. It vanished between two pinkish half-round shapes somewhere ahead. Hills? Mountains perhaps? A soft thud and she found her feet standing on polished stone. The road looked different here. But was it real?

It was foggy and damp and the air around her lingered like stale breath. Teret, still half-blinded, put one foot forward tenuously. Her feet settled on stone again and she started walking. The way rose up toward gentle slopes, and slowly the mist cleared, revealing a bizarrely alien landscape.

Teret refused to let that daunt her. *Keep going—whatever this is it isn't death. So that's good.* The pain in her body announced she was very much alive. Aches and cold—they keep you focused. Teret pursed her lips and pushed on through. It were as though she were visiting someone else's dream. She hoped she would awaken soon with Tam smiling beside her. But until that happens she must needs walk.

What choice had she but to follow the road toward those distant hills and whatever else lay ahead? Teret had no sense of time or place, but as she walked on she heard the chimes of a distant bell. A town? Teret's stomach rumbled, demanding food. She set her teeth and kept walking. Eventually the chiming ceased.

As her vision cleared, Teret saw the road led arrow straight, plunging between two oval-shaped hills the color of freshly caught salmon. Above her head the sky had cleared. It loomed heavy and low, the hue of bronze, and triangular dart-like birds shrieked way up there as they clawed at each other with metal talons. Teret heard a distant roaring which became louder as she approached the pink hills. Teret followed the road between them, climbed a third hill—round as a ball—and then from its top gazed down upon a wonder.

The ocean. Vast and blue-green and calm as a milk pond. It filled her vision—a silk canvas of aquamarine unbroken by island or vessel.

This cannot be!

Teret had only seen the ocean once when she'd travelled with Tam to his birthplace in Port Wind on the far west coast of Kelwyn. Half a world away. That water had been a fierce mass of surge and wave. This sea had a dreamy look about it. Surreal, it lapped an empty coast a mile from where she stood. Teret stood staring in wonderment until something sharp cut into her arm. She cried out, wrenching the arm free from the golden-eyed bird clawing at it.

Black and featherless with huge barbed feet, the evil-looking bird had settled on her shoulder and was pecking her flesh. Teret swatted it away, but others were winging low toward her. Bald ugly things, their cries almost human. Loathing filled her. Teret ran and the birds cried out to each other, swooping and diving at her, sometimes clawing at her hair and face. Teret batted them away. Whatever this nightmare was, she determined to survive it.

Tiring of their game, the birds gave up quickly, vanishing into the copper-colored sky which seemed to suck them out of view. Teret wiped blood from her sleeve. She walked on, her body on the brink of collapse and her mind wandering dangerously.

I'm exhausted. I need food.

Teret stopped, noticing what looked to be a town off to her left. Her heart jumped. The road steered toward it. Oval-shaped roofs huddled close like small round people sharing secrets. They reminded her of bee hives though she could tell they were made from stone. The village ribboned around an inlet with docks and jetties thrusting out spiky into the water. Teret saw a dozen boats moored there, motionless and silent, and one large square-rigged vessel, its bronze colored sails hanging limp like damp sheets spread out to dry. The large ship looked as out of place as she felt.

Teret entered the village. She saw no one; not even a dog challenged her as she strode between oval buildings and walls. A stony mass of hut and store. This place appeared deserted, and to Teret it seemed no one had lived here for months, despite the vessels parading the jetties close by. At last she saw a low wooden door cracked slightly open, spilling yellow light from within. An inn perhaps, or a fisher's abode? Someone still lived here. Teret felt a rush of hope quicken her heartbeat. There would be food inside.

She entered beneath the low portal, pushing the heavy door wide. Once inside, the lone lantern flicked out with a menacing wink. Teret stood in darkness, trying not to panic, turning sharply as she heard the door thud shut behind her.

"Welcome to the last lonely tavern," a rich voice said. Teret tensed, and her eyes adjusting to the light, saw a bulky figure clad in fur and iron hunched at a table, a large tankard clutched in his tanned hands. His hair was shaggy and long the face hidden beneath.

"I need food," Teret told the hunched shape. "I haven't eaten in days." She approached the table where the man sat. He gazed up at her and Teret glimpsed keen brown eyes dominating a ravaged, heavily tanned face that might once have been handsome. "I'm sick of asking this," Teret said. "But where the fuck am I?"

"I have no idea," the man said, his voice filled with irony and his accent strange to her ears. "I keep asking the same question. I'm lost too—ship hit a storm. My crew, everyone, swallowed by waves." His voice was bitter and he appeared on the brink of tears. "I've been here for days. Maybe weeks—hard to tell."

"I'm sorry to hear that," Teret said. "But I have my own problems. So tell me where I can get something to eat and I'll leave you to your grieving."

The stranger set tankard on table and lurched across the room. Teret noticed the door was open again behind her, though no wind blew outside. The man fumbled at a hatch in a corner, pulled out a bundle of what appeared to be small well-wrapped pieces of fish. Teret's mouth watered. She snatched them from him, unwrapped the contents and stuffed them into her mouth. There were six of them, salty and cold, and she swallowed them whole.

"This will help wash that down." The brown-eyed stranger grinned slightly, producing another tankard from somewhere and handing it over. It was brimmed with thick honey-colored beer and Teret took a gulp.

"This is good—thanks." Teret, stomach nicely groaning with satisfaction, had time to look around. Just a dark empty space, low ceiling, some cupboards and the odd empty table, a few wicker chairs strewn here and there. Clearly no more than a fisherman's hut. It sufficed. "So where is everyone?"

"Gone." The stranger shrugged and motioned she join him at table. "I was washed ashore close by. This village is deserted but mercifully its former occupants left fish and beer. Good of them. I've been living on both for some time. As to where this place is—your guess is as good as mine, lady. I'm a very long way from home."

"Me too, and with scant notion how to get back there." Teret sipped her beer and wiped her mouth. She wasn't a drinker normally but she'd take anything today. Besides, the ale was rich and strong and steadied her frayed nerves. "I've had a rough couple of days," she said. "Name's Teret."

"I'm Carlo, of House Sarfe," he said.

"Carlo the lonely sailor," Teret smiled slightly, cheering at the company of another soul in this creepy alien landscape. She clinked her tankard against his. "Delighted to meet you, Sir Carlo. Where is House Sarfe?"

Carlo's brown eyes clouded over. "Sarfania—it's a province in Gol. I'm a baron's son. Hard to believe that now." The sailor slurped his ale and stared at the door. It had just slammed shut. "Oh—its back again," he said.

"What's back?" Teret turned to the door then something nagged her memory. "Did you say—Gol?"

"You have heard of it?" Carlo laughed. "So happy to hear that."

"Only what my husband told me. But enough to know it no longer exists."

"Now you are jesting with me."

"No, sir." Teret grabbed Carlo's arm and pulled him close. "The continent called Gol sank below the sea more than a thousand years ago. It's just legend—a myth. My husband's ancestors came from there. The Crystal King is a direct descendant of Kell, the warlord who escaped Gol's ruin and founded the Four Kingdoms west of my country. So my Tam told me."

"What nonsense is this?" Carlo stood shakily and pointed down at her. "Are you another ghost intent on tormenting me? Come in amiable guise to hoodwink me? Deceiver, haven't I suffered enough?" Carlo shook and swayed as if ill, and Teret could tell he was drunker than first she'd thought. "Why are you lying to me?" Carlo almost sobbed. "Stealing hope—the one thing I still retain."

"Sit," said Teret. "Listen. I'm Rorshai—we are an honest people. I don't know what's happening here but I can tell you this much. The continent Gol drowned in millennia past. The survivors were led by a man called Kell, a direct ancestor to both Queen Ariane of

Kelwyn and the Crystal King over in Kelthaine—the country named after him. I'm not lying, Carlo Sarfe. Why would I do that? I'm as lost as you are."

Carlo stared at the door. "Those countries mean nothing to me. I don't understand what's happening here. Gol was very much alive and above waves when I left. You tell me it's legend—that makes me a ghost. Or are you a ghost inside my head feeding poison? Perhaps I'm possessed?" He shuddered and walked over to the door, opening it, letting the bronze sky creep inside, while gazing out into the hazy strangeness of ocean beyond. He turned and surveyed Teret, the copper glare glimmering around him like sparks dancing off his fur.

"Three years ago, I sailed from Reveal, stopping briefly at Galanais and Xenn City before sailing on past Xandoria's other cities. After that we fared south to the Island States and beyond into territories none I know have ever seen. At first things went well for my crew and me. But then the Gods turned against us."

"Those Gods are dead now," Teret told him. "I saw them die. And the places you mention no longer exist." She felt a sudden shiver and looked at the door again. It was shut. "Is there something in here with us?" Teret gazed around but saw only gloom.

"'Tis but a zephyr, or some wandering spirit—I care not which." Carlo appeared lost to thought. "The door closes and opens. I've got used to it. Just happens."

"So, what's your plan, Carlo of House Sarfe?" Teret, stronger now she'd eaten, was struggling to come to terms with what had happened.

"Plan?" Carlo raised his tankard but Teret grabbed it and stopped his hand.

"You just going to sit here alone and drink yourself stupid until someone comes back and murders you? Or else this creeping invisible—whatever it is—steals your breath while you're sleeping?"

"Guess so," Carlo said. "I haven't thought much about it."

"You're as pathetic as my husband." Teret growled at the door as it swung open again. "And you—thing! Just piss off. I've seen enough nonsense for one day. Either murder us or begone." She heard a faint clatter like the tiptoe of tiny feet then the door opened and slammed shut with sudden silence. A noise outside hinted someone leaving. "Good," Teret said, turning to look at her companion again.

"What do you propose, fierce lady?"

"We take what food there is and walk," Teret said, her eyes on the door again. It remained shut.

"Walk . . . where?" Carlo held his filthy hands out wide. "And for what purpose? I'm a sailor, I like to keep my walking minimal."

"Staying alive."

"We're alive here. And there is ale."

"Things happen when you walk," Teret said. "There are two of us now so we can keep an eye out both ways. There has got to be someone around who can help us. We're here for a reason, Carlo Sarfe. Nothing is random."

"All right, I'm with you," Carlo nodded. "Just let me finish this." He slurped and then looked up in surprise as the door crashed open and a huge figure burst through it.

Teret leaped to her feet as the giant decked in glittering armor and face hidden by helmet reached for her, and two smaller men entered behind and grabbed Carlo before he could rise.

"The Rundali ghosts will come for them after they're dead," the leader's voice was muffled beneath steel. "We'll set torch to them tonight."

And Teret screamed as the steel giant and his men dragged her from the oval hut. Her bad day had just got worse. Beside her she saw, Carlo Sarfe blink and stagger in disbelief.

Chapter 7 | Jynn

"How many?" Tam asked, as Stogi's sharp eyes watched the riders cantering in file through the low hills toward where he and Tam lay hidden. They'd seen the horsemen just in time to take cover, hiding their horses in a thicket behind them.

"Hard to say, a score maybe?" Stogi squinted; the noon sun weighed down hot. They watched for several minutes as like a steel worm the column wound eastward along the Great Trade Road.

"Ptarnians?" Tam asked.

"Who else?"

"I thought maybe Tseole—friends of yours coming to greet us."

"I haven't got any friends," Stogi shook his head. "We Tseole are loners."

"Maybe if you washed more often," Tam nudged his companion and then glanced back at the riders. "They appear well armed."

Both riders and horses were covered in steel. So much glinting armor it was hard to stare without getting momentarily blinded— even from this distance. Unlike some of his friends back west, Tam had never crossed swords with Ptarnians—though he'd knifed more than a few in alleys during the last seven years. Their soldiers were known for precision and drill, and iron discipline, obeying their officers' commands on pain of flogging, branding, or—in extreme cases—execution.

"They're a long way from Caranaxis," Stogi frowned. "I've not seen them this far out before."

"Perhaps our reward money went up?"

"No chance—this lot are up to something but I'm pretty sure it don't involve us."

"And more coming. See over there!" Tam pointed to the horizon where tiny sparkles turned into ranks of soldiers marching along the trade road. "Croagon's tits, how many are there?"

"Lots. And more important, where are they going?"

"Shen?"

"Too far," Stogi shook his head. "The Shen River lies seven hundred miles east of Caranaxis, with little to nothing in between."

"You've been there?" Tam was impressed.

"Once– many years back when my father was alive. Nothing to see; a big brown slug of a river trawling through fog. Could scarce make out the other side." Stogi shook his head. "Cold and drizzly as I recall. Vowed never to return."

"Where else then?" Tam could see the helmets clearly now. The riders wore chain masks obscuring their faces, and on closer inspection their armor was painted in yellows, blues, and reds. "Gaudy lot," Tam said as the riders trotted past, their steel-clad steeds kicking up a mile of dust. Far behind the foot soldiers filed along the road like steely ants. Somewhere in their midst Tam noticed banners and a kind of cart. "Looks like someone important."

They waited for an hour sipping cactus juice and water, occasionally commenting and calming their horses as over one hundred heavily armed soldiers marched by, just half a mile below their hide.

Purple banners and gonfalons flapped on poles as the wagon approached pulled by six heavy horses, each attended by what appeared to be half-naked slaves, their bulging arms and legs chained to the wagon they strained beside. Gilded and ornate, the cart was square in shape with tiny windows.

"The emperor?"

"No." Stogi glanced at Tam as though he were mad. "Some official—a merchant perhaps."

"A wealthy one, with a lot of clout."

"Don't make much sense," Stogi said, watching the last footsoldiers march out of view. "No one travels the old roads these days."

"Doubtless they have a reason."

"Well, I don't like it," Stogi said. At last those stragglers faded into distance and Tam and Stogi could resume their journey. "Ptarnians seldom venture this far from home," Stogi said. "Whoever that was in that cage is up to no good, and I'd sooner not enquire further."

"How many miles until we turn south?" Tam asked Stogi. The two had been together three days and a rough friendship had grown between them. Tam liked Stogi, mainly for his matter-of-fact way of thinking. Besides, he needed all the friends he could get these days.

"Less than a hundred, more than fifty," Stogi said. "As long as we steer clear of Rundal Woods we should be in good shape. That shouldn't prove hard as the Laregoza highway lies well this side of the forest."

"I don't like woods," Tam said. "They bring back memories."

"The Rundali are rumored to be spiteful," Stogi said, urging his steed pick up pace as afternoon wore on. "The forest surrounding their country is so big it hedges both Shen and Laregoza. They say enchanters abide somewhere within its midst."

"The cactus makers?" Tam eased back in his saddle as Stogi passed him the gourd with his new favorite liquor inside.

"No, they're the Rundali," Stogi explained. "I'm talking about the ones who dwell in the forests."

"They sound similar."

"They're not—Rundali are men like you and me, though they dabble in sorcery. The other lot are something else entirely." Stogi seemed unsettled by the subject and Tam decided to let him be. Why worry about something that didn't concern them? It was around dusk that Stogi noticed the lone tracks leading down into a small copse of firs.

"Someone diverted here recently," Stogi said. "A lone rider." They dismounted and followed the hoof tracks to a little stream where Tam noticed boot prints and then something else. The bare footprints of what must surely be a woman.

"They were here," Tam looked around in sudden anguish, as though expecting to see Teret tied to some tree. "It has to be them!"

Stogi nodded. "Looks like some kind of fight. And look there—she got away! See those foot prints leading up to that ridge?"

They tied off their horses quickly and sprinted up through the brush. Teret's prints—if that's what they were—were shadowed by the larger scuff of boot on soil. Tam controlled his fury as he thought of the mad killer Sulo chasing his wife.

Stogi stopped so suddenly that Tam crashed into him and the two of them almost tumbled off the cliff they'd reached. "Fuck," Stogi said as he gazed down at the rocky river winding far below. "That was lucky." Beside him, Tam sunk to his knees as the thought hit him. Teret was dead. She'd fallen from the cliff, and Sulo too most likes.

"He chased her here and now she's gone." Tam blinked back tears of rage as he stared down at the river. "Broken on those rocks below. I've lost her, Stogi—I've fucking lost her!"

"You don't know that." Stogi folded his legs neatly and perched beside the drop. "It's impossible to tell as the ground here's too rocky for prints. "Come let's follow this ridge, see if we can get down to that river. Once there we'll walk the banks—see what we find."

Tam said nothing so Stogi rose to his feet and started cutting through the brush, the river churning to his right far below. Pale and drawn, Tam staggered behind his companion. He was feeling ill again and in desperate need for a smoke, or failing that a stiff hard drink.

If she's dead . . .

Occasionally he'd stop and gaze down at the river. Each time he had to will himself away, the temptation to jump was so strong.

At last they found a way down through the tangle of briar and thorn. A valley lay ahead, the river running through it, and the odd tree scattered here and there. Stogi rubbed his chin. "I've no memory of this place," he said. "There shouldn't be a forest here."

They flanked the river, the progress painfully slow. Tam's eyes were on every log jam or floater, fearing the worst. But they saw nothing save the odd lone crane beading eyes at them from the opposite banks.

"It should be dark by now," Stogi glanced up at the sky, clearer and bluer than it had been when they left the road. "I'm not liking this."

They entered the valley. A long green sward of freshly cut grass led to a lone standing stone, its chiseled top looming forty feet above them like a forbidding finger, ominous and stark. Beneath it a well-kept road ran straight ahead vanishing into trees. The men exchanged glances.

"We should return for our horses," Stogi said. "Before we lose ourselves entirely."

"I'm not going back," Tam said and walked toward the lone stone. Ahead the river faded into hills and mist.

Stogi glared up at the stone. "I don't like this place—it stinks of enchantment."

"You are perceptive, Tseole." The voice came from the river bank. Both Tam and Stogi seized a weapon as a figure hopped into sight. A small, chubby man dressed in immaculate green leathers. He carried a silver pipe and placed it to his lips, producing a string of notes before stopping in-front of them and smiling broadly.

"I'm called Jynn, in this place—at this time. In other places I have different names. But today I'm Jynn. Delighted to encounter you, noble wayfarers."

"Well that's interesting but we don't have time for pleasantries." Tam reached forward to grab Jynn's arm but stopped as he swiped air. A laugh behind him. Tam turned and saw Jynn grinning at him. Stogi had backed away, his tough face taut as leather and dark eyes wary.

"Tam, we need to go back to the road and horses. We can start fresh from there. Quickly now, before we fall into this trickster's trap." Stogi made to turn but Tam stood his ground.

"I'm looking for a woman, blue eyes, dark hair. A man too—a killer." Tam leveled his sword at Jynn who laughed and wagged his hands.

"You can't prod me with that," Jynn said. "Best put it away, Tamersane of Kelwyn. You are a long way from home, my laddie. And you, Stogi of Tseola, have no home since your family drove you away for murder. Nobleman and thief—quite the pair."

Stogi bridled but Tam waved him back. "This bastard knows something about Teret's whereabouts; I'm not leaving until I get the details out of him." He slid the sword back in scabbard and folded his arms. "So, Master Jynn. Who—or whatever you are. How can we help you? You obviously want something from us, else why block our road?"

"I want nothing from you!" Jynn looked flustered, as if surprised by the change of tack. "I don't need anything from anybody." He played a short-hurried tune of the flute as if aggravated. "I just watch the road and try to guess where it's leading. 'Tis an honest profession I have."

"Tam, you're on your own," Stogi said, turning to head back up the ridge.

"She passed through here a short while ago, your lady." Jynn had stowed his flute in a deep pocket and now mirrored Tam's stance with chubby arms folded.

Tam felt a flood of relief. "Alone?"

"For the meanwhile; she took to the crossroads."

"Stogi wait!" Tam called out as his friend made for the brush, intending to climb back up to where they'd first seen the river. "Teret's alive."

"So he says," Stogi shouted back. He stood for a moment and then cursed. "Damn you, Lord Tam—you're the only fucking friend I have. Guess that means I have to stick by you, even when you're being incredibly stupid."

"Thanks!" Tam smiled at his companion as Stogi jumped back down to join them. Jynn bowed as Stogi stopped short of him.

"Nice to have you back," Jynn said. "You were missed." Stogi glared at him. "Teret took the left fork," Jynn wagged a hand down the road, and for the first time they saw how it split into three forks scarcely a hundred yards from where they stood. "I suggest you follow."

Tam stared at the crossroads. Why hadn't he seen that before? Stogi's face was white but he said nothing. "And the man—Sulo. He's been here too?"

"Oh, yes. Sulo arrived just an hour after his quarry. He was in a rare foul mood so I advised him to take the middle path."

"That was good of you," Tam said.

"I like to do what I can," Jynn caught Stogi's black stare and for a second his smiling blue eyes glittered like winter ice. "Best you pair get going." Jynn waved a dismissive hand and turned and retreated back into the brush by the river. Seconds later he was lost to sight. Tam heard a brief flurry of pipes and then silence.

Stogi stood staring at the crossroads ahead as though a hundred heavily armed enemies were guarding it. "You intend to take his advice?"

"What choice do we have?"

"We?" Stogi cursed as Tam left him standing and walked with brisk steps down to where the road forked at the entrance of an open windy field. "Sodding sorcery—I can smell it all around here," Stogi yelled. "Whole region stinks of witchcraft." Tam heard his friend slam his sword in its scabbard as he ran to catch up. "What if we get the lane wrong? This could end badly for us!"

Tam turned and grinned seeing the Tseole hovering at the crossroads. "You coming?" he said as he started down the left track, his boots crunching on stone.

"Stupidity is infectious," Stogi said as he followed his friend down the left lane. "And will most likes prove lethal too."

"She's alive!" Tam grinned at his companion. "I'm going to make it up to her, Stogi." Then the cloud fell upon them, smothering visions and sounds, and they stumbled through blackness and choking smoke.

Tam coughed and choked as thick air assaulted him, forcing him to his knees. He could hear Stogi cursing but the Tseole sounded far away is if locked in some distant room. Tam's throat burned as the acidic air clawed inside his mouth. He heard a rushing noise like tumbling rocks, felt something hard strike him, roll him onto his back and then drag him through space until he crashed into a softness that pawed and sucked his body down beneath the ground.

Tam felt that invisible heaviness pulling him down as though a ship's anchor was tied to his ankles. Long time he fell, through darkness and smothering smoke. At last Tam crashed through clouds and floated leaf-like to settle on a carpet of pine needles; the dark trees looming over him like grim silent sentinels.

"What happened?" Tam checked his body and saw nothing untoward. "What a trip, and I've been sober for a week . . . Stogi?" Tam looked about for his friend but there was no sign of the Tseole. "Stogi—where are you?" Nothing. Just the silence of pines looming over him.

Tam rolled to his feet, checked his sword was still in its scabbard, and loped like a wounded bear out of the trees. Close by, a road wound through more pines leading up to dark wooded hills. It was cold—colder than he'd felt in months, and Tam shivered as his feet found the road. This wasn't the same track that led out from the crossroads. Stogi was right, someone was playing games around here. No matter, Teret was alive and he would find her. Time to redeem himself. Keep moving—his only option.

Chapter 8 | Laregoza

Garland swatted a fly from his arm and glanced up at the heavy skies above. They were six days out from the Lake of Stones. Almost a week of grueling riding through bleak deserted terrain, his men grumbling and cursing every step. Apart from Doyle, who kept grimly silent, and Tol the bowyer who so often wore a smile. Life was a joke to Tol. But the others hadn't taken Garland's decision to journey further into the east well. He didn't blame them but wished they'd shut up now and then.

There had been quarrels and objections—mainly from Pash and Kargon, the former argumentative and latter just stubborn. But Garland had overruled their complaints and, as ever, Loyal Doyle had supported his captain. They were good men he'd known for years and Garland empathized. But they'd volunteered just as he had. No one else to blame. Open ticket until the job gets done. You're a soldier so suck it up.

Queen Ariane's vague orders had been to journey to Ptarni and discover news of her wayward cousin, Lord Tamersane formerly of Wynais—a drunken fool in Garland's opinion. A fallen man who had stabbed his treacherous brother in the dungeons of Wynais.

Garland would have let the fool be. But Tamersane was loved by the Queen and had been a hero of the last war. So, they say—Garland had never fought beside him, so couldn't comment on that. But Ariane had dreamed of the Lake of Stones, a place shrouded in mystery until their visit last week. In her dream she'd had a vision of the seeress Ysaren whom the dream told her had the answer. Queen Ariane had learned to trust her dreams—so she'd told Garland back in Wynais.

They all loved Ariane of the Swords, bravest and strongest of queens. A young ruler who had stood alone against the all-powerful sorcerer Caswallon, and somehow survived to turn the coin. She was worthy of everything they had. Hence Garland's acceptance of this quest, despite his misgivings. The men too loved their Queen. What else would they do? She'd asked and they'd complied. They were veterans growing old, restless, and grumpy—Garland's stoic crew. So back in Wynais they'd leapt at the chance, and Garland knew the boys wouldn't let him down. That said, they were not happy. These former fighters needed action.

"Laregoza." Doyle held the glass to his eye and scanned the horizon. "All I can see is a haze of brown sludge." He wiped his face after handing the glass back to Garland. Day on day it had warmed up, and now a hot humid sun weighed heavy upon the eight riders.

"It's there somewhere," Garland said, shaking his head as Doyle offered the spy-glass. "Your eyes are younger than mine. Keep them peeled; we have to cross that border before we can stock up. I don't know anything about Laregoza, but if we're apprehended here in Ptarni, we're dead men. So best we keep riding—hey," he grinned at Doyle. "Been through worse—you and I."

"The men are edgy," Doyle muttered.

"The men will shut up and put up," snapped Garland, tired of the subject. "We've discussed this, Doyle. Tenuous or not, I have to follow the only leads I have. We all signed up for this."

"Tenuous—really?" Doyle chuckled. "An abandoned seeress

seduces you by a lake and then bids you find some ancient artifact that will free her, so she—in turn—can save our renegade boy."

"Yes," Garland smoldered at Doyle's half grin. "I'll not say more on the matter. Yah!" He heeled his mare pick up speed and Doyle, still smirking, followed suit. Ahead, the dusty road faded into haze, a monotonous continuation of stony outcrops breaking free of wild spiky grasses, the occasional rushing brook winding through. At least they had water. A terrain not dissimilar to Northern Permio. Garland had served there as a boy soldier during the bitter conflicts between the rebel Permian tribesmen and their sultan. So many years ago. A lifetime.

Two days passed, and the sun blazed hotter, the heat oppressive and muggy and the riders' faces grimed by trails of sweat. The brown smudge on the horizon had swollen, hinting a vast area of swamp and low-lying trees. Garland balked at the thought of riding through that. Doyle rode close and yelled in his ear.

"Over to the left—maybe a mile!" Doyle handed Garland the glass. He held it to an eye, easing his horse to a slow trot. The men behind rode up close and surrounded their leader and lieutenant. They passed drinking canisters around and blinked at the road ahead, brushing flies from their sweating faces and cussing sporadically.

"What is it?" Pash scowled, his scarred face wary. "Trouble?"

"Tents," Garland said. "Some kind of settlement. Over there. Maybe nomads passing through."

"Or else soldiers," Kargon said, spitting out the rye grass stem he'd been chewing all morning.

"We'll soon know," Garland said. "The road winds close to that camp. Keep your weapons handy lads. Tol, Coife—have those bows ready for ambush. We've made good progress and the border can't be far. Don't want trouble this late in the hour." The men exchanged glances. Pash looked edgy, Kargon grim. The rest shrugged and urged their mounts follow the captain. Tol calmly nocked a shaft to his bowstring and whistled a merry tune. Garland wished the others would follow Tol's suit and stop looking so glum. He overheard Pash muttering behind him.

"Think you he's lost it?" Glancing back, Garland saw Pash riding alongside the dour-faced Kargon.

"Maybe," the other replied. "Best we keep an open mind." Garland stored those comments in his memory bank and turned ahead to face the road again. Pash was a good soldier but had always been trouble. If anyone would give him problems it would be Pash. Garland would mention it to Doyle so together they could keep an eye on things.

The eight riders followed the road, eyes scanning for movement. There was no sign of life, and they passed the tent camp to the right, soon leaving it behind. Riding close, Garland had gazed at the camp, seeing nothing but flapping canvas and abandoned cooking trestles, and the odd rudimentary fire pit—just ashes and half burnt logs. Whomever stayed here had departed a while back. Garland wondered why they had left the tents standing, like so many pointed wizard hats studding the scrubland.

Riding close, Doyle wiped sweat from his face. "I think this entire country is deserted. Have we ridden to Permio by mistake? It's almost desert though the air is too moist. Where is everyone?" The answer came almost immediately when an arrow thudded into dust to their right. Garland swung in saddle and gazed back along the road. He counted twenty riders galloping at speed toward them.

"Ride!" Garland yelled, and his men urged their horses speed behind their captain. "I think you spoke too soon," Garland shouted at Doyle as another arrow thudded close. "Next time keep your trap shut."

Doyle nodded grimly and spurred his beast to greater speed.

Chapter 9 | Marei

It felt like morning—somewhere. Tam trudged along the road, heart heavy and mind giddy with confusion. Above his head, a whisper of thin clouds pursued each other like smoky dragons fading off toward distant slopes. Tam felt a familiar dampness in the air. A moist saltiness that reminded him of his childhood.

The ocean. He looked up half expecting to see gulls swooping and crying above but saw only clouds and pale blue sky. He was alone in a strange land but somewhere ahead he'd find Teret. The only thought that made sense. Despite the agony of the last week Tam's head was clearer, and he was surprised how little he thought about smoke and strong wine. he wouldn't go back to that. Lesson learned. Tam pictured Teret's lovely face as he walked. Clutched the image close like a cherished child; the thought of his love back in his arms.

Soon. *I'm coming Teret!*

He walked for hours, the sky and distant smell of brine his only companions. No bird flew above, and Tam saw no sign of beast or human as he trudged toward the distant line of hills, hungry and tired yet unswayed in his determination. By dusk he'd reached them and, after following the road to their crest, gazed down on an idyllic scene of wood, winter, and a lonely thatched cottage thrust amid them.

Tam felt his heart surge as he quickened his steps. A house in this empty land! A stone cottage or croft perhaps a mile past the hills. It looked welcoming and Tam hoped that whoever dwelt inside would feed him and give him news about Teret. Perhaps she was there? That thought spurred him on to greater speeds.

Almost there!

The homestead was surrounded by trees, and surrounding them were white patches of what must be snow lay scattered around, with square empty fields leading off into the distance, where the thin ribbon of the road continued before vanishing in haze and the distant murmur of water.

Tam eased to a slow walk when he approached the cottage. Best he keep wary—these could be enemies holding her hostage. *You can't let your guard down in this life—it's moments like that that get a man killed.*

But the place looked friendly enough, suggesting reasonable honest folk lived within. He walked through a cluster of fences and gates, his breath steaming in the chill. Tam saw bee hives silent and deserted, the ice clinging to their tiny roofs. To his right a frozen pond was fed by a small gurgling stream.

The cottage lay amidst a collection of stone buildings: a stable, barn, some kind of storehouse, and a large thatched roof hinted another dwelling a little further down the lane. Between stables and cottage lay a square paved courtyard; a well stood at the center.

Tam stopped, seeing the woman leaning over as she hoisted bucket from its depth. Long chestnut hair shadowed her face. She was slim, though shorter than average.

"Hello there!" Tam held his hands out in greeting as the woman turned and glared at him. She looked annoyed and flustered. Alarmed at his presence. A white hand brushed the hair from her face.

"I'm sorry," Tam waved his hands about. "Didn't mean to startle you." The woman stared at him in patient silence, so Tam continued. "I'm lost. Haven't a clue where I am, but I'm looking for a woman."

"It appears you have found one." Her blue gaze hinted at humor. She placed the bucket brimmed with water carefully on the ground and wiped her hands on her apron. "How can I assist you, Sir?" She appeared older than he was. Perhaps forty, though her elfin features and long wavy chestnut hair made her look younger. Those blue eyes were wise and she had fine lines where sorrow and laughter had left their mark.

"I'm Tam." He walked toward her, and the woman smiled slightly showing even white teeth.

"I know. I've been expecting you." The woman turned and, without further comment walked toward the cottage, leaving the bucket where it stood.

Tam leapt behind her his heart surging with sudden joy. Teret was here! "Here, lady—let me carry this. You forgot your water." Tam picked up the bucket, spilt half the water in his excitement, and followed the woman inside the cottage. He looked around but saw no one present.

"Where is she then?" Tam almost dropped the bucket and more water splashed the slate floor until the woman reached out and took it off him.

"Sit," she hinted at a wooden chair over by the fireplace. "You look in need of good ale and food."

"That I am," Tam nodded urgently. "But first tell me where my wife is."

"Your—wife?" The woman frowned slightly. Despite his anxiety Tam marked how attractive this woman was. Not beautiful, just something about her. The way she tilted her head, the soft smile and humorous glint in her eyes hiding a wry sadness below. Tam was impressed how she kept this place so trim with no man around.

"Lady Teret of the Rorshai," said Tam. "She passed through here, maybe yesterday? That's how you know my name." Tam smiled but his eyes hinted desperation. The woman rested small white fists on table and frowned, her brows crinkling slightly.

"I know of no Lady Teret," she said. "It was a man who bade me look out for you. I'm sorry."

"A man?"

"A soldier—he had kind eyes. Called himself the Journeyman. Didn't say much and wouldn't stay around. Said he was seeking Lord Tamersane of Kelwyn, and it was imperative that he found him in the next few days as time was running out—what he said," She shrugged. "Made little sense to me. That was a week ago and he hasn't returned. Shame, I liked him."

Tam grabbed her arm with sudden violence and the woman cried out in pain and alarm. "What trickery is this, woman? Are you in league with that villain at the crossroads? The trickster? What's happening here?"

"Sir—let go, you're hurting my wrist," Tam looked down and saw how his fingers had dug into her skin. He felt sudden shame, relaxed his grip and slumped into gloomy slouch. "I'm telling you the truth," she said. "I know nothing about Teret or a villain at the crossroads. What crossroads—have you been to the city?"

"Caranaxis?"

She shook her head. "I don't know its name. We call it the city— only one we know. I've never journeyed that far. Few have."

"We?"

"My son, Dafyd, and I. My husband perished in the raids six years past."

"I am sorry," Tam leaned back in the chair. "But nothing makes sense. You, this place. I mean—where the fuck am I? Pardon my language. It's not the smoke, that never gave me visions. Forgive me, but I'm not sure you are real." Tam smiled ironically. "I'm finally losing my mind," he said. "Stogi was right. Fuck it . . ." Tam felt the tears welling at his eyes again. "I'm sorry."

She just stared at him for a moment and then disappeared into another room. She came back moments later and shoved something on the table. A cup of brown ale and a large steaming platter of turnips, carrots, leeks and what smelt like roast lamb. Tam glanced at it in amazement.

"Mad or sane, this will give you strength," the woman said.

"You just cook that up?"

"I'm not a magician," she smiled. "Been stewing for days. Ever since that journeyman fellow told me you were coming. Eat up, you look like you're about to collapse."

Tam gazed deep into his stew for a moment and then grabbed adjacent spoon and started heaping piping hot contents into mouth. It was delicious and he hadn't realized just how hungry he was. Long day didn't cover it. The woman took seat close by the window and gazed outside, her calm blue eyes hinting loneliness.

"Where is this place?" Tam managed between mouthfuls. He felt stronger, fueled by the nourishment, and the ale was better than he'd expected. He hadn't tasted ale in so long. Hard to find in Ptarni.

"Torrigan's Tavern," the woman said, her dreamy gaze on the courtyard outside. "By some called the Last Lonely Inn. Nothing between here and the city—so they say."

"I hadn't realized this was an inn," Tam looked around seeing four walls, a cupboard, some cups and what looked to be a tea pot. He'd seen one like it before, strange looking object with a spout. Queen Ariane his cousin drank the stuff by the bucket as he recalled. Tam didn't see the point of drinking hot water infused with dry leaves, but tea was fashionable now in Kelwyn. Ariane was quite the trend setter.

"Where's the tap-room?"

"Out the back across the yard," she shrugged at the door. "We've a skittle alley too."

"A what?" Tam hadn't heard of skittle, maybe some kind of animal kept for meat hereabouts. She laughed seeing his expression; it made her look younger.

"A game," she said. "They play it in the Hall too. Though the stakes are higher there, of course. I'll show you when you've eaten. Are you done?"

Tam nodded. "That was excellent, and the beer . . ."

"There is plenty more next door." She turned and he followed her outside. Close by, a rooster crowed and something that sounded like a pig snuffled and snorted behind a hedge.

"Quite the farm you have." Again Tam was impressed. He knew little about farming but thought the life a worthy one.

"Homestead," she corrected him. "The Inn was busy once and the road much travelled. Before the raids. Nowadays it's just those down at the Hall as visit when the mood takes them. Sooner they didn't bother."

She guided him through a tangle of dead looking vines and tall dry stalks until another door appeared, worn and shabby, the paint faded dull yellow.

"You need a handyman," Tam said, but the woman didn't respond. She opened the door and Tam followed her in. He blinked through the gloom seeing tables, trestles, and benches and three large oak barrels propped up on more tables. Impressive for such an out of way place. To the right a door creaked ajar, the chilly drafts working it back and forth.

Tam spied a long narrow room, stone floor funneling into a wall where six wooden bottle-shaped objects waited like soldiers expecting a charge. "What are they?" Tam enquired.

"Skittles." The woman picked something up and shoved it in Tam's hands.

"A ball," Tam blinked at the heavy sphere of animal skin gripped between his fists.

"Yes." The woman glanced at him askance. "You are perceptive. Have a go," she said pointing down the room at the far wall where the skittle soldiers waited.

Tam shrugged, balanced the ball in his hands and then hurled it at the distant objects. It crashed into the wall three yards to the right leaving a dent in the plaster. Tam looked at her.

"Like this." She produced another ball and leaning forward, rolled it long and steady toward the skittles. The ball clipped the corner of one, and before Tam could blink in surprise all six were wobbling and tumbling as the ball rolled past.

"Wow, you've some skill."

"Just practice." The woman's gaze was on the window again. She looked pensive. "Let me replenish you." She walked back into the taproom and refilled his cup.

"I expect your son will be back soon." Tam smiled reassuringly as he followed her in. He felt for the woman all alone in this place. That said, it wasn't his problem, but the ale and food had cheered his heart. He felt certain Teret must be close by—maybe in that hall the women kept mentioning. He'd eaten well, so next Tam needed sleep. Then he'd press on and find her.

She's around here somewhere.

"I hope so," the woman said. "I don't like him going there; Dafyd's very young, though strong and able-handed. Naive and trusting, and they are what they are in the Hall."

"What's with this Hall?" Tam had a sudden sinking feeling that Teret could be captive there.

She shook her head, unwilling to discuss the subject further. "Let's return to the cottage; you can help me build the fire. I've usually got it going by now but have been distracted."

Tam nodded, and after several minutes assisting her he'd carried in enough logs for a healthy roar. An hour later with three ales downed, Tam felt his senses relaxing. He was ready for a smoke but put that thought away.

Teret was somewhere in this vicinity. Whether this was real or his imagination didn't matter. It would lead him to his wife. He'd visit this Hall at first light and get some answers.

Tam studied the woman as she poured herself an ale and wiped her mouth on her sleeve after taking a long slurp. She was small, slender with curves in the right places. She wore long leather boots, and the green woolen skirt and sleeveless sheepskin jacket clung to those curves. Her arms were covered by the loose linen shirt beneath, pale white and flared at the wrists. Strange garb, but easy to imagine what lay beneath.

The woman glanced at Tam sharply as if reading his thoughts. "You haven't told me your name," Tam said.

"Marei."

"I like it—unusual."

"Common. My father was a fisherman. We lived in a village close by the Hall, least until the raids started all those years ago." Her eyes looked lost and Tam changed the subject.

"Tell me about this Hall—is it far from here?"

"No, close—not ten miles. Wish it were further. An easy ride or walk as needs must. The other stranger went there, despite my misgivings—so perhaps you should go too. Might know where your wife is. But be careful if you do."

"A castle?"

"Not really."

"Fortified house then?"

"You might describe it so—we just know it as Graywash Hall, or the Hall for short. Always been there at the water's edge. A place of secrets, whispers, and dark silent corridors of stone."

They'll know where she is if they're not hiding her themselves. And why would they do that? Tam allowed the ale to let him relax. Things would work out as long as he kept his cool.

"I don't know this journeyman fellow," Tam drained a fourth glass. He was dopey tired now, sleepy, his eyelids drooping. Marei appeared not to notice.

"Well, the journeyman knows all about you, Lord Tamersane. Said he'd been looking for you for months and time was running out. He described you as tall, fair-haired, glib of tongue, and handsome, though arrogant and uppity."

Tam blinked. *What?* He'd been handsome once but those days were past. Arrogant? Uppity? Who was this man who claimed to know him?

"He was insistent, so I suggested the traveler seek answers in the Hall, though I urged him to be wary. They know things there—though most often they keep that knowledge well hidden. But your friend was determined so departed without spending the night."

"I don't know this 'friend,'" Tam said. "Maybe I should wait here until he returns. He might know where my wife is."

"If he returns." The woman gazed at Tam shrewdly. "Been gone over a week. Not everyone returns from the Hall." She tilted her face slightly and her eyes narrowed. "What happened to your wife?"

Tam looked awkward, ashamed. His weakness had always been attractive women. And the more he drank the lovelier Marei looked. "I love her—so much. But I let her down, and now I've lost her. I'm a fool, Marei. I don't know why your journeyman fellow is seeking me. Not much to find here."

Marei took seat beside him and rested chin in hand, her elbows on the table, her calm blue gaze studying his. "I doubt your Teret would want you moping her loss like a sick cow," Marei said. "I can see the man hidden in there." She poked his chest. "Buried beneath layers of denial, self-loathing, and despair. The three roads leading to oblivion."

Tam nodded. "Guilty as charged. We had a good life, but I couldn't settle—either in Wynais or Rorshai. Too much had happened."

Tam realized he was drunk, his words slurring, but he'd always opened up to women, and Marei's eyes were perceptive and sympathetic. "I acquired a habit in Ptarni," Tam said. "That helped me for a while. Reason why we moved there, my wife and I."

"I do not recognize these names; you must have journeyed very far."

"I could use a smoke, been a while—beyond a week. Feels like I'm falling apart." Her face was very close, scarce inches away as she leaned toward him. Tam could smell her soft scent. On sudden impulse he slid a hand through her thick copper hair, kissed her lips and hugged her close. She pushed him away and stood up, her face flushed with anger.

"I thought you were concerned for your wife, Sir?"

Tam placed his ale on the table. "I'm sorry," he said. "That was unfortunate. A moment's weakness brought on by this worthy brew. I shall sleep in the stables and be away before dawn. I'm going to get answers from that Hall."

Marei nodded slowly. "As you wish," she said, her expression unreadable. "There's plenty of fresh straw, and I daresay the rats are sleepy this late in the year." She left him to his thoughts as the fire cracked and eventually faded to faggots and flickers. Bone weary, Tam fared out into the cold.

Chapter 10 | Elerim

This isn't happening. Teret kicked and writhed as her giant captor led her up a steep incline towards a rocky outcrop. She saw wicker structures and almost swooned as she guessed their purpose. There were animals up there, goats and sheep, the odd cow. Chickens squabbled and capered about. All were contained in cages, waiting to be put to fire.

A sacrifice!

Close by she heard Carlo Sarfe curse and lash out before being buffeted to silence. The sky above glowed deep bronze and weighed on her heavy as the metal it portrayed. "This is a dream!" Teret whispered to herself. "A nightmare. Not happening. I refuse to accept this reality!" The armored hands gripped her and she lost consciousness for a moment.

Tam—where are you? I need you now!

Teret was hoisted high, her head lolling back so she could see the track they'd followed ribboning down through shrub back to the village far below. The sea lapped lazily around the village edge, and Teret wished she could reach those waters and sink beneath, deep into cold void and oblivion. What had she done to deserve this?

The armored giant and his silent obedient men reached the plateau of rock where the wicker cages stood silhouetted against the copper sky. Those cages were fashioned in the shape of men, women, and beasts.

Worse, they were occupied—not only by fowl and livestock, but by humans too. Teret saw men and women there. Weeping and sobbing. Crying out in terror. Clothes torn and ragged, faces lost to despair, arms clutching chests; some stood with hands clenching the cages, their expressions pleading, while others sat staring like lost things at the distant ocean. There were children too. Teret closed her eyes to deny this horror.

She heard a rasping sound like steel scraping on stone and realized it was the giant speaking. "We wait till midnight. Moon's full—the Emerald Queen will claim them before morning breaks. Put these two in with the others."

The Emerald Queen—where had she heard that name before? A memory flashed through Teret's mind but vanished as panic swelled to overcome her.

I have to stop this monstrosity.

The silent men obeyed their armored leader, and Teret and Carlo were tossed into the nearest cage. Teret rolled to her feet as she landed, and glancing sideways saw Carlo crash into the wicker frame. He turned, stared at her, his dark eyes wild and savage and his brown fists clenched.

Teret shook her head.

Easy now—we'll work this through.

Carlo nodded seeing her expression. She watched him study the framework shaking his head. No give there. "Methinks we'll be warm tonight," Carlo flashed her a grin. Teret glanced at the other occupants of the cage. Three women and a man. Garbed in dun tunics and trousers, the cloth grimed with dirt and badly torn. They stared blankly back at her, the tears dried on their pale haunted faces.

"We're going to escape," Teret told them. "I don't know how but we will survive this night. I haven't come this far to perish." The nearest—a young woman, perhaps twenty--approached timidly. She had large almond eyes, and her face, though pretty, was almost yellow in sheen. Her hair was straw-yellow and strewn across her face.

The girl stared at Teret as though she were mad. Teret reached out and touched her arm and the younger woman jumped back in alarm. "Settle," Teret said. "Do not succumb to fear." To her right Carlo barked a wry laugh. But the woman reached out and touched Teret's sleeve.

"They say the Emerald Queen always comes," the girl said, her voice thick with accent. "The Grogan feeds her needs in return for power."

"The Grogan?"

"The giant in the metal case."

"Oh—that bastard." Teret exchanged looks with Carlo who shrugged.

"Best learn what we're dealing with," he said.

"And those others were his servants?" Teret asked the girl but she didn't respond. Teret noted how the remaining occupants of the cage had loomed close and were listening intently, like frightened birds perched above a stalking cat, waiting for it to jump.

Yards away, she could see the faces of people staring out from the other cages. The weeping, crying out, dismal low of cattle, and occasional cock crow surrounded the stone plateau. What a terrible sight. Aside that, watchful silence and a feeling of impending doom wrapped tight beneath those deep leaden skies.

"His slaves." The almond-eyed girl summoned up the courage to speak again. She curled her lip down. "Once they were our people but the Grogan turned them into what they are."

"Which is what exactly?" Carlo asked.

"Mindless, soulless beings. The Grogan sucked the life-force from them, leaving physical shells. The Emerald Queen gives him knowledge while his slaves fuel him strength. One of them was my husband," she said, her gaze blank.

"Who is this Emerald Queen?" Teret asked the girl, but her face looked blank, so the man answered instead. *And where have I heard that name before?* Another image flashed through her, the face of a young dark-haired woman gazing out a window in a city far away. Ariane—Tam's cousin . . .

"The witch in the woods," the man said. "Not our business to ask about her. The Grogan does her bidding, keeps her supplied with flesh." Teret stared at the man in bewilderment. *Not your business?*

"Where did this Grogan come from?" Teret's keen blue eyes examined the cage's structure. There were splits here and there. She had sharp fingernails and this enemy clearly wasn't used to retaliation. It was a chance. Teret poked a finger at the wicker, worked her nails within the strands.

"Outside the sky," the woman said, not noticing what Teret was doing. "Up there, beyond limbo—another place."

"Was there a piper there?" The woman shook her head, confused by the question. "It doesn't matter," Teret smiled at her as her deft fingers prized a small crack between the wicker strand. Two nails had broken painfully but she'd spilt the wood and now had a hand through.

"Tell me your name."

"Carys." The woman barely mouthed the word.

"And this land is?" Teret winced as a splinter cut deep into her palm. She ignored the pain. "We are strangers here," Teret explained, and the woman nodded slowly.

"Gwalen," Carys said. "The last free province."

"There are other lands occupied nearby?" Carlo Sarfe loomed close and the girl shrank away from him. His hands were bloody too and Teret guessed that like her he'd been trying to tear open a crack, but so far without any success.

"He's my friend," Teret said, and the girl relaxed.

"Yes, though I know not their names," Carys said. "The village has always been our home. We were peaceful fisher folk before the Grogan came. There was a war years ago. Invaders came from across the sea. The other lands were conquered and their peoples put to the sword. But Gwalen survived because of its closeness to the forest. Like us, the invaders feared the reputation of she who dwells within."

"Tell me more about this Emerald Queen, Carys—is it? Did I pronounce that right?" Teret's fist bunched and she shoved an elbow through the strand working it wider. If Carys noticed she showed no sign. Carlo was away struggling at the cage a bit further on, tugging, tearing, and cussing.

The girl nodded, but before she could speak the man in the cage leaned toward her and smudged her lips with a filthy hand. "It is forbidden to mention her name," he said.

Teret slapped his hand away from Carys's mouth as though it were a fly.

"And who might you be?" she said, pulling her bleeding hand from the cage and standing square with arms folded and blue eyes smoldering. "A willing sacrifice, some kind of weird fatalistic priest? Or just a witless fool?" The man stepped back, alarmed by Teret's speed of movement and steely stare.

"He is Boal," Carys said. "Once a fisher. Now . . ." It was evident Carys had no love for this Boal. "The Emerald Queen just is," Carys explained with a shrug of hand. "She and her people come out of the forests at night and take what they need. We used to offer fowl and fruit, sometimes fish. Then the Grogan came and upped the stakes."

"And now he offers people," Teret nodded. "But tonight, this queen will starve." She turned and with both hands tugged hard at the wicker pulling a rent wide enough for her shoulders to squeeze through. The weasel-faced Boal gasped and threw up an arm in alarm, Carys blinked rapidly, and to her right, Carlo laughed.

"How did you achieve that when I couldn't?" Carlo said.

"I'm Rorshai," Teret said. "Got tough little fingers." She showed him her bleeding hand. "Our people are taught how to fight as children. Hands, feet, and elbows and knives. We are not easily defeated. And I'm no fucking victim, Carlo Sarfe." She turned and began tugging at the cage again.

"Let me assist," Carlo said, offering a hand. Teret, after a moment, nodded and stood back. Carlo looked strong—much stronger than her.

He flashed Teret a grin and leaned into the wall of wicker, pulling, tugging, ripping, and wrenching, until he'd prized open a space almost a foot across. He flashed a grin at Teret, who nodded.

"Good enough." She turned to the girl. "You need not be a victim either, Carys," Teret said, as the girl looked on with almond eyes wide. "We will free every man, woman, and creature here down to the last chicken, and the Emerald Queen and your Grogan friend can go fuck themselves."

"You've a way with words, Teret of the Rorshai," Carlo laughed as he pulled the wicker struts apart, breaking open a hole wide enough for them to squeeze through easily. But Boal scolded and pushed Carlo hard from behind, knocking him off balance.

"This is heresy!" Boal yelled as he made to shove Carlo again.

"What—you want to burn?" Carlo said, wiping fresh blood from his hands. Boal raised his hand to strike Carlo, but then his head snapped back as Carys's small fist crunched into his nose. Boal fell back into the other women gathered close behind.

"Well done," Teret said smiling at Carys. "Now quickly, all of you, climb down through that hole. That Grogan monster might return at any time." She hinted Carys go first, and the younger woman nodded and squeezed her skinny white body through the crack in the cage. The others followed including Boal, who seemed to have changed his opinion. Carlo urged Teret jump after Boal.

"Watch that bastard," Carlo hinted toward Boal, now standing close, his eyes bulbous and manic. "He's clearly insane."

"Don't worry about him." Teret watched Carlo Sarfe throw his body free from the cage. Once done, they set about tearing rents in the other cages, Carys and the other women helping. This took well over an hour and it wasn't until they were done that Teret noticed Boal was missing.

"I told you to watch that crazy bastard," Carlo snapped at her. "He could have warned the monster, clearly he's mad enough."

"I don't take fucking orders from you!" Teret said.

Carlo held up both hands. "Fair point. But methinks we should leave this place soonest. And before nightfall."

"I agree. But where should we go?" Teret said as she gripped Carys's arm. "I see some kind of forest over there." She'd see it earlier, a misty mass of leafless trees marching off over gray hills. "The same woods the invaders shunned?"

Carys nodded her head vigorously. "That's where the queen comes from," she said. "Those woods are haunted. Forbidden."

"Well that leaves open hills or sea," said Carlo. "That Grogan fellow will surely find us should we take to either. Unless there's a boat nearby I can commandeer. Not in the village of course."

Carys just shook her head, her earlier courage lost to new fear and indecision. A shout announced someone coming their way. The villagers froze in terror, but Teret looked down at the road as the light faded to crimson-copper dusk all around them.

The giant had returned. The deep glow glinted off his armor. The Grogan, huge and shouting, marched toward them, a long steel mace swinging like a pendulum in his metal fists. A squad of shabby men swarmed around the giant as his steel boots crunched up toward the broken cages cresting the hill.

Animals scattered and people fled—all terrified by the noisome one approaching. Boal was there with the silent men. Teret saw him shouting up at the Grogan and pointing to where they stood.

"I'm going to kill that weasel," Teret said to Carlo, then, "Hold fast!" The villagers were breaking up in small groups as panic fell among them. "Not that way!"

Most had started running along the ridge leading down to the plateau. Some of the Grogan's slaves broke off in pursuit, and minutes later Teret heard the screams of the victims apprehended. Fools, throwing their lives away. She turned from the sight, eyes bleak, and instead gazed down at the shroud of trees clustered amidst the valley below.

"You coming?" Teret croaked at Carlo, who nodded and joined her, trotting down from the plateau. Carys followed, as did a few of the others still gathered there. The rest stayed put, their limbs frozen in terror.

"Poor bastards," Carlo yelled in her ear as the first screams echoed down the valley. The Grogan's mace was already splitting skulls.

"Their choice," Teret said. "And a quicker end than burning. We must look to ourselves, Carlo Sarfe."

The way was steep and rocky but they descended at haste. One of the women tripped and tumbled but Carlo caught her arm and heaved her back on her feet. She managed a brief grin at the strong man helping her. Teret could hear the Grogan's metallic voice calling after them. Screams and shouts faded as they reached the first trees where the ridge sloped away into deeper, denser forest.

The surviving villagers ran, driven both by the terror of what chased them and a dread of what might lie ahead. At the fore, Teret and Carlo Sarfe jogged on with grim determination. Both were intent on achieving some result in this forest—whatever the outcome. Teret thought about Tam as an image of his face flashed through her mind. Stay alive! She would find him again in time. Until then she had to keep moving forward. Ride this nightmare or whatever it was. Were Teret to hesitate once she would crumble. Faltering meant death. That wasn't an option.

The trees reached over and pulled them in, a moist dankness filling the atmosphere and smothering their frightened whispers. The runners tripped, tumbled, and fell as the trees crowded close around them, the steep slopes leading down to deeper forest below.

Teret stooped and helped an old man find his feet. They were scarcely hanging on, needed protection and rest—and soon. Teret had no idea how long these people had been prisoners, but clearly, they were beyond exhaustion.

"Keep going," she said, turning around and bidding them keep up. "Flight, then refuge. Food and then a plan. One thing at a time you people. We can do this!"

Nobody replied, but Carlo swept her a warm smile and for the briefest moment Teret smiled back, a glimmer of something passing between them.

They reached a wall of rock from which a waterfall spilled and cascaded, noisy, lively, spray veiling the atmosphere, the water crystal bright. A beautiful sight were this on any other evening. Its constant voice chimed, crashed, drowned out all sound as they headed toward it, the only break in the forest leading them there. Large gray rocks loomed overhead, vines trailing from them, and the steady thud and tumble of icy clear water filled their ears. The deer path, or whatever it was they followed, led straight beneath that deluge.

"Looks like we're getting wet!" Carlo winked at her.

"Better than burning," Teret said, and without further word ran headlong into the torrent, gasping as she plunged through. A shout announced Carlo behind her, then the icy chill and thudding in her ears eclipsed all other sensations.

Teret stumbled blindly forward, pushing her tired body on, gasping as the sheer weight of chilled water threatened to knock her to her knees. She staggered, gulping breaths, and at last almost fell into a hollow cave opening on what appeared to be a warm sunlit glade, just yards ahead.

Teret emerged gasping, Carlo jumped alongside. He grinned at her, his beard and hair flopped down like a soggy dog. "That was refreshing," Carlo said.

They waited as the others emerged. Teret counted nine, led by a determined- looking Carys. The old man stumbled in a few minutes later, Teret smiled at him. These people had some strength left in them.

"Are we all here?" Teret asked Carys. The girl nodded, wiping water from her face.

"We are thirteen," Carys said. "The others . . ." She shook her head and the old man rested a palm on her shoulder. He looked a kindly soul and Teret saw a determination in him the others lacked. This old one was a survivor.

Teret took stock of the new environment, gazing about as water dripped from her hair. A clearing. Warm sunshine filtering down through fully-leafed trees, and birds singing somewhere close. Summer had stolen a march on winter. More trickery no doubt.

Whatever she'd expected it wasn't this. Another enchantment, but at least a pleasant one. Again, Teret wondered if she were still under the influences of that Piper at the crossroads, or maybe the fungus she had eaten earlier. If this were a dream she would follow it through to the other side and emerge safe and strong. That was the only thing that made sense.

"Come on," Teret said. "Let's see where this takes us." The path led away from the waterfall, now a veil of mist and music fading like stolen memories behind them. It was warm and very quiet, and Teret knew they were being watched by someone or something hidden in the trees. "It's not the same forest," she said to Carlo who looked surprised.

"I don't take your meaning?"

"That waterfall was a gateway, like the one I passed through earlier before I found you back there in the village. A portal. It's summer here, Carlo. Back in Gwalen it was winter, or autumn. But here it is summer and these trees are heavy with enchantment."

It was then that she saw the woman seated quietly on a rock.

Teret froze and Carlo almost crashed into her. Behind them Carys's pale features were stricken with terror, and some of the others already turning to flee.

"Stop!" Teret said. "You cannot keep running, people. We will face this—person—together. Is she the queen?" This last to Carys. But the girl just stared as one transfixed.

Teret exchanged looks with Carlo who shrugged. "After you, my valiant Lady of Rorshai." Teret's cheeks flushed annoyance, but she walked on up to where the woman sat, observing them coolly in the sunshine.

Teret stopped a few feet away, and the woman cast her green-eyed gaze upon her. Teret saw a beautiful face, symmetrical and perfect; the eyes a milky, dreamy, mysterious pale green, and her skin a sheen of viridian and teal, flecked with freckles of star-shaped luminous gold. Her hair was long and fine, the color of sun-ripened wheat. The woman wore a shimmering dress that clung to her lissome figure like a second skin. A deep green dress, Teret couldn't help noting.

The Emerald Queen.

She appeared young yet ancient, and her eyes were filled with potency and power. Eyes far colder than the waterfall had been.

"You are the Emerald Queen." Teret folded her arms and gave the woman a hard look. The stranger didn't answer but Teret saw a flicker of amusement in that glacial gaze. "These people think you a murderer, some kind of flesh-eating witch. But I'll try another tack. Maybe you're not that bad. Besides, we need your help, Queen," Teret said, not in the mood to prevaricate.

A musical sound filled the glade, a chime of chords, melodic and whimsical, and it was a few moments before Teret realized the woman was laughing. The laughter emanated from leaf and tree all around them, yet no quiver moved those pale lips. Teret relied on her instincts.

"Are you going to eat us then? Or torture us like your Grogan friend? Come, at least have the dignity to answer me, Queen. Or is it a witch I see before me?"

"Does a dog address the fleas on its back?" The woman said, her tone bored and her pale green eyes pinning Teret. There was venom in that stare. The queen's voice was raspy yet alluring. And a tone deeper than Teret had expected. This was a very strange being seated before them. "What care I for you sorry creatures, save that you trespass in my forest? Mortals have no mandate here."

"That may be so," Teret said. "And I apologize for any intrusion, but we didn't have a choice. So, fry us or free us—but stop wasting our time."

"Fry you?" The laughter again. "Why would I do that?"

"Why wouldn't you?" Teret clenched a fist.

"You cannot use that on me," the woman said. Her eyes flickered at the rag-tag group still poised like deer at edge of flight. "You, woman, appear interesting at least. The man there—Carlo Sarfe—I like the look of him. Strong." Her thin lips hinted a different kind of smile, and Carlo muttered a curse behind her. "These others appear as empty shells. I've scant interest in such hopeless things."

"They are my friends," Teret said. "Freed from the wicker cages erected in your honor, Emerald Queen. You've a foul reputation. Does it please you to watch children burn alive?"

"It neither pleases nor displeases me." The woman appeared puzzled by the question. "That is a game played out by another."

"So, the Grogan doesn't work for you? The giant in armor? The metal monster who has tortured, butchered, and burnt most the occupants of these poor people's village, and stolen the minds of the rest?" The Emerald Queen said nothing, her perfect lips parting ever so slightly. Carlo stepped forward and she eyed him with sudden interest, as a hawk focuses on a sparrow in flight.

"Know you Gol?" Carlo said. The woman didn't reply, and instead slipped from her rock and glided like spilled silk toward him. Teret held up a fist but the woman laughed, making the trees shiver in the glade surrounding them.

"I am Elerim," she said, looking straight into Carlo's eyes. "Not She who you think I am. That was another. I'm just a woman. Though once I was very powerful, now I am in decline."

She was taller than Carlo and stooped over him as she breathed huskily in his ear. "You look strong and healthy enough." Her slender palm rested against Carlo's chest. Teret noted the long, dark green fingernails. Carlo jumped slightly and looked alarm at Teret.

"I can't help you with that," Teret said, raising a brow. "But I think you at least are spared from any immediate danger." Carlo coughed as the woman's hand worked inside his shirt, stroking the hairs on his chest.

"Is this really necessary?" Teret said. Elerim turned and awarded her a frosty stare.

"Our Lords had little interest in carnal matters. They neglected their Ladies, poor fools, so we always got what we could when chance allowed—my treacherous sisters and I." She smiled at Carlo—the kind of leer Teret had seen on a cat dissecting a mouse.

"We are trapped in this frail frame of life, as are you. Yet we are wise and ancient but driven half mad by boredom. Diversity feeds our monotony. And you, Carlo Sarfe of Gol, divert me. For the moment. A temporary distraction. Though a pleasing one."

"So, you have heard of Gol?" Carlo gripped the ice-cold hand on his chest and gently removed it. The woman's milky green eyes flashed annoyance.

"Of course," she said, turning away as though no longer interested in him. "You live as long as I have, you get to hear of many things. Different worlds and strange dimensions, the wheel is always turning—even though the Gods have moved on, they do say." She flicked a knowing gaze at Teret. "But you know something of that—don't you child?"

"Even if I do, I don't care. So, if you're not the Emerald Queen then where is she?"

"How would I know? And why should I care that those frail fools you're protecting mistook me for another?"

"I'm looking for my husband," Teret persisted, tired of the nonsense. "You clearly know something, whoever or whatever you are. So . . . I dare you, Elerim the enchantress. Help me find Tamersane—what have you to lose?"

Elerim raised an eyebrow. "You're a spiky little one, aren't you? Follow me." Elerim showed them her back and glided to the edge of the glade, her long green gown brushing the carpet of pine needles. Within seconds her willowy form had faded into the trees beyond, and with it the afternoon sun paled and evening stalked close. Teret glanced at Carlo.

"Best we comply," he said.

Teret nodded. "Come on, friends," she said to their silent companions. "I don't think she means to kill us. Though what she's up to is hard to guess."

"Yet," Carlo whispered in Teret's ear, as Carys and the old man urged the other villagers follow them from the glade.

The path widened to a level and smooth track, and as soon as they set foot on it the light fled from the trees surrounding and a sudden hush filled the air as darkness cast its cloak over them. Ahead, just yards away, Teret saw a yellow glimmer. A flickering will-o-the-wisp. She walked towards it, saw the shadow of the woman Elerim poised, a lantern swaying from her right hand.

"Stay close to my light, else the forest spirits fall upon you. There are perils in this wood. Ancient beings dwell here less benign than myself."

"I find that hard to believe," Carlo muttered as he strode alongside Teret, the lantern swaying and dancing along the path just ahead, and the shadow of the woman fading into gloom.

"Where are you leading us?" Carlo called out, but woman didn't reply. He glanced at Teret. "Guess we'll find out. Interesting sort of day. How are you faring, Lady Teret?"

"Just Teret—I'm no lady. Stop saying that."

"Oh, but you are." He awarded her that warm smile. "Your husband is a lord, then that makes you a lady. Least where I come from. He is also a fool deserting you."

"I didn't say he deserted me," Teret snapped as anger flushed her features.

Carlo shrugged. "I'm just saying."

"Well don't bother. You know nothing about my life, Carlo of House Sarfe. And I know nothing of you. Let's keep it like that."

"As you wish," Carlo said, and then stopped, seeing Elerim had turned to allow them catch up. Her eerie beautiful face flickered in the lamplight.

"My sisters would like you," Elerim said. "Cille would be cruel though, in her blood-red dress. So dramatic—she likes to play hard. That stale hag Ysaren—were she free—would be more attentive to your needs."

"And you?" Carlo asked, giving Teret a sidelong glance. "What about the lady Elerim who insists she isn't a queen?"

"That you will find out soon enough." Elerim turned again and vanished into shadow and lamplight.

"I hope there's food and ale wherever you're taking us," Carlo called out. "I've a rare thirst on." He reached across and touched Teret's arm lightly. "I'm sorry," he said. "I'm sure your husband's a worthy fellow. I left my manners in that fisher's hut."

"My husband is a tortured soul," Teret said. "Which is why he needs me with him before he destroys himself. None of your business but I accept your apology. Come, that green witch is leaving us behind again."

Teret quickened her pace and the man strode silent and thoughtful beside her. Behind them Carys and the others stumbled wearily on, their eyes huge and fearful in the ominous dark. Teret pursed her lips. Odds were they'd all survive this night and come morning they would know more. That knowledge was all she could handle for the moment.

Chapter 11 | The Bruhan

"They're gaining on us!" Pash called out from behind.

"How many?" Doyle yelled back, as Garland urged his beast kick up more speed down the track.

"Hard to say—thirty or forty? Hope your border's close, Captain." Garland ignored Pash's shout as he focused on controlling his horse, as more arrows struck the way beside them.

"Whoa!" Doyle almost screamed to his right. "More ahead, and coming this way!" Garland raised a hand to shield his eyes and groaned, seeing at least a dozen horsemen cantering up toward them from the road a half mile ahead. He glanced back to see the main force gaining slowly. Nothing for it.

"Cut across country!" Garland yanked the reins and kneed his horse, turning the beast and urging it crash into the brush and strewn rocks leading down the slope away from the road. The others followed suit as a dozen shafts fell all around them.

Glancing behind him, Garland heard Taylon holler and witnessed him almost pitching from his horse, an arrow having pierced his arm. Tol rode close and supported his friend. "You all right?" Garland heard him yell.

"Never been better!" Taylon shouted back, gripping his arm and trying not to scream out at the pain.

"We need cover!" Doyle said from beside him, and Garland nodded grimly. The pursuing riders had reached the place where they had left the road, and were guiding their beasts down the bank, though slower and with a deal more care than Garland's crew had. The other party were close too, and Garland heard more shouts as these newcomers rode up and joined their comrades.

"Must be a border patrol," Garland said, as he urged his horse through the rough terrain. Ahead a steep rise crested on broken rocks—as good a place as any to shore up and face what was coming. They'd take it at the gallop and just hope the horses didn't tumble. Poor beasts were getting shredded in all this brush.

Garland pointed at the rise. "That's our best bet," Doyle agreed, but behind Garland heard Pash curse and Kargon mutter disapprovingly at the decision.

"Horses ain't going to make that climb, Captain," Kargon's gruff shout reached him from behind.

"They'll fucking have to!" Garland yelled back and spurred his own beast on.

But the horses fared better than even he expected, with all eight cresting the steep rocky rise without mishap, the odd arrow still biting the rocks behind them. Once up there they dismounted and took stock. The rocks crowning the hill were bigger than he'd dare hope so there was plenty of cover, and at no point could the enemy surprise them.

The riders realizing this slowed their assault below, fanning out wide and looking up at the hill ridge where Garland and company had dismounted to tend to their beasts as best they could. Once that was done the captain and his men crouched low and watched the riders below. Garland saw that most carried spears and swords, and only half a dozen were archers. Tol leaned close, arrow nocked to string.

"Can you and Coife take those archers out?" Garland asked the bowyer.

"Watch us, Captain," Tol grinned, being in his element. Beside him the short dour-faced Coife grunted acknowledgement. Tol rolled lithely to his feet, pulled back on bowstring and sent a shaft high. Garland watched it arc up, then slide down with a precision that never failed to amaze him. An enemy archer cried out and pitched from his saddle. Doyle whooped and slapped Tol's back. Tol grinned at him.

"Too easy," the archer said.

Coife jumped out from behind a spur, nocked, drew and loosed, and a second archer fell. The other archers scrambled back in alarm and began circling the lone hill. "This could take some time," Coife grumbled as he squatted down beside his fellow bowyer.

"Nothing else to do," Tol smiled. "Let us see what they're made of."

Garland left the archers watching as he made his way through a hole in the rocks to where Taylon lay with hand clutching arm, his face pale, Mullen standing over him.

"How fare you lad?" Garland bid Mullen join the others with a gesture.

"Not too bad." Taylon managed a grin. "Wasn't my best knife throwing hand, but it does fucking hurt."

"We got to get that out—and quickly, else your arm rots in this stinking heat."

Taylon grinned. "Ready when you are Captain." Garland nodded, and fumbled with his flint kit, at last striking flame with some brush wood he'd gathered. Once a little fire was ablaze, Garland whipped out a knife and shoved the blade deep amongst the faggots.

He waited, Taylon panting beside him. Doyle appeared and crouched alongside. "The boys all right?" Garland hinted through the split in the rocks to where he could glimpse some of the others scanning the enemy below.

Doyle nodded. "Tol and Coife are having fun. They've enough shafts to keep the bastards busy jumping about, though not indefinitely."

"They better not waste any," Garland snapped. He leaned over Taylon and gently gripped his wounded arm. The shaft had pieced his left bicep and narrowly missed his shoulder behind.

"You ready?" he asked Taylon.

"Can't wait," Taylon said through gritted teeth. Doyle rolled a swab of cloth from his saddle bag and winked at Taylon.

"Bite on this. I soaked it in brandy," he told Taylon. "Had a tiny drop left." Taylon grinned though the fear showed in his eyes. "Hold steady, old lad." Doyle passed a wood axe he'd brought across to Garland who rested Taylon's arm against the rock, aimed carefully and then hacked down, snapping the shaft in two. Taylon jerked then relaxed.

"Now to push it out through your arm," Garland gripped the shaft and shoved quickly. Mercifully it cleared the wound without splintering, and Doyle held Taylon still as his body shook.

"Last up," Garland said, retrieving the knife from the fire and checking the blade for heat. "Good enough. Now hold still, this will hurt."

"Get to it Captain," Taylon mumbled through the wet cloth he was chewing, then tensed and hissed as Garland set the flat of the heated knife against his arm, sealing the flesh.

"You all right mate?" Doyle said, leaning over, taking the swab from Taylon's mouth.

"Not enough fucking brandy," Taylon complained.

"We'll get more once we've dealt with those idiots down there," Doyle said. Garland bid his second stay put with Taylon and returned to the rim where the two archers and the rest of the men crouched low and watchful. They'd lashed the horses' reins together and the beasts were being monitored by Kargon, who also made sure they'd had plenty of water.

"So, what's the plan?" Pash said as Garland joined them.

"We wait and see what they do," Garland said gazing down at the riders hovering just out of bowshot. They'd circled the hill but soon realized there was no way for them to climb without risking more casualties. They were soldiers and not wild tribesmen and Garland was grateful for that. Permian nomads would have been scampering up the hill by now, yelling and cussing, ferocious savages that they were. These fellows were timid by comparison.

"Look, here's someone," old Mullen grunted and pointed down to the far left where a lone rider eased his horse closer. The rider raised a stiff palm in parley and Garland stood forth in reply, studying the other, who looked like the leader with his brightly polished breastplate and helm with a crimson horsehair plume.

"Careful Captain, could be a ruse," Tol said, taking aim with his bow. The rider bid two archers accompany him to the base of the hill, well within range and earshot. Once there the leader called up. His accent was strange but Garland could just make out the words.

"Ptarnian slavers are not welcome here!" The voice was not only foreign but muffled by the helmet.

"Good to hear! We are not slavers!" Garland shouted down. "Nor are we Ptarnians!" This seems to cause a stir between the officer and the two archers next to him. Eventually the leader looked up.

"If you are not slavers then what are you?"

"Wayfarers making for Laregoza! We're lost and mean no trouble — but must needs defend ourselves, of course."

"I think you are lying!" the officer called. "No one crosses this terrain except slavers and border patrols. This is treacherous countryside."

"Yeah, I noticed," Garland said. The officer wheeled his horse about, clearly unsure what to do. The two archers glared up at them and Tol waved at them. "Stop that," Garland told him, and the archer shrugged letting his hands drop by his side.

A few tense moments followed as Garland and his men watched the riders guiding their mounts to and fro, as their leader and the two archers sat their steeds in silence just staring up the hill. Doyle appeared and gazed down at the scene.

"Taylon will be fine," he told Garland, who nodded. "What's happening here?"

"Buggered if I know," Garland said. "I don't think they have a plan." Enough was enough. He approached the steep rim of cliff and held palms out wide. "I'm Captain Garland of the Wynais Garrison." The officer just looked at him. "We're a long way from home, seeking a cousin of our Queen's. A man feared lost in Caranaxis."

"You're a long way from Caranaxis," the officer shook his head.

"I know, and we've heard it's best avoided. Besides, I've reason to believe our countryman has journeyed farther east. We have no quarrel with Ptarni," Garland added glancing sideways at Doyle. "Worth a try," he whispered and grinned at his second.

"That's a shame because we do," came the answer.

"You're Laregozans?" Garland waved his hands. "That's excellent news! We've been seeking your country's border."

"You crossed it ten miles back—the River Laros."

"We saw no river!"

"It's dry this time of year, though a wide-ranging flood before reaching the sea twenty leagues south of here. We are out of Talimi Garrison, and you are now our prisoners. We execute slavers in Laregoza."

"Then it's fortunate that we are not slavers," Garland called down.

125

"Do you have a name, sir?"

"Bruhan Dahali of the Fifteenth."

"Well, Broo-Han Da-Haa-Lee of the Fifteenth, it's like this," Garland said. "We can stand all afternoon yelling pleasantries at each other, or we can exchange arrows. My lads have lots of spare arrows and—allowing that your boys clearly outnumber us—we can put a lot of holes in your little army before you climb this ridge and eventually murder us. We're seasoned veterans hard to kill. Won't look good when you return to Ta-whatever Garrison, a rag-tag force with your tails between your legs. Where is your garrison?"

"Scarce two miles away," Bruhan Dahali said. He circled his horse and spoke to his archers. They looked up and scowled. Tol cheerfully waved down at them again.

"I said stop that," Garland snapped at the grinning archer. "That lot down there don't seem to have a sense of humor."

"Nobody has his sense of humor," Coife said, and Tol nudged his arm.

Bruhan Dahali steered closer and looked up from the edge of the hill. "What you say is true enough, and I have no wish to lose any more of my men."

"Good. What do you propose?"

"We escort you to Talimi Garrison, once there you can speak with my superior and convince him you are not slavers."

"Do I look stupid?"

"I don't know—I cannot see your face." Bruhan Dahali sounded puzzled by his question. Garland glanced sideways at Doyle who shrugged.

"This could take some time," Garland said to his men gathered about. "I suggest you rest up while we try sort something out with this pompous Laregozan imbecile." He turned and yelled down at Bruhan Dahali again. "You see our quandary? Once we're down from

126

the hill your men will surround us and murder us.'

The archers looked shocked hearing that and the officer glared up at the hill. "How dare you say that? We are honorable fighters here," he yelled in outrage. "My word is trusted in nine counties."

"Sorry, but I don't give a shit. We are not coming off this fucking hillock until you and your shiny-arsed gathering bugger off and leave us be."

"That told him, Captain," Tol said.

"Your attitude is unreasonable." Bruhan Dahali glared up the hill.

Garland rolled his eyes then blinked back surprise as the officer snapped at his two archers and slid his long legs free of his stirrups. "What's he doing now?"

"Perhaps he needs a shit?"

"Shut up, Tol."

"I'm coming up. I'll meet you half way," Bruhan Dahali said. Garland exchanged glances with Doyle who shrugged. "Shoot me, and my men won't stop attacking until you're all dead. What say you, foreigner?"

"On my way down . . ." Garland made to step down but Doyle grabbed his arm.

"Captain, he's calling our bluff."

"Maybe so, but daylight's passing. At nightfall those bastards could creep up here unannounced, and though they don't appear over-bright they might grasp that notion before dusk and change tactics. Best we comply with his wishes. Besides, I'm curious to meet this Bruhan What's-his-Name.

"Keep me covered, lout," this last to Tol.

"I got you Captain, or should I say Bruhaha?"

"Shut up."

Garland slung his sword across his back and painfully picked his way back down the slope. Below, he could see Bruhan Dahali making swift jerky progress up through the scrub. The man seemed energetic at least.

Twenty minutes later, Garland almost crashed into the younger officer. Bruhan Dahali saluted him with a sharp wave. Garland returned the gesture with a wry grin.

The officer stood pencil straight. "Bruhan Da—."

"Yes, I know—honor to meet you. Let's cut the crap, shall we?" Garland took seat on a small rock while the Laregozan loomed over him, his dark eyes glaring from under that tight-fitting helmet and a tanned hand on his scimitar stored neatly in its polished steel scabbard. Bruhan Dahali looked hot, stiff and very uncomfortable. Unsure how to proceed. Perhaps twenty—just a boy. Out of his depth.

"Rest easy, lad," Garland waved him settle. "Tongues are better than swords most times."

Bruhan Dahali hesitated, then, after an awkward glance at his men watching from below, he too found a small rock to sit on, adjacent from Garland's.

"You are a strange fellow," Bruhan Dahali said.

"I've been called worse." Garland picked a blade of stubby grass and placed it between his teeth. He partially closed his eyes and yawned, leaning back as he chewed the blade.

"What are you doing?"

"Resting up—been a long day. Need my strength for fighting." Garland almost chuckled at the officer's expression. He now looked alarmed—scared even.

"Fighting? I thought you wanted to resolve things between us."

"I do." Garland winked open an eye. "But I'm a practical man. You seem upset, and obviously have to impress your men. That doesn't give me confidence in your negotiating skills. So, I expect we'll have to fight each other. Shame, but shit happens."

"What—hand to hand?"

"You and me, yes. More cost effective. Whoever wins gets to lead his lads away."

"Not sure I want to fight you alone," Bruhan Dahali said.

"Only sensible way forward," Garland yawned. "I've killed over a hundred men in single combat. One more won't harm my sleep."

"This is irregular." Bruhan Dahali looked increasing worried. "I mean, we don't usually operate like this in Laregoza. I've only been a Bruhan six months, posted way out here to keep an eye on slavers.'

"Which me and my lads are not," Garland growled.

"I . . . believe that's so. You don't have the look now I come to think of it. You, foreigner, appear more wholesome."

"Wholesome? I'm not a fucking loaf of bread, Bruhan Dahali. Do I have to keep calling that, it's quite a mouthful? Have you another name?"

"Yurillion Masparis Dahali recently of Largos Heights. A Bruhan in the army of Laregoza."

"I'll call you Brew. How's that sound?"

"Tolerable."

"Good. So, what's it to be, Brew—swords or knives? Or bare knuckle, if you'd prefer—I was regimental boxing champion once. Old now, but still have a few nifty moves."

"This isn't necessary," the Bruhan said. "I mean, I have no wish to inflict dire wounds upon your person. Far better you and your men accompany me to Talimi Garrison and we get this sorted out."

"So, we can be strung up for being slavers?"

"No. I've agreed you are not slavers, Captain. Upon my word as a Laregozan Bruhan you shall be tried as raiders, infiltrators, spies, or invaders—but not slavers."

"Oh well, that's good I suppose." Garland's gaze had drifted to a column of smoke rising above the road in the west. High above, he heard one of his men shout out a warning.

"I think . . ." The Bruhan noticed Garland looking at something behind him. "Is something amiss?" The Bruhan turned, his young face paling on seeing the dust trail in the distance.

"How many?" Garland leapt to his feet, yelling his question up to Tol who he could just make out silhouetted against the rocks high above.

"Hundred, maybe more?"

"Fuck, but that makes things complicated." Garland rubbed his eyes and reclaimed the rock. "Your boys?"

The Bruhan shook his head. "Ptarnians. We are outnumbered."

"Well, I'm sure you can deal with it, confident fellow you appear."

"What—you're trapped here too."

"Not our fight," Garland yawned. "So, we'll slip away while you worthy Laregozans deal with that lot out there. Our horses have rested enough. Been good visiting with you, Brew."

"Wait!" Garland turned and saw the panic in the officer's eyes. The lad looked almost in tears. "The Ptarnians are professional killers," the Bruhan said. "We're just conscripts trying to protect our borders. My father paid for my commission. For over a year the Ptarnians been brutalizing our people. We try to fight back but they win every time. And now we are outnumbered too."

"A sorry situation," Garland shrugged. "But not my affair." He turned to walk back up the hill.

"You could help us," the Bruhan said.

"And why would I do that?"

"They are your enemies too."

"Are they? You'll have to do better than that, Bruhan."

"We need your . . .I personally would appreciate your help as a veteran warrior."

"In return for?"

"Safe passage and assistance with your quest into the east lands—
or whatever you are up to. I can offer no more!"

Garland could see the distant riders clearly now. They wore
armor, the bright glare glancing off helmet and breastplate, their faces
hidden beneath chains. They rode in orderly fashion two abreast,
kicking up a thick trail of dust as they cantered toward the lone hill
where Bruhan Dahali and Garland of Wynais conducted their affairs.

"I suppose we'll have to learn to trust each other." Garland thrust
out a hand and the young Bruhan, after a moment's doubt, shook it
firmly.

"Order your lads up this hill," Garland said. "Tell them to mind
their manners, some of my lot are touchy. Up there they can
dismount and we have the mutual advantage. What say you, Brew?"

"We are with you," the Bruhan smiled for the first time that day.

Chapter 12 | Cille

Among other things, Marei had lent him a pony. Tam guided the mare down the lane, his head cloudy as the skies above, and mind racing with anticipation. Ahead the road wound down through open hills leading to a pale strip of water and more low-lying cloud. The sea—just ten or so miles to go. It was cold and a stiff breeze whipped Tam's face as he nudged the pony down the road, his mind churning with anxiety.

She'd said nothing that morning, just led him to the stables after cooking up some porridge for his breakfast. "I'll find your boy," Tam had promised as he mounted up. Marei had just nodded and left him to the morning and his ride.

An hour later Tam eased his steed to a slow walk and studied the terrain. Bare hillocks parted, opening on a low-level strand, where gray greasy water washed pebbles and a wide creek surged in from beyond.

Straddled across that creek at the edge of the ocean stood a rock. Or at least it looked like a rock, vaguely square in shape with the odd lump or point jutting out. On closer inspection, Tam saw walls etched along the surface, almost invisible. And as he got nearer Tam discerned what might to be crenellations and roofs, and even a few windows winking pale light from afar. Creepy and disturbing. He could see why Marei disliked this place. Whomever dwelt inside had limited design skills.

Graywash Hall looked hostile and was confusing on the eye, like a huge distorted rock that had tumbled from the sky and didn't belong in this cold calm seascape. Tam set his teeth. None of that mattered. Time for some answers! He urged the pony down the road where it joined the noisy rush of creek leading to a half-crumbled arching bridge spanning the fast-flowing stream.

"Steady girl." Tam heeled the pony's sides. "I don't trust this bridge any more than you." As Tam crossed the narrow arch, he glanced down at the silvery surge of water thirty feet below, an urgent stream pressing down through broken rocks on its voyage to the ocean just a few miles away. After bridge and stream, the road followed the bank down a steady slope, the ominous rock called Graywash Hall staining the horizon like inkblot on parchment.

Tam saw no sign of life, though as he got nearer he spotted the tiny shapes of houses and huts huddled close by the stream where it fed into sea. A village—must be where Marei's people came from. But the Hall dominated the skyline, a smudge of blue-black quartz stamped across a line of lowering rushing clouds, the ocean a paler brittle gray expanding way out beyond. Not a cheery sight.

Tam urged his hesitating pony on as a few stunted trees appeared like crippled sentinels on either side of the road. There were hedges and ditches and the odd sign of recent work in puddle-strewn fields beyond. Tam shivered as damp cold crept inside his clothes. He felt the pommel of his sword and hoped that it wouldn't be needed. Comforting though it was to have the weapon at hand.

Tam thought briefly about Marei. Had he offended her last night? She must have known how desperate his situation was. Another mistake. But no point dwelling on that. Teret was his only concern, he reminded himself.

He pushed the thoughts of her away too, lest he become useless with emotion. Instead Tam wondered how Stogi fared. Hard to keep track, events had happened so quickly. *Keep moving forward. Concentrate on the task ahead.* Moping achieved nothing and was only worthy of contempt. Tam pictured Teret's worried face, and wielding an expression gloomy as the sky above, he urged the pony approach the monstrosity of stone looming just a mile ahead.

Tam felt the presence of many watchful eyes as he approached the gates to Graywash Hall. Dark heavy wood embossed with black straps of iron, the gates looked as if they hadn't been opened in years. No guards stood there, but a wall of blue-black shiny rock rose sheer, broken by the occasional wink of window hinting inhabitants high above. He dismounted.

To Tam's left, he saw stones arch up spanning the stream, the water rushing beneath the bulk of Graywash Hall and on into the sea. To him this place appeared as one great rock, chiseled out and occupied. But by whom? Uncanny folk Marei hadn't wanted to talk about. But people who might help him. Will help him—Tam corrected. *Time for answers.*

"Greetings the Hall!" Tam called up as cheerfully as he dared to the windows high above the gates. "I'm seeking brief lodging, having travelled far through lands I do not know." No answer. Just the wind whipping up from the pebbly strand, lost beyond the mass of rock and stone. "Anyone home!" Nothing. A cry of gulls in the distance and the distant rumble of wave striking beach.

Tam shivered. That's that then. Forlorn hope. Next up try the village. He placed a foot in stirrup and heaved up, stopping when a long slow scrape announced the gates opening outwards. Tam slid back off the pony and turned. A man stood there, clad in heavy dull-red coat and gloves, a floppy wide-rimmed black hat occluding his features. Tam frowned, recalling someone similar from a time gone by.

"Greetings friend. I'm—"

"Lord Tamersane, recently of Kelwyn. Yes, you're expected." The man had a very deep voice but his face was hard to define. He shuffled inside his coat, producing a satin-gloved hand the color of dried blood, and hinted Tam lead his pony through the gates. "I'll take the nag," the man said reaching for Marei's pony.

"She's not mine," Tam told him, but the man just nodded, and without further word left him standing alone in what appeared a spacious empty courtyard of stone. Tam took stock, no longer surprised by anything he saw, nor by how the man in the red coat knew his name. Clearly there was sorcery here too. But Tam had seen much in his thirty years and, after last night, his craving for smoke and ale had returned again, forcing away fear and curiosity. A relapse and a bad mistake, but no time to dwell on that now.

A door emerged at the far end of the courtyard. Tam swore the door hadn't been there moments earlier. A trap? It didn't matter. He'd get a response one way or another. Tam slid a hand down to grip his sword and strode purposefully toward the door. He turned the handle; it snapped off and a cloud of dust exploded in his face.

"Fuck." Tam coughed and pushed hard against the door and it fell off the hinges. Tam shook his head. Not encouraging. He walked through the mess of dust and splinters, emerging into a large oval room lit by a single lamp standing tall on a table in the distance. As Tam approached the table, it slipped backwards seeming to distance itself further from him. He quickened his pace and the table withdrew again.

"Stop that!" Tam heard the faintest hint of laughter. At last he got closer and saw a figure hunched at desk, a parchment in thin hands and a quill clutched between narrow twiggy fingers.

An old man, frail and gaunt yet icy sharp of eye. Thinly mustached, he wore a shabby jacket three sizes too big for him. His eyes were black as jet. That acerbic gaze lashed him, as Tam finally reached the table and gripped the musty ink-stained surface, making sure it was real. The scholarly ancient glared up at him with hostile curiosity.

"You're in the wrong room," he snapped. "Cille's quarter is at the other end. The east wing. A month away if you take the wrong door." He motioned another door that had just appeared behind Tam's shoulder. "That's the right door—today anyway. Might be the wrong door tomorrow."

"I'm new here," Tam said, uncertain how better to put forward his case. "A casual visitor, and I don't know anyone called Chilly."

"Chi-Ley." The man made a lingering "click" with his lips as though slowly spitting out the word. His lips drooled. It wasn't endearing. "Pronounce her name wrong and she'll slit you open like a sack of grain," the old man said. "Iron fingernails. Go now! I have studies to attend." He hinted the door again with his quill.

"Been a joy," Tam said, his sarcasm wasted on the ancient. "Doubt we'll meet again." Tam turned making for the door. He stopped when something fluttered past his face. A crow or rook; it croaked once and then vanished from sight. Tam felt a shiver of familiarity and deja vu. Crows had served the corpse-gatherer. The one-eyed wanderer called Oroonin who had played a crucial role in the recent war. But that being was dead, his enchantments lost forever.

The Gods are dead, and the world has changed.

Crows are just birds. Tam mouthed the mantra as he approached the door. The only way to survive was to keep moving forward, let go of the past. Focus. Tam gingerly placed a hand on the door knob. This one appeared solid enough, and he turned the brass until the door eased open without the hint of a creak. He left the room with the old man without a backward glance.

Ahead loomed a passage, long and flat, hemmed by walls that seemed to press in towards him as he walked. The odd sconce winked flame and guided his passage. There were paintings of faces, dark, faded, and hard to make out. Maybe the Lords and Ladies of this fine hostelry. They had an ominous look and after glancing to and fro as he walked, Tam chose to ignore them.

The passage neither veered nor cornered, and beneath his feet a shabby worn carpet hinted dull rose and smelled of mothballs. Tam walked for an hour before the murky light suggested another door. This one was arched and high with pale gilded birds carved at its apex. Tam pushed it open and was immediately greeted by a wall of blinding light.

Tam staggered, blinking against the dazzle assaulting him. He stepped forward gingerly and fell, not seeing the wide staircase spreading out before him. Tam rolled and crunched down the steps painfully, at last coming to rest on a smooth polished floor, the surface chequered in bold red and black squares. Quiet cruel laughter surrounded him, crisp and clear as breaking glass. A woman's voice accompanied it with words he couldn't understand.

Then the floor slid sideways beneath him and Tam threw his hands up to grip its surface as he slid down and down, faster and faster.

What the . . .?

"Nothing is as it seems." The voice changed tone and drifted across to Tam, this time with words he could decipher as he half fell, half slid down through the blinding glare. Tam braced himself for inevitable impact, but the floor leveled slowly and his bruised body came to rest inches from the stone hearth of a roaring fire. The flames spat at him as he rolled to his knees and blinked.

The light dimmed at last as he kneeled, panting, coughing, clutching his sword hilt and flinching as the flames crackled close. "That wasn't funny," Tam said to the room around him. He soon regretted his comment because the room started spinning, becoming a whirl of light and shadow.

Sick and giddy, Tam gripped the stone hearth beside him, hanging on despite the heat, and his fingers scorched. "Damnation, stop!"

The laughter surrounded him again like invisible jabbing fingers, or small birds pecking, and then the room ceased moving and Tam pitched hard onto his face.

He looked up painfully. The light had withdrawn to distant corners chasing spider-shaped shadows along the walls. A woman watched him from a desk much like the table the old man had sat behind. A triple candelabra flickered yellow light across her features. Its shadow clung to her back but stayed put as she moved. Her eyes glinted with firelight.

Tam saw a perfect face framed by flame and shadow. Oval, the skin creamy white, eyes jade-green with gold flecks, and long black hair smooth and oily, thick and curling around beneath her ears and disappearing down her back. She wore a deep red gown, and a wicked smile adorned her full carmine lips. Grape-sized rubies dangled from her earlobes.

A looker, in a scary, witchy kind of way. Tam rolled into a sitting position and stared at her, pain, confusion and giddiness banished as he studied her beauty. Such was the effect of this woman on his senses. She just gazed back dreamily, so Tam clambered to his feet and put a hand on sword hilt.

"You won't need that," the woman said, her voice a rasp dry as winter leaves crunching under boots. "Besides, you lack the strength to draw it." Tam heaved at the sword but it wouldn't budge.

"Sorcery," he glared at her. "You *are* a witch then, and this place is—"

"Graywash Hall. What were you expecting—a welcoming committee?"

"The woman—Marei."

"Mentioned me?"

"Er . . .no," Tam said. "Not in person. She was—"

"I don't care about her," the woman glared at him.

"She said you people might be able to help me," Tam persisted.

The woman arched an eyebrow. "Help . . .you? Well, that is intriguing. Another random thread in this game of life—or death, depending on which side you're gazing in from. Come!" She curled a finger, urging him approach. Those full lips were mocking and cruel but her beauty held him trapped like bug in jar.

"You are the Lady Cille?" Tam made sure he pronounced the name right.

"See these pathways before me?" The woman beckoned him close and Tam, hesitant, loomed over the desk and gazed down at three large cards placed on its ebony surface, Cille's white fingers brushing over them. The finger nails were crimson and filed to pristine points, Tam couldn't help but notice. "They represent your journey, Lord Tamersane."

"You have my attention, Witch. Or whatever you are."

Cille's lips parted in the faintest smile. "Your recent dependency on opium and alcohol has stolen your wits. Fool." She turned the card, and Tam saw the picture of a man garbed in yellow chequers, a strange triangular hat on his head and a mask hiding his face, the word "Fool" written beneath him. The man looked familiar, and for some reason Tam recalled the Piper at the crossroads, the villain that had sent him here.

Tam held back an ironic chuckle. "Accurate but not overly helpful," he said.

"Its meaning is more complex," Cille said. "You are entering a period of change, morphing into someone new." Her green/gold eyes glinted up at him and she almost smiled. "Someone more interesting perhaps. But then again . . ." The smile fled her face replaced by a stern accusing stare.

Tam held his ground. "And the others?"

"Not time to draw them yet," Cille said. "Everything happens only when it must. We can push and prod all we like but to scant avail until the time is right."

"Eloquently put, but I for one am out of time," Tam said. "Trapped inside a dream conjured up by some evil imp in a forest, himself an illusion. And now lost in this creepy castle whose residents have not proved very welcoming. No offense," he added after a moment's thought.

"Graywash Hall is no castle," Cille said. "It is a living thing. An entity that exists outside the confines of your limited perception of what reality comprises. Time itself has no meaning here because the Hall lies outside the confines of Time. That's how Garland met Marei before you did—how she knew you were coming. The journeyman crossed to this dimension when time was running backwards at the Hall. But in your own world—Ansu, he has yet to arrive. A riddle, yes?"

"That's terrific—but not sure I care. And I don't know anyone called Garland. Not why I'm here. I need to get back to my wife, Lady Cille. And for some reason I think you might help me."

"Might I?"

"You have the ability, I'm sure, even if you lack the incentive."

Cille crackled like the fire. "You hold to optimism. I like that. You, Tamersane of Kelwyn, still have strength despite your many failings."

"My strength is my love for my wife," Tam said. "I fucked up and now she's gone. I need to get her back before that slime kills her. If Teret dies . . ."

"What care I for that!" Cille snapped at him, her voice harsh and eyes suddenly cruel. "Why should I care a jot for your situation?"

"Because you need me."

"I . . . need . . .you?" Cille arched a brow and her razor-sharp fingernails drummed the middle card. She lifted it slightly and gazed underneath. "Interesting."

Tam wished he could see what that card read. Cille's features relaxed into another smile, the curious smile a cat wears as it studies its helpless victim. Almost he liked her at that point, being perpetually drawn to dangerous women.

"Perhaps I do," she said.

Tam nodded. "Else why summon me here? The Piper at the crossroads—that trickster. He serves you, doesn't he?"

"The Jynn serves himself. I have no power over such a one." Cille shivered suddenly as an icy draft crept into the room. A dull thud echoed from outside and Tam spun about, eyes wide and hand gripping sword hilt.

"What is that?"

"The other ones returning home." Cille looked pensive, uncertain, and Tam noticed her lips tremble slightly.

"Other ones?"

"There are many occupants in Graywash Hall," she said. "But not all share the same dimension. Not all are as equitable as myself. Some of them come and go, shift in and out. Others remain stuck for years then fade into memory."

"Ghosts?"

"There are no such things as ghosts. Spirits, yes. Shades

frequenting different times and spaces, certainly. But ghosts are just rumor and shadow. Ghosts are a lie." The thud again, followed by the sound of something heavy sliding across the floor somewhere out beyond the door.

"What is that?"

"You need to leave now," Cille said, her voice suddenly urgent. She reached and out gripped his arm, the nails digging in. "Listen before you go. There is something I require most urgently. A weapon of considerable power—sought also by my enemies. The emerald bow—Kerasheva. I need it brought here before they get their filthy claws on it. Do that and I will ensure you recover your dear Teret before mad Sulo's curved knife cuts open her heart. I see the blood dripping from his blade! Time is running out for your little wife."

"How the—?"

A blast of light hurled Tam back against the wall beside the fire. Roaring filled his ear, and he felt his body lifted up and hurled violently through space. Correlations of color assaulted his eyes, dazzling him, the sickness returning, as Tam was blasted up and out into the atmosphere. Half stunned, and again expecting to impact the walls at any moment, Tam instead felt his body slow, the air sucking at him, and slip down, almost floating through a warm cloying atmosphere. He had the sensation of tiny invisible hands lowering him gently.

Tam settled like snowflakes in soft grass as the sound of hoofbeats approaching filled his ears. He opened his eyes, blinked, and gasped, seeing Stogi leaning over him.

"Glad you're back," the Tseole said. "Things are getting out of hand."

Tam saw twenty or so riders bearing down on them, amid dust, shouts, and gliding steel.

Chapter 13 | Carlo

They came at him like rolling steel towers, cranking and grinding, ten-foot tall machines in the form of men, armored, hefting battle-axes and flails with chains swinging.

Carlo rolled to his feet; a sword gripped in his hand. The nearest metal giant hewed down hard striking the soft soil where Carlo had lain. Carlo stabbed up and under the metal knight's armpit. A clang of sound and flash of light and the monster faded from view. The others clanked toward him, Carlo braced his legs, leveled the sword. He waited until they were almost upon him, three towering figures, their faces hidden behind the visors of heavy round helmets.

An ax swung down at him. Carlo eased his left knee and slid sideways, striking out with sword gripped with both hands. His blow struck iron, sending sparks through the air. A metallic shout echoed in his ears and the second giant knight vanished.

The other two circled him; they seemed unsure, puzzled by his victory over their companions. Carlo leaped at the one on his right, shoulder charging into the knight's groin as the giant swung frantically with his flail. Carlo stabbed up, both hands on sword. The metal knight cried out—a distant vacant sound like a lone lost bird driven far by wind and gale. Then the knight vanished. That left the biggest. A master of steel bearing two huge flails.

This one had cunning. A low intelligence that had learned from its companions' errors. As Carlo tested and lunged, the creature blocked easily enough and struck down hard, flails swinging like well-timed pendulums.

Carlo felt the wind knocked out of him as he dived free of one swing, but got caught by another, the blow sending him sailing through night air. He rolled to his feet again, almost vomiting as nauseating pain cramped his guts. Carlo gazed down and saw the huge rent in his belly.

I'm dying.

No—this is was test or some dream. An illusion. The little voice inside his head assured Carlo.

I have to survive this test.

The giant loomed close, the morning-stars swinging in unison. Carlo tried to stand but an iron boot lashed out, knocking him onto his back. He rolled, then screamed in agony as another boot kicked hard into his groin, sinking inside the gaping wound. The knight loomed over him, both weapons held high, Carlo noted how his breath smelled like attar.

"You don't exist," Carlo spat up at the metal knight, then blinked startled as his adversary vanished in a soundless bubble of air exploding in his face. "Just a nightmare?" Carlo choked, holding back the pain as he felt the ground rising up and then falling away. He heard laughter, cruel, ironic. A woman's sultry tones.

"That all depends on your perspective, Carlo Sarfe," The Emerald Queen or the Lady Elerim—one of them for sure.

"We all dream—do we not?" The voice was soft, flowing like wheat grass in breeze all around him. Carlo felt the warmth of her presence like summer in his face. The pain had gone, and glancing down he saw no wound. He sighed, gazed about for the owner of the voice, but saw no one.

"It's joining the dots between each dream that defines the reality of what surrounds us." Her voice trailed off like distant thunder.

"Where are you and what do you want?"

"I want you."

Carlo fell. Black wings strummed close by as dark things snapped at him. Down he fell, seeing an orange light far below swelling like morning sun as it rushed up to greet him. Fire? *Not more fucking fire* . . . Carlo closed his eyes, damning this new nightmare to the confines of she who had sent it.

I'm not your plaything witch!

As he fell, Carlo saw eyes blinking at him from corners. Insect's eyes. There were fine sticky wires glinting with dew. His body struck one and it immediately folded around him, pulling him across to the greedy eyes watching. Carlo struggled, but more wires tangled his arms and legs, trapping him. Below the fire blinked and went out as though extinguished by some massive invisible glove.

Carlo's sword fell from his hands. He saw it flicker and twist then vanish far into the blackness below. He struggled but the wires cut into him, pinning him and trussing his body tight, like the shell shielding the urchin within.

The insect eyes were closer. A dozen at least. Like a cluster. Green and cruel and sharp as daggers, lancing into him. Probing. Carlo could make out a rough shape around those orbs. A large bulbous body, a number of legs twitching and clawing toward him. A black mass of crawling, creeping evil, approaching him as he twisted and writhed in terror.

Laughter again. Carlo recognized Elerim's green gaze in those pale lamps. The spider teased toward him, those sinister green eyes mocking and victorious.

"Play your games witch," Carlo closed his eyes. "It's just a sham, a rough etching—there are sorcerers in my land who could send your soul screaming!" The spider rushed upon him and Carlo Sarfe screamed, losing consciousness in the void of terror that consumed him.

He woke when a small determined fist battered the side of his head.

"What the . . .?"

"You were dreaming," Teret told him, her blue eyes intent and wary, and her lean body squatting close to where he lay.

"It was more than a nightmare," Carlo said as he came to his senses. "Metal giants attacked me, then she appeared in spider form and started eating me."

Teret smiled. "Hardly surprising considering what we've been through. Those giants were the Grogan, obviously. And the spider represented your horror and confusion. And Elerim's eyes hinted how we're are under her influence. Whoever she is. Emerald Queen or some other enchantress. Just a dream. Best not delve too deep, Carlo Sarfe."

"Maybe you are right," Carlo said and sighed, rubbing his tired eyes. "And I'd sooner forget it. But where are we? For some reason I cannot remember much after our encounter with the witch."

"Don't call her that," Teret hissed. "She is around; I feel her presence."

"So? Let the witch explain what game she is playing. I'm not easily spooked. And where is here, exactly?"

"You are in my woods, Carlo Sarfe. An honored guest." Elerim glided toward him, her green eyes mirroring the spider's in his nightmare. Carlo tensed.

She smiled. "I'm not your enemy today. Were it another day then who knows? But you need fear no harm while you are here. However, be wary of those dreams. That's where the others will find you."

"The others?" Teret blinked.

"My sisters."

"Is the Emerald Queen one of them?" Carlo rolled to his feet and glared at the dark-haired beauty gazing upon him.

"She has nothing to do with us." Elerim's beautiful face flushed with sudden anger. "Stop mentioning her name. Her spirits frequent these woods and will harm you if they can. My power protects you while you are awake, but her spirits can and will enter your dreams and steal your souls. It's what they do."

"I dreamt of you sucking the life out of me." Carlo felt for his sword and then noticed it wasn't there. "What plans have you for us, Enchantress?" ·

"Plans?" Elerim laughed suddenly. "Why would I have plans for such as you? Foolish exile from a drowned continent. What are you to me?" Her voice crackled like embers and those eyes glinted icy jade. Elerim's lips curled down and she turned, and without further word departed the glade where they were resting, her long green gown floating like reeds on water behind her.

"Why must you provoke her?" Teret's blue gaze flashed annoyance. "We live or die at her mercy in this place. Whatever she's up to, it's stupid to annoy her."

"Because I'm tired of people pissing on my plans," Carlo said, noticing the slight smile on Teret's face and feeling the soft sense of movement below. She wasn't beautiful. Not like their host. But Teret was earthy and warm, and Carlo found her very appealing. Her skin dark as his, but with striking blue eyes—something he'd not encountered before. And she had such spirit! Hard not to like her. Her husband sounded like a Galanian noble: full of hauteur, arrogance, and foolhardy nonsense. Carlo could see Teret watching him, her lip still curling and curiosity in her gaze.

"Where are the others?" Carlo said, feeling awkward for some reason.

"Gone," Teret shrugged. "I woke to blue haziness and you lying snoring beside me."

"You paint a delightful picture, Teret of the Rorshai."

"It's what I saw." Teret turned away and left him gawping at her. "I think we have to wait out our time here until Elerim chooses to show her hand. She won't kill us. That much I believe."

"I do not hold to such optimism," Carlo said, watching the girl wander off to a nearby stream to wash her face. He studied her strong brown legs, the way she walked—almost as a warrior struts—and the way she held her head and tied back her long black locks.

"You are a beautiful lady, Teret of the Rorshai."

"And you, Carlo Sarfe, are a restless vagabond. Forget it. I'm a married woman. Your advances are wasted on me, sir."

"Just trying to be friendly." Carlo held up his hands as Teret walked by to the glade where he waited. "I mean, not much else to do here." She said nothing, just sat quietly by his side, her blue gaze on the trees framing their little shared world.

After a moment Teret reached and gripped his callused brown hands with her own. "I would have us be friends, though," Teret said.

Carlo reached down and kissed her hand. "Friends it is then," he said.

***

A blue haze filled sky and forest, the melodic rhythms of cricket and bird melding off into dreamy nothingness. The blue-eyed girl slept beside him, exhaustion finally having claimed her. Carlo had let her sleep, wishing he could do the same, though fearing the dreams would come back. Instead he turned his mind to face the confusion and disaster of his own story.

A ship's voyage, so many months ago. His carefully chosen crew. Twenty-two bright, laughing, sunny-faced lads had toasted their captain as they'd sailed out of Reveal harbor into the west. A brave sight that day. Carlo's speech had raised the fire in their bellies. New lands, new adventures, women, wine and wealth—all a young man desired, plus the glory of staking claims on lands not yet discovered.

For well over a year they'd sailed, until the storm took both his memory and his crew. Shipwrecked and lost, at first Carlo had blanked out his emotions. But the hollow days spent alone in the hut, and then his meeting Teret and what she had told him, had left Carlo reeling with the knowledge that the home he'd left so valiantly no longer existed. The fire, the Grogan, Teret's arrival at the village, and now this strange lady, Elerim. All factors churned inside his head as he struggled to hold back sleep. Not going there yet. Those nightmares had nearly unmanned him.

But drowsiness found him despite his struggle, and Carlo slumped into deep slumber as his head hunched forward, the girl sound asleep beside him. Thus, for a second time that day the dreams fell upon him.

In this visit, Carlo lay in a huge downy bed, the scent of pollen and stamen twitching his nose. Carlo rolled to his knees, saw huge petals rise up like steel fences surrounding him and, realized he was captured within the prism of a tall sentinel flower, its petals the color of freshly-spilled blood. The stem swayed and the flower lifted its head in the wind, and gazing down between the petal fences Carlo saw the grass and trees far below him. He relaxed, assuming this to be another vision, but kinder than the last.

Elerim came gliding toward him through the deep red blooms, the pollen dust lifting and encircling her green dress, staining it crimson. She smiled, for once the green eyes friendly, and Carlo sat back, folded his arms and waited for this next outcome.

"Stranger in strange lands," she said, taking seat beside him in the soft downy yellow, and placing a pale veined hand on his arm. The touch was silky, but soft and cold as wet fish sold at winter markets.

Carlo almost recoiled at that touch but, instead forced himself relaxed.

"You call my country dead, and Teret says it's just a legend. A rumor. That may be so, but I sailed from Sarfania only last year—my parents and brothers waving farewell, as our people cheered from the walls of Reveal. I don't understand."

"There are many worlds," Elerim smiled as she stroked his arm. Her cat stare fixed on his chest and then dropped further.

"Please—no riddles. Oblige me, just this once?" Elerim's weird green gaze left its playful peruse, and instead pinned him like butterfly to board. For the first time Carlo realized that this woman—or whatever she was–was ancient beyond his concept.

"I'm a simple creature, unlike yourself, Witchy Lady."

"I'm not a witch," she said. "Just someone old and wise enough to see around the bends." Elerim's green gaze washed over him as though he were sand and she the ocean. "We were a great people once," she said, her eyes now dreamy with distance and memory. "A race like none other.

"But we overreached, and the Gods turned against us. Like treacherous, cruel harridans, spiteful and jealous in their lofty towers. Those same Gods who themselves have but recently been blasted from the heavens. And for good reason. They were our guardians—back then. We learned much form their wisdom. But they turned against us."

"You became sorcerers," Carlo croaked the word out. "And now my new friends and I are trapped in your game."

"We are all trapped in someone's else's game," Elerim said, her hands on his chest, the fingers searching. Carlo tensed at that touch. "But the nets constraining me are much stronger than those binding you, lost voyager. You have the strength–the woman also—to find yourself back from whence you came. For me there is no such hope.

Which is why I'm not inclined to empathize with your plight."

"The Emerald Queen and her creatures—these are your enemies. Your captors?"

"Ugh! You mention that name again. She is not part of this. She is a lie!"

"That's not what Carys's people think," Carlo said. "They are terrified of her. What manner of creature is she?"

"Dead!" Elerim spat the word out. "She perished in the war that shook our universe. She is no more. Do not mention Her again."

"And yet she still haunts this wood?"

"Her essence perhaps. A memory, nothing more. Her people too. They perished with their mistress but some spirits lingered, became echoes, phantoms. The shades of a departed menace, and the rumor of twisted memory. But true, they are not my friends, but rather are a remnant of the people who rebelled against our race who ruled them long ago. They're the Dark Faen—or rather what has become of them.

"I had five brothers—all dead now," Elerim said, her hand sliding lower. Carlo stiffened. "Just my sisters and I remain, though they are lost to me. Their fickle hearts stolen by treachery and time. I doubt I'll see them again, which is just as well."

Carlo coughed as she worked deftly at his drawstrings. "So where is this place and why are we sitting inside a massive flower?" It was a fair question, but judging by her irritated expression she wasn't about to answer him. "I mean, when am I awake and when dreaming? All seems the same, if you don't mind me asking." Her hand stopped, pulled away. Carlo breathed a sigh of relief.

"That's because you are riding the hub of the wheel that turns the nine worlds, the spokes circling and whirling ever faster around you. This is the place between places. The world fabric is thinnest here. Possibilities are endless as planets collide, slipping through dimensions. The wheel turns and the spokes must follow, but each one represents a different dimension."

"I fail to grasp your meaning," Carlo said yawning. "Something momentous happened several years back—I gleaned that much from Teret."

Elerim looked irritable, much like a teacher challenged by an obtuse student's foolish questions. "Obviously, an event resulting in the annihilation of the old order would leave some reverberations," she said, looking peeved. "Those of us who could withdrew to the sacred places, those steeped in earth magic, for protection, such as this forest in the center of the world. But there were risks involved. Ansu's core is thinner here, that's how the Grogan creature broke through.

Too much to take in. Carlo was feeling sleepy. It seemed strange to feel weary inside a dream. But her words were like incantations drumming inside his skull.

"Every action has a reaction, and any single event can change not only the future, but past, and present too. You sailed through time as well as water."

"So, Gol still exists, just not in this dimension, and time?"

"Yes," she said "Gol exists in one, but in others is gone—ravaged by water and fire. The woman Teret exists in yet another, close to yours but separated by time. Were you to return to your land somehow and intervene it could result in her oblivion. Her never having existed."

"But I have to get back there, somehow."

"Unwise," she said. "You wouldn't last the journey, much less the arrival."

"I intend to try."

She ignored him. "These other mortals with you come from yet another spoke. Same wheel, different strut. The Grogan creature, from somewhere else—a cold place at the far corner of the cosmos.

"All these dimensions are turning and crashing into each other as the Gods, the maintainers of order—and recently chastised and driven out—have neglected them, and the wheel races out of control and random, crashes reckless through time and space.

"That make sense?" Elerim's eyes pinned him again.

"Not really," Carlo yawned, and then smiled at the recurring thought of feeling sleepy inside his own dream. "I need to know how to get back to Gol—the Gol I left, and not the one Teret tells me was destroyed a thousand years ago. I need to return and warn my people of what is about to happen, or even better—prevent it."

"Even though that could kill you and might even alter the future of mankind—break the spokes of the wheel asunder?" She smiled cruelly. "I can help you achieve that." Her eyes were crafty. "But first I need you to find something for me before my siblings acquire it. But for now—enough talking." Her fingers found his drawstrings again.

It was that precise moment that Carlo woke, slightly disappointed, and saw Teret washing her naked body in the stream. She turned and glanced his way, the small bird tattoo standing out on her cheek. Funny how he'd hardly noticed that before.

Carlo studied her nakedness absentmindedly, his mind still partially addled by Elerim's weird gaze. He saw a flash of annoyance flush Teret's face.

"Enjoying the view?" she said.

"I am."

"Well good, now you've had your fun, you need to get ready for a journey." Teret showed him her back. Carlo could hear her muttering to herself as she pulled on her trousers.

"A journey? First, we have to escape from this wood," Carlo yelled at her back, feeling disappointed.

"That's not a problem," Teret said.

"I admire your optimism."

"Is that all?"

"Nope," Carlo said, watching her dress, holding back the desire to rush across and throw his arms around her. "I think you are a beautiful woman, Teret of the Rorshai."

"And you, Carlo Sarfe, are full of crap," She turned away again but he caught the ghost of a grin fleeing her face. "And why are you still sitting there like an imbecile when you should be getting ready for departure?"

"But I thought we were trapped here?"

"And so we were, until I negotiated a deal with the Lady Elerim."

"Without my input?"

"You were asleep. She left you that— said you might find it useful."

"You could have nudged me," Carlo said, his eyes on the broadsword resting against a tree stump. Useful looking. Hand and a half grip, the steel hidden in a shabby leather scabbard, abelt and buckle alongside.

"She needs us Carlo," Teret said, turning to face him, her eyes big in the sunshine. "I knew that when first we encountered her. Elerim is trapped here, and there is something we can do to help her escape. But there are others she does not trust that want the same thing."

"Yep she hinted that to me while I was asleep. That and something she needs. Very mysterious." Carlo strapped sword belt to his waist and tugged on his boots. "And I don't think she likes her sisters much. But, yes, since you've arranged it so nicely—I'm happy to leave, so you can fill me in on the way."

"Will do." Teret turned to get busy.

"I'll go get the others." Carlo made to depart.

"Don't bother—they are not coming."

"We can't leave Carys's people at the mercy of that woman!" Carlo said, rounding on Teret, angry and surprised she'd abandon their new companions so easily.

"Carys and the others will be fine." Teret's eyes softened as she saw his expression. "I'm sorry, Carlo. I don't want to be short with you, but we need to move and I can explain all this better on the road. Elerim can only hold the portal open for a short time."

"Portal? Fine. Best you lead on then, Blue-Eyed Lady." Carlo smiled again. "I'd follow you anywhere."

"Oh, shut up," Teret said, as she left him and faded into the twilight of trees and pale blue shimmering skies. Carlo shrugged, clasped his heavy cloak over his shoulders and followed the woman's fading shadow. Teret was right. There would be time for answers later.

Chapter 14 | The Shaman

"Ptarnians?" Tam's head was buzzing and his stomach churning, but the riders heading their way funneled his thoughts to the present. Which was just as well under the circumstances.

"Wish they were," Stogi said, standing and shaking his head as the riders whooped and shouted and spurred their horses faster toward them.

"Who then?" Tam said, bleary eyed and trying to adjust to the reality that he was suddenly back in Tseola. "And hadn't we—?"

"Too late," Stogi quashed his question before it had left his lips. "We cannot outride this lot."

"They're Tseole?" Tam saw the worry on his friend. "Isn't that good news?"

"Family." Stogi shook his head, folded his tattooed arms and waited for the riders to surround them with their horses amid shouts and gleeful banter. "I prefer Ptarnians."

Tam counted two score riders, most clad in fur and iron with various weaponry protruding from saddle and back, or gripped savagely in fist. They sported wild hair, mostly black or red, though a few yellowish-fair as was Tam's. All had tattooed faces, and any flesh showing was painted too. Spirals and studs, images of wild beasts and various outlandish weaponry—all dramatically traced out in vivid blues and reds and yellow. Tam had never seen such painted folk. The Rorshai ritual brands were plain by comparison, and Tam had always been impressed with those.

A garish brazen host surrounded them. They wore loose and baggy brightly colored trousers tucked into floppy dun-colored riding boots. Many had large hoops of gold hanging from their ears like Stogi, though some displayed hooks and miniature daggers and battle-axes. Tam noticed several women among the riders, just as outlandish and hairy as their men.

"Hello there!" Stogi stepped forward in friendly fashion, stopping when a brace of spear tips pinned his neck forcing his chin up. Tam closed his eyes. He didn't have time for this. Every hour, Teret was slipping further away. He'd failed at Graywash Hall, though he wasn't sure what he'd hoped to accomplish. But he'd missed Teret again, and now she could be anywhere. Almost he wished he was back in Graywash Hall. Tam felt sick to the bone, but the painted faces staring at him brought him back to the present.

Rough hands grabbed his arms, and a fist impacted his face. Next thing he knew, Tam was being dragged toward some trees. "And this is your fucking family?" he called. Stogi couldn't reply as his head was buried beneath a hood, a rope lashed around his neck. Tam strained his eyes to see how Stogi fared but then was sent sprawling face-first into the mud. Someone laughed as a boot thudded into the back of his neck.

An hour later, while tied to the post, Tam had time to reflect on Stogi's little speech.

"I can win them over," he'd said, before being kicked to the floor again, and horse-whipped by the leader. A distant cousin, he explained later.

"Horse thief!" The leader loomed in front of them, broad of chest, hard of face, with drooping mustaches and the bow-legged stance of a man who spends too much time on his horse.

"Villain!" A woman approached behind the leader, reddish hair wild, with freckled round face and angry dark eyes. And the snake tattoo replacing her left brow was most impressive—although Tam wasn't about to tell her.

"Hey Hulda," Stogi said, waggling his ear, the only body-part he could move. "Greeting Broon. You both look well." Stogi groaned as the woman—Hulda—kicked him hard in the groin. "That's a nice welcome," Stogi choked.

"And you, Stogi, look like a piece of rat shit," she said.

"Fair point," Stogi coughed. "Been a rough few days. I'll scrub up handsome, so don't fret darling." Stogi grinned heroically, and Tam, watching, wondered if his friend had lost his mind.

A third man approached. This one was older, unusually tall and whip lean, a long scar curving from below right eye, cutting cheek and cleaving upper lip. Tam noticed how Stogi's smile fled his face. He looked genuinely worried for the first time. Not only did the newcomer look different from the rest, with his pale features and large gray eyes, his apparel was plain by comparison. A long black coat, reed-thin trousers and shabby black boots. He wore a tall hat that accented his superior height, and his scruffy gray hair spilled out beneath its rim. There was something unnerving about him.

"What's to be done with them?" the newcomer said, voice growl-deep, eyes the hue of winter clouds, their gaze cynical, flat, and questing. He stooped and grabbed Tam's forelock heaving his head up. "Westerner. Soft and decadent. Heavy drinker. Rendered slow and bloated by inaction."

"Up yours too," Tam mumbled. The tall man ignored him.

"Where did you come by this one, Stogi?"

"Caranaxis," Stogi muttered. "And he's not soft as you think,

Seek."

"Don't pretend you have a glimmer of what I think, fool." The man in the hat continued to examine Tam, who replied in silent measured defiance. "I see fallen pride, a man once held in high office, now but a lonely shadow haunted by past actions."

"We all make mistakes," Tam said. He forced a smile. "And I've made bad ones. But I don't give a sparrow's fart for your opinion, scarecrow. What are you, a hedge lurker or a child catcher? That dreary apparel might impress these honest folks but it does nothing for me."

Seek glared back at him surprised, his sharp features flushed with annoyance and disbelief.

"Hang him over hot coals," the woman Hulda urged the men beside her. "Disrespectful bastard, addressing the shaman like that. But do it tomorrow, bros. I might like some time with him tonight. He's not as ugly as you lot."

"You're not my type," Tam said, and wrenched his head back as Seek tugged his chin, staring deep into Tam's eyes. "Get off!" Tam spat into Seek's eye. Hulda and the raiders' leader Broon looked askance and Stogi's black eyes were bleak. Seek just stared at him as though he were a viper. His mouth tightened and his eyes misted over.

"You shouldn't have done that Lord Tamersane," Stogi told him. Seek calmly wiped the spittle from his eye with a flared sleeve and smiled coldly upon Tam's person. "Not a good career move, upsetting the shaman," Stogi said. "They seldom have a sense of humor."

"Take this grubby specimen away," Seek said. Broon and some others dragged Stogi off. "Slit his throat or hang him, matters not. This one will serve well enough to satiate the spirits. They are always after foreign blood."

"Seek, I've done nothing to you," Stogi hissed the words out as they dragged him away.

"Going to murder your own brother?" Tam yelled after them. "Don't recommend it. Believe me, he'll come back to haunt you!" The fist impacted his stomach and Tam buckled forward spewing in the dirt.

"Untie him," the shaman said. "Put some food in his belly then bring him to me."

"Broon says we're to ride back to camp tonight." A rider stared down at the shaman, his dark eyes furtive.

"We stay put, Hanadin," Seek said, and the rider took the hint, urging his beast join the others clustered a few yards distant on the top of a small hill.

Tam stood, straightened slowly, his eyes never leaving Seek, currently looking at the road just a mile to the south as though he were expecting someone.

"Stogi is a good man," Tam said. "Kill him and you will regret it."

"Will I?" Seek turned his venomous gaze upon Tam. "You've known him—what, a week? Two? Not thinking straight, are you? You crave the smoke—is that it? I can see it in your eyes, laddie. Need that release from past crimes."

"You have some?" Tam felt a sudden rushing urge, an excitement blanketing his other emotions. "Give me some—I'll leave, never come back."

"Why are you here?" Seek said. The shaman's eyes were slightly humorous as though he were enjoying Tam's desperation. Evidently this character was a bully who had something on the other riders. Shaman? More like a charlatan. Tam wasn't buying any of it. He'd come across Seek's kind before.

"A man stole my wife," Tam said. "I have to find her."

"In Caranaxis, a long way from here. Seems like you got lost."

"Stogi believed he'd sell her to Shen slavers, or else Laregozans. So, we took the east road. I nearly caught up with her but things got a bit . . .altered."

"Stogi is a fool," Seek said, his gray eyes studying Tam with a hawk's tenacity. "Laregozans are not slavers. They're cowards, weaklings, and peasants, but not slavers. Ptarnians are slavers and so are the Shen. Rundali too when they can be bothered. But particularly the Shen. Many of our people toil and suffer in Shen mines. Imagine that Westerner. Men and women like these, from the wide desolate plains, their lives spent grubbing underground, never seeing the light. Dying a slow cruel death under whip and leash and chain."

"Can't you free them—a raid or something?" Tam steadied his nerves and shut out the urge for release. He wasn't going to get that here. Stay strong. He'd learn what he could from this freak then break free—somehow. And best he do that before sun-up since they were planning on murdering him too. He'd find a way. Incentive helped channel the mind.

But Seek looked at Tam as though he'd just lost his mind. And maybe I have, Tam thought to himself. *No great surprise after what I've been through.* Tam struggled to keep a lid on his anger, as the yearning for smoke and release, the fear for Stogi's situation and his own, combined with an intense dislike for this unpleasant individual addressing him.

Seek must have read his mind. His gaze turned quizzical.

"The smoke helps occlude the past, doesn't it? How you plunged cold steel in your brother's heart. Most men would want to forget that. And now you've lost your wife to the brutal whims of another. Careless, Lord Tam. And your anger so transparent, I can so easily read your mind," Seek said, lips curling downwards.

.W. WEBB

"You're a bastard," Tam said, then jumped, hearing a scream cut short. Stogi was dead. They'd had killed his friend. Some family. Tam grimaced. Perhaps Stogi was the lucky one—what point carrying on when the fates had sold him short? Stogi's problems were over, but Tam had to get out of here and find Teret. That was all that mattered now.

"Give me a smoke and then cut my throat too, I'm all done with this existence," Tam said. "You'd be doing me a favor."

"But this existence is not done with you," Seek nodded as the rider Hanadin returned.

"Pork's on spit, supper won't be long," Hanadin said. Tam noticed how his gaze avoided Seek's.

"We'll be over in a few minutes," Seek said, waving the rider away.

"You have to reach the bottom before you climb back up." Seek folded his arms and smiled at Tam. That was more alarming than his scowl.

"What?" Tam could smell the pork and now realized he was starving.

"Yours is a story yet to be written." Seek's flat eyes hovered inches from Tam. But Tam's mind was on something else. He'd scooped a parcel of hope from the rich smell drifting across.

"That scream I heard was the pig squealing, wasn't it?" Stogi was alive! They never intended to kill him. It was just a wind up. Bad joke. Odd people these Tseole.

"Did you see the Gods die?" Seek's pupils were distended, his long face inches from Tam's, the scent of stale garlic and tobacco strong.

"I did," Tam said. "Would that I hadn't. But, yes, I witnessed their fall seven years ago."

"A great battle—they tumbled from the sky?"

"It wasn't like that," Tam said. "The poets claim it was, but they're fucking liars. Nothing heroic. I saw confusion, heard a lot of

62

noise. Witnessed distortions and saw the despair on men's faces. Felt the rush of wind, earth tremors, and eerie silence that followed them. The fabric of existence blown apart—or so we thought back then."

"We felt the tremors here." Seek glanced across at the smoke drifting down from where the horses were gathered. "The Gods have moved on, they say—left us to self-govern this world."

"The Gods are dead," Tam said, but the shaman ignored him. "And the dark things that accompanied them have crept back beneath the earth. Though some still linger it seems." Tam awarded Seek a meaningful glance. He braced for another blow.

Instead, Seek laughed, a crow-sharp chuckle. His tone and manner almost friendly, as though the whole business between them had been but a joke. "Go," Seek said. "Join them. You must be hungry. Eat and drink. We'll smoke and talk later."

"You do have smoke?" Tam felt a rush of excitement.

"I have questions too," Seek said. "How you answer those will decide on whether I'll slit your throat afterwards." The crow laugh followed, but there was something in that last sentence that hovered over Tam like the headman's axe suspended. Wasp in the room. Joking or not, this Tseole shaman was not one to test.

Stogi sat by the fire looking thoroughly miserable, the redhead Hulda hunched beside him. He caught Tam's gaze and pulled a face. Hulda nudged a younger woman seated beside her who turned and glanced Tam's way. Comely—in a broken nosed, tattooed-cheek, pierced-lip, wild and unkempt ginger-haired kind of way. She grinned up at Tam as he approached the fire, her brown eyes alive with mischief.

"Not bad, Hulda," the younger woman said. "Don't seem to have much spark though. Looks like all the go's been sucked from him."

"We can liven him up, Shel." Hulda nudged her again and the other woman smiled evilly.

"That we can, big sis."

"Better looking than our brother."

"That pig we're grilling was better looking than him," Shel smirked. "Cheer up Stogi, we're talking about you, not to you." Stogi buried his face in his hands.

"You're his sisters?" Tam looked baffled as he shuffled in to sit with the group gathered cozy around the fire. Besides the two women, Tam counted seven men, the messenger Hanadin among them. The younger sister shuffled closer to Hulda and hinted he sit beside her. "I thought you were going to murder him." Tam said to her as he claimed the log.

"We might yet," Shel winked at Tam unashamedly. "Wouldn't be the first time I'd tried to gut the bugger."

"It's true," Stogi muttered. "She's rough is Shel. Hulda too, but my other sisters are worse. I so hate family reunions." In a softer voice he leaned forward and whispered to Hulda, "Why's Seek here?"

"He just arrived and took over like they always do."

"What did Broon say?" Tam noted how the leader was missing.

"Nothing. No one questions the shaman, Stogi. Except you— that's why you're outlaw and vagabond. You upset the wrong people."

"I don't trust the shamans," Stogi said, grabbing a leg of pork and ramming it in his mouth. "They spend too much time out alone at night howling at the moon like deranged hounds."

"You had best keep your lips together on the subject," Hulda told him and Stogi gave Tam a long-suffering stare.

"Tell me about your homeland." Ginger Shel sidled closer to Tam. He wasn't in the mood but answered readily enough.

"Born by the sea." Tam munched through his pork, offered across by Hulda's grubby fist. "But brought up in the city."

"Never seen either." Shel reached forward and pressed her palm between his legs. Tam almost spewed his pork making the women laugh and Stogi chuckle. "Got something good down there!" Shel said, while Hulda and the others slapped their knees with sweaty palms.

"Fuck off—I'm married."

"Where is she then? You don't strike me as the loyal kind," Shel said. "Besides, Rholf over there has three wives, but still prefers poking me."

"They won't do the things you do," Rholf said, a wiry looking rider with long black hair and bristles surrounding the pipe he sucked at. "You're a wild lass, Shel," Rholf said. "It's why I like you."

A shadow loomed over the fire and faces turned. Tam saw the shaman standing there, looking down on them, his large gray eyes far away and misty.

"Where's Broon?" Seek said.

"Away scouting the road," Hulda said. "What's up, Seek?"

The shaman looked at Tam for a moment. "Your friends are close," Seek said.

"I have no friends, save perhaps Stogi here."

"You've got me," Shel grinned grabbing his groin again.

"Who has come?" Tam wriggled free of the girl's grasp and caught an annoyed glint in her eye. Broon jogged into view, his fierce face red and flustered.

"Riders coming this way—a hundred, maybe more."

"Two hundred and fifty-three," said Seek. "I saw their faces, felt the arrogance exuding from the aristocrat who leads them."

"I just saw riders," Broon said, confused, then bitter. "But then I don't have shaman powers."

"Ptarnians fresh out of Caranaxis." Seek was staring at Tam. "They're planning a visit with the Ministers of Shen. I have seen this unfolding—the smoke told me."

"What do we do?" Broon asked.

"Follow." Seek knelt beside Tam and tore of a hunch of pork.

"I'll not risk my men against so many. Best we stay clear," Broon said, squaring up to the shaman, though his eyes were downcast, and some of the group nodded at their leader's words.

"We follow close on their heels," Seek said, crunching through crackling. "I need to know what they are up to."

"Who cares what they are up to?" Broon's bristly face was redder than before. "Not our affair, Seek. I lead these riders, not you."

"I am shaman," Seek said imperiously, wiping his sleeve and leaping to his feet, the long coat flapping, and the hat tilted on his head. Seek turned to Tam and pointed. "I will ride up ahead with this one. Stogi too—the fat slug has his uses. You, Broon, will follow with the rest close behind."

Broon looked furious; he fingered his knife on his belt. Tam sensed the tension building between them.

"Think you're a match for me?" Seek said. Broon let go the weapon and hunched his shoulders. "Good. Now get ready to ride, I want to see where they camp at dusk," Seek said, and strode off, his long coat tails flapping. Tam followed, ignoring Shel and Stogi's protestations. He noticed Broon glaring at him.

"This is your fault," Broon said, but Tam ignored him too. He caught Seek up on the ridge that allowed clear view of the road ahead.

Tam shaded his eyes, saw the first riders emerge like hazy shapes a mile or so along the road. "What do you want from me?" Tam said.

"Answers," Seek replied as he studied the distant horsemen. "You're here for a reason, and I need to know what that is."

"Chance," Tam said. "Serendipity." The irony was lost on Seek. "I told you I'm seeking my wife and the bastard that kidnapped her. That's all I've got for you."

"Maybe you are looking in the wrong place," Seek said, turning and staring hard at Tam, who met him look for look.

"That I do not doubt. But where the fuck should I be looking?"

"You should have asked the right questions when you had the opportunity," Seek said. "The Wayfinder is contrary but will answer when the question is put correctly."

"Wayfinder?"

"The man you met in the woods, before you and Stogi were parted."

"Jynn the Piper? How do you know about that?"

"I know about many things. One is that your time is running out, Lord Tamersane. The net closes on your wife—Sulo will kill her. And I know this isn't the first time you've been warned."

Tam started to reply but Seek merged into woods ahead, his gawky strides leaving Tam behind. Instead Stogi and Hulda, with Shel close behind, rushed up and urged him to lay low.

"Where's he going?" Tam asked the woman, but Shel placed a warm hand over his lips and bid him be silent. Tam nodded, seeing the nearest riders passing along the road below. One cough and they'd be on them.

Tam counted two hundred and fifty-three riders decked in bright polished mail and helms, the faces hidden behind steel-mesh masks. They looked disciplined and durable. Ptarnian cavalry were feared by all in this part of the world.

The Tseole waited a half hour until the last riders had vanished and then took to their own mounts, filing down the road keeping their distance from the dust trail ahead. Seek rode at the head, the coat and hat making him stand out, his posture arrow straight and whip lean. Tam wanted to question Seek but when he rode alongside, the shaman's eyes were cold as serpents, and Tam knew this not to be the time. Beside him, Stogi bit his lip and bid Tam ease his steed back so they could ride side by side.

"How is it Seek knows about me and Teret?" Tam asked his friend. "He mentioned that Piper in the woods too. What's going on, Stogi? Who is that man?"

"He's up to something," Stogi said. "They always are, but we won't know what it is until it's happened. Take heart from the fact that he needs your help."

"What makes you think he does?"

"Because you're still alive. Ride on, Lord Tam!"

Tam nodded grim-faced, his thoughts on Teret and Sulo, and how he was determined to save her despite the odds slipping away like spilled water diluted in a fast-flowing stream.

"I won't let him kill you," Tam muttered beneath his breath. "Just stay alive until I find you. Do that for me, Teret."

Stay alive! I will find you—somehow.

Part Two
Shadows and Mirrors

Chapter 15 | The Killer

But I had the bitch.

Teret had thwarted him and she'd pay dearly for that. He would find her and finish what he'd started in that wood. *Revenge*—the only thing that gave him purpose. Hurt those who'd hurt him. Sulo didn't hate Teret more than the others in her clan. Just a means to get at them. Teret was loved by her brother the Kaan, a man Sulo loathed more than any other, and number one on his death list. A man who would prove hard to kill.

But Teret should have been easier prey. She'd married that pale-haired westerner and that alone earned her a cruel death. Rol Sharn's suggestion of slavery had appealed, not only as a lure to catch the bigger fish. To see her suffer, proud bitch that she was.

It was cold here, and wet. And the sky above dripped copper rain. Terrible place. Sulo knew that trickster Jynn had meant for him to fail. Didn't matter, Sulo wasn't going to fail. This was *destiny*. She was here, somewhere. He knew it. *I'll find her and kill her.* Didn't matter what color the sky.

Keep walking. Sulo crouched low and broke into a trot, the cobble lane weaving up through round shaped hills that reminded him of women's breasts. *What had happened back there?* He'd stabbed her, but she'd evaded him and then vanished in that cursed wood.

After that he'd run for hours through those trees, snarling and spitting as rage tore into him. Then Sulo had seen the river far below. Dived, breaking through the water surface like a hammer hitting ice, its cold embrace quenching his rage but filling him with eager energy.

He'd swum out, allowing the current take him, the mist-wrapped trees leaning low on either side, dark willows with witchy-fingers brushing the water. A gorge had funneled into rocks, leading through rapids. Sulo had laughed as his battered body was tossed like a child's rag doll.

After the rapids, the river had eased back to a steady course, its surface weed-strewn and idle. Sulo had swum for the bank, stumbled up through the maze of briar, bracken, fern, and bramble, the small thorn trees stabbing at his eyes. He'd won through to a deer track and paused to get his bearings.

Sulo had known the river wouldn't take him. Not his destiny to drown.

"You can't kill me!" Sulo had yelled at the trees, his anger returning.

"Seems that way."

Sulo snarled as he ran, picturing that trickster at the crossroads. The man had emerged like mist through the trees. Seated on a rock, his lips playing a merry tune on that silver flute.

"Who are you?" Sulo had tried knifing the fat man, but he'd faded back into mist again. *Sorcery.*

"Hard to answer," he'd said. "I have several names depending on time of week, or year, and whether or not they suit me on that day. Today is a black kind of day, hence my choice of drab dress. You may call me Jynn."

"This your forest?" Sulo had asked.

"My forest? Some presumption. The wood owns me, not the

other way around. A forest of many dimensions, so in a sense I belong here in the place between places."

Again, Sulo had felt the lava rage rising through his veins. Sorcerer or not, he'd have killed this creature if he'd got near enough. But Jynn had kept his distance in those woods.

"Listen, Trickster," Sulo had said. *Days ago, or hours? Impossible to tell.* "I don't care who you are or what witchery you command. I'll cut you open from guts to gizzard, unless you tell me where I am, and how to catch the little bitch I'm chasing. And don't tell me you haven't seen her!" But the fat man had laughed at him—again.

"Teret? But of course," he'd said wagging that flute. "Nice girl. Passed through here scarce an hour ago."

"You're lying, Toad," Sulo had said. He'd been looking for her all day and night in that forest. "Cut your crap and tell me where she's hiding."

The Piper had nodded, feigning sympathy. "It is hard to define time in this place. Even I struggle occasionally." He'd pointed through the trees. "She took the middle way at the crossroads."

Sulo hadn't seen any crossroads until Jynn waved his fat hands and a clearing had appeared through the trees. Sun had shone down there like treachery luring him forward. Sulo recalled how the hairs had stirred on the nape of his neck seeing the old battered sign and what looked to be a gibbet, rusty and creaking. *Not natural.*

"Where am I?" Sulo had said, feeling the icy fingers of fear creeping along his spine.

"The wood between worlds—just a place among places." Jynn had smiled. Sulo, recalling that smug expression, pulled out his knife and stabbed the rain drops as they tumbled from the copper sky.

When this is done I'll kill you too—trickster.

"What manner of being are you?" Sulo had crept closer to the Piper, wanting to slice away that smile.

"One who engages in polite and pleasant conversation," the fat man had told Sulo. "An art I think you've forgotten, master Sulo."

That did it. Sulo had hoisted his knife and leapt for the rock, narrowly missing where the little man had been seated. But again, Jynn had faded from view, and Sulo, turning, had seen the Piper standing behind him.

"That was clumsy," Jynn had said, folding his arms as addressing a small belligerent child. His congenial face turned serious. "I suggest you get moving if you want to catch Teret. She could be anywhere by now."

"Which way do I take?" Sulo had demanded.

"I told you she took the middle fork," he'd said wagging his flute. "So perhaps you should too. But I cannot guarantee it's the same road. Things change often around here. Except the crossroads and their wayfinder—they remain constant. But the roads leading off— they can carry you anywhere. Ah . . . Now I'm thinking you should try the one on the left. Yes—that's it. The left road is your best bet today. Goodbye!"

"Sly little bastard." Sulo cursed the cold rain as he pictured Jynn's round smiling face full of dagger holes. The joker had vanished, leaving him alone at that crossroads: three roads, three choices. He'd relied on instinct. Taken the right fork. The only path the Piper hadn't mentioned.

As soon as his boots touched stone the lane had exploded in his face. Sulo had gasped as a sudden hot wind scolded him, and blinding light dazzled his eyes like tiny daggers jumping about inside his head. The air was on fire and Sulo had screamed out loud, his voice lost in that searing heat. The trickster had fooled him after all, and Sulo was being cooked alive.

But the pain had passed swiftly, leaving only memory. And a deeper, hungrier rage. Sulo had staggered blindly upon this cold alien landscape of pink round hills and windy arid plains, the odd dead tree silhouetted like a deserted tower in the distance. And that wet sky above his head the copper-brown of freshly polished bronze.

There'd been strange birds up there circling. Others had glared at him like accusers from the round rocks, their wings droopy and soaked. Weird triangular creatures; they'd called across to him with sharp metallic voices. Sulo had paid them no heed and the birds had gone when the drizzle turned to downpour, puddling the track ahead.

A nightmare realm, but Sulo wasn't swayed. Teret was here too. The only thing that made sense. *Keep moving.*

"I'm in Yffarn," Sulo said, as he picked up his pace. He had little fear of the underworld. If the villain at the crossroads had duped him into choosing this awful place, so what? Not his destiny to die here. He'd find his quarry and cut her open for the trouble she'd given him. Then Sulo would work his way back to that witch-wood and murder the treacherous Piper that had sent him here.

Simple plans work the best.

Sulo slowed to a walk, saving his strength, not knowing what or who was waiting for him around every turn. A bleak place; it suited his mood.

The road angled dusky up toward more round hills; their hue had turned to an inky blue-black as light faded. A mile later, he'd crossed beneath high walls and gazed down at the broad horizon of field and rocks, fanning out to a blur of level grayness, with neither form nor substance. Sulo had never seen the sea before. He stared for long moments before the occasional glint of movement and the shifting sheen and the reflection of one pale star informed him this was water.

Real fear stabbed his groin for the first time in weeks. Sulo dreaded that water. It defied his distorted sense of reason and surpassed anything his imagination had allowed. But the road led down there, so he must follow. Sulo saw small buildings scattered like dead beetles along the rim. *Teret must be down there.* That thought spurred him on. She was the first domino he'd topple. Teret *was* down there. This was destiny. Sulo grinned, his ravaged mind at last making sense of the conundrum.

The Gods were dead and that spook in the woods was clearly a distant relative or servant of theirs left stumbling in the void of their departure. Jynn had tried to hoodwink, maybe even murder Sulo. But Sulo had his vengeance to achieve, so the Piper had failed.

Besides, the only God Sulo listened to was the acid worm churning inside. He smiled, shook a fist at the distant sheen of dark water, and commenced jogging in slow measured bounds down the long ribbon of road leading to the buildings mirrored by fading light.

"You can't escape me, Teret!" Sulo called as he gathered pace, the dark mass of water filling his horizons. "I'll heat the knife before I take your eyes." Sulo reached the village just as the rain ceased and darkness stole the copper sky.

Chapter 16 | Stand Your Ground!

"Hold easy," Garland growled at Bruhan Dahali's men. Now he'd seen them up close it was clear most were just boys. Wet behind the ears and shitting themselves at the hard-looking professionals dismounting in orderly fashion on the rocky ground below. The odd Ptarnian veteran would point up slowly and then make a swift chopping gesture. Arrogant bastards in Garland's opinion. Some of his men responded with raised fingers, and Tol showed them his naked arse, lightening the mood on the hilltop.

The Laregozans stood silently in little groups, gripping their spears, shields, and swords with white knuckles, the fear showing like flags on their faces. "Fucking virgins," Garland saw Pash spit tobacco on his boot. "Looks like we'll have to settle this ourselves, Karg."

"Known worse odds," Kargon said standing beside his friend, and then cursed as one of the Laregozans dropped his spear and fainted dead away. Pash looked at Garland with a lopsided grin.

"Better we run now and take our chances, Captain."

Garland ignored him. Instead he rounded on the Bruhan standing by his side. "They need to pick him up," Garland said. "Those bastards smell fear they'll tear you apart. We have the high ground, Yuri. It's a steep climb. The Ptarnians are on a hiding to nothing. Tell your people!"

Bruhan Dahali stiffened at Garland's sharp tone, but nodded and turned to his soldiers. "Stand fast, Laregoza!" Bruhan Dahali hissed. "They are only men, and we have better fighters with us. Learn from these foreign veterans and hold to courage. We can prevail!"

"We *will* prevail," Garland said.

"We will prevail!" Bruhan Dahali said in a firmer voice, and some of the Laregozans nodded. Garland studied them for a moment. He shrugged, satisfied. These boys had nowhere to go and realized it. *Time to grow up—that or die.*

But they needed a sign. Inspiration. A random show of strength to embolden them. The balance of battle is like walking on thin ice: one misjudgment, slip, or error, and you're through, plunging into endless cold, and no way back. It was past time they showed those armored tossers below what they were up against.

Garland gazed down, glaring coldly at the enemy, already clanking and creaking up the hill, their plate armor and weapons glinting in the sun. Garland wiped sweat from his face; the humidity was horrible, but it would slow the enemy. They'd be thirsty, their strength sapped by the climb. All that armor and steel weighing them down.

"They'll be tired before they reach us," Garland said. "See, they stumble already. We have this fight lads!" There was nervous laughter among the Laregozans as they witnessed one of the warriors tripping below. But the Ptarnian soon regained his feet and raised a crooked bill at those watching him from above.

"And you, Arsehole," Garland pointed down at the warrior. "My sword is waiting for your throat!" Garland shouted though he knew the man wouldn't hear him. The Laregozans did, and that was what mattered.

Garland's military eyes were impressed by the enemy. He'd heard how the Ptarnians had fought at the Gap of Leeth, the last great battle in the war against the sorcerer Caswallon. Caught between two enemies, the Ptarnians had been slaughtered to a man, their bodies swept away like dry dead flies on dusty flagstones.

But Garland had heard from men who'd survived that fight extolling the bravery of the Ptarnians that day. A warrior race. Well disciplined, tough, and fearless. He watched them now. Organized as ants, Garland thought. Most of the enemy sported colored chains hanging from their helmets and covering their faces, but those few he could see appeared ruthless, eager, and determined as they climbed ever closer to where the defenders held their ground. The Ptarnians must be melting inside that armor but they didn't show it. Garland chewed his lip. This would be close.

"Tol, Coife! We need a show," Garland said to the two archers standing close by.

"Just thinking the same thing, Captain." Tol appeared, grinning. The rangy bowman nocked arrow to string and waited calmly as grim-faced Coife moved alongside.

"We need to spook those bastards; they're far too confident," Garland said. "Pick your quarry and loose."

"They don't know what they're up against," Tol said. He leaned back, pulled and released, sending a shaft arcing across high and wide. Garland heard laughter and guessed the Ptarnians were smug with the knowledge that some fool had loosed a wild shaft in terror. But the dart fell true, taking a young officer in the left eye as he gazed up at his men above, oblivious of the death descending on him.

Coife's arrow pierced the chest of the standard bearer beside him. The result had the other officers urging their mounts back out of range. Enraged, they yelled at their men on the slopes above. The attackers took heed and rushed and panted the last thirty foot up toward where Garland's crew and the white-faced Laregozans waited with weapons held ready and feet braced for impact.

"They're tired, they will make mistakes," Garland told Bruhan Dahali. The Laregozan said nothing, his mouth dry and dark eyes pinned to the enemy advance. "Hold your nerves lads. Stand fast and the day will be ours!" Garland said, and braced his feet wide, flexing his knees while waiting for the first enemy to crest the rise.

"Stand strong!" Garland stepped forward, cutting low with his sword as the first Ptarnian vaulted onto the ridge and leaped at him with spear. The thrust went wide, Garland's sword broke the spear shaft, but his own swing missed. The man reached for a scimitar but Garland rammed a shoulder into his chest knocking him backwards. No room for a lunge, so Garland reversed his blade, smashing the pommel hard into the enemy's visor, knocking him off his feet. Garland stepped forward again; this time he had room and cut down hard and clean. The Ptarnian's head rolled free to settle in the dirt. Garland sucked in air and regained his balance before the next man arrived. Minutes later, the rest were upon them.

Screaming, shouts, and cries of agony surrounded Garland, as men fought, fell, and were trampled bloody in the melee. Garland held his ground with his men alongside, yelling and stabbing, sweeping their swords from side to side as enemy warriors stormed up towards them. They were outnumbered and the sheer weight of Ptarnians was pushing them back.

"Hold!" Garland shouted, fighting for breath. He gripped an enemy spear in his left hand and jabbed forward while swinging from behind it with the sword.

A man fell screaming. Garland stepped over the body and ducked under a scimitar arcing past his head. He brought the spear up and under the attacker's arm, piercing armor and cutting through the tendons supporting his shoulder. The man screamed and fell away. Garland jumped forward and opened his throat with a clean thrust of his broadsword. Close by, he could see his lads were doing well, but the Laregozans were lost to sight and Garland could only pray they held their nerve.

Time passes differently on a battlefield. Garland felt the usual distance from emotion, hacking, lunging, wounding, and killing. Unlike many surrounding him, Garland never opened his mouth. His lips were tight, eyes hard—a killing machine, whose trained body responded without thought. Not bad for a man well past his prime.

But they kept coming, and soon Garland was surrounded, his arms and legs leaden and tired and breath running ragged.

Could be this is my lucky day . . .

***

Further back, and sheltered behind the rocks cresting the hillock, Lieutenant Doyle crouched low and bid wounded Taylon sit back. "Save your strength, those bastards are getting nearer," Doyle said, as Taylon fretted to join the fight.

"I've got strength aplenty," Taylon told him, "and an appetite for murdering — not lying here like a stunned slug while our mates get a trouncing. We need to help them, Doyle!"

"Garland said for you to wait here. You can't fight one-handed, so stay put and shut the fuck up while I go see what's happening." Taylon spat blood and cursed, as Doyle carefully rose and peered over the rock ledge they were hidden behind.

"I'm going out there," he said. "Stay put!" Taylon shrugged and spat again.

"Yeah, right," Taylon said. "Anything you say, Lieutenant."

Doyle left him and slid out from behind the rocks, almost crashing into a Laregozan whose dented shield was taking a battering from a huge Ptarnian wielding two scimitars like spinning scythes, his face covered by yellow-painted steel mesh hanging from his helmet. The young Laregozan had dropped his sword and clung to his shield with both hands, but the Ptarnian's lightning swift blows soon brought him to his knees.

Doyle cut in quick and low from behind, slicing through the big man's armor and opening his back through the lungs. The Ptarnian pitched forward, knocking over the exhausted shield carrier. Doyle hacked down, finishing the job.

"You all right?" Doyle flashed the lad a grin and the Laregozan blinked back, too stunned to respond. "Big bugger, wasn't he?" Doyle said.

"He was," the young Laregozan managed after moving his lips a few times.

"Your name?"

"Calicastez," the soldier said as he shoved the Ptarnian's corpse aside and found his feet.

"I'll call you Cal," Doyle said. "Here—take this." He handed Cal one of the heavy scimitars the Ptarnian had carried. Cal blinked at it.

"That's bigger than I'm used to."

"If you can lift it you can use it. Come on!" Doyle turned and jumped clear of the rocks, landing close to where Garland's troops were surrounded by two score heavily-armored enemy. Over to the right Doyle got a brief sight of Bruhan Dahali's men holding their own against the enemy. For the moment. Doyle reached Garland's side, cutting and stabbing at the foe as he caught up with his Captain.

"I told you to stay put," Garland cursed, as a scimitar narrowly missed his head. Doyle's Captain caught the assailant's arms and pulled him close. Caught off balance, the Ptarnian stumbled and Garland rammed his short spear up under the man's helmet, killing him instantly.

"Two-handed work!" Garland grinned at Doyle, his sword and stolen spear working perfectly together as he readied for the next attackers. "Still got it, Doyle Lad!"

"Yeah, I noticed." Doyle grinned at the Captain, whose face like his own was covered in blood. "But don't get cocky!"

Doyle leaped at a Ptarnian with a sweeping backstroke that sent his head spinning. The men beside him backed off, eyes wary. Doyle spat at them and gripped his sword with both hands. Enjoying himself at last. "We've got this," he said.

The enemy were used to winning, and the combination of fierce resistance, the weight of that armor pulling them down, and sheer heat exhaustion after their long climb, were combining to tire them fast. Another soldier vaulted a rock and swung down hard at Doyle with his scimitar. Doyle glided past the blade's arc and rammed his sword up into the man's groin, piercing armor and flesh. The Ptarnian screamed then fell twitching. Doyle despatched him with a mercy cut.

Even though they were exhausted, the enemy's superior numbers kept Garland's troop hemmed tight like cattle in corral.

"Laregozans?" Doyle looked about but couldn't see the Bruhan's soldiers. He yelled in his Captain's ear. "How fare they?"

"Holding their own," Garland said between thrusts. "Pleasant surprise, these boys are doing better than I expected. Bruhan Yuri should be proud." Doyle turned, hearing a roar of triumph somewhere close behind him.

As if hearing Garland's voice, the Laregozans had taken heart witnessing the Ptarnians fall back. They now advanced with rare confidence and discipline, a wave of leveled spears jabbing forward in precision at the Ptarnians and taking the initiative for the first time.

Doyle whooped in delight, seeing Bruhan Dahali's plumed helmet amidst the knot of his spearmen, his hoarse orders barking out in Laregozan.

The Ptarnians were breaking. Doyle had seen this happen before and sensed their uncertainty. He smiled, splitting the crusted blood covering his lips as he saw the coin settle in their favor. The day was theirs with just the mopping up to do.

The last stubborn enemy surrounding Garland's troop turned to face this new attack from behind. It was the break Garland's men needed. "Now!" Garland growled at his men, including Doyle. Like snarling wolves scenting blood, they leaped after the withdrawing Ptarnians and cut them down from behind.

Doyle saw Taylon amongst the boys, not wanting to miss out despite his arm hanging useless by his side. Doyle glared at him for an instant before returning to the task at hand.

Even the Ptarnians' thick plate mail was no match for the cunningly placed stabs and slices. At last, caught squarely between Bruhan Dahali's youngsters and Garland's pros, the remaining Ptarnians had no choice but to flee back down the hill.

Doyle, giving chase, saw the enemy officers watching them for a moment before turning their horses about and cantering off back to the road, abandoning their men to those chasing them and cutting them down from behind.

"We won!" Bruhan Dahali's face was splattered with blood but he was grinning like a loon. The Bruhan stood beside Doyle and Garland, laughing and shaking in delight. Doyle took a soberer view. He was relieved to be alive but feared this was just the start. They'd be back and soon, and in greater numbers. So much for keeping a low profile. Instead they'd stirred the hornets' nest.

"How did we fare?" Doyle asked Tol, who was stowing a long knife he always used for close quarter work.

Tol shrugged. "Mullen took a hit. He's sitting on that rock over there. Doesn't look good for the old fella." Doyle saw the hunched shape of one of his men clutching his belly.

"Mullen, how fare you?" Doyle approached and saw the old

warrior looked pale and drawn. "Is it bad?"

"I've felt better," Mullen grumbled.

"Here, drink this." Doyle placed his battered water canister in Mullen's shaking hands.

"I don't want any fucking water," Mullen said.

"It's not water." Doyle fumbled with the stopper and held the canister to Mullen's cracked lips. The older man took a gulp and coughed.

"Fuck—that's good," he said, coughing again. "Think I'm done for Lieutenant."

"Don't talk crap," Doyle said, but his eyes betrayed him. Mullen's belly was soaked with blood, oozing and spilling at his feet. A spear had torn into his guts and twisted; the pain must be horrible, but Mullen was a tough old bugger. "You're good for another twenty miles' ride after you finish that."

"You're a good lad, Doyle," Mullen choked. "We all thought you were a bit of a knob when you first arrived, fresh and green. Doodle—we called you that, remember?"

"I do."

"Doodle . . ." Mullen's eyes glazed over and he slumped. Doyle sat beside him for a moment longer and then stood shaking, draining the last contents of the brandy he'd kept for moments like this. He looked up, feeling shaken and exhausted and saw the Captain standing there.

"Mullen's dead," Doyle said, stating the obvious.

Garland nodded. "He will be missed, and the rest of us will join him shortly if we don't get moving. Bruhan!" The Laregozan leader emerged and stared down at Mullen.

"Captain Garland." Bruhan Dahali's face had sobered seeing Mullen lying there.

"We need to leave this place soonest, Brew. How are your men faring?"

"We lost a dozen or so, and I've twenty wounded, though most will pull through," Bruhan Dahali said. "I can't believe we won the day. They were crack Ptarnian troopers."

"They were overconfident," Garland said. "A mistake they won't make twice. How far to this city of yours?"

"Talimi Garrison is a fort some twenty miles southeast of here. The city—Largos—the nearest large settlement, is over two hundred miles away. But we'll need to go there as Talimi cannot withstand any major attack from Ptarni."

"Well then best get moving as soon as we can," Garland said. "We can restock at your depot and then on to the city with fresh supplies. What say you, Doyle?" Both his Captain and the Bruhan were staring at Doyle.

"What about Mullen and the Laregozan dead?" Doyle motioned the old soldier, still hunched forward as though sleeping on the rock.

"We leave them be," Garland said, his eyes hard.

"Captain, we—" Doyle blinked as the Bruhan cut in.

"We must attend to our fallen, Captain Garland. We need to take the bodies to the station for honorable burial."

"We leave them here beneath the sky."

"But," Bruhan Dahali looked appalled.

"They need . . . attending to, sir." Doyle said, feeling for the Bruhan. "We can't just leave them here."

"We can and we will." Garland stared hard at him. "They're dead—so hardly likely to care either way. We, gentlemen, are still breathing. For now. We won't be for much longer unless we get off this fucking hillock."

"Captain, at least let us perform the rituals, send them on their way," Doyle said, looking up at the birds circling high above. Strange how the things appeared from nowhere at times like this. "Captain?"

"They are dust and shadows." Garland shrugged, glanced briefly at Doyle then turned away and started walking briskly back to where the other men waited.

"It isn't right," Doyle said glancing up at the carrion birds again.

The Bruhan looked at him and nodded. "There is wisdom in your Captain's words, though he is a hard man, I think."

"He's changing," Doyle said. "Something's eating at him." He walked over to Mullen's corpse and gently closed the old soldier's eyes. "Farewell, old friend," Doyle said quietly. "I will see you in time."

Doyle turned away then, his eyes moist and mood suddenly grim. They had been eight and now they were seven. And for what? How many more of them would fall by the road before they achieved what their Captain wanted?

He glanced around, eyes bleary. The Bruhan was already mustering his men amid grumbles. Within an hour both groups of warriors had departed the hill, the buzzards, vultures, and crows settling noisily behind them.

Chapter 17 | The Road to Rundali

Teret smiled as the hot sun tanned her face, reminding her of home. Hot and dry; the wind was blowing and the distant line of mountains in the south rose up, mile by mile. The dreamy forest seemed but a memory, the harrowing events surrounding it mingling between nightmares and confusion. The mists had lifted inside her mind as well as all around when they'd left Elerim's realm and found themselves alone. Two lost travelers walking the empty road to Rundali.

She should be worried to the core, not knowing what awaited around the corner. Instead Teret was content in the knowledge she was moving forward. Making things happen. She'd find Tam in one piece. Call it a hunch or wishful thinking, but Teret knew they'd catch up with each other again. What happened after that she wouldn't dwell on. First things first. She had a task to perform.

Carlo was good company in the main. Positive and strong. He'd refrained from his flirting and gawping at her, and instead acted with polite deference. He was a charmer despite his battered face, but there was more depth to Carlo Sarfe; a tough determination lay hidden beneath the veneer of that glib smile. Teret was glad he accompanied her.

Carlo had an easy smile, and warm brown laughing eyes that

almost hid the sorrow and loneliness beneath. He was witty too, just as Tamersane had been before the darkness clouded over.

In looks Carlo much resembled the Raleenians she'd met years ago. A proud race dwelling across the mountains from Rorshai. Paradoxically, Carlo insisted they were his younger brother's Kael's descendants. Thinking about such things hurt her head so Teret let them go. Better to concentrate on what you understand. That way you've a chance of pulling through. Suffice to say they were similar to this man walking beside her: dark skinned, lithe, energetic, and quick.

"How long?" Carlo asked, as Teret strode ahead, her strong legs carrying her up the steep climb. The road had led higher for miles, the brush of trees hazy in the distance and many miles behind them.

"A week. Maybe two?" Teret said. "Hard to say."

"And you trusted her?"

"It's not like we had a choice," Teret said. "But yes, surprisingly, I do. As I said before, Elerim needs us."

"And as I said before, I admire your optimism."

"Among other things, as I recall."

"Yep."

Teret paced up the road. "We have supplies enough in that pack you're carrying, and I'm hefting three water bottles, with plenty of streams around to fill them. We should be fine."

"You still haven't told me the plan," Carlo said.

"Tonight. We'll light a fire, eat some provisions, and I'll explain what's happening."

"Sounds cozy."

"It won't be, so don't get any ideas."

"You are a hard woman," Carlo laughed behind her.

By the time evening found them the walkers were exhausted. They had covered a score of miles and reached the nearest shoulder of the Rundali Mountains, the main slopes folding up in brown-gold ridges and mingling with the clouds.

They made camp close by the road. The land appeared deserted and they'd seen no beast, or even eagle flying overhead. A deserted realm but not a desolate one. Their small fire gave off sufficient warmth and would keep any night visitor at bay. Unless there were creatures here Teret didn't know about. And no point dwelling on that.

They shared a blanket and huddled close. Teret told herself it was to keep out the cold, as it was chilly at night on the shoulder of the mountain. Truth was she was lonely. She missed Tam horribly, and this stranger's warmth proved no small comfort.

Teret felt stronger and fitter since she'd escaped from Sulo. Her body was leaner, suppler, and her reactions sharper. She had always been athletic but had felt herself slipping toward indolence and depression while living with Tam in Caranaxis.

How had she let that happen? The love between them had grown stale like week-old dough. Sour even. She needed to know Tam was safe. After that . . .Time would tell if there was a future for them. It was hard to dwell on such issues with another man sitting in thoughtful silence beside her.

Teret watched as Carlo poked the fire and sent sparks winking. "I'm glad you're with me," she said. "And thanks for your patience. So much has happened that's strange. I don't know who I am sometimes."

"Me neither—like I've fallen inside someone else's dream," Carlo said. "Maybe Elerim's? Or the Emerald Queen's." He gave her a sharp look. "Are you sure you can trust her?"

"No, but I trust my intuition. And Elerim needs us, or rather needs what we can bring her."

Which is . . .?"

Teret grinned at the fire. "A bow."

"That's not the answer I expected."

"It's one of the lost treasures of the Aralais."

"Ah—that explains everything." Teret swatted his ear, and Carlo laughed. "I'm sorry but you'll have to do better than that. A bow? What? So she can shoot this Emerald Queen that bugs her so? Or maybe her sisters?"

"I know, an odd request," Teret said. "And it's taken me time to process, but now I think I know who she might be. The key is her sisters and the mystery piper—he's part of this too."

"The crossroads man you told me about?"

"Part of it for sure."

"Might I enquire what 'it' is?" Carlo nudged her shoulder and she smiled.

"Coming to that. Involves sorcery."

"Thought it might."

"Elerim is trapped in that forest, and she has another sister trapped somewhere else. Who put them there I don't know— perhaps the Emerald Queen? We can only guess. Thing is, Elerim believes this bow will free her, and with it she can avenge whomever it is that imprisoned her and her sister.

"As to how, I have no idea, but Elerim promised to harbor Carys and the others until we returned, and more important to me, promised to help me find Tam before he is lost to me forever. He still lives, Carlo—Elerim told me that much and I believed her."

"Good to know." Carlo didn't look over happy despite his words. "So where is this Aralais artifact, and what's so special about it?"

"You know of the Aralais?"

"I think so. A race of warlocks long extinct. There was a twisted individual dwelling in the south of my country. A dangerous type who called himself 'The Aralais'—all I know."

"They were a mighty people once," Teret said. "I think Elerim is one; she has the look. Those green/gold eyes. Unlike you, I encountered one long ago. An enchanter who helped Queen Ariane and the Crystal King defeat Caswallon. He was odd-looking—very tall. Unsure what became of him."

"That's fascinating, but you haven't answered my questions." Carlo stoked the fire again. "It's getting late, Teret. We'll need to sleep soon."

"The Castle of Lights."

"And where is that?"

"An island, or rocky outcrop—not sure which. Somewhere just off the coast of Rundali. The land waiting for us across these mountains."

Carlo's eyes gleamed in the firelight. "So, we are making for the coast?"

"Thought you'd be happy about that."

"I've got to get back there, Teret—back to my home. Somehow. In all this craziness there has to be a way." Carlo's tanned face was flushed with excitement in the firelight. "Elerim hinted she might help me, though she warned against it."

"I believe so," she said. "Just as I have to believe I can save my Tamersane. Keep my sanity. You have to work with the tools you're given. Elerim is using us, so we can use her too."

"Sounds fair, but what of the other sister?" Carlo said. "Elerim said they were three, and five brothers now lost."

"She mentioned her name only once; the other sister she spoke of freely. Ysaren—or something like that. Imprisoned like Elerim somewhere in this corner of our world. She and Ysaren are close though not friends—her words. The other one is more mysterious."

"They all seem mysterious to me," Carlo chuckled. "Perhaps this third one is the Emerald Queen, and the other two want her dead. You know how sisters are."

"They are old," Teret said. "Steeped in sorcery—witches, as you call them. Enchantresses for sure, but I think the third one is the most powerful. It would make sense that she's the Emerald Queen and the others want to pull her down. Some ancient grudge. Elerim said that sibling alone could pass through the realms and that she lived in a great castle on the coast."

"Sounds like where we're heading."

"No, it's different. A cold place, remote and lost."

"A bit like us then."

"Quite." She turned and stared at him, and he sighed. "What's the matter?" Teret said.

"This seems like a lost opportunity," Carlo said, smiling. "Good night, Teret of the Rorshai." He turned and grunted, and a few seconds later was snoring into the blanket.

Teret envied him. She couldn't sleep and spent most that night staring up at the stars winking through the black. At least she was resting her body.

Next morning, they reached the high mountain passes, and three days later they dropped down into the jungles of Rundali.

Chapter 18 | The Shen River

They followed the Ptarnians for almost a week, keeping discreet distance and making sure they weren't seen. No hard task for the Tseole riders, who were born in the saddle, but for Tam it was agony. Seek had hinted that Tam's time for saving Teret was running out, and every mile weighed heavier than the last.

It would help if he knew what Seek was planning. There was something underlying here. Spying on these Ptarnians was not only dangerous but most likely worthless too. Not their affair. Seek—clearly no fool—had an agenda, and Tam determined to find out what it was. That meant staying close to the shaman as often as he could.

But that was easier said than done, especially as Tam's emotions tugged at him, pulling him every which way, and his nagging need for smoke drove him to the brink of madness. More than once Tam considered cutting loose from the clan and riding off alone. Chancing the wild in the vain hope he could find that wretched Piper and demand some answers at sword-point.

But in more rational moments, Tam quashed such notions as reactionary and reckless. His best chance of finding Teret was to stay close to Seek. The scarecrow knew things. In the meantime, put up and shut up. The shaman was part of this pattern, and Tam believed he could help were he but persuaded.

The other riders kept their distance from Seek, with the exception of the leader Broon, who occasionally consulted the shaman. Tam noticed how Broon always looked angry after such exchanges. Seek was disliked as much as feared.

Stogi steered clear from the shaman and advised Tam to do the same. But Tam needed answers and so watched and waited until chance allowed. Unsurprisingly, it was the shaman who approached him first.

The Ptarnians had set up camp three miles away on the banks of a wide sluggish river that Stogi informed Tam was the gateway to Shen and shared the same name as the mysterious country beyond. They'd turned in early, and Tam had strolled off to attend to nature. He stopped midstream when he heard the voice behind him.

"You are burning from within, Lord Tam! On the brink of doing something reckless," Seek said, his voice serpent soft. The quiet crunch of leaf under boot was the only warning Tam had that someone had followed him into the bushes.

Tam laced up his drawstrings. "Not polite, creeping up on a fellow when he is–"

"You want to know my part is in this . . .situation?"

Tam turned, saw the shaman's gray eyes glinting, the tall hat shading his face.

"I do, but only because I need to find my wife. I don't much care about the grander scale of things. Been there, done that. It's all shite."

"A jaded opinion. I'm sorry you've lost your spark," Seek said, a smirk creasing his features.

"Just tell me how I can find Teret."

"He is stalking her—I have seen it," Seek said. "Just as I saw you and Stogi leaving Caranaxis after the fight outside the tavern. I can far-gaze." The smirk widened, giving Seek a smug look "A gift from the Gods," he said. "My inner eye roams wide in the dark hours, gaining me knowledge, wisdom, and foresight. 'Tis a rare gift I have."

"You're a sorcerer then. It's as I thought."

"I'm a shaman from Dunnehine—I don't dabble in sorcery. Far too dangerous. A shaman is a conduit, Lord Tam. A link between the greatness above and the smallness surrounding us. A translator am I."

"I don't care what you are. I just want results."

Seek ignored him. "Sorcerers attempt to bend and warp the fabric of this world and fashion it for their own purpose. Risky that, as the forces of nature are not to be tangled with." Tam settled his rump on a log and waited for Seek to continue. Whatever his game the man was about to reveal something. Listen and learn. Act later.

"My people live north of here. Far north." Seek angled his hat toward the closest bushes, hinting what must be north. "A realm of ice and cold and dark where the Giants' Dance floods winter nights and strange voices ride out upon the wind."

"I thought you were a Tseole?"

"We're related," Seek said, waving a dismissive hand. "Dunnehine is a waste of grinding ice and roaming bears. The winter nights last days on end—perfect for storytelling and the study of lore. Broon's people call it the witch-realm, say we are all shamans, though in truth only a few have the gift of visions."

"So, what do you want from me?" Tam asked, picking up a stick and placing it between his teeth. His back hurt; he was weary and ready for sleep. But first, he would glean some answers from this stranger. "Clearly you want something, or you'd have either told me where my wife is or else slit my throat."

"Been listening to Stogi?" Tam could see Seek grinning openly beneath that hat. "There is a new pattern forming," Seek said. "You, Lord Tamersane of distant Kelwyn, are part of it. Your Rorshai wife—Teret—is another, and the voyager accompanying her, yet another strand. Stogi, these riders, the Ptarnians and their depraved emperor. And the three conniving sisters—all part of it. A new dance."

"Voyager—you mean that bastard Sulo?" Tam bit through the stick in his mouth and swallowed half of it. He coughed as it went down. "What's happened to my wife?"

"Careful," Seek said. "No choking. I need you alive—for now at least."

"I'm not planning on fucking dying yet. Just tell me how I can find Teret, and I'll help you in any way I can. Piss me around and I'll gut you open, I don't care if you're a shaman, warlock, or just a big-talking tosspot. I'm past patience. Time you delivered."

"I don't know where your wife is," Seek said, the smile sliding from his face. "You have a temper, laddie. I'd rein that in were I you." Tam shrugged, and the shaman glared at him for a long moment and then forced the smile back on to his lips.

"My visions are . . .well, visions, Lord Tam. Glimpses of things that sometimes come to pass. Some are useful and some not. The skill in shamanism is knowing how to read them and then learn which ones to use."

"And you possess that skill in abundance—don't you?"

"Better than most, yes," Seek said. "And I've a curious, inquiring mind. It keeps me young." Tam noted that quiver of a smile again. Maybe this was Seek's attempt at humor. It was lost on him.

Tam waved a dismissive hand. "The less you know the happier you are. That's my take on this existence."

"It's not about being content, it's about survival," Seek said. "Same for everyone. Seven years ago, something changed that altered the axis that spins our world. An event of such momentous—"

"The day the Gods died. I was there, remember?" Tam

interrupted, losing patience again. "Just tell me what you want, Seek. I grow weary of our conversation."

Seek's eyes narrowed but he didn't reply. Instead he gazed back through the bushes to where the Tseole were preparing evening meals and setting up camp, although it was only early afternoon. "We'll cross that river tomorrow," Seek said, after a moment's gazing at the bushes.

Tam closed his eyes, summoning patience. "And then what?"

"They are not dead."

"What?"

"Death is an illusion," Seek said. "Just a portal to a different place. The Gods have moved on—most of them anyway. Though I've come to suspect some still linger hereabouts."

"Trust me, they are dead and gone," Tam said. "And what's dead stays fucking dead." Tam closed his eyes, recalling that fight in the dungeons below the Silver City. The knife in his hand and how it plunged so easily into his brother's heart. That day Tam's soul left him. That day the old Tam died.

"Well, that's a very one-dimensional way of looking at it, and I know you have your reasons. I see things differently."

"Good luck with that."

"I'll repeat what I told you earlier," Seek said. "The Piper, the three 'witches', your lovely wife, yourself, this Sulo character—all players partaking in a new dance."

"Yep, heard you the first time."

Seek ignored him and continued emphatically, his gray gaze intense, hungry even. "Nothing is random, despite what you think. The fabric of the earth was damaged seven years ago. It's why we can cross through the dimensions. Couldn't do that before. There are advantages but also great danger. Things can break through, and I'm starting to believe some already have. Those doors were closed before and for good reason. Lots of bad stuff out there."

"Well, maybe you should have sent a request out for the immortals to close the door after they were blasted from the universe," Tam said bitterly. "It was a battle fought in the sky while we mere humans struggled below, pawns in a far bigger game. The Gods paid the ultimate price but our puny race paid too, caught in the crossfire."

Seek smiled. "Is that how you see it—all about you? I know who Cille is," Seek continued, his voice dropping to a whisper mentioning that name.

Tam glanced hard at the shaman. "You've been to Graywash Hall?"

"No, but I've seen it and spoken with she who lives within those cold walls."

"For what purpose?"

"Knowledge, of course. The gateway to wisdom," Seek said. "Cille is one of three once powerful sorceresses who ruled these eastern lands. Perhaps the most powerful. She it was who told me about your role in the new fabric stretching before us."

Tam smiled wryly. "And what, pray, is that?"

"Stay with us, cross the river. The answer lies in Shen!"

"What about my Teret? You told me time is running out. I keep asking and always you evade the question, wittering on about 'world fabric,' dances, and other crap."

"Time is running for all of us, Lord Tam. You are not a special case." Seek's gray eyes flashed at Tam. He lifted a bony finger and tilted his hat, turned, and walked briskly away.

"Bastard," Tam muttered as he watched Seek stride back to where the tents were being erected. "I'll learn your game, shaman, or whoever you are. And if Teret dies I will hold you responsible. So, watch your back!"

Tam walked into the camp his face torn with anger, frustration, and deepening despair. He caught Stogi's eye, and his friend wandered over.

"Eat," Stogi hinted the campfire where Shel and Broon were seated on a log tearing at strips of jerky with their teeth. "You'll feel better."

"That I doubt," Tam said to his friend.

"Stronger then."

"I need a smoke," Tam said and took his place by the fire. The others ignored him, sensing his mood.

Morning found them mounted and gazing down the rolling slopes of stubby grass spreading out toward the wide brown slug of the river three miles distant. A thin steely worm, the Ptarnian column was making for a straddle of buildings barely visible in the distance.

"How will they cross that? It must be a mile wide," Tam said, watching from his saddle alongside Stogi and Shel.

"There's a raft, some kind of ferry the Shen operate," Stogi said. "It's kept at the far side so the Shen can spy on these lands. I've been here before, remember."

"You're quite the rover, my friend."

"Needs must." Stogi curled a lip. "With my past record you have to keep moving."

"They seem to have forgiven you."

Stogi flashed him a look. "Mine's a big family; this lot are the gentler side."

"Except Seek."

"He's not family," Stogi said. "Speaking of whom," he hinted as five horsemen appeared over the crest of a rise where they'd been scanning the Ptarnians and the river they approached. Seek and Broon led them and urged their mounts across to where the three waited; the other Tseole were gathered close by and these too guided their horses across.

Seek had abandoned his usual gear and now looked resplendent in a long white coat. Fur, Stogi explained that had been stripped from some great bear found roaming those wild northern wastes. Seek reined in and stared at them coldly as though he knew they'd been talking about him.

"They are boarding rafts. Horses, provisions, and all," the shaman informed them. "There are Shen boatmen manning them. Looks like a pre-arranged visit."

"They are allies then; what we expected," Stogi said, chewing on a blade of grass. Tam watched him turn and address the shaman. "So now your curiosity is sated we can return west—yes?"

"No." Seek glanced across at Tam and smiled slightly. "Ask your new friend. We've business across that river."

"And I don't know what he's talking about," Tam said to Stogi.

"No one ever does," Shel added beside him.

"We've no business in Shen," Stogi said, and Tam wondered why Broon was not saying anything. The Tseole leader sat silent on his horse, his tough face grim. Broon seemed sold out to Seek's plan, though judging by his expression, clearly unhappy about it.

"We've prisoners to free," Seek said.

"At what cost to ourselves?" Stogi challenged.

Seek shrugged and patted his horse's neck. "We are following them across. You, Stogi, can remain here if you wish to, but I suspect your foreign friend will join us."

Tam nodded. "I need to know what your game is Seek." The shaman flashed him a crafty grin.

"First I have to know that myself."

Hulda appeared on horse beside Stogi. The redhead looked flustered and annoyed. "Am I missing the obvious here, but how do you propose to cross that river, Master Seek?"

"I was coming to that," Seek answered, but instead of explaining further, turned his horse about and cantered down the slope toward the distant road ahead.

"You coming?" Tam asked Stogi.

"Not much choice, have I?"

They reined in a half mile short of the river, a cluster of thick shrubs allowing plenty of cover for horse and rider. Seek and Broon dismounted and pushed their way through the brush, crouching low. Tam glanced at Stogi, who nodded. They followed suit and soon were lying low next to the shaman and Tseole leader. Both ignored them.

"That's a sight to see for sure," Stogi blew through his teeth. Beside him, Tam wriggled into a better position and watched the hive of activity down on the river bank.

The Shen River was a brown crawling slug. A great foggy mass of churning water, the sky leaden gray above it. Tam frowned, barely making out the low shades of humps that must be the far bank in the distance.

The rafts were huge and sturdy, and the men working them knew what they were doing. Tam was fascinated by his first sight of the Shen people. They looked like no one he'd encountered before. Unlike the metal-clad Ptarnians surrounding them, the Shen wore no armor, though it was obvious there were men of rank scattered amongst the soldiers and ferrymen.

Instead, they were garbed in long ornate coats that flared out at sleeve and tail, the colors ranging from deep purple to vivid orange. Their hair where visible was jet and glossy. A few wore conical hats, though most were bareheaded, the hair tied back in neat pig or pony tail. It was too far to see their faces.

Tam noticed the glint of swords at waists, and on closer inspection he saw that many of these Shen carried long curved blades on poles, weapons he'd never seen before.

"What are those spikes on poles?" Tam asked Stogi.

"Jiang—a kind of spear used by the personal bodyguard of the First Magister and his Secretary, and other top Shen people. Hard to wield but deadly in the right hands."

"Magister and Secretary? Don't they have a king, or an emperor like normal people?" Tam looked across at Seek, who had briefly glanced his way.

Yes, I'm watching you, shaman.

"Never have as far as I know," Stogi said. "Keep themselves to themselves, do the Shen. Queer folk. My guess is there are some important individuals down there."

Tam nodded and watched alongside his friend as the heavily armored Ptarnians lined up in ordered ranks and began leading their horses onto the first raft. Tam noted how the rafts must be tied to ropes as he saw the ferrymen dig long poles into the river and thrust hard upon them.

"How do they—?"

"It's a pulley system. I know—clever," Stogi said. "They have a covered house at each bank. Inside are two huge pulley wheels where the steel ropes are wound back and forth feeding out and pulling in across the river. Two steel ropes spanning the entire river. It's very impressive."

"How do you know all this?"

"Because I've been across!" Stogi flashed him a grin.

"You've what?"

"Shish—keep it to yourself." Stogi flicked his head in Seek's direction, but the shaman was preoccupied with his study of the maneuvers down by the river. "I was curious, so I slipped on a raft guised as a beggar and took a ride across. Big fucking river—the crossing took time. Stayed a few days on the other side and came back. Interesting visit."

"You are one reckless, crazy bastard," Tam said, and Stogi grinned. "So, what's over the other side?"

"Same as here—wind and grass, the odd crowy wood. Oh, and there's a village several miles beyond the river. The road runs through it. Tawdry place, occupied by silent suspicious people, and plagued by endless drizzle as I recall. I found a tavern eventually, pilfered some crap food and watery ale, and then rode back to the river in the morning. Happy to cross back over."

"Sounds like a fruitless trip," Tam said.

"I had my reasons for the visit," Stogi said. "And I learned what I needed."

"You're as mysterious as he is." Tam jerked his head toward Seek, still currently occupied with his survey.

"Aye, we Tseole are mysterious folk."

"He told me he was from Dunnehine, wherever that is," Tam said. "But said his folk were related to the Tseole."

"They're different," Stogi said, and would comment no more on the matter. "Look, the first raft is leaving." They strolled over to join the others.

"What do we do?" Tam asked as no one present seemed to be addressing the situation. "I mean, do we just ride down, say hello, and ask for fucking portage?"

"Shut up," Seek said, his gray eyes flickering Tam's way. Tam held that gaze and Seek shrugged. "We wait until dark," he said. The others nodded, except Broon, who glared, and Stogi, who shook his head in disgust.

"You don't know what you're getting into, shaman," Stogi said.

Seek smiled at him and turned away.

"Get some rest," Seek said, addressing them all. "We'll need to be ready at dusk, the ferrymen should be done by then, and our friends down there off on their way to the meeting."

"And where will that happen?" Tam asked Seek. "I know you know, so why not enlighten us too."

"I've a notion," Seek smiled slowly. "Be prepared for a long trip—it's many leagues to the coast."

"He's lost his marbles," Stogi said as Seek left them watching the rafts being manned in the distance. "And will get us all killed."

"Possibly," Tam said.

"Probably," Stogi insisted.

"He said you don't have to come, Stogi." Tam grinned at his friend, who glared back, offended. "But I'm not leaving shifty Seek's side until I find out what he's up to. My wife's life may depend on it. He's the only thread I've got to go on, thin and fragile though that may prove."

"And your own life might depend on me watching your back." Stogi grinned for the first time that day. "I'm knee-deep in this nonsense too, so I'll not quit now. Just think it's a bad idea, and I'm worried about Seek. Even more than usual. He's dodgy, Lord Tam, even for a shaman. But that's all I'm saying on the subject." Stogi blew out his cheeks and crinkled his nose. "I must be mad," he said, after a moment's reflection.

"We all are," Tam said. "World we live in. But I for one am happy you're on board." Tam slapped the Tseole's back. "Let's go rest up while we can."

Chapter 19 | Largos

Garland sat his horse and wiped sweat from his features. Ahead, the gates opened to allow their column inside the city. A week's hard, sweltering ride through brush, heath, and skirting the occasional swamp had brought them to the coast.

The young Bruhan had done well, convincing his superior at the garrison that Garland and his men were renowned veterans from a war overseas, now searching for a lost hero. A noble venture which impressed the portly commander enough to allow the Bruhan and his men ride on to Largos as personal escorts to Captain Garland's crew.

After restocking at Talimi Station, they'd followed the Larg River as far as they could south before making out across country, the fear of pursuit weighing heavy upon them. Garland had seen enemy horsemen watching them from afar, but mercifully the Ptarnians stayed away.

Garland suspected they would be planning something more rigorous than ever before. The new self-styled emperor was not a man used to defeat. When he got wind of the events in the south of his country, Callanz would be furious. Garland almost felt sorry for those cowardly officers who would have to report their failure. Doubtless some would lose their heads.

Not his problem, nor even his concern. But Garland's six surviving men were.

Predictably, Pash had started it. Complaints, jibes, and subtle challenges at what they were doing and why they were here. Garland had ignored it for the most part during their long ride, but now they were at Largos City he needed address the problem. Garland respected and loved his men, even Pash. But that relationship was straining harder by the mile. Even Loyal Doyle had been unusually curt of late.

The gates swung open, revealing a wide piazza opening into three streets, these teeming with brightly-clad, talkative folk, all eyes on the riders entering their city. The Bruhan saluted the guards and they waved him through, his soldiers riding in file behind. No one spoke until Garland bid his horse cross beneath the gatehouse.

"Stop." The nearest guard lifted his visor and approached, spear leveled and dark eyes staring hard at Garland. "What business have you here?" But the Bruhan had anticipated this and had turned back to consult with the guards.

"Let them through," Bruhan Dahali said. "These men are our friends and deserve the full hospitality of this city."

The guard captain wasn't happy, but he nodded reluctantly and waved Garland and his men on through. Garland saw Tol wink at the fellow who glared back angrily. He'd have to watch his boys over the next few days; they hadn't seen a city in months.

Garland guided his horse across the broad piazza, the people watching him pass with curious expectant expressions. Some were affable, most suspicious. But Bruhan Dahali, now riding alongside, smiled and waved away any concerns or questions they might have.

"We'll get your men settled in a decent tavern," Bruhan Dahali told him as he rode next to Garland. "Then we two will go visit with the Rana."

"Rana—who is he?"

"She," Bruhan Dahali corrected him. "The ruler of this city, third cousin to the Ran, our 'king' if you like, though we do not call him that. Ran and Rana means something close to lord and lady in our language, but the Ranai are a family who have ruled Laregoza for decades."

Garland nodded, absorbing the details. He gazed at the citizens as he rode through the streets. Mostly they were dark of skin, small, wiry, and quick of eye. The women wore veils, though some of the younger ones went bare-headed. Those looked pretty, with dark questing eyes and their skin a soft mocha. They wore flared jackets and baggy striped trousers, brightly colored, some with bells attached to hem or ankle.

Garland heard Tol whoop and call out to one, causing him yell back at his man to be silent. "We are guests here," Garland growled, "so no bloody nonsense."

Largos was large and sprawling, so unlike the cities Garland had known back home. This place was triple the size of Wynais, but it lacked the beauty, and had no clear definition or order. One street merged into another with no orderly layout. The buildings were ugly haphazard tumbledowns, in the main comprising low-roofed dun colored huts, and the odd tavern wedged between, with twin wicker doors hinting soft light within.

After a good twenty minutes' ride, the street opened out into a large common area where trees spilled moss over wide lush lawns. Cattle and wild horses were cropping at the grass. Garland saw clumsy wingless birds wading through a pond. Mercifully, there was a breeze here that drove both the city-stink from his nostrils and sweat from his face. Garland smiled. This was more like it.

Ahead lay a spread of stone, random walls, and general masonry, which was hard to describe. A colossal building of sorts; it looked old, and a large section appeared crumbling and neglected.

"Not much of a palace," Garland heard Pash mutter behind him. Like the Captain, he must have assumed this the ruler's demesne.

"Barracks," Bruhan Dahali said. "My men will remain here. Your people can take lodging in the merchant quarter beyond. The taverns there are comfortable enough, and I've already ordered my second to ensure they award proper treatment and respect for such worthy fellows as your men."

Garland thanked him and, as the Bruhan's men led their horses over to the ramshackle mansion which comprised the barracks, asked if Doyle could accompany him to meet the Rana.

"As you wish," Bruhan Dahali said, and Garland noticed Doyle's smile. Good. He needed Doyle behind him, and the boy had started to waver.

Bruhan pointed out the nearest taverns shaded by olive trees at the far end of the street they'd just entered. "Your men can take their pick of any of those," Bruhan Dahali said.

Garland thanked him and bid the five go quench their thirst. That got him a few smiles, even a smirk from Pash.

Once parted from their men, the Bruhan and Garland, with Lieutenant Doyle riding close behind, entered a narrow lane that wound crisscross up a long slow gradient, eventually leveling out and depositing into another grassy area.

They emerged onto a high plateau that awarded grand views of the city sprawling below. The air was fresher up here, and a cool wind lifted branches on a line of cherry trees, and Garland saw banners and gonfalons flapping from towers close by.

We must have arrived.

Ahead were more moss-laden trees, shading crystal fountains, and opaque statues and wide verandas trailing with vines. Beneath those, Garland could see people taking their ease or chatting politely then looking up, distracted, as they rode by.

At last, he saw a building that impressed him. The Rana's house, so Bruhan informed Garland. The oldest structure in Largos. It looked both solid and square, not beautiful like the lofty towers of the Silver City. But it was stately and orderly in fashion, constructed with a longevity in mind which he hadn't noticed anywhere else in this teeming mess.

The seneschal met them at the door. A tall, studious man, with long drooping mustache and thin face. His look was mournful and his manner dismissive. "Bruhan Dahali, is it? You are a long way from your posting, soldier."

"Lato Topaiz." The Bruhan dipped his head. "This is an acquaintance of mine and a shrewd captain of war. We just survived an attack by the Ptarnians and need to speak with the Rana. It's urgent," he added, when the older man didn't respond.

"Why wasn't I informed? And dare I ask why you have allowed foreigners, whom you call friends, enter our city?"

"I'm just passing through," Garland said, not liking the seneschal's manner. The old man awarded him a withered glance.

"I'm sure you are, though you've a roguish look about you." Garland stiffened hearing that but kept his lips together. "No matter, we can get to the bottom of this business soon enough. I shall inform the Rana at once, and we can conduct our interview right away." Lato Topaiz smirked slightly and turned about, his heels clicking and long cloak trailing, moments later vanishing in the corridors beyond.

"Unpleasant fellow," Garland said, but the Bruhan shrugged.

"The Lato is an important man, though not as important as he thinks he is. The Rana is the voice of power here. Do not concern yourself overly with Topaiz."

"I wasn't," Garland said. "Just wanted to punch him." They waited a half hour before the seneschal returned with two brightly clad retainers, both younger than Doyle, who stood several feet away, dreamily taking in the views of the city below.

"This way." Lato Topaiz flicked a gloved finger toward the nearest corridor, and briskly set about striding in that direction, the young retainers following him side by side. The Bruhan followed without comment, and behind him Garland glanced wryly at Doyle.

"Wake up! You wanted to be part of this," Garland said, as Doyle shuffled over. "Never a dull moment, hey lad." Doyle didn't respond, but his sharp eyes were everywhere as though expecting some sudden attack. "These are allies," Garland whispered reassuringly.

"Captain, I—"

"We'll discuss it later; I need to talk to the lads, too." Garland smiled, and Doyle shrugged back his questions. Things were reaching a head, Garland thought. Garland needed his lads onside and Pash was getting to all of them. Even Doyle—judging by his behavior of late.

They entered through two large doors held open by more smartly-clad retainers and revealing a spacious airy room with all manner of tables and furniture draped with rich cloth and laden with finery. At the far end was a larger table with several chairs occupied by studious-looking individuals. A woman sat at the biggest chair, her face hidden behind the scrunched parchment she was reading.

She looked up, hearing their approaching footsteps, and Garland knew this must be the Rana. A handsome woman in her forties, maybe even older. She had a stern square face with a large crooked nose and bright curious eyes. She was larger in build than most women he'd seen here, though strangely appealing. Those keen black eyes looked shrewd. Clearly this Rana was no fool.

Lato Topaiz swept his flared arms dramatically in a wide announcement. "This young Bruhan has left his post at Talimi and begs an interview. He tells me he has good reason."

"And these others?" The Rana's expression was cool but not hostile.

"Friends, he calls them. Acquaintances," Lato Topaiz said, glancing at Garland and Doyle and making it very clear he thought those descriptions a mistake.

"Friends are always welcome here." The Rana's sharp dark eyes locked on the seneschal's, and he stiffened. "Take a seat, the three of you. I trust you've eaten?" She dismissed the other men gathered at her table. These stood up and departed quietly, polite curiosity showing on their faces, though a couple looked annoyed and stared hard at Garland as they left.

"Not for a while and not much then," Doyle cut in, and both Garland and Bruhan Dahali glared at him. Topaiz looked outraged, but the Rana's eyes were moist with humor.

She chuckled and turned to her seneschal. "Topaiz, would you be so kind as to organize some food and wine for our starving guests. I can't believe you kept them waiting at the doors for so long. This young one looks on the verge of collapse."

"I'm fine, just hungry."

"Shut up, Doyle," Garland said, annoyed at his second's impertinent manner. "Forgive my lieutenant. We've been together a long while and haven't shared refined company for many months. Doyle spoke out of place."

"A man should speak his mind," the Rana said, and Garland decided he liked the woman. She possessed common sense and appeared the practical type, unlike her stiff and pompous seneschal. He was still hovering behind her seat, Garland couldn't help noting. The man was clearly at odds with the Rana's instructions.

"Topaiz, why are you still here?" The Rana turned in her chair and motioned him depart. Topaiz stood glaring at Garland and Doyle; he looked furious at being dismissed in such a way.

"Rana, I—"

"I can handle these good folks until you return, seneschal." Her eyes narrowed dangerously, and Topaiz took the hint, departing with brisk important strides, the two retainers flanking him as before.

"Please do sit." The Rana hinted the vacant chairs, and this time Garland obliged happily. Doyle took seat beside him, and a stiff, nervous-looking Bruhan Dahali perched warily at the far end of the table.

"Rana, may I speak?" The Bruhan held up his hand but she waved him to silence.

"Eventually," the Rana said. "First I want to hear from this one." She smiled at Garland who straightened awkwardly under those careful, intelligent eyes. "This 'acquaintance,' whom my young Bruhan holds in such awe."

Bruhan Dahali blushed at the end of the table but Garland pretended not to notice. "Or are you going to let your hungry, blunt-speaking lieutenant do the talking for you?" The Rana pinned Garland with her dark eyes. "Well?"

Garland glanced briefly at Doyle who still looked uncomfortable, though not as awkward as Bruhan Dahali. He turned to the Rana.

"My Lady—"

"Rana is both my title and name. You may use it."

"As you wish. Rana. I . . . we are . . ." Garland waved a hand. "Just brief visitors in your city. Your officer, Brew . . .," Garland caught himself. "The Bruhan, I mean, has shown us courtesy in allowing our passage through to the east. His commander at Talimi spoke highly of him." Garland flashed a supporting smile at the Bruhan who still looked uncomfortable.

"To Rundali?" The Rana looked baffled and turned her gaze to Bruhan Dahali. "Dahali, have you told them nothing of that country, the perils they risk venturing there?"

The Bruhan made to speak, but Garland cut in.

"Rana, your Bruhan is a fine captain who held off a savage attack by Ptarnians just over a week ago. My men and I were in the vicinity and the Bruhan rightly wanted to question our reason for being there, when the Ptarnians arrived and we were forced to defend ourselves."

"How many men have you?"

"Seven including Doyle here. There were eight, but Mullen died in the fighting."

"A large force. Clearly you're not planning on invasion." The Rana's eyes sparkled as she chuckled. "A joke, forgive me. Ah, wine at last. For a moment I thought we'd have to get it ourselves." She leaned back and allowed a servant place a heavy crystal decanter on table. He filled her glass first and then the three men's. Moments later, Lato Topaiz returned with his two retainers and informed her food would soon follow. The seneschal hovered at the table until the Rana dismissed him again.

Garland sipped his wine. Sweeter than he was used to but not unpleasant. He noticed Doyle gulping and flashed him a warning stare. The lieutenant placed his glass on the table and pretended he hadn't noticed. The Rana's artful eyes were on both of them.

Topaiz returned, and this time insisted on taking seat at table and pouring himself a glass. "What is your business here?" he cut in without any attempt at courtesy. If the Rana was annoyed she didn't show it, and Garland found that strange.

"We are passing through on our way to . . .Rundali, as I've already explained to your Rana here," Garland said, irritated by the seneschal's lingering presence.

"No one visits Rundali," Topaiz said. "I think you are spies. That is the only thing that makes sense." His eyes flashed at the Rana but she didn't respond. "Why else would you be here?"

"They helped us defeat the Ptarnians." Bruhan Dahali found his tongue at last. "They may be few in number but are valiant fighters. We couldn't have held that hill without them."

Both the seneschal and his Rana were looking at Garland. He shrugged and motioned the Bruhan continue.

"Go on, Brew, don't let me stop you."

The Bruhan nodded, and then excitedly went on to explain everything that had happened, including his challenging Garland's men and their combined defence against the Ptarnians. No one spoke until his account was over. Garland rubbed his eyes and sipped the wine feeling suddenly weary after hearing all they'd been up to.

Fortunately, he was revived by a series of servants entering with trays of food, which they spread upon the table. Doyle fell upon the trays ravenously, and Garland and Bruhan, also hungry, followed at a more mannerly pace.

"Slavers?" The Rana glanced sharply at Bruhan Dahali. "These men are nothing like slavers, Bruhan. Believe me, I know." She turned to Garland who sat with arms folded.

"Your queen seeks a lost family member in Rundali, is that it?"

"Sort of."

"A bit tenuous," Rana smiled. "Topaiz here thinks you are spies, but he's always suspicious of strangers."

"And you, Rana?" Garland raised a quizzical brow until she flashed him a reassuring grin.

"I think you are rogues," the Rana said. "But honorable ones, good fighting men welcome in our city. Tell me, is your queen a strong ruler?"

"She is, Rana. None more so."

"I like the sound of her, this western queen. What name does she go by?"

"Queen Ariane of the Swords. She would like you, Rana," Garland said.

At that point the seneschal stood and rested neatly manicured hands on the table. "Rana, forgive me but we cannot trust these people. They are either spies or knaves on the run from their own land, or most likes both. We should have this soldier and his people interrogated properly by your brother the Ran's inquisitor in Corloza. We cannot risk Ptarnian wrath. This young Bruhan's foolishness will likely bring that empire down on us. Young fool," Lato Topaiz flashed Bruhan Dahali an annoyed look. "Hoodwinked and browbeaten by this glib foreigner. Such naivete deserves a flogging."

"You do not rule here yet, Topaiz, although I am aware you are working on that. Nay, don't object sir! You are not the only one who creeps around in the corners. I have my people too, seneschal. I am well aware where your sympathies lie, so I suggest you have a care with that acid tongue lest you lose it."

"Rana, this is preposterous and a slur on my person. I—"

"Shut up and sit down, seneschal. Else I'll order your head sent to Callanz—your real master—on a golden dish with 'no longer required' carved on it." Topaiz obeyed in stunned silence, his face white and strained. Garland wondered what was occurring here. He looked hard at the Rana for a moment and decided on taking a chance.

"There's something else, Rana."

"I thought there might be," the woman smiled. Beyond her, the seneschal looked about to self-combust. "Pray, do continue, Sir Garland."

"Queen Ariane has the Dreaming," Garland said, and when no one responded went on to explain what that was, and how her vivid prophetic dreams had been the reason for their journey here.

"I met a strange lady at the Lake of Stones, a witch I think she was. But she needed something and in return promised to help me."

The Rana's expression changed suddenly, and for the first time Garland realized how tough this woman was. "A witch—she has a name, this witch?"

"Ysaren."

"Rana, I warned you of this!" Lato Topaiz was on his feet again, his knuckles white as he pressed down on the back of his chair. The Rana glared at him for a moment and then motioned he sit yet again. Topaiz obliged but his expression was grimmer than before. More worryingly, he looked scared, and the Bruhan beside him terrified.

"A name not often mentioned in this country," Rana said. "Though you weren't to know that." She took a long hard swig at her wine. "This changes matters entirely."

"I don't understand. Who is Ysaren, and why do you fear her?"

"She is one of the three sisters who ruled these lands long ago. They were banished for nefarious deeds, but I'd heard rumor of their return. This is bad news. If Ysaren is here the others must be too. Even she . . ."

"Ysaren is trapped by some incantation and remains at the Lake of Stones," Garland said. "She cannot leave that place without the sacred object she requires."

"The emerald bow," Rana said, nodding, and Topaiz looked about to explode. "They, all three of them want it. Mainly to use on each other. That and all manner of wickedness. They are rumored spiteful, vengeful creatures."

The Rana sipped her wine and then covered the glass as the nearest servant stooped to refill. "I need to think," she said. "There is purpose in your coming here, Sir Garland. We need discuss this in detail later. But for the moment, take your ease in this house. My good seneschal will escort you to suitable quarters, won't you Topaiz?" Lato Topaiz stiffened but nodded. "Enjoy the day," the Rana said, waving them go.

"This way please." The seneschal ushered a perplexed Garland and Doyle from the hall. A confusing walk along narrow passages led to a room where he said they could spent the night. It was early yet, and Garland had questions, but he'd prefer not to put them to the seneschal, a man clearly at odds with his ruler. And possibly a traitor too.

"Enjoy a rest. You will need it." Lato Topaiz stared coldly at Garland for a moment and then departed the room, closing the door behind him.

"Home for the night," Doyle said, after a moment staring at the room. A single cupboard, two tables, a wonky lamp and a shabby mirror were not what one expected in such a grand estate. But the two beds looked comfortable, and Garland was sorely tempted to take a nap. The quiet knock on the door dissuaded him immediately.

Garland motioned Doyle relax. "I've got this."

A servant stood outside, flustered and nervous. "What is it man?"

"The Rana. She would talk further with you, stranger." The servant hinted the corridor. "This way, please."

"Of course." Garland exchanged glances with Doyle. "See you later. Doubt I'll be long."

"Be careful, Captain," Doyle looked worried, and for good reason. Something was evidently amiss here.

"Where are we going?" Garland said as the silent guard led him through a maze of corridors and passageways. Soon he'd lost his bearings and wondered how he'd find their room again. "I thought the hall was back there."

"We aren't going to the hall," the servant said. "The Rana wishes to speak with you alone."

"Suits me," Garland nodded, wondering where this was going. Afternoon light glinted golden through windows, as he followed he servant, his soldier eyes scanning each turn. They left the main building behind, crossed through courtyards chiming with fountains, and continued out to a shabby looking, low-slung house with a poorly hung door. The servant knocked, and a deep voice answered, "Enter."

Garland was hit by a sweet thick aroma and lingering smoke stung his eyes. Barely could he see through the gloom. But he noticed the woman seated there. The Rana. She looked different than she had earlier.

She wore a shawl gathered loosely at the hip, her long thick graying black hair tied back, and her bare legs showing beneath the lamplight. Garland froze.

"Come in." The Rana sucked hard at the pipe in her hand, and she leaned back, revealing another two inches of deeply tanned thigh. Garland turned, saw the servant had vanished, and warily stood by a chair in the corner.

"You are a strange man." The Rana's voice was deeper than it had been earlier. She seemed different, almost another person entirely.

Garland watched her eyes sparkle in the lamplight. "I'm a soldier and a journeyman," he said. "And I've been given a job to do."

"And you mean to get it done." The Rana blew out smoke and coughed slightly. "The only way I relax," she explained.

"I do."

"Because you love your queen?"

"Not just me, the men too. We owe Ariane everything. Her, and the Crystal King." The Rana shifted on her cushion and Garland tried not to notice.

"Do you find me attractive, Sir Garland?"

"I do, though that's not why I'm here."

"I'm forty-nine years old."

"Younger than me," Garland said, "and in much better shape."

She croaked a laugh hearing that. "You look worried, man. Relax.

We can speak freely here."

"Hmm."

"Come, take a seat. I'm just teasing you," she said, smiling slightly. "I can tell you're a man of honor in love with his queen. Written all over your face, Sir Garland."

He didn't know how to respond to that so changed the subject. "Why are you scared of the woman Ysaren? Your people should be more concerned with Ptarni. That twisted emperor has his eye on your country."

"And fair sweet Laregoza cannot withstand the might of Ptarni and possibly Shen too falling upon her." The Rana crossed her legs and sat up, her dreamy eyes suddenly focused.

"Shen?"

"The land beyond Rundali, where the bow you seek is rumored to lie."

"I thought that it was in Rundali."

"And maybe it is, everything becomes tangled outside our borders, particularly our eastern borders. Come, smoke with me."

"I don't partake," Garland said.

"Once won't hurt, and it might help you focus on your conundrum."

"I wasn't aware that I had a conundrum."

"Your men, you worry about them. I saw it in your lieutenant's eyes. They will desert you, even him, if you seek to help Ysaren."

"You said she is one of three sisters?" Garland sighed, accepting the pipe as she passed it to him. "The man I seek smokes this crap. Reason why he's where he is—so I've heard anyway."

"You know this man already?"

"I knew him, or rather knew of him once."

"Before the Gods died." The Rana smiled and shifted on her pillows. "Funny how people still say that in the hope that they are wrong." She took a long suck at the pipe and blew smoke in his face. "You saw that happen, didn't you?" the Rana said, her voice raspy with smoke. She passed him the pipe again.

"I don't know what I saw." Garland's head buzzed as the rush hit him like a mallet between the eyes. "It was a long time ago." And yet now at this precise moment it seemed like yesterday. Vivid. He could hear the screams, see the orange flames licking the walls of their city. The destroyer in white falling upon them. The memories tore at him like tiny knives. *I can't go back there.* Garland sucked in smoke again and choked.

"Careful, easy." The Rana leaned forward and took the pipe from him. "You are tired, and this drug is strong."

"Are you going to kill me?"

"That depends," the Rana said, with a faint smile, and Garland laughed, the smoke driving his cares into oblivion.

***

Doyle stared at the fading light outside. Two hours had passed with not a sound bar that of his own worried heart beating. What was going on here? And why was his captain so remote and strange? A man he admired beyond any had become a stranger of late.

The men were talking—especially Pash. Even cheerful Tol was questioning why they were here in this alien city. And for good reason too. Garland needed to tell them what his plans were, if indeed he had any. And that was the problem. Doyle suspected he didn't but rather was under some spell brought on by his visitation at the Lake of Stones. The captain hadn't been the same since that encounter.

The fight last week had been good, except for poor Mullen, though he'd gone the way they'd all go eventually, and had had a good run for this money. They all loved Garland, a man whom Doyle had come to respect beyond any other. A good plain honest man. A soldier, uncomplicated and strong. But Garland had changed over the last few weeks. Whatever had happened at that lake had had a profound effect on his captain.

A knock on his door.

The handle turned slowly, and Doyle tensed. "Enter," he said, and then felt a rush of relief seeing Tol standing there. "What's up?"

"We need to talk, Doyle." Tol stood at his window looking out at the gardens below, now shrouded in mist. "I don't like it here."

"They seem friendly enough, these Laregozans." Doyle noted how Tol looked tired. Strained, the familiar smile replaced by constant frowns. "We're just a long way from home, mate."

"Aye, that we are, and that's fine. If we knew why." Tol turned and stared hard at his lieutenant. "The boys are getting restless, Doyle. They are losing faith in Garland."

"And you?"

Tol looked uncomfortable and ill at ease. Doyle knew it wasn't easy for him to speak. "Me too, though I'm sad to say it."

"Garland said he'd hold a meeting," Doyle said. "He wants to brief us on what we're doing next. What he said."

"So where is he now?"

"I don't know. Either with Bruhan Dahali or that woman the Rana," Doyle said. "No doubt trying to discover what he can."

"I think he's lost it, Doyle," Tol said. "Captain's changed since his encounter with that witch at the lake—or whatever she was. Not the same man."

"Everyone changes, Tol." They both looked up as Garland stood in the doorway, his eyes dilated and his features flushed red.

"Are you all right, Captain?" Doyle motioned a chair and Garland nodded, slouching into it and sighing.

"So the men are unhappy?"

"They are, sir," Tol said, glancing at Doyle who shook his head.

"We need to know what's going on here."

"We're going to Rundali, that's what's going on," Garland said, and Tol shrugged, and without asking their leave departed the room. Doyle watched him leave with worried eyes. If Tol was this dejected, the others would be a lot worse.

"Captain, we need a clear plan. You've told us nothing save hints and innuendoes. We are plain fighting men, not mystics."

"We were given a task, Doyle," Garland said, and Doyle felt increasing concern about the state of his captain. Garland looked tired, disheveled, and depressed. "A job to do. A man to find, or at least discover what's become of him. That's turned out to be more complicated than was expected. Doesn't matter. We swore to our Queen, or have you forgotten our vow?"

"Of course, I haven't forgotten," Doyle snapped, feeling irritated. "And we are the loyalest of men and will not divert from our task. But you need to explain what you hope to achieve by venturing further into unknown lands. You've told us nothing. Tamersane is still most likely in Caranaxis, so why the fuck are we going in the opposite direction?"

"I made a promise."

"To a witch, yes, you told me."

"She will help us, but first we must free her, although I now believe that might prove hazardous. But we'll discuss this tomorrow Doyle. I've said enough for tonight."

Chapter 20 | Allies

Sulo paced through the deserted village, a lone hunter poised and ready, with long knife gripped in palm. He was uneasy under the brooding copper sky above with dark surge of ocean beyond. Both were so alien to him, beyond the confines of his narrow imagination. He walked on, found a building that opened to a cozy room with vacant chairs and tables and evidence of recent occupation.

She'd been here, Sulo felt certain. Teret, and someone else, had recently left this place. A big man judging by the boot scuffs near the door. And what's this—he crouched—more scuff marks, and a couple were huge and clearly made by steel reinforced boots. Sulo straightened, sensing danger.

But Teret had been here, so he'd chosen the right path. He smiled, pleased with his earlier decision, and then tensed, hearing hoarse shouts from somewhere outside. Sulo dropped and listened. People coming his way.

Eyes narrowed to cunning slits, Sulo stowed his knife and slipped silently from the tavern, or whatever this shabby place was. He trotted slow and steady through the deserted village, toward the approaching sounds of voices. He found a low wall to hide behind and waited, poised for ambush, as long moving shadows hinted men coming his way.

There were five of them, tall and thin. They appeared half-starved, gaunt and weakened by some mindless toil or drudgery. Worthless things. Sulo relaxed. Rural peasants or maybe even slaves. Sulo knew he could take them if needs be. But then he saw the creature leading them, and he tensed in sudden alarm.

A huge monster of a man encased in steel, the weird copper sky-light glinting and sparkling off his armor as though it were ablaze. A figure eight-foot-tall or more, the giant cranked and creaked toward the wall where Sulo lay hidden, crouching lower, well aware his knife would make small impact on that mountain of steel. The other men walked in silence beside him. Like empty drones, and judging by their faces, terrified of metal giant too. Sulo heard the monster speak but couldn't make out his words.

They were getting close, so Sulo lay flat on his belly and gripped the knife in its sheath. Just for comfort. He held his breath, listening to the crunch and thud of heavy boots cracking clay. In moments they'd passed the spot where Sulo hid. He watched them fade into the village, the cranking giant surrounded by the shuffling half-dead creatures, the copper sky deepening to rust above their heads, the ocean smudging the distance like a blot of ink.

A terrible place, but one where he'd find his quarry. Time for action.

Against his better judgment, Sulo rose slyly to his feet and started making for the spot he'd last seen them. It wasn't long before he heard that metallic voice again. Despite his misgivings, Sulo dared get close enough to see the giant and his companions crash noisily into the building he'd recently visited.

Again questioning his actions, Sulo crept closer. And closer, but coiled to break into a sprint should anyone see him. At last Sulo reached the wooden walls of the building and pressed his ear to the door.

He couldn't hear anything because the door was too thick, so he prized it open very carefully, freezing when it creaked slightly. One of the men turned, looked briefly toward the door, and then turned back, his eyes dull and dreamy. Sulo let loose a slow release of breath.

Hold your nerve—they'll know where she is.

Through the crack in the door he could see them clearly. The giant seated at table, his huge girth barely contained by the chair he smothered. Metal elbows pressed onto the wood. The five scrawny men were clustered around him as though expecting an important announcement.

Moments passed. An icy chill crept in through the door, and Sulo felt the draft pierce his clothes like damp probing fingers. He shivered. Something amiss here.

Crack!

Sulo almost fell back out into the street when sudden bolt of lightning struck the giant's armor and scattered his men to the floor. The giant endured the blast without movement, sitting up straight, and issuing a canine growl from deep within his helmet. A gravelly sound that sent shivers up Sulo's spine.

The shock faded, replaced by a sense of numbness and confusion. The men staggered to their feet and clustered around the metal giant, who still hadn't moved. Sulo wondered if he lived or was some kind of sending or manifestation invoked by alien sorcery. He looked hard through the gloom that had replaced the lightning's glare and tensed when he saw a shadow crawling along the wall at the other end of the room.

Sorcery!

So his instincts were right again! The shadow took form, becoming a monstrous spider or some kind of insect. Sulo gaped, caught halfway between terror and morbid fascination.

Then the shadow dropped from the wall, peeling off like rotten plaster, half sliding, half crawling to where the metal giant sat with the men clustered around. The giant barked again, and Sulo was amazed how his servants didn't jump in fear or flee from his fell voice and the creeping ugliness manifesting on the floor.

That ugliness was changing, congealing from quicksilver shadow to solidified gold, then back to shadowy smoky black, shifting from one shape to another. Sulo stared in horrified wonder. What corner of Yffarn had he arrived in? Even if he'd wanted to run his legs lacked the strength to carry him, such was the terror he felt.

The insect-thing became a nameless snarling beast, then crumpled back to scaly insect again. It shifted shape again, swelling into a beetle-like creature. Then, as Sulo stared witless, the crusty skin on its back exploded, spilling out chunks of yellow steaming flesh across the wooden floor boards. The flesh mingled and crawled, separating and congealing again until finally the shadow-creature rose up and manifested into humanoid form.

The room shook, and another lightning bolt hit the roof of a house nearby. Sulo jumped and blinked, adjusting to the weird, shifting light, too terrified to breathe.

A woman sat cross-legged on the floor, her naked body facing the armored giant. The metal monster and his companions hung their heads as she stood slowly before them. A tall, ancient looking, yet eerily beautiful woman with pale yellow hair and milky blue eyes, her skin an ivory white with hints of pale blue, and tiny gold stars freckling her breasts and upper arms.

"You need not hide any longer, Sulo of the Rorshai." The woman's voice was crusty and hoarse. She turned and stared at the door. Sulo felt his bowels loosen. He tried to flee but the malice of the woman's stare kept him locked in place.

The giant broke free from his chair, the wood snapping apart like twigs as he moved. Even while stooping, his massive helmet scraped splinters from the beams on the ceiling.

"Relax Grogan, I've been expecting this one." The woman was still watching Sulo. Behind her the giant froze, and Sulo felt those hidden eyes blazing down on him from inside that featureless helmet.

"So, come on in," she said, a twiggy finger curling his way. "Not polite to linger skulking and eavesdropping in doorways." The woman drew a circle in the air with her fingers forming a square with a throbbing light contained within.

"The fabric of chaos," she said, pulling the square down until it resembled a doorway and then stepping through and vanishing. She emerged seconds later dressed in a deep green gown. It clung to her curves, and Sulo couldn't turn his gaze away. "My secret wardrobe," she said, smiling at Sulo, who now hung limp in the doorway expecting the worst. She turned to the giant stopped motionless beside her.

"This is the one I told you about, Grogan. He will help you return to you own dimension, a skilled hunter filled with malice and cunning." The helmet cranked sideways and Sulo was aware of a faint red glow emanating from the eye slits—the giant assessing him. Sulo felt the fear threatening to unman him.

He leaned hard against the door frame, mouthing little noises until the words finally came. "You don't exist, none of you," Sulo said. "Just a bad dream I'm having."

"That may be so," the woman in green said. "The things you've done, it's small wonder you have nightmares." She smiled cruelly and her milky gaze swept over him like a judge passing sentence. "Dream or not; you cannot escape it. Like the Grogan here, you Sulo of Rorshai, are trapped in a different dimension, sent here by the watcher at the gallows. The man called Jynn."

"Tricked, you mean." Despite his dread, Sulo felt his anger

return, fueled by the fury of how his fear had unnerved him.

"You crossed of your own volition I seem to recall," the woman said, folding her arms and wrapping the green gown tighter as though she were chilly. "Small matter. Now you're here I've work for you. Your kind of work, murderer, and the Grogan's too."

"What is that thing?" Sulo glared up at the metal beast in armor. The helmet was still tilted towards him, and Sulo knew the creature was weighing him up.

Yeah—keep looking. I'll murder you if needs be however hard it proves.

An odd coughing sound came from inside the helmet and Sulo wondered if the creature was laughing at him.

"The Grogan is an unusual specimen," the woman said, resting white hand on the giant's armored thigh. "A lost stray from an ancient warrior race who once inhabited the far side of the universe, almost beyond the gates to the void. There were many once, but they are now almost extinct after the third great war of the Gods."

"He is from the outer dark?" Sulo found his voice again. "A place outside time?"

"Beyond it. During that last phenomenon, the Grogan fled in his space capsule and escaped the catastrophe occurring in his realm. Some of the Gods had fled way out there to the fringes of the universe, seeking escape from certain retribution. Their father, the Weaver, found them there and tore up the world fabric of that region, having no further use for it. He thus left those rebel Gods nowhere to hide. The Grogan here escaped. But he lost bearings and spun out of control, whirling blind through space and time, until landing in Gwelan. Here, in this sorry forgotten realm, with its cold dreary oceans and heavy brown skies."

"But you are not from here either?" Sulo had recovered some of wits. Part of him still believed this a dream yet he determined to find a way out of it. And in doing so to get back on the trail of his prey.

"I am from everywhere and nowhere, not restricted like you mortal folk. My body may be trapped at present, but my essence is free to roam, unlike my sisters, who are fettered within and without. Those two would foil me with their schemes if they can. I mean to ensure that doesn't happen."

"What do you want from me?"

"The same thing that you desire for yourself. Vengeance, by stopping those who have hurt you so badly."

"What do you know of my situation?" Sulo pressed his back against the wall as the woman leaned forward, seeming to float towards him.

"You're a black-hearted killer. That's the reason why I asked the Jynn to send you here. I have the Grogan's help already, as he knows I can assist him. But such a creature is unreliable, therefore of limited use. I need someone with low cunning, and a will to achieve. I know you have those, Sulo of the Rorshai."

"How so? And that trickster at the crossroads advised me take another road. The road was my choice—not his."

"Ha! Do you think so?"

Sulo tried another tack. "So how can I assist you?"

"Fetch me something I have a need for," she said, smiling faintly.

"Why should I care?" Sulo's anger had given him strength. He reckoned he could run now if he had to.

"Because the woman you desire to kill is seeking the same thing I need."

Sulo tensed with sudden excitement. "You know the whereabouts of that bitch, Teret?"

"More or less." The woman's smile was colder than the room surrounding him. "She and some others escaped the Grogan here a while ago. They entered my sister's realm, or a part of it that lies within this dimension. Elerim entertained her and the man she journeys with."

"What man? Tamersane of Kelwyn?"

"No, a stranger. A voyager from the past seeking a way back there. Like you and the Grogan here, he too is lost. Elerim has promised both of them aid in return for the artifact I myself desire. Elerim wants it too, so she can use it against me."

"Why do you hate each other?" Sulo was excited now. This spirit woman would help him find Teret. All that mattered.

"Ours is an ancient rivalry," she said. "Elerim and Cille would thwart me as they did before. That is the reason why I blasted them from your world. They in return duped me into eternal confinement at a place called the Lake of Bones."

"I have been there." Sulo recalled his flight from Rorshai years ago. Half-starved and crazy, he'd arrived at this desolate lakeshore only to find the water undrinkable. He's almost died there but sheer willpower and hatred had seen him arrive in Caranaxis days later.

"What is it you seek?" Sulo said, then twitched nervously. The Grogan had swung around to face him, the barrel-shaped helmet tilted slightly as though the giant were listening.

"Grogan rest," the spirit-woman said, bidding the giant take seat again on one of the vacant chairs. Sulo noticed the men surrounding him were asleep. They appeared drugged, or stupefied, as though their minds were scrambled, their heads lolling on table. Sulo paid them scant heed, the armored giant and this strange lady being more than enough for him today.

"A bow," she said holding his gaze. "The Emerald Bow of Kerasheva. A weapon of my people, once potent and powerful, but long ago lost in a forgotten corner of Ansu, your earthly realm. It can be used for good or ill by those who possess the skill. As I do, and regrettably my sisters also."

"What's special about it? A bow shoots arrows."

"Emerald arrows that puncture the confines of time by piercing the world fabric. Spell-crafted shafts that can alter destiny and reshape both future and past."

"Can a man shoot such a weapon?"

"That depends on the man. I already have someone looking for it but fear he has lost his way. You, Sulo, are insurance. Both my treacherous siblings and I suspect we know where the bow lies. What will follow is a race to recover it."

"You mean to kill your siblings?"

The woman's pale eyes narrowed to cat slits. "Possibly," she said. "In that last great conflict of the Gods, things got messy. You were there, remember?"

Sulo had heard things. Cosmic booms and shifting light. The ground shaking beneath him. But he'd been too busy fleeing Rorshai to pay much heed of the cause, until weeks later when the rumors started spreading through the markets of Caranaxis.

The Gods had gone for ever.

"I have a dim memory of the times," Sulo said.

"Do you know why the war happened, why the Gods were broken?"

Sulo shrugged. "I wasn't paying much attention at the time. I was fleeing dogs and men with torches. Hiding in streams, and ignoring the weird color of the sky, and the throbbing of the earth beneath my feet. I only learnt later what had happened," he said.

"Well then, let me refresh you," she said, placing hand on the Grogan's shoulder. The giant looked asleep, slumped motionless in the chair. "The Gods tore each other apart that day, resulting in the cosmic balance getting unhinged, and everything warping badly. Both throughout our own world, Ansu, and beyond out into the future fringes of the multiverse. A ripple effect. Tectonic plates shifted, things were lost, and other things found. A nasty tangle ensued as the Weaver's Dance distorted and fragmented. Souls were trapped, and others found freedom, the doorways through dimensions opening and closing more rapidly than ever before. The world spins faster now."

"But why did it happen? Why should I care?"

"Because everything is different," she said. "New rules to live by, new rules to break. Twice before, the old rulers in the sky rebelled against their father, the Weaver. The first time he forgave them, much as a doting parent ignores the tantrums of his favorite child. The second time, the Gods warred amongst themselves, some siding with the Weaver, and others, led by the First Born, Cut-Saan—or Old Night as He is more commonly called—seeking to topple the Weaver and set up a new order.

"The loyalists won through, but the price was high, and the Weaver moved on to fashion new worlds in different parts of the universe. Old Night was broken and dismembered, and His body parts placed in tombs spread amongst the nine worlds, His head beneath a mountain in the midst of this planet—Ansu. They set a demon to guard it. But the Sorcerer Caswallon delved too deep, and his reckless behavior broke the bonds set around the God, enabling Old Night rise up again, resulting in the third war in the heavens. The Weaver destroyed Him but only after the other Gods had fallen, save that fragment who fled."

Sulo let that all wash over him. Too much information hurts the head. Instead he focused on his situation.

"And Teret is also looking for this bow? Why?"

"Why do you think?"

Sulo said nothing for a moment as he struggled to absorb the manifold emotions battering his head. "It doesn't matter, as long as I find her and kill her, and then do the same for her bastard husband.

Because of those two I lost everything. I would have revenge, Sorceress or whomever you are. That is all that matters."

"Then you need accompany the Grogan and his slaves back to your realm. The giant will be of limited use until you reach the Castle of Lights. Once there, the Grogan's terrifying battle skills shall prove invaluable. Let him deal with any conflict while you focus on getting that bow. Once you have that, you can deal with your own little distractions easily."

"I know of no Castle of Lights."

"It lies at a far corner of Rundali, so you need to get back there," she said. "But there are portals, and I can assist your passage. It's important you arrive before the rest."

"Teret and this stranger."

"Among them, yes. But there will be others, as there is a lot at stake here. And a limited time gap. The constellations must be aligned perfectly."

She let her slim hand drop from the Grogan's metal shoulder and glided toward Sulo, her ancient face taut with excitement.

"Bring me the Emerald Bow of Kerasheva, Sulo, and you shall get what you desire, and much more besides."

"I shall do it," Sulo said, then blinked in alarm as the room filled with steamy mist that blurred his vision and stung his eyes. The floor melted beneath his feet. Sulo yelled as he fell through the hollow gap, cold air and space rushing past him as he tumbled down into black emptiness.

I shall see you in time. The sorceress's voice echoed around his head. Then Sulo saw dark trees far below and braced himself for painful contact.

***

A world away, Ysaren gazed deep into the cold slimy water. She smiled cruelly, seeing the accusing face looking back at her. Almost a mirror of her own, yet younger-looking and more beautiful, untouched by the scars of endless exile. Her sister gazing back up at her with such vehemence.

"I took your form, Elerim. Borrowed your image, just like I used to. Posed as the Emerald Queen herself. My power returns, sister! The love that foolish soldier gave me has fueled my ancient fires. He seeks the bow, but now I have others working for me too. One good man, and two evil creatures. That's a useful balance. Small matter who succeeds, as long as they bring me Kerasheva."

The water rippled as Elerim's face distorted and her green-gold eyes blazed in silent rage. "You are overconfident, sister, a common failing of yours I recall."

"No longer," Ysaren said. "I've had years to think and plan." Ysaren folded her arms and rocked slowly from side to side, her sister's beautiful face watching her anxiously beneath the water. "You trapped me here, Elerim. You and Cille—Gods curse that evil bitch. Well now you're trapped too, in that forest. Caught in your own webs and machinations, and herself lost in another dimension. She cannot help you this time. Too clever by far, the pair of you. Shame you've messed up so."

"You are most unkind, sister." Elerim's beautiful face distorted out of focus for a minute then drifted back into view. "And as usual have your facts distorted. Too many years alone have addled your wits, Ysaren. Neither Cille nor I were wholly responsible for your predicament. You brought that down upon yourself. We wanted to help."

"Lying bitch!" Ysaren spat down at the water but Elerim persisted.

"Nor are we trapped like you, crone-sister, despite what you may think. I can't speak for Cille, but I for one would make peace between us. We are no longer young—not by our standards anyway. And you look rough, Ysaren. A frail stick who could snap apart in a strong breeze."

"I'm tougher than you think, sister."

"The game is shifting, Ysaren. We are all merely reflections of what we once were." Her lovely face twisted into sudden anger. "It was *his* fault, Ysaren. Our brother, the Wanderer. Arallos drove a wedge between us."

"Only because you were fool enough to love him," Ysaren scoffed at the face looking up at her. The ripples twisted Elerim's features again, and Ysaren felt the age-old jealousy and resentment rising up and betraying her emotions. Her sisters were solely to blame, no matter what silver-tongued Elerim said. Ysaren's memory was crystal. They had deserted her, so now they would pay.

"Arallos is gone, sister—our sweet, wayward brother. Your . . . *lover.*" She lingered cruelly over the last word, a vicious smile creasing those dry lips. "Blasted into limbo, lost forever in the realms beyond space and time. A restless shadow with no place to call home." Ysaren smiled, remembering her brother's pride.

Golden no longer.

"A shade he is now," Ysaren said. "A being without form or substance, blown every which way on the four winds—and serve him fucking right. We were a mighty folk before Arallos the Golden goaded us into ruinous war with our kin."

"I don't remember you objecting back then," Elerim's watery voice drifted up and was carried high and far by the chilling winds surrounding the Lake of Stones. "At the van were you, Ysaren, as I recall. Always the most impressionable sibling. Cille and myself had our doubts. But not you. A golden host led by the greatest and noblest families, our brother riding at the front. How proud you were that day. 'Nothing can stop us,' were your words, sister. Well do I recall them on the eve of that disastrous war." Elerim's image looked smug until Ysaren's palm slammed the water, distorting it again.

"So what?" Ysaren unfolded her arms and smiled down, the ripples smudging Elerim's face. "Arallos duped us, like he tricked everyone, including the Urgolais, our deformed cousins. Especially them. He used them to advance his ambition and caused the hatred to grow between our peoples. Those crook-backs would have kept to their mines without our dear brother's intervention. Because of him, both our race and theirs are all but extinct."

Elerim laughed then, her soft sultry chuckle rising up above the water. "They are dead, so who cares? Arallos, his arch foe, the Dog Lord—all dead. History. Just another war to forget. You dwell on the past too much, sister."

"What the fuck am I supposed to do, stuck here all these years? And you, bitch Elerim, are culpable, and very soon will pay, as will Cille—Gods curse her brittle bones, the conniving witch."

Ysaren felt a rage, dry as winter leaves blasted by sudden furious gust. It took hold of her and she struck the water's surface harder this time, as if she could impact the smirking face below. Elerim had kept her beauty intact, whereas Ysaren's thousand-year exile had worn her to dry flesh stretched over bone. Just another reason to hate Elerim.

Elerim's face was sinking further beneath the milky water, fading as Ysaren's charm broke up, her emotions having scrambled the control she needed.

"You're too rash, sister," Elerim said, her voice almost lost to the deeps and her face barely discernible. "Driven to extremes by your own fragile mind. You have only yourself to blame for exile. Cille and I sought only to protect you from your own machinations."

Elerim's visage drifted and broke apart as the stiffening breeze provided fresh ripples. Soon there was nothing but Ysaren's own distorted reflection, a cruel reminder of how ragged she appeared compared to the one who had departed. Ysaren stood, wrapped her skinny arms round her person and spat down at the water. The wind buffeted her ears. She looked up at the cold empty sky above and felt a stab of the loneliness that was her constant companion. It should have been different. He should have loved her, not Elerim—shallow creature that she was back then. But Elerim's words were chiseled inside her head.

Perhaps I am mad, and are not those two to blame if I am?

Ysaren clenched her small fists and screamed at the sky. It was hard to recount the precise details of millennia past. But the hatred remained. She had been wronged. And to redress that, Ysaren needed the Emerald Bow. With Kerasheva's power she could tap into her sorcery freely, break her bonds, and then trap her sisters instead, nulling their potency so she could escape this perilous world and drift at peace through the dimensions as she had back then.

But Elerim and Cille—especially Cille—were unpredictable and volatile. Ysaren dared not let them live long once she was free. Elerim was seeking the bow too; she had her own players. Cille was involved in her own game. Not time to disturb big sister yet. Ysaren feared Cille more than anyone.

The noble clown Garland would do his best. But it would be naive to back one horse. The others were a safer bet, as they were less complex than Garland. Her insurance, Sulo and the Grogan creature, would serve well as back-up. It mattered not who, as long as someone brought her the bow. And soon! Ysaren forced a cold smile to her lips. Elerim would regret her mocking tones. The bitch was running on borrowed time.

Chapter 21 | The Green Maze

The storms were the worst. For three days, they'd struggled beneath purple skies spilling torrential rain and worse. The mountain passes gave them some respite with hidden crags and places to shelter. But when they reached the highest incline and looked down on the land far ahead, it wasn't inspiring.

Those storms they'd endured looked benign compared with what waited for them down there. Rundali sprawled outwards from the mountains, a vast green maze comprising dense jungle, the sky above lanced by ceaseless spears of lightning, jabbing down, the thunder growling seconds later.

Hard to find a way through that. Teret gazed down, shivering. A mile-high sign saying "Do Not Enter" would have fitted perfectly down there. Through the gloom, Teret saw a maze of trees shimmering moist beneath the violent skies. She hoped the road continued down there, though there was no way of telling.

"That weather's getting closer." Teret could smell the rain rising up the valley, and her hair hung limp from the moisture in the atmosphere. "We'll get drenched before we reach that forest down there."

"We need shelter," Carlo said, stating the obvious. "It's a long trek before we're down. You're right, we'll drown if we stay on the road much longer." He smiled that warm smile that said *That's fine by me as long as we drown together.*

Teret shook the rain from her face. "Let's return to those caves we saw a while back, rest up, and start again in the morning," Teret said, though she hated the thought of retracing their footsteps. Every hour lost could see the end of Tam. But small choice. This storm had legs and was striding up the mountain slopes towards them.

The heaviest rain found them just before they stumbled into the nearest cave, scarce more than a yawning crack several yards across from the lane. They rushed within as the deluge unfolded from above.

Refuge. A shoulder of mountain had splintered and the fissure it left revealed a deep maze of tunnels reaching far back and underground.

Carlo got nimble with his hands and soon had a fire going, and— mainly to warn off predators but also to satisfy curiosity—he wrapped some furze around a stick and set it alight too.

"Let's go explore," Carlo said with a wink. "This furze will serve as a makeshift torch." Despite misgivings, Teret let him lead her deeper into the cave.

It was cool and deep and deathly quiet. Teret glanced through the murk as she stepped low under thresholds of stone.

So creepy in here. But she was curious too, and besides there could be creatures back there they needed to kill. *Better that than being preyed on while we sleep.*

They reached a wider section where space allowed a better look. Teret strained her eyes, seeing odd marks on the closest rock wall.

"What's that?" Teret pointed to the strange markings on the walls. Depictions of people and animals, hard to define. There was something disturbing about them; the carvings appeared warped, twisted, and distorted out of proportion. Whomever had done this must have had a troubled mind. They were sinister and alien, and Teret wondered what kind of twisted individuals carved them. And why.

"These caves must have been occupied once," she said in a whisper, as a shudder wracked her body. "Those etchings would have taken days."

"Yes, but long ago," Carlo said. "Creepy. Those drawings don't look right to me. But the artists are long dead, so we can relax on that score. Still, I've seen enough. Let's return to the light before we get lost, or the torch goes out." Teret nodded, happy to comply.

They fared back and decided to stay as close to the cave entrance as they could without getting soaked. They huddled close, but neither slept that night as the creepy atmosphere crawling from the tunnels behind kept them wary as owls.

The rain streamed ceaselessly outside, a sheet of warm spray, the breeze carrying it into the cave and dampening their tired faces. Far out there, a veil of mist hinted the forests below. Lightning still lanced, and the constant rumble of thunder rose and fell beneath the torrent of water cascading all around them.

The steamy hot atmosphere reached them in the cave. Hotter than it had been. Teret woke several times, feeling fidgety and edgy. She turned once, deep in the night, and thought she saw pale eyes gazing at her. She blinked and they were gone. In the morning, the storm moved off past the mountains. Time to try again.

As they took the arduous descent from the high mountain passes, the leafy mantle of the jungle seemed to float up and swallow them whole, choking their breath as the damp heat and closeness stifled sounds. Rundal Woods.

Teret remembered the maps she'd studied back in Caranaxis. A huge forest surrounded and penetrated the land of Rundali. Unlike neighboring Laregoza and Shen, Rundali had no cities marked, no roads or infrastructure. Nor was there any detail of what lay within. Just a green smudge on the map. A mystery land shrouded by forest. Or jungle, more precisely; the haze of green engulfing them, too stifling for a wood.

Gloomy, oppressive, and very hot. The cry of alien birds, slithering sounds in the undergrowth, and a distant roar of hunting predators were their only companions. At least the road stayed with them. Though Teret half expected it to vanish in the murk at any moment. Hard to follow with fallen limbs blocking their way, and vines and thorns tripping legs and tearing at flesh.

They continued in glum silence for hours, their progress slow. Teret felt hungry, tired, and lost, her clothes heavy with sweat and rain water. The diminishing thread of path was the only hope she had that they were moving toward their destination.

"There seems no end to this jungle," Teret said, as she tripped over a vine and struggled to follow the path through the tangle of tree and fern. The path barely existed at this point, its ancient pavings broken and cracked, split open with roots crawling through and weeds choking them. It must be old, but built by whom? And why so abandoned?

Carlo nodded his head but kept walking in silence. She knew his mind was focused on reaching the sea, with fresh hope he could find his lost home again.

Teret hoped that wouldn't prove a false hope. She couldn't imagine how lonely he must feel—his entire world and time destroyed, and now but a myth.

For her part, Teret tried to focus on their task, keep things simple, though she had no notion how to achieve it. But one thing led to another, and her head would be clearer once free of this foliage.

The Bow of Kerasheva. An Aralais artifact wanted by Elerim—

herself a witch or sorceress playing a sinister game Teret couldn't begin to comprehend. But Elerim needed their help, so surely she would use her powers to aid their passage through this wood. Small comfort, but focusing on it helped Teret hold herself together.

Do as she requests, bring her the Aralais bow, and she'll save Tam.

Teret smiled at her optimism. She kept mouthing the words "I will find you" as she struggled through the brush, finding it harder each step to hold positive. Hope was the key to survival. Lose hope and you've lost everything.

And what else did Teret have? She and Carlo were as lost as two strangers could be, in a land that hinted seeping menace and witchery at every step. Again Teret tried to remember details on those maps in Caranaxis. Rundali had been marked as one big fuzz, the only definition the mountains and sea enclosing it. Now here, she could understand why, but someone had lived here once.

"How far to the coast?" Teret asked, her small voice almost buried by the heavy atmosphere.

"Your guess is as good as mine," Carlo said, then froze and Teret nearly crashed into him as a huge crunch and scrape erupted closely.

Some large animal perhaps?

"Coming this way!" Carlo grabbed her sleeve and the pair jumped from the path and clambered beneath a fallen limb. Teret shuddered as she wiped the greasy mould from her face and hands; the limb was rotten and stinking.

The crashing and tearing approached nearer. She glimpsed trees bending and snapping and heard a whooshing of something huge striding toward them.

"What is it?" Teret hissed in Carlo's ear, then gasped as a tottering, shambling figure strode up the path toward where they lay hidden. Impossibly tall, his dark face lost in the mantle of leaves above, and ragged, his raiment ripped and sucked at by tendrils as he passed. In seconds, the walker was gone, and the forest surrounding closed back in again, rustling as though discussing his passage.

Teret shook her head and vented a silent yell. Carlo winked reassurance at her and she nodded she was fine. Neither spoke, but they carefully returned to the path and then hastened their steps as best they could.

An hour later, the path fanned into a glade. Teret stared disbelieving, seeing a garden. Wide, trimmed lawns led to borders paraded by hazy golden flowers; beyond these, a house sat comfortable and welcoming. Teret and Carlo exchanged worried glances. There was enchantment here.

"Best we turn back," Carlo said. "See look, the path is bending away from here!" Teret saw now, realized the path that opened into the glade was not the same path they had followed, but rather a spur jutting off, the main track barely visible in the gloom of the jungle beyond. They needed to get back there fast. She turned but stopped, hearing the sound of muffled feet approaching. Teret felt a shiver crawling up her spine.

"You're welcome here," a voice behind her said. A sickly voice that reminded Teret of the fungus on that branch. She turned slowly, eyes wary and fists ready. A man stood beside the door of the house. They hadn't moved, yet the house was closer, and a wide gate opened onto gardens all around, encasing the glade they were in, and the jungle was pushed back to hazy distance, like some nightmare looming beyond the fringe of reality. "Come! Eat and drink!" the man said, beckoning them approach. "It's not often we have visitors here."

He wore a wide-brimmed white hat. A mask covered his features, and a long black coat hugged the skinny frame. Gloves clung to his fingers, and the only flesh showing on his face was the hue of alabaster. "Come!" The figure stepped forward and bid them approach. Teret saw the door behind him open of its own volition into a room hinting firelight and welcome. "You'll be safe inside; the forest creatures can't reach you there."

Carlo stepped forward, but Teret grabbed his arm and pulled him back. "Carlo!" she yelled in his ear. "What are you doing?"

Carlo stared at her then stopped. The stranger in the mask had gone; instead, a huge black bird with a skull for its head lifted and settled like judgement on the nearest chimney, black wicked eyes surveying them, waiting for its moment.

"We need to move!" Teret shook Carlo hard, then jumped as a heavy crash turned her around again. The house had fallen in upon itself, folding and flattening like playing cards, then disappearing from sight. Carlo and Teret gasped as garden and glade vanished too, only to be replaced by a mass of rotten limbs of some long-dead spidery tree carcass.

"Thank you," Carlo said, shuddering as they stumbled back onto the pathway, just a hint of stone in the thicket. "Gods, Teret, I'm sick of this maze." His face was drenched with sweat, and Carlo Sarfe looked sickly as one ailing with illness. "I was about to go in that house. I don't know what madness took hold of me!" He appeared shaken to the core.

"Doesn't matter," Teret said, squeezing his hand with hers. "We're still alive, Carlo. All that matters, and scant reason dwelling on things we can't understand."

"You are right," Carlo said. "Lead on!"

"We have to channel our minds and not allow random intrusion. This place works like a canker sucking resolve. Elerim didn't mean for us to die here or be trapped in some beguilement."

"Except of her own making," Carlo said, but she shook her head.

"She needs us," Teret said. "We have to stay strong, Carlo. I think the biggest danger in this forest is what our minds might do to us should we allow it."

"You are right," Carlo nodded. "I'm fighting myself here. But where did that illusion appear from? Gods, but it was so fucking real."

She shook her head and kept on going. They would find a way through—just a matter of placing one foot in front of the next.

Time passed slowly, and they lost sense of progress and direction. The path weaved and twisted and the forest darkened around them, step by step. Dusk beckoned and still no break in the thicket. Teret stopped, hearing the distant jingle of water, and suddenly she remembered that they had neither eaten or drunk that entire day. She grabbed Carlo's arm and he turned back to look at her.

"Do you hear that?"

"Could be another illusion," Carlo said, glancing around. His eyes were wary and mouth set grim.

"Water is Elerim's conduit," Teret said. "She might be trying to help us."

"Careful, Teret," Carlo said, forcing a smile. "Personally, I don't think we should touch anything around here unless we have to."

"I know, but we need to drink to keep our strength up. I hadn't realized how thirsty I am!" She strayed from the path just a short way, and Carlo followed. Within minutes they saw the distant glimmer of water and heard the chime of ceaseless cheerful splash on stone. Carlo hung back, but Teret ignore him and hastened toward the waterfall.

She entered another glade, and sudden panic took hold, but there was no house or garden. Just the waterfall, and bright blue butterflies lifting in the sunshine. Evening sunlight filtered through a gap in the haze. Teret nearly cried out feeling the welcome breeze accompanying it and filling her heart with yearning.

"It's all right—no danger here," Teret called, turning to wave him forward. Carlo screwed up his eyes and nodded, entering the glade alongside. She smiled at him, reached down and cupped her hands, then drank long and deep from the water.

"Ooh, that's good," Teret said. "Nice and cold."

"It will give you strength." The voice surrounded them like the drone of bees, and Carlo's eyes were wild as he glared at Teret.

"I thought you said . . .?"

"It's Elerim," Teret insisted. "Don't you recognize her voice?"

Carlo shook his head. "Sounds like insects to me. I do however, recognize more sorcery." He stopped speaking as the butterflies erupted skyward exploding in a blue and yellow cloud. The cloud split into two, congealing and becoming eyes. Beautiful wise eyes—green with golden flecks, smiling eyes that looked down upon them. Gazing closer, Teret looked inside that gaze and saw the tiny form of a woman riding upon each butterfly. Elerim was within and without.

"We are lost, Lady, and need your help," Teret said, as Carlo gripped his sword belt beside.

"You have done well and are nearly through the Rundali jungles," the butterflies spoke in hovering drone-like tones. "I twisted the pathway, shortening the distance, thus keeping most the enchantment at bay and allowing you safe passage. But the man here started flagging, so I feared you would come undone."

"Me?" Carlo stiffened hearing the ice-cold laughter settle in the glade. "I've a stout heart."

"Aye—You, voyager!" The butterflies curled inside those huge eyes, the tiny riders on their backs blowing kisses at the man beside her. "The male species is ever the first to fail when beguilement looms." The butterflies danced and hovered, and the two eyes changed from green and gold to deep, constant purple.

"I was not failing—" Carlo began, then stopped as the voices fired into now-deep tone. Elerim.

"There is more peril than you think." The butterflies and tiny riders had congealed like beeswax, their wings melting, melding together and becoming a face. The purple eyes settled into the midst of that face, and Elerim gazed upon them.

"Night falls. You are almost through the forest, but danger awaits you at the other side. There are others seeking that which I desire. My sister Ysaren is cunning and twisted and knows of our plans. She too has sent men to get the bow. Evil men I suspect. If they succeed, and Ysaren uses Kerasheva against me, you, Teret will lose her love forever, and the man here will never return to his home. The stakes are high for all of us."

"Your sister—I thought you had two?" Teret said, exchanging worried glances with Carlo beside her.

"Ysaren is mad," Elerim said, her tone brittle. "She would destroy everything in her bitterness. For all our sakes, we cannot let that happen."

"We need more information," Carlo said.

"You know all you need to at present." Elerim's face exploded with violet light, and the butterflies spilled out, filling the glade as the last sun faded to a shimmer of pinkish red. "I will help you when I can," Elerim's voice said, coming from all around them again. "But know this. The way ahead is marked, and your journey might prove more troublesome than first you thought. Be wary!"

"And I thought us on a light-hearted romp through woods," Carlo said, but both butterflies and waterfall had vanished. Instead the trees closed in tighter than before, as evening folded toward smothering dark. Best they move on while the meagre light allowed.

"Well, that was enlightening," Carlo said, pushing vines from his face. "We are headed somewhere to retrieve something two sorceresses want so that they can destroy each other, and probably us too if we get caught in the crossfire."

"That's sisters," Teret said.

"What about the third one? And the Emerald Queen—where is she in all of this?"

Teret didn't respond, because at last they had reached the end of the forest. Like curtains falling, the land opened out, the dense foliage parting, revealing a sultry sun setting like spilled blood into water framing the far distance.

The sea! Their destination in view. A coastline comprising low sweeping hills and scattered forests, the thin ribbon of path chiseling through—all this teased them briefly before the sun sank beneath that distant water, and night stole their vision. But that glimpse had been more than enough.

Teret sighed and almost slumped. They were through the green maze. Rundal Woods were behind them. Carlo wrapped his strong arms about her and kissed her lips. She smiled, pulling away, and then kissing him back. Both were happy for the first time in days.

Chapter 22 | Beyond the River

Dusk smothered the slug of a river below. They rode down carefully in single file, Tam's eyes scanning the banks for movement. A lone lantern swayed at the crossing, a barge resting alongside, the gentle thud of water slapping its stern as they approached.

Seek led the way. Tam could see him leaning forward in the saddle like a hound hungry on scent. Broon rode alongside, the others bunched close behind with Stogi and Tam riding at the rear. Both were lost in thought, but Tam kept his gaze on the water ahead, suspecting trouble at any moment.

They dismounted just short of the river bank where a small cluster of trees awarded brief cover. Tam watched Seek confer with Broon for a moment, who nodded and hinted at the closest building: the one Stogi had said contained the wheels and steel ropes.

"We had best check that first," Broon said as they joined the others, and Stogi and Tam followed him into the wheel house. It was empty, but a battered table and haphazard chairs showed signs of recent occupation.

"Do you think there are guards still occupying this side of the bank?" Broon asked Stogi, who shrugged.

"Better for us if there were, then we could slit their throats, and jump on board. Most likely they're waiting at the other end—a nice reception committee."

"Let's hope they're asleep," Tam said. "Safe in their knowledge that only madmen would cross behind them."

"And they'd be right too," Stogi grinned, while Broon glared at Tam, not appreciating the wit.

"Best you keep that tongue in your head, foreigner," Broon said. "Not all of us want you here." Tam gripped a forelock and bowed his head in mock salutation. Broon glared and let them be.

"Don't mind him," Stogi said as they led their horses down onto the ferry, amid noise, jostling, and tense whispers. "But you shouldn't bait either—got a short fuse."

"I couldn't care less about him," Tam said, but he'd keep an eye on Broon all the same. Tam couldn't afford to get knifed while his mind was on more pressing matters. The Tseole leader was brewing nicely, a blend of resentment and distrust that could erupt at any time, and Tam the easiest target for his anger. Best he sleep with his knife in one hand.

The ferry crossing took an hour. Stogi and Rholf worked the steel ropes, their hands muffled by cloth and their sinews bulging under the strain.

"Those Shen ferrymen must be iron-hard," complained Stogi. "This work is murdering me." Tam didn't offer to help, and Stogi muscled through amid grumbles. Ahead at the prow, Seek leaned into the gloom with arms stretched wide as though ordering the distant bank to reveal to itself.

"What's he doing?" Tam asked Stogi.

"Who cares?" Stogi said, his face serious with concentration. "This is the tricky bit." Stogi took rest from his pulling at the ropes and glanced at the approaching bank. "An arrow in the dark would be most unwelcome."

Tam nodded, taking scant comfort from the thought. But they were lucky: the guards were either at rest or had abandoned their posts, safe in the knowledge that no one would be foolhardy enough to enter their country uninvited.

They drew alongside a jetty. Seek leaped onto the plank and made for the bank, as Stogi, Rholf, and young Hanadin cranked the ropes into clasps and lashed the ferry to the jetty. The other Tseole guided the horses over to the safety of the bank and waited until everyone was gathered.

Close by, on a low hill, Tam could see pale lights framed by the shadow of buildings. He suspected that was where the guards spent their nights, as there was only the empty wheel house here, just as on the far side.

"Is that the village?" Tam asked Stogi as he mounted his horse.

"Just out-houses and storerooms, and doubtless the odd ferryman and guard snoring within."

"Let's hope they keep snoring," Tam said, looking across at the shadow of Seek already guiding his horse onto the broad paved road ahead. "I think he's in a hurry."

"In a hurry to get us all killed," Stogi grumbled behind him. Tam, inclined to agree, refrained from comment.

They rode two abreast. The road beneath them was well made, Tam noted. Round, even cobbles, with no grass growing between, washed clean with recent rain, gleaming like a black snake under the glint of crescent moon. Whatever their faults, the Shen impressed Tam with their construction skills. He'd never seen a road so well made.

It was colder this side of the river; strange how a span of water could make such a difference. This country had a bleak feel to it, and as night closed in Tam shivered, hearing a wolf's cry somewhere far away.

"Cheerful place," Tam said, as Stogi passed him a flask to sip. "Thanks—that's better." The evil juice went straight to his head as normal, but the rush was very welcome and gave him fortitude. "So, where is this village?" Tam said, after some serious belching.

"Not far—a mile or so, and there's a curve in the road. But I suspect we'll keep going."

"Probably wise, as I doubt they'd welcome us."

"True, but that's not the reason. We could raid for supplies—easy targets. But no time. I know what Seek's up to."

"Rescuing prisoners?"

"Hah, right," Stogi said. "Nope, he wants to find out what these people are up to, and then intervene."

"In what way?"

"Disrupt supplies, raid, and make life hard for the new alliance between Shen and Ptarni."

"Dangerous," Tam said.

"Mildly put," Stogi said. "I'd call it fucking reckless, witless, suicidal, and none of our business."

"You should say what you think." Tam grinned at his friend.

Stogi glared at Tam, his dark eyes glittering in the night. "No joke. We Tseole are few in number, Lord Tam. What matter if those countries pass through our land? Tseole is so vast and empty we couldn't police it even if we wanted to. They are fleas crossing a dog's back. The odd raid wouldn't hurt if we were careful. But Seek wants to control things. It's a shaman thing; they're all like that. Though he's worse than most."

Tam slowed his steed, seeing the flat shapes of stone merging into vision. The village looming out from the gloom. "What about the occupants?" Tam asked his friend as they approached the broken gates that hadn't been in use for some time, judging by their state of disrepair. "Shouldn't we prepare for some king of trouble?"

"Timid, mind their own affairs. Like we should," Stogi said.

"Point taken." Tam let the matter rest as they cantered through the village, soon leaving the dreary hovels far behind.

After that they rode in silence for a time. Hours faded into night. Tam dozed in his saddle until Stogi nudged him. The others had reined in, seeing firelight in the distance. Tam, following suit, could see a sparkle of small fires flickering through woods somewhere close to the road, perhaps half a mile on.

"Campfires for sure," Tam said, and screwed his eyes up, seeing Seek loom out of the murk. The long coat flapping in the wind, tall hat, and sharp features rendered him a child's nightmare.

"You'll want to accompany me," Seek said, crouching down alongside Tam.

"What?" Tam blinked at him.

"I need to hear what's going on in that camp, and you, foreigner might find that useful too. Trying to be helpful here."

"I doubt that," Tam said. "Stogi here says it's none of our business," Tam said, noting how Stogi squared his shoulders beside him.

"Everything is our business," Seek said. "Knowledge is survival. Ignorance, extinction. Were it down to Stogi we'd stay starving thieves, driven from every corner of the land until we are finally hunted down and eliminated. We need to know their plans so we can fight back."

"That's crap," Stogi said, rounding on the shaman. "We've always been outlaws and fugitives, ever since our people fled the destruction of the Great Continent a thousand years ago. That civilization crumpled, but we're still here. Empires come and go, shaman. Their soldiers hunt us and we raid their trains. What we do."

"What we did," corrected Seek, his gray eyes flashing with annoyance. "You coming, Lord Tam?" Without further comment,

Seek turned his back on them and vanished in the dark. Tam exchanged glances with Stogi.

"Like I said, I need to stay close to that bastard," Tam said. "And maybe he's right; perhaps we will learn something to our advantage."

"To Seek's advantage maybe." Stogi slid from his horse and grabbed his weapons. "Come on, I'll ask Hanadin to mind our horses as we can better stalk that camp on foot."

"You don't have to come."

"Stop saying that," Stogi said. "Someone has to look after you."

Chapter 23 | A Mutiny of Sorts

"You've lost it Captain."

Doyle straightened in alarm hearing Pash's words as the veteran faced up to his long-time commander. "We're going home," Pash continued. "The lads and I have been talking, and it's obvious you're on some kind of personal quest, which you're keeping close to your chest, and all the time dragging us deeper into peril."

"We didn't sign up for this, Captain," Coife said, adding his support to his friend.

"It's exactly what you signed up for," snapped Garland. His eyes were hard, but his face looked strained and weary. And there was something else, a strange remoteness hovering on uncertainty. The captain looked haunted by self-doubt, and the men were sensing it too. Most held back, still respecting the man they'd fought with for so many years.

Pash didn't. He'd been spoiling for trouble ever since Mullen had died on that hill. The Captain's fault, that—in Pash's opinion. Unfair, perhaps, as most soldiers die in battle at some point, and Mullen was no youngster.

"We volunteered, Pash," Doyle said. "The highest honor is to serve our Queen."

"I love the Queen," Pash said. "But I didn't sign up for no goose chase across four countries. Queen Ariane dreamed of that Oracle, and we were sent to find out about her cousin—who's most likely gutted and long past rotted in a Caranaxis alley by now."

"Tamersane lives." Garland's face was straining, and Doyle worried he would lose patience any moment.

"And how the fuck do you know that?" Pash said.

That did it. Garland's heavy blow knocked Pash to the floor. The captain stared down at the soldier, his gritty eyes fueled with rage. "You'll obey me Pash, so you will. That or I'll hang you for the traitorous shit-stirrer you are."

The rage passed, and Garland slumped his shoulders. "I'm sorry," he said, to the men gathered around staring. Pash he ignored. "But I'm tired, lads, bone weary, and looking for answers wherever I can find them. You have to have faith."

"Bruhan Dahali warned us not to venture near Rundali," Tol said. "I'm with you, Captain, but you need to explain things."

"I was about to do that when Pash . . ." The captain turned and glared down at the rebel. Doyle watched as Pash struggled to his feet, dusted his shirt and turned his back on them.

"I haven't finished with you," Garland said.

"Fuck off, Captain," Pash said and left the room, his companions gaping after him. Doyle saw Garland's hand reach for his knife. The captain half slid it from the sheath and then paused before slamming it back in.

"He's out." Garland hinted the space where Pash had departed. "No longer part of the troop. I doubt he'll survive long on his own, and serve the fucker right." Nobody spoke, so Garland waved them take seat at table.

Doyle sat opposite and studied his Captain's eyes, worry and concern filling his own head. "Lads, forgive me." Garland waved a hand. "I know it's been difficult, but Pash should have heard me out.

I spoke with the Rana."

"Is that all you did?" crafty Kargon put in, and Doyle motioned him to silence.

"These are strange folk, and we need to play by their rules," Garland said. "The Rana . . . she had her specific way of conducting an interview. It involved some intimacy—though not in the way he thinks." Garland shot an accusing glance at Kargan. "And who am I to challenge that?" Garland said. "At least now I think we are allies. The Rana has her own problems, and her house is threatened from within. There is trouble brewing in Largos. We shared a certain . . . familiarity. Her idea, not mine, and it helped me get the gist of this strange country."

Kargon sniggered, but Garland ignore that too. Doyle didn't like the way this was going. A growing distrust between his Captain and the men. One bad apple, Pash, might be out, but the rot he'd started was spreading through the crop.

"I like Brew," Garland said. "But he's a junior officer, therefore naive—all brass and spangles. Best not listen to him. But the Rana is shrewd; she knows things and can help us."

"Why should she?" Doyle couldn't help asking.

"It's complicated," Garland said. "Hard to explain."

"I thought it would be," Doyle smiled slightly. "But do enlighten us all the same." He studied the faces of those gathered around the table: Garland, tense and torn; Kargon, wary, slightly sardonic; Tol struggling to remain cheerful; Coife, flint-eyed and clearly in Pash's camp. And then there was Taylon, his arm still in its sling and his face expressionless. Taylon could go either way.

Garland sighed. "What we seek is in Rundali, not Shen—so I suppose that's good news, as Rundali lies east of this country. So not much farther. It's where the Emerald Bow can be found, at a place called The Castle of Lights."

"The Emerald Bow?" Doyle shook his head slowly. "Castle of Lights? What's this about, Captain? You're speaking in riddles."

"The bow I promised Ysaren I would fetch for her and use to free her from her captor."

"What nonsense is this?" Kargon said, face flushed in anger.

Doyle waved him to silence again. "Hear him out," Doyle said.

"Kerasheva will free Ysaren," Garland mumbled the words. "Then Ysaren will help us find Tamersane, who she told me still lives but is under great threat."

"And you expect us to believe that witch?" Tol looked at Doyle, who shrugged in return. The lieutenant masked his worry. Doyle now suspected their captain was under some illusion, the witch having cast a glamour over him. He'd hardly spoken about his encounter with Ysaren. Perhaps they should have listened to Pash. Doyle slammed down that thought. Pash was trouble, one problem they no longer had. Time to forget Pash.

"Ysaren needs that bow, and she's the only lead we have. We were given a task, gentlemen. Find Tamersane the Queen's cousin and bring him, or news concerning him, back to Wynais. Not a soldier's job to ask why. Ariane dreamed of Ysaren, and Ysaren needs that bow. That's all I have to work with."

"You should have told us this before," Doyle said.

"There wasn't the time or place."

"Even so."

"Enough Lieutenant," Garland rounded on Doyle. "I am journeying to Rundali, entering this Castle of Lights, retrieving the bow, and returning to the Lake of Stones to learn how I can find Tamersane. That's my quest. You're welcome to accompany me thither," Garland said to all of them, "but I see how things are going here. With that in mind, I free you from your pledge; you've come as far as you need go, but my journey continues. That said, I would remind you all that you made a pledge to our Queen. If word gets out you broke it, I'll not vouch for you."

No one spoke; they hadn't expected that. Doyle felt a flush of relief but also a feeling of betrayal, abandonment. As though their Captain no longer trusted them. That hurt.

"Sleep on it," Garland said. "I'm seeing the Rana in the morning, then I'll be heading out as soon as I can. I bid you goodnight, gentlemen." He turned and left the table, his men gaping after him.

"What the fuck?" Tol said.

"Pash had it right," Kargon muttered. "Our Captain has lost it."

Taylon shook his head slowly, and Coife laughed.

"What's funny?" Doyle said, irritated by Coife's manner.

"Fucking sheep, the lot of us. Following him blindly, then when we challenge him, Garland tells us to piss off. Some gratitude."

"He didn't say that," Doyle said.

"Might as well have." Coife stood up and dusted his sleeves. "I'm done with this foolishness." Kargon followed his friend, and after a moment Taylon made to depart, but Doyle stopped him.

"Taylon, what's your opinion on this; you've scarce said a word all night."

Taylon turned and awarded Doyle a withering look. "What's there to say? As our Captain reminded us, we were given a job to do. We swore a vow, Doyle. I'm with the Captain." Taylon turned and shut the door, his footsteps fading off down the corridor, leaving Doyle and Tol alone.

"He's right," Doyle said. "You call me 'Loyal Doyle,' but Taylon deserves the name more than I do. I'm wavering, Tol. If only I could believe Garland knew what he was doing."

"That witch cast a glamour on him," Tol said, his face unusually grim.

"Yep, I've been thinking the same thing," Doyle said.

"It's the only thing that makes sense," Tol said. "Ysaren bewitched him, and now we're all caught in her trap."

"You and me too? You heard the Captain. We are free to leave."

"But we won't, will we?" Tol laughed. "We're stupid buggers who would follow that fool to the ends of the earth if we have to. He's our Captain—our leader."

"That he is," said Doyle. "Though I think he might have forgotten that. But you're right of course, and if he has lost his wits we need to be there to find them for him."

Tol nodded and said goodnight, leaving Doyle alone, watching the fire flies outside the window, his thoughts brooding and hollow.

Next morning, Doyle found Garland sharp and ready for the day ahead. His face was shaved clean, the beard he'd worn for years scraped away. Garland looked like a man who'd crossed an invisible line and could never go back.

"You look younger," Doyle said, offering comment and joining Garland at table for some breakfast courtesy of the silent servants. "Suits you."

Doyle wondered why his Captain had chosen that morning to remove his beard; it was just another change in a man who was slipping further away from them every day.

"Better in this climate," Garland said, but Doyle know that wasn't the reason.

"Pash is gone," Doyle said between mouthfuls.

"So?"

"He took Coife and Kargon with him. The Bruhan informed me on the way here."

Garland said nothing but stared silently at the window. "Another hot day," he said after a moment.

"Tol is with you, and Taylon too."

261

"And what about you, Doyle?" The Captain's gray eyes pinned Doyle.

"I'd love to go home—but it's not about what I want, is it? We made a vow; both yourself and Taylon reminded me of that. Shamed me—as I was sorely tempted. Especially as you've been so remote of late. We three are with you Captain, though we fear you are bewitched and will lead us to our ruin."

Doyle saw Garland smile for the first time in days. "You might be right lad, and sometimes I think I've lost it too. But then I remember our promise to Ariane, and all the days we fought alongside our Queen. 'Trust your intuition, Garland,' what she always said. Ariane of the Swords. The only woman I've ever loved." He smiled again, appearing warmed by the memory. "I can hear her saying it now."

"I miss our Queen," Doyle said. "And I miss green Kelwyn, more even than I thought I would."

"Then return thence, Doyle," Garland said.

"Haven't you been listening, Captain? I'm in this for the long haul, not a quitter like Pash and those others!"

"I know that," Garland said, "but I've been thinking about this." Garland nodded as a servant poured hot tea into his flask. "For the journey ahead," he told Doyle, bidding the man pour a cup for them both. He sipped for a moment and then waved a hand. "This is good. Never took myself for a tea drinker, but this I like." Doyle waited.

"I need to contact the Queen, and I'd trust no pigeon over such a vast distance," Garland said. "Ariane needs to know we're still out here, alive and—though tenuous—have gathered clues regarding her cousin."

"What clues?" Doyle shook his head in exasperation. "Ysaren—a very strange individual by all account and certainly one not to trust—wants this Emerald Bow and has promised to help us find Tamersane when we bring her it. Tenuous doesn't cut it Captain."

"I know, but Ariane has the Dreaming. She will understand, and perhaps be able to help us too. I need you to journey back to Wynais, Lieutenant. Leave right away."

"It will take months . . ." Doyle tried to stop the wave of emotions flooding his mind: excitement, tension, apprehension—and disappointment.

"No more than six weeks, if you don't tarry," Garland said. "The Bruhan has two fresh horses for you and a good supply of dried meat, plus three water canisters."

"You've spoken to him already?"

"I have—and he's coming with me to Rundali."

"He's what?" Doyle was failing to keep up. "Why . . . why would the Bruhan do that?"

"Because the Rana asked him to," Garland said, smiling at Doyle's confusion. "I sought her out last night, Doyle, after our meeting. I couldn't wait until morning and I needed her counsel. She's a shrewd woman and capable ruler."

"So that's it?" Doyle sipped his tea. "I'm excused and we part company just like that?" Doyle was struggling to come to terms with what had just happened.

I'm going home, my heart's desire!

"Tol and Taylon will journey with me to Rundali, Yuri too, with a score of his men. Better than I could have hoped for. The Rana says that this Castle of Lights lies on the southern coast at the far side of that country. A dangerous place, but where the Emerald Bow— Kerasheva—is rumored to lie."

"You seem to have it all worked out."

"Had time to think," Garland said. "The Rana needs help here. Support and a strong arm to fend off the scheming crows feeding at her scraps. I mean the seneschal and his friends. That treacherous old slime has growing support in this city. I fear for the Rana and would help. So, we came to an arrangement."

"Hardly your concern," Doyle said.

"Mutual advantage. Besides, I like it here." Doyle suspected that a lie but said nothing.

"Go home, Doyle," Garland said. "Report back to our Queen all that has happened, and inform her that I'm following this lead based on my intuition. Ariane will understand."

"I don't know what to say, Captain."

"I'll miss you, boy," Garland said. "Miss your support, but I'll be happy in the knowledge that you're back in the west. May happen we'll meet again if destiny allows. Stranger things have happened. But whatever the outcome, I know you for my friend."

Garland thrust a callused hand in Doyle's palm. "I don't do farewells, Doyle." The Captain winked at him and stood, wiped his face with cloth, and departed the room, leaving Doyle blinking back tears, his heart racing, and a thousand emotions battering his head.

I'm going home . . .

Chapter 24 | Interlopers

Seek strode towards the midnight camp as though intending to announce himself to the enemy. Stogi and Tam hung back, keeping low and under cover of whatever brush they could find. Tam had his sword, Stogi, a bow with full quiver alongside, plus six throwing knives hanging from his belt. He wore a short sword too. If Seek carried a weapon there was no sign of one, but then he could hide a lot beneath that shaggy dark coat he wore. At least he'd left his hat behind. His long shaggy hair glinted in the moonlight.

Seek found a lone tree and faded behind it, but Tam could see his sharp eyes glittering as they studied the camp, scarce fifty feet away. They crept close and took cover behind the huge oak. Seek ignored them.

"So, we're here—now what?" Stogi said, as Tam tried to see any sign of movement around those campfires.

"Seems oddly quiet," Tam said. Usually camps of soldiers meant laughter, curses, and the odd fight, even singing. Instead, just silence.

"The Ptarni commanders would have put their men on curfew," Seek said, and Tam wondered how he knew. "As for the Shen; they don't say much anyway."

"Aye," Stogi whispered. "They're rumored sneaky fellows. They say the Shen can tie a man's boot laces together without him knowing they are there. Slippery."

"And devious fighters." Seek nodded his head sagely.

"Fascinating," Tam said. "And good to know. But how the fuck do we steal into that camp without being seen?"

"Just follow me," Seek said, flashing Tam a grin.

Tam exchanged wary glances with Stogi, who shrugged his shoulders. "I expect he's something up his sleeve," Stogi said.

But Seek just wandered into the camp as if invited. The guards—and Tam saw several—didn't see him, and more important to Tam, didn't see them either. No mist or fog, and yet they were able to steal close to the largest tent and creep low to listen.

"How did we just do that?" Tam hissed in Seek's ear.

"I tweaked the dimensions," Seek said, preening his coat collar. "You wouldn't have noticed but we crossed into another realm. Very briefly—we're back now. I cannot keep us there indefinitely as we'd be torn apart. Takes concentration and requires careful timing. But a useful trick that helps in these situations."

"Nice of you to tell us," Tam said. Seek ignored him and started cutting a man-size slice through the bottom of the tent. "He's not?" Tam stared in horror as Seek slipped his coat off and rolled inside the hole he'd just made.

"You two wait here," Seek hissed back at them before disappearing inside.

"Shit," said Tam. "He's going to get us murdered for sure."

"I've been telling you that for days," said Stogi, and jumped through the hole in the tent.

"Stogi, wait," Tam scanned around, seeing the guards huddled over by the closest fire. One of many flickering all around him.

I don't believe I'm doing this.

Tam pulled back an edge and heaved his body through the rent, making sure his sword didn't get trapped in the canvas.

Inside the tent, dazzling firelight and heat hit him like a wall. Tam blinked, rolled, and lay still, sweaty palms gripping sword by scabbard and hilt. His initial worry was soon quelled as the tent was framed by vacant heavy tables and benches awarding ample cover. The three imposters huddled beneath a table.

The tent was huge but appeared mostly unoccupied save for the odd retainer or guard stationed here and there and at the entrance. Aside that, five important-looking men sat around an oval table, their faces flushed by torchlight, among them—Seek informed them in an excited whisper—the Ptarni ambassador and a senior Magister from Shen.

The ambassador, easily recognizable by his costly and gaudy attire, was speaking in crisp clear tones addressing the Magister, who was neatly garbed in crimson velvet, as though they were comrades playing at dice. The other men looked on, three Ptarnians—hard-faced fighters, swords at their sides but no armor, their masked helmets resting on the floor. Obviously, men of rank and discretion. Opposite these were three Shen, clad in plain black gowns—cruel-faced, silent watchers, their eyes flicking back and forth like glinting knives.

The ambassador's tone was rich and he spoke with comfortable assurance. A fat man with shaven head and large red face. "The Emperor has dreamed of this day, Magister. A day when the two greatest nations in Ansu unite against a common foe, and in doing so start an alliance that will bless us both for generations."

"I'm glad he's happy." The Magister's face was lily-white, resembling bleached parchment. He wore a long, well-combed mustache which he rubbed through his fingers every now and then. Tam could see the Magister's narrow eyes. Flat, hard currants set well back in his face. He looked by far the more dangerous of the two leaders present.

"But Callanz must understand this is not all about him," the Magister said, interlacing neat fingers, with velvet-covered elbows on table. "However powerful your 'emperor god' now believes himself to be."

"The Emperor is a man of peace." The ambassador spread his fat hands wide, tone patient yet slightly irritated. Clearly used to getting his own way, but the Shen Magister wasn't about to oblige. "Trade is essential between our nations. We can flourish, Magister."

"Your Emperor is also a man of vengeance as I recall." Tam saw the Magister's thin smile disappear as though swallowed by whiskers. "Peace and revenge seldom sit well together."

"Well, yes—there is a score to settle, and with Shen's help we can settle it fast." The Ambassador was waving his hands again. "Think of the advantages, and how your family, Magister, in particular, will rise to prominence. Once you gain a hold on the western ocean. Between us, Shen and Ptarni will control the trade routes on sea and land throughout the entire world. A stranglehold on the fools who dare stand against us."

"Tell me of this crystal king in the west and why your emperor hates him so much." The Magister leaned forward, his lizard eyes locked on the ambassador. Tam shuffled and held back a sneeze, aware that the slightest noise would trigger his throat being cut, or worse. Far worse.

"A common man who gained the throne through sorcery and happenstance," the ambassador said dismissively. "Seven years ago, after the event that shook the foundation of the world."

"A warrior-leader who destroyed the Ptarnian armies." The Magister almost smiled, and neatly combed his long mustache again with his brightly-colored painted fingernails.

"Our general was foolish and caught off guard." The ambassador's tone was annoyed now. "He served the old regime.

Emperor Callanz would never have sent such a craven fool out at the head of his armies. Our soldiers were lost in the carnage, caught in a war they had no part in."

"Wiped out in the crossfire?" The Magister smiled, enjoying his opposite's discomfort.

"It was unfortunate," the ambassador allowed. "Ten thousand Ptarnians died that day, all because of a general's folly."

"And this commoner made king was solely to blame?"

"The Crystal King he calls himself," the ambassador nodded emphatically. "The crown he wears fashioned that way. Yes, he led their armies. But there are others the Emperor would see in his dungeons. The little Queen Ariane being one such."

"I know nothing of whom you speak, and I still cannot see any evidence of Shen advantage for investing so much finance. I—"

Tam nearly choked on his tongue when Seek chose that moment to rise up from the table behind which he'd be hiding. Stogi cursed beneath his breath, and Tam saw faces turn and stare in amazement at Seek.

What the . . .?

Tam saw Seek's hand retrieve something from his sleeve. A blur of metal flashed inside the tent as the knife Seek hurled lodged itself in the Shen Magister's throat. The Magister gaped and choked as his lifeblood spilled onto the table.

Beside him the two other Shen leaped up seizing hidden knives. Quicker than Tam could blink, they slit the throats of both the Ptarni ambassador and his officers, and then rounded on the guards, Seek having already vacated the tent amidst the confusion, through the entrance.

Stogi grabbed Tam's arm and pulled him back through the tent hole. Outside was quiet until a harsh shout from a lone survivor who had escaped the Shen knives, and pitched face-first into the open air outside.

"Assassins! Murderers!" His yell split the night like thunder.

Tam almost crashed into Stogi as they sprinted for the distant dark, weaving around campfires, stabbing and kicking the odd stupefied soldier in the face. Tam could not see Seek anywhere, which was just as well as he'd happily stick a knife in that bastard should he show his face.

Steel clashed. Shouts filled the night. Men were mounting horses, the clatter of harness and hoof following on road. Tam and Stogi ran full pelt until gaining the sanctuary of relative safety in the gloom outside the enemy camp.

"What the fuck do we do now?" Tam asked his friend. "It will be a hornets' nest out here for days."

"Aye, best we warn the others, and sharpish," Stogi said. "And then head deeper into Shen. Hopefully they'll keep themselves occupied with murdering each other, so we few can slip away in the confusion."

"I admire your optimism," Tam said, running behind his friend and crashing back into the camp. Broon was there and the others, all mounted and ready for swift departure. Seek was there too, smiling as he straddled his horse.

"Told you you'd learn something, didn't I?" Seek said, grinning at Tam before wheeling his horse about.

"I'm going to murder that bugger," Tam told Stogi as he mounted his horse.

"Join the queue," Stogi said, urging his own mount kick up dust.

They rode east at speed, keeping a mile south of the road, the distant clash of steel and shouts fading off and finally disappearing. The riders continued until daylight and then set up a hurried camp on a bank by a river. They were deep into Shen and deeper into trouble, and Tam still had no idea what was going on.

Chapter 25 | Illusions

Pash reined in and stared at the shifting horizon. His heart was racing and a growing panic rising up from his belly. They were lost through no fault of their own. The road the three riders had followed for miles had just disappeared before their faces, replaced by a steep wooded valley, a busy river working its way through rocks far below.

Pash sat his horse grim-faced and silent. Alongside Kargon guided his steed close, and Coife emerged behind him, face tight with fear.

They were three days out from Largos and should have been well inside the Ptarni border. Instead they had lost all sense of direction several hours ago when a fog, thick as winter broth, settled over the land surrounding, panicking the horses. They'd lost the road in the chaos that followed but managed to stay in saddles despite the nervousness of their beasts.

Eventually they'd found another road. That proved a false path. The track looked the same but it wasn't and instead had led them Gods only knew where. And worse, night had stolen upon them, leaving them alone and powerless.

"Maybe we should have stayed with the captain," Coife said. But Kargon and Pash glared at him, and the dour archer shrugged. "We wouldn't have got lost then-- all I'm saying."

"We don't need the captain and his new friends," Pash said.

271

"We'll find—or fight—our way out of this region. We must have switched roads in that sudden fog, got off track."

"Oh, you think?" Coife's sarcasm dug deep.

"I daresay there'll be a village or hamlet somewhere close," Kargon said, not sounding overly optimistic. "Countryside looks hospitable enough, and I assume we're still in Laregoza."

"That might be, but where has the road gone?" said Kargon. "Nor do I remember seeing evidence of a forest before we were immersed in one."

"Come now, it's not as bad as it seems."

The voice came from the branches of a tree high above. Meanwhile, the mist was clearing fast to allow a pale moon slide into view high above the beeches, its white light filtering through.

"Who's there?" Pash slid his sword from his scabbard. "Show yourself!"

"But I'm in plain sight—you have only to look!" Laughter accompanied the voice, and Pash, looking up again, saw a man framed by moonlight, sitting neatly amid the branches some thirty feet above them. Beside him, Coife nocked fletch to bowstring with shaky fingers. Where had this fellow come from?

"Oh, you won't be needing that," the man said. He was small, clad in dun brown trousers and jacket. A broad belt hung at his waist, and from it Pash could just make out a bag of sorts with something long and thin inside.

"Come down," Pash beckoned the stranger climb and join them.

"I prefer it up here—more vision, even at night—though clarity's perhaps a better word." He laughed as though he'd said something clever.

"Are we in Ptarni?" Kargon said, shielding his eyes to see the man better.

"No indeed, that's far from here."

"Where then?" Pash demanded.

"You are deep within Rundal Woods, many days ride from Laregoza and even further from Ptarni."

"That's not possible," Pash said. "I think you're a liar, a trickster, and you serve that witch, or else the Rana in Largos."

"The Rana?" The laughter again. "Interesting idea. As for a witch, I know three and have no intention of serving them. Dangerous ladies."

"Either you come down here or Coife will shoot you out of that tree," Pash said, pointing up at the man. "I don't know what you're up to, but you don't want to tangle with us. We are weary, lost, and need provisions and guidance. Unless you can help us, I suggest you clear off before you get hurt."

"You cannot hurt me." The man's voice hardened, and his tone changed from light to menacing. Moonlight shimmered, and the man disappeared for a moment and then re-emerged further up the tree.

"That ain't right," Kargon said, and Pash heard Coife's bowstring twang beside him.

"Wait!" Pash hissed. Too late, the arrow shot true, but the target had vanished. Above them were bare branches, breeze, and night air.

"Why did you do that?" Pash snapped, his nerves on the brink of eruption.

Coife said nothing, just gaped at the branches above.

"Let's get moving," Kargon said, "no point us lingering here." It was pitch dark now, the moon swallowed by sudden cloud, and the trees closed in around them, stifling the atmosphere.

Suddenly, where none had been before, Pash saw twinkling lights in the distance. He felt a glimmer of hope. Sanctuary? A village perhaps? Somewhere where they could take refuge from the strangeness of this wood, and regroup in the morning. They were lost, yes, but Pash told himself that freak had been lying. Rundal Woods were far from here—if they existed at all.

"I don't like this," Kargon said, guiding his horse through the dense canopy of brush close behind the other two, the twinkle of lights luring them on.

"What choice have we?" Coife said. "I'd sooner not spend the night creeping about in these woods."

They reined in, startled. An opening in the trees hinted a wide green lawn fringed by neatly trimmed bushes. The sky had cleared above, showing a diadem of stars, and the moon rode past defying cloud. Again, Pash felt the hairs lift on the nape of his neck.

Something isn't right here.

But what choice did they have? Coife was already guiding his beast into the glade. Pash exchanged looks with Kargon, whose hard face looked tense and edgy. "After you," Kargon said.

As Pash entered the glade the distant lights winked into dazzling brightness, flooding the lawn and surrounding trees with silver glow, and chasing shadows like skulking night creatures into dense corners of the garden.

That was it for the horses; they reared and frothed at bit until Pash dismounted and his friends followed suit. The beasts were uncontrollable and soon broke free from their riders.

"We'll find them in the morning," Pash said, waving his arms in desperation. "They won't stray far in this thicket."

"Pash." Kargon's voice, sounding alarmed behind him. Pash turned.

A man stood there smiling; the long black coat he wore brushed highly polished boots. His face was hidden by a mask and a cap covered his head. He wore white gloves and used these to beckon them closer.

"Welcome to the Manor in the Woods," the man said, his voice warm and friendly, though faintly hollow. "I am Solace—the custodian of this forest. You are weary and confused, as is to be expected. You can rest here for the night, or longer should you wish to. We don't get many visitors in the Manor, being so far from the road."

"Where is this place?" Pash said, but the masked man just turned and walked back through the garden leading to the shadow of distant buildings, a hint of brick and stone almost hidden in the glare.

"You won't need those horses tonight." The man called Solace turned again at the entrance, and Pash started as pale figures emerged from behind the light and surrounded them.

"Something's wrong here," Kargon said. "Where's he gone?"

"Coife!" Pash turned shading his face with a hand. He could just discern Coife's silhouette surrounded by silvery figures that were guiding him toward the shadow of the house. Pash flashed Kargon a look. "Come—let's not leave him with them alone." Pash took a step forward. Behind him, Kargon cursed and followed suit.

"Come, your supper awaits!" The masked man vanished inside the house, and the lights dimmed, just allowing them to find the wide stately entrance and walk through the gap between doors. Inside was a large foyer leading to wide sweeping alabaster stairs. Pash saw candles everywhere, sconces flickering, parading the walls, and from the ceiling a huge diamond chandelier chased more shadows from the hall.

The three men were led through countless rooms, all lit with candles but deserted and deathly quiet. Pash felt a warning tremor along his spine. But what choice did they have but to follow? At last they reached a door that opened into a long dark room dominated by a single table of polished oak, with a fire flickering at stone hearth at the far end.

The table brimmed with all manner of meat, fruit, and forest fare.

Crystal vases with ruby studs held wine and liquor, and there were three fine-stemmed glasses lined in a row—all brimming with the same wine, the colour of freshly spilt blood.

"Please, be seated." The man in the mask bid them forward with his white gloves. "The family will join you shortly. In the meantime, help yourself to everything you see."

He faded from the room like a lantern being slowly shuttered. Pash found himself staring at the table, his stomach rumbling but his mind unwilling to sample anything lest it be poison.

"Leave that!" Kargon shoved Coife's hand away as he reached for a chicken leg. "Don't eat anything. We should never have come here. Can't you sense it? This place reeks of enchantment."

Coife grinned at him and snatched up the chicken leg, biting hard into it. "That may be so, but this chicken tastes better than anything I've had in months." He crunched and reached for the wine, took a long slow sip and sighed. "Oh—that's good, boys!" Coife said, the wine staining his lips in a way that sent a shiver up Pash's spine.

"Coife, be careful!" Pash warned his friend. "Let's wait and find out more before we get too deep into this food and wine."

"Too late for him," Kargon said, and Coife laughed at him, his eyes dilated and face flushed red with excitement.

Pash felt a brush of sharp air as a zephyr glided past him. He turned. A woman stood there, tall, her long pale hair and white skin flawless. She too wore a mask, but Pash could tell she was beautiful, and the dress that clung to those curves revealed her nakedness beneath.

The woman smiled and brushed her icy fingers along the back of Pash's neck. Pash shivered at that touch, but felt his manhood rise up and blood surge hungry within.

"You can relax," she smiled beneath that mask, the corner of her lips just visible. "There are many pleasures to be had in the Manor in the Woods." She slid her icy, dry fingers down and found what she sought. Pash sighed as she worked his breeches loose and then kneeled low before him.

"Pash, no!" Kargon shoved the woman aside. She stood without sound, her manner cold and remote, and took seat at the table opposite. Others were entering now, all silent, their faces hidden by masks. The woman's domino was focused solely on Pash.

"Your friend is foolish not to partake in our pleasures," she breathed, and those half-hidden eyes flashed briefly at Kargon. Pash caught just a glimpse of the ice within that gaze. He exchanged looks with his friend.

Need to get out while we can.

But Coife looked happy. Seated at the far side of the table, eating and drinking apace, his long face uncommonly merry. Almost he appeared a different person entirely. Kargon looked more uncomfortable than ever, and Pash, despite his lust for the woman across the table, determined they make a move before things got even stranger.

Solace reappeared and removed his hat and gloves but retained his mask, taking silent seat at the head of the table. As though that were a signal, the hearth behind him roared into flame like dragon breath.

"Why do you not eat like your friend?" Solace asked them. "You will feel better for it. See how Coife enjoys this evening."

"How do you know his name?" Pash asked, but another pale-eyed woman had seated herself beside him and she rubbed sharp fingers along his thighs. Pash closed his eyes and then, with heroic effort, lifted her cold, spidery hand from his leg.

"We would have answers, Master Solace," Pash said. "We are lost and need to return to our home. Been away far too long."

"That is no longer possible." Solace folded his gloves and set them neatly on the table. "You are now my honored guests, and as such must remain here forever. You, gentlemen, will neither grow old nor weaken, and every day you will eat and drink and flood your seed inside whomever you desire, be it man or woman. All is on offer here."

Pash glanced at Coife, currently kissing the woman next to him, as she slid her long fingers inside his shirt and stroked his chest. "Stop that," Pash warned his friend, but Coife didn't hear him.

"Love me." The first woman had appeared by his side again. She clutched his hand in her own and pressed it to the hot damp spot between her thighs. "Love me!"

A noise to Pash's left brought him back to his senses. Kargon had leaped up from his table and kicked it away. "Pash, wake up! Let's get out of here while we still can!"

Pash nodded, pushed the woman away from him, and rose to his feet. "We got to leave," Pash told Solace, and all eyes watched him from the table, apart from Coife and the woman disrobing him. "Coife!" Pash yelled at his friend.

"It's too late for him," Kargon grabbed Pash's arm and made for the door, which creaked open to allow them out. Pash lingered just long enough to witness the woman, now completely naked—her white thighs straddled across his friend—lean forward and sink neatly filed teeth deep into Coife's neck, just as the masked man beside her stabbed him with his thin eating knife.

Horrified, Pash watched for frozen seconds as man and woman lapped at Coife's lifeblood like greedy carrion birds after a battle. Blood oozed from Coife's shuddering corpse. Worst of all was the expression on Coife's lost face. His lips smiled, but those eyes were glazed in terror. Pash turned and fled the room.

***

Kargon crashed through lamplit rooms with no idea where he was going. *Got to get out of here!* Corridors led to more rooms and these opened into more corridors, a maze turning within itself. Kargon ran, crashed through furniture, regained his feet, and ran on.

Never should have come here!

He sensed rather than saw shadows following, and the sconces flickered as he stumbled half-blind and confused through the dusty silent rooms. At last he almost fell into the entrance foyer and gasped in relief.

The front doors were open. Kargon didn't waste a second, pelted through the gap, and sprinted across the lawns until he was immersed in the deep cover of the forest, and the moon-haunted night surrounding it. Only then did he realize Pash wasn't with him. No time to fret about that now.

Kargon distanced himself from the glade and its house, walking fast as he could beneath the thick canopy, the dense undergrowth tripping him and stabbing his legs. He didn't notice. Turning back twice saw the distant lights of Solace's manner winking and then finally vanishing as night and distance swallowed them whole.

He walked and ran, staggered, tripped, and crawled, for what must have been hours, the terror of the forest eating into him and pushing him on. Throughout the night Kargon heard weird noises, beastly snarls, screams, and the distant stomp of heavy feet. He stopped once, hearing a young girl sobbing close. "Who's that?" Silence, followed a by the shuffle of tiny feet. "I said who's there?" Kargon's eyes scanned every nearby bush. He saw nothing through that maze of thorn, root, and vines crawling over rotting mulch and fungus, the latter giving off sickly faint glow like corpse lamps at graveyards.

Kargon pushed on through the forest, weariness and fear battling to consume him.

Have to keep going—must be an end to this wood . . .

As though the forest heard his thoughts the canopy changed around him. A faint breeze lifted his hair. Above his head, the sky shone black, and ahead Kargon saw tall pines like sentinels marking the way. A hill loomed close, a track leading on up.

Kargon felt his legs buckle beneath him as he struggled up the steepening slopes of that rise. He climbed, exhausted, his legs like lead. He should have reached the top long ago. He felt sick and dizzy, but after an hour's climb Kargon crested the rise and filled his lungs with fresh clean air. He stood on the crown of a bald rocky knoll. A lone island, surrounded by stalking cankerous green, the dark whispering canopy of forest below.

High above, the horned moon rode free again, shedding silver on Kargon's face. The sky had paled, and far to the east Kargon glimpsed the first hint of pink that promised dawn. He felt a flood of relief and turned to see the tall man watching him from the cover of trees that flanked the knoll's bare crown.

The man wore a deep blue cloak, almost black in that half-light, his features shrouded by a wide-brimmed pointed hat. The figure strolled towards Kargon, hefting a long spear across broad shoulders, its tip glinting in the moonlight.

"You, deserter, should have stayed with your captain." The stranger's voice was crow rough. He pointed the spear at Kargon, who fell to his knees and felt his bladder loosen.

"Who are you?"

No answer—just the sudden rush of wind through pines above his head. Then the racing moon slid behind a rack of cloud, allowing the darkness regain the hill, hiding the stranger and his deadly spear.

Kargon found his feet again.

He ran back down the slopes, re-entering the woods. Morning was nearly here; Kargon had only to hold on and stay alive until it found him. So close. Kargon turned sharply, cursed as his arm entangled in a bramble. The poisonous thorn dug deep, ripping his flesh and sending a shot of pain from wrist to shoulder.

He fought himself free as the briar clung and twisted, cutting his face and neck too, the hot blood blurring his vision as fresh pain throbbed. Kargon broke loose from the poisonous vine, shook the blood from his face, and then froze. The figure stood yards away, hat covering his features, gloved hands resting on the spear shaft.

"You cannot escape; I already own your soul."

Kargon heard the cry of a wolf close by, while far above his head a questing owl hooted, its cold voice answered by its mate seconds later.

"Yffarn take you, Specter!" Kargon crashed free of the undergrowth, sword loose in hand, slicing, cutting at trees, limbs, and roots. "Out of my way!"

He blundered into a path that led to a clearing, where expanding pale light hinted the end of the forest.

I've made it!

Kargon sprinted toward the clearing in the trees. He'd made it! But just as his feet crashed through the leafy mantle at the forest's edge, the ground parted beneath him. A pit; it swallowed him whole. Kargon screamed as the stakes at the bottom pierced his flesh and the hard ground beneath them shattered his bones.

Broken and helpless, Kargon looked up and saw the shadowy figure gazing down at him, his face hidden beneath that pointed hat.

"You are mine now," the specter said. Kargon felt cold fingers pulling him down through the earth and choking his life with wet soil and icy stone.

***

Pash had found the doors leading to the garden without any

difficulty. He'd walked from the feasting hall in a half-daze, his clouded mind still full of the image of Coife being devoured at dinner. He had almost crashed through the entrance without noticing. After that he'd been lucky, finding one of their horses staggering as though blind, and after soothing and mounting the animal, Pash soon reached the road.

He rode without any sense of direction, like Kargon his sole focus on morning's arrival, and escape from this accursed wood. He reined in once, hearing a scream trail off into the night. Pash blanched—he knew a man's death cry when he heard it.

Kargon?

No point thinking about that. Pash had his own skin to save. Survive—all that mattered. Pash thought of the captain and young Doyle. He felt the tears race down his face as he regretted his choice to abandon their quest.

"It's your fault, Garland!" Pash said, as he urged his horse pick up pace down the lane. The beast was exhausted but like its master yearned for freedom from this witchy wood. "You led us astray— never would have left you else." Pash reined in suddenly, the sweat shining his face. He'd reached an end to the forest. Like parting curtains, the vista opened welcomingly before him. Dawn pinked the sky ahead, and Pash, clearing the last of the trees, gazed in wonder upon a vision of beauty.

Horse and rider gazed down from a wide slab of rock. A high place, the shoulder of a mountain frowning from either side. Ahead, the road cut zig-zag down through deep rifts, before disappearing in a hazy valley below. Beyond that, in the far distance, Pash saw the ocean sparkling as early morning sun settled on its surface.

The sea—I am alive . . .

Pash scanned that distant horizon until his blurred exhausted gaze settled on a sharp promontory capped by a tall green tower. The tower seemed to call across to him, and Pash knew should he reach it, he'd find sanctuary within. A single green light flashed on and off like a beacon from the top of the tower. Pash guessed it was scarce more than twenty miles distant.

Mind drugged by reckless joy and relief, Pash urged his mount down the steep twisting road until he reached the valley below. There he stopped, hearing voices in the distance. Men approaching. They'd seen him.

"Hey there!" Pash called out, but when someone shouted behind him, he turned, his voice trailing off in terror.

A giant was striding toward him. Clad from head to toe in metal, the face hidden beneath a huge canister of a helmet. Pash urged his horse about but the beast panicked and threw him from saddle. Pash cursed in pain as he collided with the floor of the valley. He looked up just in time to see the mace swinging down on him.

***

Sulo watched the Grogan standing over the body of the rider, his mace rising and falling until there was nothing but fleshy pulp. "What's the matter with that bastard?" Sulo said to the Grogan's men who surrounded him and watched their leader doing his work with detached repetition.

"The Grogan kills." The man addressing him was thin, his face ravaged with self-loathing and his eyes half-glazed like the damned.

"Makes no sense," Sulo said. He was a killer, but to butcher a stranger without any reason was beyond even his mandate. "That man could have helped us!"

The pitiful creatures around him just watched on without a word until the Grogan finished his gory work and rejoined them in silence. Sulo glared at the giant for a moment and then leaped back up into his saddle.

Means to an end.

He'd be free of the Grogan creature and his mindless slaves soon enough. That monster would help him get Elerim's bow, and once Sulo had that he'd find those fugitives, Tamersane and Teret, and cut out their treacherous hearts. The Grogan might be a machine of death, but Sulo's heart was blacker than the monster's. Sulo had a reason to kill, and that made him far more dangerous.

Chapter 26 | Rundal Woods

"A ship would serve you best," the Rana had told him, and Garland had heeded her advice, taking passage on a schooner bound for distant Shen and the far coast, regions Garland knew nothing about.

Three days out from Largos Port, their first destination was Sorloza in eastern Laregoza; from there they'd purchase fresh horses and cut north, and then head due east to the Rundali border, and beyond to the far coast.

Garland had inquired why they couldn't sail right up to the Castle of Lights, as it was clearly marked as being on the coast. He'd scrutinized the old map the Rana had shown him in her study and memorized the journey as best he could.

She'd told him the coast near Rundali was almost impassable: a chain of rocks called the Scrapes had torn apart endless ships. And to sail further out to sea would risk encountering Shen galleys, or merchantmen on their way to the south lands. Shen were hostile and sank any ship not recognized.

The Bruhan was with him, and twenty chosen men who'd accompanied him from the garrison at Talimi. Good men, Brew had told him. Garland had grunted they would need to be. But it was hard to hold on to pessimism on a day like this. Warm sun, the sea's freshness, and salt keening his eyes. A coastline of sandy red cliffs, a mile to port.

Sailors were busy, the helmsman standing silent on the aft deck, gulls swooping and mewling, timbers creaking beneath his feet, and warm breeze ruffling his hair. A good day to be alive. Garland would be happy today were he not weighed down by worry.

How had things gone so awry? Had he failed his men—veterans he'd been through so much with? Tough, loyal lads. One dead and three gone, and Loyal Doyle more than happy to leave too, despite his protestations otherwise.

Tol and Taylon were the only two left with him. Garland hadn't shown it, but Pash's desertion had hit him hard. The men had been with him for years. More than just soldiers, they were Garland's comrades and friends. They loved him, as he loved them. They'd survived a score of battles spread over three decades, only to quarrel and break up here on the edge of the world.

My fault.

Was he wrong to pursue this quest? Pash had been right to say their mandate was to discover what they could about Tamersane and his lady. And they'd achieved that at the Lake of Stones, and since then little—were it to be measured that way.

I must not lose faith like Pash did.

Garland knew there was a reason why he was continuing this journey—now a voyage into the unknown. He knew it was meant to be, but also knew he could have handled things better. Too late to change that now. Best he leave those doubts behind. The inner voice Queen Ariane had told him to heed still urged him, despite every logical thought tugging at him and questioning why.

"I like this craft." Tol stood alongside, his long dark hair tied back in a pony tail and a new earring studding his left ear. He was smiling, handsome and tanned under the hot Laregozan sun.

"You look like a bloody pirate," Garland said. "Where did you get that earring?"

"Gift from one of the servants at the Rana's palace," Tol said. "Pretty lass; she took a shine to me. Wearing it for her—I promised."

"Doesn't suit you." Garland turned away and watched the gulls following their wake. "You're not a gypsy, or a sailor." The schooner cut crisp and clean through aquamarine waters, her sixteen sails taut and billowed in the blow. Garland managed a smile. "But you are right," he said. "A fine ship; I've not seen its like before."

"I have, while on leave at Port Wind," Taylon said, joining them. "Beast of a thing. Had a ram, fourteen sails—out of the far north. Boys in the tavern told me its Captain was a giant, some hero from the war with Caswallon." Taylon wiped fruit from his mouth and smiled at the sunshine. He'd just joined them from the galley below where he'd been eating mangoes. Taylon looked good, Garland thought. His arm was fully healed, and a rare sunny expression was on his face. He'd cropped his fair hair short and grown a stubble beard to match. That made him look tougher, sharp. Like Tol and their captain, Taylon was enjoying the voyage.

"Sounds like Barin of Valkador," Garland said. "Captain of the *Starlight Wanderer*. I met him very briefly—a terrifying fellow. Not easily forgotten."

"Good with an ax," Tol said.

"None better," Garland said. "That man is a legend. Doyle was with Barin at the siege of Calprissa when he was just a lad. Told me he'd never seen an ax wielded with such skill and ferocity."

"Did he survive the war?" Tol asked, but Garland's eyes were on the Bruhan approaching via ladder from the main deck below.

"A fine morning." Bruhan Dahali looked fresh and sharp, his clean-shaven face almost shining in the sun. "Captain says we'll make Sorloza by nightfall." Garland was almost disappointed hearing that; he would have liked a few more days at sea.

"How far then?" Garland asked the Bruhan.

"A week, maybe two?"

"That long?"

The Bruhan shrugged. "depends on the weather, Captain."

They docked late that night, the harbor lit by crescent moon. The Bruhan paid up front for lodging for his men and Garland, Taylon, and Tol. A scruffy tavern on the quayside, it sufficed, and the ale was good. Garland spent an hour in the taproom with Tol. Taylon, the Bruhan, and his people had sensibly retired right away.

Tol's eyes were on the dark-skinned girl with sleek black hair weaving between tables, the plates she carried perfectly balanced. "I like these eastern women," Tol said. "They move well."

"You like all women." Garland wondered if this place stayed open all night. Dawn was not that far away. But it was good to think and relax with a cool dark ale. And Tol was right, the smiling lass was pleasing on the eyes.

"True enough," Tol said. "But these Laregozan girls have style, so graceful the way they saunter about. And that dark skin . . ."

"Shut up, Tol," Garland said. "I'm trying to think."

"Taverns are for drinking not thinking." Tol drained his cup and nudged his captain's shoulder. "I'm done for the night, Caps." He winked at the girl, who curled a lip as she drifted by. "I'm just upstairs," Tol told her.

"I don't care," she said, the smile falling from her face.

"Worth a try." Tol grinned and vanished from the room.

Garland sighed, envying Tol's easy manner and lack of worry. A cheerful demeanor got you through lots in this life. Again, he thought about Pash and the others.

Not my fault—their choice.

If only he could believe that. A soft sound to his left. Garland raised an eyebrow as the girl settled beside him, her chores finished for the moment.

"Your friend is overfamiliar," she said, brushing dark hair from her face. She was even prettier up close, those huge brown eyes intelligent and curious.

"He means no harm," Garland said quietly, wondering what she wanted.

"And you?"

"Me?" Garland placed his ale on the table. "What about me?"

"Look like a man drowned in worry."

"Oh—it's not like that, but I do have things on my mind."

"Another ale?" The girl smiled.

"In a minute—no rush," Garland grinned back at her. "You are working late tonight."

"Always," she said. "My father's inn stays open beyond dawn, ready for the fishers returning for their breakfast. She paused, her body shaking slightly, and those dark eyes misting over.

"Is anything wrong?"

Her gaze narrowed to flint chips, and she jabbed a finger into Garland's chest. "Stay away from Rundali, Garland of Kelwyn. You will find nothing but death in that land."

Garland gasped and clutched his chair in alarm. The young woman's face had changed completely. Instead of her bright dark eyes, he was staring deep into the pale hard eyes of a woman who much resembled Ysaren at the Lake of Stones, though Ysaren's hair was dark as jet, the dress she wore like liquid rubies.

"Who?" The vision passed, and instead he saw the girl looking at him askance.

"What's the matter?" she said. "Your face went white—are you sick?"

"I don't feel too good," Garland said, made his excuses, and stumbled out of the taproom, aware off the girl's eyes watching him in puzzlement. Other less friendly faces watched his departure from the far corners of the room, and Garland was relieved when he found the stairs and slipped up to the stall where Tol was already snoring next to Taylon.

Garland sank into his cot and gazed up at the ceiling. What was happening to him? Garland tried to sleep, but the memory of the woman's face drifted through his mind. Ysaren's sister—but which one? And why warn him? Too many riddles for his tired mind. So, Garland gave up trying to sleep and just lay staring until dawn's light spilled gold through the drapes.

That morning they bought horses and provisions for a long ride. The Bruhan handled everything, much to Garland's relief, as his head was foggy and full of doubt. The woman's face branded in his memory--pale eyes, white skin and long silky dark hair. And something else. A cruel hard way about her. That beautiful face—alien and cold—was almost Ysaren's. But last night's mystery woman had looked younger.

"You ready?" Taylon said, his words jolting Garland back to the present as he and Tol guided their horses alongside the Captain's. They were lined up outside the market stable yard where they'd purchased the beasts. Fine stallions, sleek and chestnut, and bought for a good price too, so the Bruhan had told him.

"I'm more than ready," Garland said to Taylon and urged his horse forward. "Past time we got going."

An hour's trot led from port into city. Sorloza was much like Largos, with its maze of streets, low-roofed houses, and the occasional bigger building hinting a tavern, hostel, or wealthy residence.

Their road wound up ever tighter, until the street widened and Garland saw a white building shimmering in the heat ahead. A temple of sorts it looked. Strange in design, with pointed turrets, comprising twisting stone, and one huge central dome the color of deepest emerald.

"That's a sight to behold on a sunny morning," Tol said from somewhere behind. "Beautiful is it not?"

"Built by whom?" Garland asked the Bruhan as they wound their way beneath the temple or whatever it was.

"The Aralais," the Bruhan replied. "There are several such monstrosities in Laregoza."

"You don't like it?" Garland was surprised, as the building was magnificent, with its spiraling towers and glittering green roof.

"It reminds us of the slaves we once were."

"Slaves?" Garland shook his head, puzzled by the answer.

"To the Golden Folk." The Bruhan scowled up at the dome. "They say thousands died building that temple. Our sorry history, Sir Garland." The Bruhan's face was so grim Garland decided to let the matter rest and kept his lips together until they reached the far gates, and after showing papers, left Sorloza behind.

Three uneventful hot days found them at the Rundali River, a fast-paced stream broken with rocks and islets, where herons stood like skinny sentinels marking their approach.

"Behold the gateway to Rundali," the Bruhan said. "The river is treacherous, but there is a ford close by where we can pass without issue."

"You have been here before?" Garland wondered why his friend hadn't mentioned that.

"Posted hereabouts as a recruit before I got my commission," the Bruhan said. "Rundali is a strange place, the forest within it worse than strange. To appreciate that, all new conscripts have to spend a couple of weeks by this river."

"What's strange about it?" Taylon asked from behind.

"Hard to explain. You see things," the Bruhan said. "Things not seen anywhere else."

"Things?" Taylon grinned at Tol who shrugged. "What kind of things?"

"Emerald bows," Garland hinted.

"No," the Bruhan shook his head. He looked annoyed that they seemed to be joking about his revelations. "I'm talking about creatures, or entities, not sure which."

"Keep selling Rundali to me, Bruhan," Garland said with a chuckle. Despite his show of mirth, the Captain had a growing sense of dread.

Do not enter Rundali.

They soon reached the ford which, as the Bruhan had said, proved easy to cross, and just twenty minutes later they had guided their mounts up the steep banks of the Rundali shore. After that they crested a long ridge, awarding wide views of the land ahead. Garland saw swards of grass coating gentle slopes, a rolling swath of green beneath deep blue sky.

"Doesn't look that bad," Tol said, and Garland noticed how the Bruhan tightened his lips.

He's not wanting to be here.

"So now we ride east to the coast?" Garland had studied the map but wanted to goad some comment from the Bruhan who appeared oddly quiet, his men the same. Curt and on edge. So much so as to cause concern.

"If we can, yes," the Bruhan told him.

"I thought the road ran straight toward it," Garland said. "Looked like that on the map."

"I know, but sometimes the forest surrounds it and things get confused."

"Sometimes?"

"Not always, but often," the Bruhan said, and Tol stifled a snigger.

"So, like, the trees move around?" Garland saw Tol wink at Taylon and signaled both be quiet.

"I didn't see a forest marked on the map," Garland said. "Just a blur that could have meant anything."

"It's not marked," the Bruhan said. "And hopefully we won't see it." Once again, he refused to shed light on the mystery, and Garland was content to wait and see.

"They must have told each other stories when they were based here," Garland said to his two men late that night by the campfire, the Bruhan and his volunteers already settled in their blankets, though Garland doubted they slept, spooked as they appeared.

"Aye, scared each other shitless by the sound of it," Tol said, blinking at the fire and yawning. "Weird creatures, a magical forest—sounds like a bloody fairy tale. What's next, the wicked witch? These Laregozans have vivid imaginations. You all right, Captain?" Tol's eyes looked concerned, seeing the strain on Garland's face.

"Don't joke about witches," Garland said, and rolled over in his blanket. "Get some sleep."

"Good night!" Tol said. "At least the moon's not full."

"Shut up," Garland said, closing his eyes. He slept well for a time.

But that following morning when they awoke deep within a canopy of trees, the three westerners were as confused and alarmed as everyone else. That night they'd camped in an open field close by the road. The morning found them in a deep dark wood, and no sign of road, or even any hint of as much as a deer track.

"What the fuck?" Taylon said, his hard eyes wide with fear.

"Steady lads." Garland rose, wiped sleep from his eyes, and tried to take in what had happened. The camp was in uproar, the Bruhan's men muttering, their leader's face tight-lipped and sweat-stained, his eyes filled with dread. Garland slid his sword free of its scabbard and strode through the camp as though he meant to attack the trees single-handed. The horses, already skittish, looked on the brink of panic.

Garland grabbed the reins of the nearest. "I suggest we get moving, lads," he said. "No point us gawping and crashing into each other. You warned us of this," he turned toward the Bruhan. "I'm sorry I didn't listen."

"We must go back!" the Bruhan yelled at him. "Depart this wood while we still can—see how it thickens already." As Garland watched, it was almost as if the trees were moving, closing in around them. Listening, even.

This cannot be!

Garland turned and crashed into Tol, who was swearing, his bow gripped in both hands, fingers shaking and unable to nock arrow to string.

"Grab those bloody horses and let's get moving!" Garland swung up into the saddle of his beast and urged the animal find a way through the thickening gloom. It was darker than it should have been, and a mist was rising like steam from the ground beneath him. Garland scowled, sorcery or not he'd find an answer in or beyond these woods. *No going back.* That option had left him as behind the trees formed an unpenetrable wall, thorns as long as spears thrusting out of the dark.

That mist rose fast, and Garland soon lost sense of sight and sound, the men and horses around him just blurs. Noises became muffled, distorted. Horses neighing, confused shouts, and far more worrying, the odd clash of steel—all muffled and mingling, fading and dwindling into a distant rumble of nothingness.

Garland heard Tol cry out as though struck by something.

"Tol!" *Tol?*

Nothing. Silence surrounded him, and the shadows of trees leaned low as if trying to smother rider and horse. Garland cursed and struggled to control the beast as he guided it through the maze of wood, stooping low as damp branches wiped his face and roots snagged the horse's hoofs, threatening to trip her. *Keep moving—has to be a way out of here.* The silence grew until a tangible menace hung like spiders' webs in the cloying air. Garland turned, looked back, but saw nothing save trunk and branch, and a narrow hint of sky somewhere far above.

He reined in sharp, hearing cold laughter rising from the ground beneath him. The horse stumbled as a pit opened beneath bracken. As his steed vanished into the hole, Garland threw himself free of the saddle and rolled as the ground sucked at him. It was though icy steel fingers were pulling him beneath the earth. He heard the horse's hoofs scraping somewhere below, and then there was nothing.

Garland channeled his fear into anger, awarding him strength. Cursing, he pulled his body free of whatever force was pulling him under. Again, Garland rolled and, stumbling to his feet, hobbled and tripped his way free of the bracken. The wood lay dense and silent all around him. Smothering, deep, and moist.

His horse gone and men missing. Garland freed his sword and clutched it with both hands.

Come on—show your face! Spiteful spirit, or whatever you are.

Wings brushed his ear, and an owl settled softly on a branch. The owl became a woman, her face beautiful yet cruel. The hair dark, and her slim body draped inside a ruby dress that shimmered in the gloom. She blew him a kiss, then vanished like drifting smoke. Garland swung his sword at the smoke in desperation.

The vision past, Garland slanted the weapon across his shoulder and started walking through the murk, fully aware that he was lost and the chances of any escape from this sorcerous wood looked slim. He chewed his lip and tightened his grip on the sword. Whether this was an enchanter testing him or something worse, his only chance of survival was to keep moving forward, deeper into the trap. Face this hidden foe head on.

He walked and then, as the ground became more even, ran, crashing through brush and tripping and cursing, clambering, ripping thorns and vines from his face. Yelling and cussing—anything to keep the terror he felt at bay.

As he ran, Garland tripped again and tumbled into a dell, the sword flying from his grasp. Another hidden pit. Garland looked down and gasped, seeing Kargon lying down there. Ten foot below, his body pierced with sharpened stakes, and a look of frozen horror on his dead face.

Kargon?

Garland blinked back tears of rage. Kargon should be in Ptarni by now—far from here. The forest was messing with his mind.

I mustn't panic—stay calm and survive. This story doesn't end here. "Not by a long shot."

The voice came from behind him. He turned but saw nothing.

"Your tale, Sir Garland, has only just begun." This time the words drifted out from a rock lying a few yards to Garland's left.

"Show yourself, trickster!" Garland stopped and picked up his sword, leveling the blade at the rocks close by. Laughter, now behind him again.

Garland circled slowly, fingers greasy on his sword hilt. A man sat cross-legged on an oval stone, his round pink face dominated by a smile and the floppy hat he wore pulled down tight over his ears. Rotund and jolly, he was wrapped in a long blue coat with shining black boots, and in his left hand was a reedy pipe, which he tapped against his ample belly, as though much amused by what he witnessed.

"I've been waiting for you," the fat man said.

Garland clutched the weapon tighter with both hands and stepped slowly toward the stranger. "What witchery is this?" Garland said, glaring at the chinless man watching him with amused eyes the color of blackbirds' eggs.

"None of my doing," the Piper said, "of that I can assure you."

"Whose then?"

"One of the three, I suspect."

"Three?" Garland stuck his blade into the soil and leaned on the crosspiece, flexing his arms, ready to strike should the need arise. "Three what?"

"Three sisters who haunt this country. Or try to—they've not the power they once had, poor dears. You've already encountered one, maybe two. The third is around too—her I can feel." He shivered noticeably. "Oh, yes, Cille is biting today."

"Where are my men?" Garland's eyes flicked away from the Piper. The man was alone. Whatever game he played seemed harmless for the moment. Garland relaxed his body; no point wearing his muscles out in useless tension.

"How should I know?" the Piper said. "I'm a stranger here too. I go where the road leads me, you see. The right road, that is. I try to stay off the wrong ones." Garland hoisted his blade again and pointed the tip at the man's boots.

"I'm going to slice those off unless you start giving me some answers. What are you—a sorcerer, or some woodland imp? Don't much matter—daresay you'll bleed either way."

"You cannot touch me," the fat man's voice took on a peeved tone. "I'm just the wayfinder. A helpful soul to guide you along best I can. Trying to help, Sir Garland, and it's nice to be appreciated. You're worse than Tamersane."

Garland froze, the sword sliding to the ground again, its point digging in the soft forest floor. "You know of Tamersane of Kelwyn?"

"Indeed, he was here but recently."

"Here? When? And where the fuck is this place?"

"Rundal Woods," the Piper said as though that explained everything. "Time moves differently here. An hour, maybe two, Tamersane and another. He took the middle road," the Piper said. "I can't remember which one his friend took."

"I see no roads."

"Try looking in the right places," the Piper flicked his instrument toward a gap showing in the trees ahead.

This mist now clearing, Garland was only half surprised to see a smooth paved lane parting the trees and leading to a crossroads, the sun shining on grass that tufted through the cobbled stone of the path. A gibbet stood there, a lone black bird perched silent on the arm.

Garland felt an icy shudder reach inside his bowels. He suspected he knew who this was smiling in the sunshine. "I thought you dead," Garland said. "Are you the corpse gatherer? Am I taken already?"

"No on both counts, but things are complicated," the Piper said. "You need to choose a path soon or you'll perish. It's perilous in this wood after dark, and nightfall approaches."

"It's early morning, scarce past dawn."

"I already told you, time passes differently here," the Piper said. "You are at the Waysmeet, Sir Garland. Best you choose wisely and be about your day."

Garland wanted to slice the man smiling at him in two but realized he had to decide. Three paths showed ahead. A plain sight, however troubling. Behind and surrounding him, nothing but wood and gloom and a deepening feeling of menace. Going forward seemed the best choice.

Keep moving and stay alive.

"So Tamersane took the middle one?"

"Yes, but that was then and this is now," the Piper smiled. "The roads change, and their destination is not always the same."

"Well, which one then?"

"Your choice." The Piper showed that infuriating smile again. "I cannot decide that for you—not my job."

"Yffarn take you then!" Garland turned his back on the laughing fat man and strode as briskly as he could through the bracken and briar until he reached the road. He turned once to see the Piper waving him on.

"Hurry," the Piper called across to him. "The way through will close very soon." Garland showed him his back, and then shuddered, hearing the eerie notes of that pipe drifting through the trees.

Garland reached the crossroads and looked up at the gibbet. The crow had gone, and only a well-rusted chain hung creaking in the sunlight, that fading fast as sudden chill entered the glade. Three forks waited for him.

Which way?

No point worrying about that—they most likes will all lead to a pit full of snakes. Should he take the middle one as Tamersane had?

Trust your intuition.

Garland pictured Queen Ariane's handsome face. "For you, my Queen." He felt a shimmer of light, and on a weird impulse, Garland took the left road instead and placed his boot upon the lane.

"Good choice!" the Piper called out from somewhere off in the woods. Garland turned, but then tumbled backwards as sudden blinding light and noise erupted all around him. Garland fell, slipping down through greasy air that sucked and licked his skin. A shrill wind assaulted his ears and the brightness was swallowed by a dense dark that allowed nothing penetrate it.

I am dying. Garland closed his eyes and waited for the pain to come. He'd done his best but had failed. "I tried!" he called, but his voice was swallowed by dark surrounding him. For a long time, Garland fell.

Chapter 27 | Dimensions

It seemed like hours. Falling, spiraling through yawning void. No sound, no vision, and mercifully no pain. At last Garland's body slowed, appeared to float, drift down like a leaf released from a tree on a windless autumn afternoon. He felt at peace—relaxed, could see his body floating in front of him. The Dreaming—he never knew he had it.

Looking out, Garland saw his own image was gazing back at him, a woman's face behind it. *Ysaren?* Not her. The dark-haired woman he'd seen in the forest.

Who are you?

But both his and the woman's image faded, replaced by a pale light that grew to fill his vision. He was aware of a sensation. Cold. And something else—a dull throbbing between his ears. Garland shivered at the windy touch, found himself laughing in surprise. He was alive, his body ached, head hurt, and it was so bloody cold—all these sensations meant he was alive.

But where am I?

Garland's boots scraped against something hard, his body bumped along the ground, and his head embraced wet cold. A smell reached out to him. Familiar, damp and . . . salty?

The sea?

301

He was by the sea. Perhaps the Wayfinder had guided him right after all. But no, the decision to take the left road had been his. And this didn't feel like Rundali. The air was cold and wind buffeted his face.

Garland opened his eyes slowly, not sure if he was ready for what he would see. He sighed in relief. He was crouched alone on an empty beach. The stiff breeze lifted his hair as a surge of breakers crashed toward him. Garland rubbed his eyes, stood up, and looked about, swaying slightly like a man with too much ale in his belly.

Garland tested his legs and dusted himself off. He was in surprisingly good shape, but he was alone. Garland glanced down, saw his sword resting in the scabbard. Funny how he hadn't noticed that before.

He walked, slowly at first and then picking up pace, the sea crashing to his right, and dunes parading off to the left. Above his head a gray quiet sky yielded milky clouds, and a winter sun coated the nearby beach with pale gold. The road had led him astray, and now Garland was lost in some desolate winter realm.

Gazing as he walked, Garland saw wader birds and turnstones running along the tide. It was raw cold, the wind shrill and bitter. *Winter—how could that be?*

He left the beach, scaled sand dunes, and took a good look around. Wind and sky, beach and ocean. Not a soul in sight. The area around him deserted save the birds, and that sky so lead-heavy gray it sapped the soul. Garland questioned his sanity. Perhaps he'd fallen in that forest and lost consciousness. No—the beach was real enough. The cold too, and him hardly dressed for it, with his mail over silk. Weary and drained of all emotion, Garland sank to his knees and sobbed. He had failed. And now he was lost, the Gods alone knew where.

Walk . . .

The voice echoed through the wind. A woman's voice, rich and strong, and hearing it gave him strength too.

"Ysaren?" Garland shouted the name. No answer. "Where am I?" he said to the wind.

Walk on . . . The voice rushed around his head.

Garland cursed his luck but took the hint, commenced walking, and briskly now. He was angry—tired of being played with like mouse in cats' paws. Ysaren, that piper fellow, or someone was pissing in his pot. Why was he here, and where were his men—dead? Tol and Taylon—he prayed they were alive. The Bruhan and his men? Keep walking. Time will tell, and no point dwelling on that.

Keep walking, do as she says—need to find out where I am.

He left the dunes and took to strolling along the beach again, the birds running from his feet. He walked for hours until the sun turned crimson and fell beneath the distant smudge of sea and sky. A round moon rolled out, and Garland saw a skein of geese carving a "V" as they flew past, heading for the swallowed sun.

Garland picked up his pace again, not wanting to spend a bitter night alone on this beach. He walked for an hour as darkness settled around him, the moon marking his progress, and the sea flanking right, those dunes shadowing his left. A deserted world he was in. Abandoned. But just when he'd lost all hope, Garland spied the distant glint of firelight a mile ahead.

A beacon!

Fire meant people. Humans or some kind of intelligence. He didn't worry about whether they would be friendly, all emotion and care having been blasted from him, and thoughts of that fire's warmth overruled any concern. Garland was meant to be here. Only thing that made sense. He was alive and whoever these people were, they would help him. *Keep going!*

Garland slowed his walk as he approached houses. Square shapes that could only be cottages or fishers' huts. A sharp clear night, and the watching moon traced silver far out to sea. Garland saw stars winking high above but focused solely on the swelling ball of firelight ahead. A bonfire. Its yellow flames crackling from a hill just beyond the settlement. A beacon, or warning perhaps?

The village—if village it was—lay shrouded in silence. A dozen wooden buildings, ramshackle and shoddy, with nets and traps abandoned beside the low-roofed thatch cottages. From those roofs smoke twisted and curled up before being stolen by wind and night. Garland stopped outside the nearest house and tapped loudly on the battered driftwood door.

"Anyone home?"

No answer.

"Hello—is anyone inside?" Garland said. "I'm lost, be grateful for shelter and food. I can pay," he lied. Still no response. Garland turned away and was about to try the next house when the door creaked open, a young man standing in the entrance. Perhaps twenty years old, hard to say in the gloom.

He was skinny, but looked bright, and his pale face friendly enough, though clearly shocked at seeing someone outside at this late hour.

"Who are you?" The boy's voice was deep and he looked a bit scared. Garland heard a woman's voice somewhere inside the cottage. "It's all right Clavin—just a wastrel, most likes from the Hall."

"I'm Captain Garland—a soldier," Garland said, "and I assure you, no wastrel. But rather a traveller lost and confused. I'm seeking the Castle of Lights, presumably the same hall you mention?"

"Never heard of no castle of lights," the young man said. "You seem decent, and mother taught me to be kind to wastrels. Best you come in, Sir."

"Thanks, but I'm not a wastrel." Garland rubbed his eyes as the thick smoke half blinded him. It was blissfully warm in the cottage. Warm, dry and cozy, and better still the welcoming aroma of beef stew reminded him he hadn't eaten for hours, or maybe days—it was hard to know.

A girl was seated at a shabby table. Pretty, with large blue eyes and pale hair tied back. She looked worried as Garland stooped low to avoid banging his head on a beam. He winked at her as he took seat at table. "I'm Garland," he said.

The girl looked alarmed and turned to her beau, currently leaning over and stirring the stew. "You're hungry, I gather," the young man said. "Your sort usually is."

"You've had other visitors like me?"

"Not here, but at Mother's tavern out on the pass. Poor lost souls seeking solace from their stay at the Hall. Broken witless wanderers mostly."

"Well—I am neither of those," Garland said. "So please indulge me and tell me where this place is? As I said, I'm lost and looking for the Castle of Lights. There's a man I need to find, and a . . . something I have to collect for someone."

"He's fucked up," the girl said, and Garland's jaw dropped in surprise hearing such language. "Worse than normal. They must have gotten to him bad." She twisted her mouth in a wry grin. "Poor old bugger."

"I'm Dafyd," the young man said, as he poured stew into a wooden bowl and offered it to Garland. "This here lass is sweet-tongued Rosey. She's from the village—it explains her coarse tone. But I don't mind that—she's a goodun, is Rose." He cuffed the girl's ear and she punched him with affection. Obviously, some ongoing joke between them.

"Just because your ma don't approve of me," Rosey said, showing her crooked grin again. "We common folk don't match up with her visitors from the Hall."

Garland tore into his stew. It was good—even better when Dafyd retrieved a large flagon of ale from a barrel resting out back. "Thanks," Garland said, and took a long slow pull. "Thing is . . .," he wiped his mouth on a sleeve. "I'm in a rush and need to know where I am. I've vital business that cannot wait."

"He speaks funny," Rosey said. "How did you smuggle that from the Hall?" She was looking at Garland's sword, until now hidden by his long silk riding coat.

"I told you I'm not aware of any hall," Garland said. "I was lost in a forest in Rundali. Banged my head—sort of—and next I know I'm on this beach, and walking like a fool toward your beacon fire."

"You must have banged your head hard," the girl laughed, but beside her Dafyd scratched his head, his blue eyes baffled.

"Mother will help you," Dafyd said, and Rosey nodded beside him.

"She's wiser than he is," Rosey laughed. "And a lot wiser than I is—or anyone, saving them queer folk at the Hall. They're devilish clever."

"Well maybe I should go to this hall?"

"No!" They both yelled at him so loud, Garland jumped up and struck his head on the beam.

He sat slowly counting to ten and rubbing the dent in his crown. "Tell me of this hall," Garland said, after a long moment's steadying himself.

The two looked at each other, and Rosey shrugged. "Graywash Hall," Dafyd said. "It's hardly a mile from here. You'd have seen it, were it not so dark. The fires come from its piazza where the Lord Chamberlain watches out for any sign of the Kaa."

"What are the Kaa?"

"Invaders from further up the coast," Dafyd said "I've never seen them but once they raided these coasts, and the Hall doesn't forget."

"This Lord Chamberlain rules in the hall?"

"Sometimes," Rosey said, as Dafyd poured himself an ale.

"Sometimes?" Garland smiled. "You're talking in riddles."

"Stranger, you need rest—look worn out," Dafyd said, placing a hand on his woman's shoulder.

"I'm fine," Garland said. "I just need answers and then must get going."

"Not before morning."

"Well, no . . . I'll wait until dawn—and thank you both," Garland said. "You are kind to take in a stranger. But it's crucial I depart at first light and try to discover how to get back to where I was. A man's life may depend on it."

"Where have you just come from?"

"Rundal Woods—a very bad place," Garland said, but the young couple just looked blank.

"Sleep here by the fire," Dafyd said after a moment. "At sun-up I'll ride with you to Torrigan's Tavern."

"And where is that?"

"The inn my mother has managed these last years, since father was lost at sea."

"Sorry to hear that," Garland said.

The young couple bid him goodnight and smuggled through a side door. Minutes later Garland could hear Rosey giggling, followed by the sounds of urgent thrusting and bed creaking. Garland closed his eyes and tried to take in what had happened. His stomach was full and he was warm. Enough for today. Best he sleep hard and be ready for the morrow.

The ride didn't take long. A bracing trot along a stony road cut inland from the sea-locked village, winding up through a knot of hills threaded by deep wooded slopes. Beyond these were open fields where Garland saw the outbuildings and fences of what looked to be a farm or homestead. They'd stayed clear of Graywash Hall, though Garland had wanted to see it.

Dafyd had told him the villages kept away from the place apart from those who worked there, and they never spoke about what occurred inside the walls.

Garland had glimpsed a huge ungainly rock as they'd left the village, the beacon fire blazing behind it. It didn't look natural, and Garland questioned whether it had fallen from the sky during the war of the Gods. He'd heard rumors of such things happening.

"Is that . . .?"

"It is," Dafyd had said and urged his beast onward, Garland's curiosity unquenched. No matter; he'd return and question those inside once he'd found out what the boy's mother knew. He suspected it just a local issue with the villagers afraid of the lords frowning down on them. Such stern folk would not faze Garland of Wynais.

It was chilly and damp, and a thin mizzle coated dark hills ahead. Garland assumed this was north of his destination. But how far north? Had he drifted through time as well as space in that altered state? Surely that wasn't possible? But Rundali's climate had seemed similar to that of Laregoza—humid and oppressive. And it had been summer back there. Here . . .

They dismounted outside a small cottage and Garland saw a woman appear, a warm smile on her face as she saw her son. Marei—her name, so Dafyd had informed him. A widow, perhaps forty winters, with long chestnut hair and kind blue eyes. She was shorter than her son and reached up on tiptoes to kiss him welcome.

Garland hung back, but when the woman smiled his way, thrust out a hand and Marei shook it slowly, her blue eyes puzzled by the gesture. "You, stranger are welcome at my inn," Marei said. "I trust Dafyd has looked after you?" She glanced briefly at her son who shrugged.

"Indeed, he has," Garland said, "him and his lady."

"Lady?" The woman smiled slightly. "A generous exaggeration."

"I arrived after dark; they were kind to take me in." Garland gazed about at the homestead. It looked clean, though in need of some maintenance. He heard chickens scampering somewhere close by and could see cattle in a nearby field, their wooly coats steaming with vapor.

"Kind or stupid," the woman said. "Not wise, receiving strangers after nightfall. Still, you look the honest type. Ale or tea?"

"Tea would be good as I've a long day ahead I'm sure."

"He's come from a forest—Mandalay?" Dafyd said to his mother.

"Rundali," Garland said. "Rundal Woods actually. An unpleasant place, best avoided. I guess it's a way south of here? Warmer there."

"You have a name?" Marei glanced at her son again, her eyes quizzical.

"He's a Captain," Dafyd said. "Captain Garland."

"Garland will suffice. I am a plain soldier seeking a nobleman called Tamersane of Kelwyn—that's a country. My homeland. This Tamersane's a cousin to our Queen—Ariane. He vanished in enemy territory and she sent me and some men to find him. But the forest . . ."

"You became lost," Marei nodded. "The Hall's vortex sucked you in I expect. Not uncommon."

"Maybe so," Garland said, his patience ebbing, tired of all the mystery surrounding that place. "We were attacked in Rundal Woods; some kind of demon dwells within. Sorcery or some vile trick addled my wits for a time. I lost track of my men, and the Bruhan's—a soldier from Laregoza," Garland said, dropping that country's name in, hoping to get a reaction but receiving only blank stares instead.

Marei folded her arms and shrugged. "So, you are lost and confused," she said. "Another result of time spent in the Hall."

"Alone," Garland said, ignoring her input. "I stumbled into a crossroads where a very odd individual hinted I chose the right road and it would take me to my destination—the Castle of Lights on the far coast. There were three forks; I think I chose poorly. Ending up here, evidently some distance from my destination. Where is this place?"

"Venland, and surrounding it are the Marches, the city far beyond those mountains," Marei said, pointing back up the road to where the forest climbed into deep dark hills.

"Come," she said, "I'll put the kettle on. Dafyd can see to the horses."

Inside the cottage it was warm and cozy yet much more spacious than Rosey's place had been. Garland took seat by a window and watched birds flitting around in the gray skies outside.

"Small for a tavern," Garland said.

"Tavern's next door; a skittle alley too," Marei said, pouring water into a metal pan and placing it on the adjacent stove.

"I don't know what that is," Garland said, without much interest. "Your boy tells me you live here alone. Is that not dangerous?"

"I can look after myself," the woman smiled; it made her look younger. She was over forty on closer inspection, with flecks of gray in that wavy hair. But her eyes were both wise and sorrowful, with hints of humor around the edges. Garland found her appealing in a homely, comfortable sort of way. A woman he could feel at ease with.

Marei smiled, as though reading his thoughts. She poured the tea, piping hot, into his cup and he sipped slowly. "It's good," Garland said.

"I'll have breakfast ready shortly," the woman said. "Take your ease while you can, sir." She turned to her son, back from the stables and now lolling by the fire like a faithful hound. "Where are your manners?" Marei said, her brows knitting. "Bored? Why not show our guest around? And explain about the skittle alley—he's never seen one."

"He looks comfortable where he is mother," Dafyd said, but then rose to his feet at a look from Marei. "Not much to see," Dafyd said. "Bring your tea."

Garland accompanied Dafyd out into the drizzle, though he'd have preferred to stay put and question Marei. The homestead was ordered and neat, but far too much for one woman to handle in Garland's opinion. He saw stables for horses, a pig den, and several coops where the chickens capered. Off in the pastures were cattle and sheep.

"She does all this herself?" Garland enquired as Dafyd led him into the tavern. He ducked his head before entering a long low room with kegs stacked at the far end and a low bench with mugs lined empty and neat.

"I help when I'm here," Dafyd said, "though I'm most often in the village these days."

"Rosey seems a good lass."

Dafyd shrugged. "Mother doesn't like her much." He walked to a far door and cranked it open. Garland looked in and saw a long alley with wooden pins at the far end. He raised a brow.

"Skittles," Dafyd told him without much interest. "That's about it," he said, after a moment hovering at the door. "Hard to imagine how busy this place was ten years ago."

"When your father was alive?" Garland saw a large ball in a groove closer to where he stood and guessed this must be some kind of game.

"Aye, so," Dafyd said. "Seen enough?"

Dafyd led Garland back inside the cottage where his mother had breakfast waiting. Garland ate well, and after more tea felt ready for anything.

"I need to leave," he said, wiping his mouth. "But first tell me about that hall. Dafyd implied they might be able to assist me there."

"I never said that." Dafyd glanced at his mother, who shrugged.

"They might," she said. "But it's best not to gamble on Earle Gray's hospitality."

"Who is he?"

"The Chamberlain—a custodian of sorts."

"Who else lives at the hall and why is it such a secret?" Garland was determined to glean all he could before visiting.

"Graywash Hall," Marei said, catching his expression, "is most perilous, Sir Garland. I'd advise you stay clear."

"The Chamberlain—what manner of person is he?"

"A difficult one," Marei said. But there are others dwelling within those walls far worse than Gray. *Cille* being one such."

"Mother!" Dafyd spat tea hearing that name. "We're not to mention her name."

"I'm not scared of her." Marei's face turned hard and her lips tightened with bitter memories. "She cannot hurt me anymore than she has already."

"Who is Chee Lee?" Garland had the odd feeling he'd heard that name before. *But where?*

"Cille," Marei mouthed the word slowly. "Pronounced Chee Lay. She is also called the Red Witch."

Garland nodded, slowly finding connection at last. "Long dark hair and ruby dress?"

"I have no idea," Marei said. "Cille changes like sea winds in springtime. Everyone knows of her existence, but there are few who've encountered her and reported back."

"And yet you hate her—a woman you've never met?" Garland

suspected this Cille held the key to his questions. *One of three sisters.*

"For what she's done to our people," Marei said.

"Mother—we don't know if the Red Witch to blame," Dafyd said, looking pensive.

"Who else?"

"The Kaa," Dafyd said, but her mother waved him be quiet.

"And this Cille dwells in Graywash Hall?" Garland said.

"She resides there—yes," Marei said.

"Then I need to visit right away, as she might be able to help me get back to where I was," Garland said, standing and dusting down his garments.

"That really isn't the best idea, Sir Garland." Marei rested a slim hand on his arm bidding him take seat again. Reluctantly Garland complied. "Few enter the Hall without invitation," Marei said. "And no one sane seeks out the Red Witch. Cille and her sisters are unpredictably spiteful at best, and deadly when aroused."

"Ysaren's her sister—that explains the likeness," Garland said, smiling as pieces of the puzzle were clunking together.

"Ysaren?"

"Another witch—I met her weeks ago. Why I'm here. Ysaren was partly responsible for my quest," Garland said. "She told me that the one I sought would die without her help. That unless I freed Ysaren from her captor, all was lost."

"What did she want you do to?" Dafyd said, his eyes full of intrigue.

"Fetch her an artifact from the Castle of Lights," Garland said, waving dismissive hand. "I know—an odd request. Long story," he said. "But I saw an image of a woman just like Ysaren before I arrived here. Perhaps more striking, but they could have been sisters. This other woman had dark hair, whereas Ysaren's is gold. She it was who duped me in the woods."

"Stay away from the Hall," Marei said, resting hand on his arm. "That is my only counsel."

"No choice," Garland said, his eyes gazing deep into hers. "Unless you know of any other way I can get back to Rundali?"

"Mother, I can go with him, at least show him the way." Dafyd was leaning against the wall, his pale face intense.

"I don't like you going near that place," Marei said. "And that girl . . ."

"I love Rosey," Dafyd folded his arms in defense, and Garland guessed this was an old business unresolved between them.

"The villagers are tainted, Dafyd, and you know why. The blaze—they are too close to that corrupting fire and could fall prey at any time."

"The beacon?" Garland was confused again. "The flames I saw?"

"The Pyre," Marei corrected.

Pyre . . .? "They torch people at this hall?"

"They did once," Marei said. "The last Kaa raiding party." She looked tense, unwilling to explain more. "There was sorcery involved," Marei said quietly, after a moment's pause. "Why the flames never die. Only fools go near." Marei flashed an angry glance at her son.

"Mother, that was years ago," Dafyd said. "And the fault of the Kaa, who got what they deserved. Earle Gray relights the beacon as a warning every eve, the rest is superstition."

"So your friends at the village are told," Marei said.

"It's a fact." Dafyd glared at his mother, who shrugged. "Rosey says the Hall leaves them be these days. Anyway, it's just for now. When she inherits next month, we'll make for the city and find work. You can come too, past time you left this place."

"What city is that?" Garland asked, but received no answer.

"You're a dreamer, Dafyd," Marei said. "A fool, and if your father was here he'd box your ears for such naivete. I still might, unless you change your tone."

"I'm twenty-one years old." Dafyd's face was flustered and red, and Garland needed to summon patience. He had more pressing matters than this business between mother and son.

"With the sense of a twelve-year-old." Marei folded her arms and sighed.

"It doesn't matter what you think, Mother," Dafyd said. "This man needs to go to the Hall. We cannot help him here. Best I announce him at the gate; at least then Captain Garland will not be shot as a trespasser. Least I can do."

Garland rose to his feet a second time. "Thank you, son—but no," he said. "I'd not put you in danger. Nor would I have your mother worrying." He caught Marei's eye for the briefest second and she turned away. "I can see how much she loves you."

Dafyd rolled his eyes and left the room. "I'll be ready whenever you are Captain Garland." The door slammed. Marei chewed her lip and stared at the fire.

"I'm sorry," Garland said.

"For what?"

"Coming here. I can see you've much on your mind, and I'm content to seek entrance to this hall myself. Gods know I've been through weirder situations lately."

"I doubt that," Marei said. She sighed. "Dafyd its right, if they see a stranger unannounced they'll most likes kill him. Ever since the Kaa."

"Dafyd mentioned them last night, and you both more recently. Who are they?"

"Enemies, sea raiders from the north. Doesn't matter, they are no more," she said. "Since that fateful day they've always killed strangers at the gate, lest history repeat itself."

"Riddles again," Garland smiled. "We live such complicated lives. Would that it was different."

"You had better get used to riddles where you are going, Sir Garland." Marei placed a warm hand on his arm again. "Do you have to leave? It's a long time since I've had such polite company. Someone sensible for a change instead of Dafyd twittering on about that dreadful girl. Relax here for a day or so," Marei said. "Get your strength back. Explain in detail what's happened to you, and maybe I can help you find your way home. Or at least try."

"Thanks," Garland placed his calloused hand over hers and squeezed gently. "I feel I've found a friend where least expected. But I've got to get back. I'm in way over my head with this business, Marei. But I made a vow to my Queen. I have to save Tamersane of Kelwyn—what I promised."

"An honorable man." Marei smiled, her tired sad eyes full of resignation.

"A tired, foolish man."

She nodded slowly. "Let the boy introduce you as he's offered. They won't hurt him, as they will know him from the village."

"I hope you are right."

"I wish you well on your venture, Sir Garland," Marei said, a slight smile lifting her lip. She turned and left him standing there, fading softly through the doorway.

Garland stood for a moment lost in thought. Then, mind made up, he rubbed his tired eyes and left the cottage, blinking as cold rain drummed his face outside.

An hour later Garland sat his horse, gazing down from the high ridge at the rain-washed road ribboning below, a river running parallel. Ahead was the sea, calm and placid and dark as ink, a brooding line of cliffs flanking off to the north. He saw the village and dunes ranging beyond, their triangular shapes fading into haze. But it was the monstrous mass of congealed rock at the road's end that dominated his view.

"The hall is hidden behind that rock?" Garland asked Dafyd, as they trotted down into the valley.

"The rock is the Hall," Dafyd said. "You'll see."

They rode closer and Garland did see, his eyes widening at the sight.

It wasn't until they were quite close before Garland noticed the many tiny windows, like frozen stars in the stone, hundreds glinting. Beneath them Garland could see the sturdy iron-ribbed wooden gates. Leading across to those was a narrow bridge spanning the fast-flowing stream.

"Who built this place?" Garland said, astounded at the construction unlike anything he'd imagined.

"I do not know." Dafyd guided his horse over the bridge and Garland rode behind, gazing down at the white rush of water far below.

"Steady boy," he said to the horse, though the beast seemed less edgy than he was.

They approached those heavy doors and Garland saw a man standing there. A long black coat and floppy hat shrouded his features. Dafyd slid form his horse and Garland followed suit, handing the reins to the boy.

"I'll take it from here—thanks." Garland winked at Dafyd, who shook his head.

"I need to introduce you." Dafyd stepped forward, and the faceless man turned his head toward them. "This is Sir Garland," Dafyd said, "a nobleman from distant lands who seeks answers in the Hall."

"Captain Garland," He corrected Dafyd's introduction and took a pace forward.

"Garland, wait!" Dafyd said; his voice sounded muffled. Garland ignored him, focusing instead on the man in the coat.

The gate keeper beckoned Garland forward. "Be welcome, stranger," he said, his voice an urgent whisper. "Enter within, third corridor on left, second stairs, last door. Good luck."

"What?" Garland turned, and startled, saw that Dafyd, the horses, and the bridge they'd been standing on had all disappeared. As had the man in the coat.

Instead, Garland stood inside a wide shadowy hallway with sconces flickering all around him. He was alone and it was very cold. *Deathly cold*—Garland thought with a shudder.

"I cannot recall what you said!" Garland called out, but received no answer. "Are you there?" No response. Just bitter drafts and sconces casting shadows on the walls.

I'm so tired of mysteries.

The hall led into gloom. Garland walked toward it slowly, eyes scanning for any sign of movement. The hall funneled into a passage—*the first corridor.*

Garland reached the end, where a door opened on stairs winding up. Garland ignored that and passed through another door, leaning ajar, leading to a second corridor—this one blazing with trenchers of fire. The heat was stifling and a shock after the chill he'd left behind. Garland saw all manner of weapons hanging from the walls on either side. He picked up his pace, walking briskly past, his face sweating in the heat.

He stopped upon reaching two doors that stood like sentries either side of the hall. Garland opened the first, saw narrow stairs leading down to pitch dark. A low moaning sound was drifting up the stairs, and Garland could make out the sound of something heavy sliding.

Not going down there.

The other door opened on stairs leading up and off to the right. It smelled bad, but Garland decided this his only option, as he didn't want to encounter whatever lurked below. The stairs turned three corners, almost winding back on themselves, before yielding into a third corridor. Garland breathed a sigh of relief. He'd got it right so far.

This corridor was bigger, drafty, with a vaulted ceiling, and tall angular windows covered in moth-eaten drapes, a faint green glow penetrating through. There were long tables cluttered with empty plates and abandoned cutlery; heavy candle holders were covered in wax which had congealed, spreading across the tables and staining the wooden floor boards below.

Those creaked beneath his feet, as Garland paced the third corridor with measured urgent steps. The far wall loomed into view. *Second stairs, last door—I remember.*

Garland reached the only door at the far end, opened it but saw no stairs. Just a long narrow landing, the odd sconce flickering along the walls. Not helpful. The stairs must be at the far end. He walked. They weren't.

A door on the left opened into a spacious hall where a woman sat cross-legged, staring into the dying flames of a fireplace. She wore a makeshift gown which half covered her legs and shoulders; her skinny arms and feet were bare.

She turned hearing his approach, and Garland saw a ravaged face that could have been any age. "You've come the wrong way," the woman's voice was like parchment ripping between strong hands. Garland saw dried blood under her broken finger nails, and there was pus leaking from beneath her right eye.

"My mistake." He turned and hurried from the room.

"Wait—it's long since I felt a man inside me." Garland heard soft treads behind him and he picked up his pace, almost running from the hall. The door ahead was closed. Garland crashed through it and fell face-first down a flight of stairs. There had been only one entrance to that room, but it had changed—somehow.

He staggered to his feet at the foot of the stairs. *First staircase after third corridor perhaps?* Wrong or right he couldn't linger here. Garland entered yet another long dark passage, and almost collapsed in relief seeing dimly lit stairs at the end. These led down into deeper gloom. At the bottom were three doors. The first was open; the others shut.

Garland could hear voices coming from inside the open door. *The last door . . .*

He hurried past making for the door at the end, and turning, saw the emaciated woman staring at him, candle in one hand, a long bloody knife in another.

"Don't go in there," the woman said; she was walking towards him, her skinny arms outstretched. Garland fumbled the latch, slippery in his fingers.

Open damn you!

Click—he opened the door.

A rush of air and blinding light; Garland fell forward into open space, the shrill sound of pipes pealing chords like chirping sparrows all around him.

Not again . . .

He fell, but only for seconds this time, and crashed heavily onto a marble floor, his sword pommel digging into his hip, and his face impacting the stone and jarring his noggin.

Shit.

Garland shrugged back the pain and staggered to his feet, hands covering battered face from the diamond glare, and head spinning from the knock he'd received. He heard laughter and feared the mad woman had followed him in here, half expecting the cold kiss of her knife at any moment.

Garland glimpsed his sword lying on the marble flags, hard to see in the shimmering brightness. He thought it sheathed beside him, but he must have freed it in his panic. He reached down and retrieved it. But as Garland wrapped his hands around the hilt, the weapon was wrenched from his grip and slid across the floor.

The laughter again.

"Who's there?"

Nothing. Garland turned full circle, but all he could see was polished floor and dazzling glare, painful to look into. Garland stared down at his feet and saw his own face glancing back at him, disheveled and wild-eyed.

I look like a deer trapped by the hunter.

Enough of this. "Show yourself, Witch," Garland said. "I'm not afraid of you!"

"That's good, I suppose." The response was lazy. "You will need courage where you're heading." A woman's voice—rich and full, bored, but faintly amused.

Angry, Garland turned towards it. "Where are you?"

"Here. Waiting for you." The light faded slowly, and Garland saw a wide dais facing him, broad marble steps leading up to it. He took them two at a time and stopped at the top. A couch lay there, draped with cushions and a low three-legged table placed alongside, a bowl of fruit and flagon filled with wine resting on it.

These Garland ignored, having eyes only for the woman lying sprawled on the couch. She was beautiful in a frighteningly alien way. Sharp-faced and dangerous looking. She wore a deep red gown, loose at shoulders and parted along the sides to allow full view of her legs.

Her lips were a deeper red than the dress, and her eyes, a cunning green flecked with gold, much like Ysaren's had been. "You are the witch Chee—ley?"

"Cille, and I'm no witch." The voice was soothing and lazy, and Garland noted how she pronounced her name with emphasis on the second syllable. "Relax," she told him, reaching for the wine glass and sipping carefully. "You look so tense, soldier." She placed the wine glass on the table and sat up, her legs crossed neatly, the deep cleft in her dress showing off her ample cleavage. Garland pretended not to notice.

"Well, lost your tongue, fool?" Her mood was quicksilver. She appeared irritated by his lack of response.

"You summoned me here," Garland said. "I thought I'd let you explain yourself, witch."

Cille's eyes flashed golden for the briefest instant. "Careful . . .," she said, reaching across languidly and retrieving a grape from the bowl. She bit into it, squirting juice from her mouth and then spat the seed at Garland. "I've killed men for less."

"You'd have killed me in that forest had you wished to," Garland said. "Instead you preferred employing mind tricks and then dragging me here. Why?"

"What makes you think I summoned you here, Garland of Wynais?"

"Because you need my help."

"Oh, I do?" She laughed, a deep rich sound. "Why do men always think I need their help? The arrogance of your race." She sipped her wine again and smiled at him. "A wonder mankind survives at all."

"Only thing that makes sense," Garland said, bracing his feet as though he was facing a champion swordsman on battle ground. She noted his tension and waved a languid hand.

"Relax, Sir—I grow weary of your manner."

"And yet you need me." Garland looked about for his sword but couldn't see it anywhere.

Her eyes flicked amusement and she raised a brow. "Someone else said that to me recently, or perhaps will say it soon—so hard to tell future from past in the Hall."

"Ysaren."

"My sister—what of her?" The women in red pulled another grape free of the vine and swallowed it whole this time. "Some have stones, others don't. The knack is knowing which." She smiled at him and shifted her knees, allowing him more than a hint of what lay between. Again, Garland tried not to notice.

"Poor, stiff, honorable Sir Garland. She seduced you, didn't she, the old bag?" Cille laughed slowly and ran a long finger down the inside of her thigh. "Tell me. How do I compare with Ysaren?"

"Cut the crap and tell me why I'm here." The room had dimmed to twilight. Garland's eyes scanned the floor and he felt a rush of relief as he spied his sword lying yards away. A short spring and he'd reach it. *Good to know.* If Cille had noticed him looking she didn't respond. "Ysaren said she was imprisoned by you and the other one—her own sisters. She needs the Bow of Kerasheva to kill her captor. Once free, Ysaren will have the power to help me save the man I'm charged with finding."

"And you trusted her word—that hag at the lake?" Cille placed her wine glass on table and caressed her hair with a long white finger, the nails the bright hue of freshly spilled blood.

"Didn't have much choice," Garland said. "My Queen sent me there to consult with the oracle in her dream—Ysaren. Since then things have got complicated."

"For simpletons like you, things are always complicated," Cille said, those jade eyes flicking gold again. Garland stood his ground.

"And what choice do you think you have now, Captain Garland? Your time is running out; the portals are closing. If you want to reach the Castle of Lights before the others, then you need to move fast."

"You're not making sense."

"This is a blunt instrument before me," Cille said, her tone waspish again. "Men—I'd forgotten how dull you all are. Bitch-Ysaren tricked you, fool. She is sending others—far less scrupulous than you—to get that bow. *Insurance* lest poor noble Garland let her down. Once they—or you—deliver the bow she will feed them to the monster she claims is her gaoler. He is not. Sorcery alone keeps my sister in check. And for good reason. The Emerald Queen saw to that."

"The other sister?"

Cille's gaze drifted for a moment. "Interesting notion—and she does like green. What do you know about the Emerald Queen?"

"Nothing," Garland said. "Just assumed she was your sister—the third in this witchy triangle."

"You are testing my patience more than is wise," Cille said. "You know nothing about anything—Fool! Elerim and I have our differences, but we at least kept our minds free of madness when our reckless brother, Arollas, all but destroyed us in his fruitless war with the Urgolais. Hard to keep your sanity when enduring a thousand years of conflict.

"Ysaren lost hers—why we locked her in," Cille said. "Safest thing for her and everyone else. She is insane, Sir Garland, madder than that wretched creature you saw in the corridors, but thrice as cunning. Ysaren entered your little queen's head and filled it with thoughts of her cousin, the renegade Tamersane. That way she knew help would arrive. Mortals can be used so easily. As for Tamersane, why worry? His course is almost run."

"Why would I trust your word and not hers?" Garland said "Ysaren seemed sane enough to me—"

"She is crafty," Cille said. "And you, soldier, are not clever with women. Too honest, poor dear."

"What? I've never had a problem with women."

"As I said, there is little time," Cille said, ignoring his protest. "You need to act fast."

With startling speed Cille rose to her knees and slid from her couch. Alarmed, Garland stepped back quickly, but Cille's hand caught his arm, stopping his retreat.

She stood before him, radiant in that red dress, her weird eyes level with his own. A tall, beautiful, and very frightening woman. "You are a good man," Cille said, resting her hand on his shoulder and squeezing slightly. Garland felt pin pricks tingle at that touch.

"I try to be," he said, unsettled by her probing gaze. Cille studied him with frank interest, like a farmer's wife purchasing cattle at market. After a moment she stepped back and smiled.

"You will do," Cille said, pushing a stray lock away from her face. Barely, Garland held her gaze and noted how up close her skin shimmered like crystal and seemed thin as parchment. Inches away, she looked as old as her sister. But far less haggard. Cille's beauty was a weapon falling upon him, and Garland tensed for the blow which he suspected would arrive any minute.

"You're casting a spell over me," he said. "I'll not have it."

"And why would I do that?" Cille turned playful, and her sharp fingers traced a line along his face.

"Caprice, boredom—how can I fathom the thoughts of a sorceress?" Garland said.

Her fingers stopped their idle peruse. "*Sorceress?* Better than witch, I suppose." She grabbed his hand with lightning speed and pulled it across to her thigh. "Whatever else I am, I have a woman's needs too," Cille said. "Scant visitors here."

"Stop playing games!" Garland forced his hand away with herculean effort. "You said I was short of time. So why not tell me why I'm here and then I can get moving."

"You partook of this quest of your own volition," Cille said. "Your choice, not mine."

"You're the reason why I'm here," Garland said, trying not to look at those legs.

"I need you—yes," Cille said. "But not like Ysaren for her own spiteful reasons. Nor in the way that you think." She pressed her warm body up against him and Garland felt his face flush like fire. "And you need me too," Cille smiled, sliding a warm hand down his back.

"To help find Tamersane," Garland said. "The only thing I need here."

She stepped back and looked at him again, an almost kind appraisal on her lips. "You have done well, Soldier," Cille said. "You passed my test."

"You were testing me?" Garland shuddered slightly. "What if I'd—?"

"I would have killed you and drunk of your blood," Cille said, and then laughed at the horror showing on his face. "Perhaps not," she said. "I like you, Sir Garland."

"Relieved to hear it."

"There is more at risk here than you know," Cille said. "Tamersane and his beloved Teret. Carlo Sarfe of fallen Gol. The Grogan creature. Mad Sulo. You, as well—all are part of the crumbling mosaic. The world axis tilted seven years ago and has been off kilter ever since. We need to set it back again. Put things right."

"You've lost me," Garland said. "Can you cut to the point? As you say, I'm short of time."

"Time has no power here," Cille said. "Just another tool I can help you with. Understand this much. Three once powerful sisters seek to regain what was lost. We have our issues, especially Ysaren, but we have to unite to stop *him*."

"Who?"

"Our father."

Garland stretched his head and glanced at his sword again. Anything to avert his eyes from those mile-long legs. "There you go again," he said.

"The bow will stop him and correct the current imbalance," Cille said. "And that can only happen at the Castle of Lights. Your destination, Sir Garland."

"Well, splendid, but I could be there now if it wasn't for your—"

"I called you here so you would understand what's at stake," Cille said, "or at least realize more is at risk than your own little quest. And I saved you in those woods—you were in dire peril there."

"Why should I believe you?"

"I am not Ysaren, and though she is not our foe her foolish greed will enable his return," Cille said. "Find the bow. Be my champion as well as Queen Ariane's. Chant the words carved upon it, and then call out my real name."

"Which is?"

"You will know when the moment arrives," Cille said. "I will help you, Elerim too. We cannot let Father get to the bow first. Ysaren knows that too but wants Kerasheva for her own selfish reasons."

"How do I—"

"Go!"

Cille's image vanished as did the surroundings. Instead, Garland felt the warm grip of his sword's hilt wrapped around his palms.

"What must I do?"

Save us all . . .

A light exploded in Garland's head. He yelled in pain and felt his body lifted up and sent spinning and crashing through hidden windows. The atmosphere around him spun, noise crackled, and hot air rushed past him as he surged high into void again. Looking down,

Garland saw the uncanny shape of Graywash Hall, shrinking to a blob as distance grew between them.

Garland raced through clouds, his mind oddly calm. *This was destiny*. He saw a far distant castle radiant with light.

I'm coming . . .

Then he dropped through cloud, losing the vision. Night came and went, strange beasts thundered by, their roars all around him. Garland felt bitter cold and blazing heat then nothing at all in the space of a second.

Garland's descent slowed. He became a leaf drifting down on a summer's breeze, settling feather-light on a dusty deserted road. Again, the surge of sea close by. Shaking, Garland found his feet, and glancing around saw his sword sticking point-down in the turf.

I thought you might need that.

Cille's voice came from deep beneath the ground. Garland slammed the sword in its scabbard. He looked around, eyes wide with apprehension. He was on a track, a stone path leading down to a long narrow bridge. More like a ridge of jagged scarp running alongside the sea. Ahead, barely a mile away, stood a castle of sorts.

The Castle of Lights.

Like a beacon, the single lone tower sent shafts of emerald light up soaring up into the sky, the sea surging white and angry all around it.

Chapter 28 | Fugitives

They rode through the night in single file, passing through woods, fording streams, and staying clear of any roads, stopping twice as the sounds of soldiers could be heard close by.

Tam was furious with Seek, whose reckless action might have scuppered any chance of him finding Teret. Both sides of the Shen River would be crawling with vengeful soldiers seeking to find someone to punish for what had happened at that camp.

At first Tam thought it might help them by setting the two enemy realms at odds, as Seek had planned. But Stogi said it would achieve nothing, explaining that the Ptarni ambassador was a small fish in the emperor's eyes, and the Shen Magister just an influential member of one of the several rival families who governed Shen.

"A stupid, rash act that almost got us killed and most likes will yet," Stogi said.

"I thought the Magister a powerful man," Tam said. "Maybe the Shen will be more fired up than you think?"

"One falls, another three take his place," Stogi said. "Shen is a machine. They are practical and not likely to be swayed, especially by assassins. Seek got it wrong. He's pleased with himself, but all he's achieved is pissing them off. Sometimes, I think he just does things to draw attention to himself."

"A wonder he's still breathing then."

"Charmed by good luck and a talent for self-preservation," Stogi said. "But I'm done talking about him, lest I'm tempted to stick a dagger in his belly to soothe my fragile nerves. It'll be light soon, best we rein in shortly. Get some kip while we can."

"I doubt we'll achieve that with all the action around here," Tam said. "Ride on!"

The hours drudged by slowly with Tam dozing in the saddle, and then straightening in alarm every time he heard shouts or clashing steel far off in the distance. Despite his longing for a good smoke, or ale, or better both, Tam felt stronger than he had. The weeks of riding and living rough had almost returned him to the man he'd been. A tough, self-reliant, fighting man, with a wry wit and cunning mind. One thing hadn't changed—his growing panic that Teret would die before he got to her. Every day that worry worm grew bigger in his belly. And now Seek was fueling the monster.

"I wish I knew what he's up to," Tam said later, as they settled just before dawn and made a hasty camp in the shelter of a copse.

"Power," Stogi said. "Seek wants to rule the Tseole and lead them against our enemies for glory and certain death. The way I see it."

"Simplistic," Tam said. "Must be more to it than that."

"He's a shaman—they're wired differently than the rest of us," Stogi said. "Dunnehine is covered in ice for most the year, leaving its tenants with little to do save scratch their bellies, play with their organs, and scheme up wicked notions in the freezing dark. Seek is a troublemaker with too much time to think."

Tam didn't see it that way, but he refrained from commenting further. Stogi detested the shaman, which, though understandable, curved his opinion. Seek was playing a far more complicated game than Stogi implied. And it was Tam's task to unravel it, if only so he could find Teret and escape this situation. Though thanks to the shaman that would prove even more difficult now.

As if he knew they were talking about him, Seek wandered over when the two riders were seeing to their horses. Stogi ignored him and strode off to attend nature in the bushes.

"That fellow thinks I've lost it." Seek showed his enigmatic smile, removed his tall hat, and took seat on a log, as Tam slid the saddle from his horse and patted her down.

"And I'd say he has a good point," Tam said. After tethering the horse with the other beasts, Tam returned to see Seek smoking his pipe, legs crossed an expression of deep contentment on his face, long coat draped around his scrawny shoulders, the hat lying beside his boots.

"Pleased with yourself, aren't you?" Tam glared down at the shaman.

"Last night's events awarded a certain satisfaction," Seek said, blinking up at him.

"We could have all been killed—almost were."

"A risk worth taking," Seek said. He saw the anger in Tam's eyes and waved a hand. "Necessary, Lord Tam—I assure you."

"Why light a fire when you're standing in the hearth?"

"Opportunities must be taken when they arise," Seek said, puffing at his pipe. Tam's nose twitched at the aroma of tobacco, and wished it were something stronger.

"Stogi thinks you want power, and that's the sole reason why you're doing this. Drive a wedge between your enemies, then raid and pillage their trains while they are preoccupied with murdering each other."

"Precisely what I intend to do," Seek said. "But not purely for that reason. That horse thief Stogi should keep his lips together; thinking's not his strong point."

"His logic makes sense to me," Tam said, accepting Seek's offer of smoke and taking a long hard pull at the pipe, "if you had a force big enough and horses fast enough to pull off such bold actions. Lamentably, I doubt your rag-tag guerrillas have the capacity, or even heart for such hazardous strategies."

Seek shrugged. "Ptarni and Shen cannot be allowed to unite," he said. "They would stifle trade and grind every other country to powder—including your dreamy lot in the west. I dented their confidence, fed their distrust. Caused a ripple. Tiny, admittedly—but it will grow. And the first of many such actions I intend."

"The Crystal King can hold his own," Tam said, thinking of his former friend.

"We'll see," Seek said. "Shen possesses a huge navy which, until now, has focused on bleeding dry the wealthy nations beyond the Permian Desert. Choking their ports and holding them ransom. A thousand ships down there—they could be rerouted northwest at any time."

"A long and dangerous sail." Tam blew a smoke ring and let it drift off into the morning. "Never heard of any ship covering such distance."

"Shen craft are well made and their captains greedy for gold. Given enough incentive they will do it," Seek said, accepting the pipe back and jamming it in his mouth. "Ptarni has the army," he said, blowing smoke through his lips, "Shen the sea power. Together, these villainous realms can throttle the trade routes both over land and water and squeeze every nation in Ansu dry. They need to be stopped, Lord Tam."

"By a wizard, and a tiny crew of renegade freedom fighters," Tam smiled. "Stogi's right, you are deluded."

"It's a start," Seek said, "and only a small part of a much bigger plan."

"I thought it might be," Tam said. "So where do I fit in?"

"I need you to do something for me, and in doing so help yourself."

"Go on."

"Bring me the Bow called Kerasheva," Seek said, his eyes lighting up. "The three sisters desire it, and they must not get it."

"I don't know what you are talking about," Tam said.

"You've not heard of the Emerald Bow?" Seek said. "And I thought you an educated man."

"I slept through most of the history classes I attended back then," Tam said.

"Unwise," Seek said. "We forget history's mistakes and they creep up on us again with painful reminders. Ignorance is mankind's worst folly."

"I'm not in the mood for being lectured," Tam said. He was bone weary and wanted to squeeze some knowledge from Seek without all the dribble alongside.

"Kerasheva is an Aralais artifact with useful dynamics," Seek said, "like those possessed by your beloved High King—the sword Callanak, and his crystal crown, the Tekara. All were made by the Golden Race. Misuse of the crystal crown and that sword were partly to blame for the war that followed, and all the trouble since—a mixed blessing those sacred tools. Handle with care." Seek smiled artfully. "You played a part in that struggle as I recall."

"I not getting involved with all that again." Despite his words Tam felt a flash of excitement recalling that earlier time. He had ridden with the best during that three-year war, and against all wagers they had defeated their foe. In the desert, beneath the mountains, on the sea—they had toppled Caswallon, the first domino to fall.

"Why not?" Seek leaned forward, grinning at him as though reading his memories. "Seven years of peace has left you dim-witted and vacant. I'm offering you a chance to become the man you once were."

"I have wife to find, not a world to save."

"And I'll help you with that," Seek said, "but first I need that fucking bow to save humanity from itself, now the Gods aren't around to guide them."

"Interesting idea," Tam said. "I didn't take you for the altruistic type. Besides, I thought we'd done rather well since the Gods tore each other into pieces. Those deities are not much missed in my opinion, self-serving meddlers the lot of them."

"A cynical reflection and hurtful choice of words," Seek said, "and not entirely accurate either." Tam ignored those remarks, wrapped in gloomy thoughts of Teret, and the mistakes he'd made after the conflict.

"Life is shit with or without the Gods' intervention," Tam said, "but at least we can hold our own cocks when we take a leak."

"Eloquently put," Seek said, his eyes on the others cooking breakfast close by.

"Cuts to the quick," Tam said, his nostrils flaring and telling him he hadn't eaten for hours. "And with that in mind—how do you propose to help me?"

"Kerasheva has many useful functions, including the power to save the one you love," Seek said.

"I intend to do that without need of a magic bow."

"No chance. Teret is riding into a trap—I have seen it," Seek said enigmatically.

"Seen *what?*" Tam's calm manner was replaced by sudden rage. "What do you know?"

"Seen her throat cut open," Seek replied with sudden venom. He took another long pull on his pipe, and then ducked low as Tam's fist narrowly missed his head.

Tam kicked out, but Seek rolled free of the log and stood glaring up at him, hat and pipe gripped in hands. "You can't hurt me, Lord Tamersane."

"Can't I?" Tam said.

"No," Seek said, "because I'm the only one who can help you."

"You keep hinting that but do nothing—except nearly getting us all killed."

Seek smiled. "It's all about timing," he said. "Patience, wait for the right moment, and then strike hard and fast. You'll see! First though, we've prisoners to free."

"What about Teret?"

"Breakfast smells good!" Seek rammed the hat on his head, gathered his coat around those skinny shoulders, and left Tam smoldering.

"Told you he's mad," Stogi said, after joining Tam and the others for makeshift breakfast by the feeble fire they'd risked. "Be the death of us, so he will."

"I agree, but Seek needs my help," Tam said. "Keeps dangling bait in front of me, saying how he alone can help find Teret, providing I do something for him too."

"I'll do something for him soon enough," Stogi said. "Stick my dagger where the sun don't shine."

The next morning, they rode through sheets of rain, turning north again and crossing the road far to the east from where they'd left it. There was no sign of either Shen patrols or the Ptarni force accompanying the ambassador. Tam hoped they were well ahead of them, and the Ptarnians would be returning home with tales of treachery and murder.

The countryside surrounding them rose and dipped in steady folds of green. A grassy open terrain that, even in this deluge, allowed good vision for many miles. Tam squinted through the rain and shifted uncomfortably in the saddle.

Shen appeared an unwholesome land, but mercifully also sparsely populated. Stogi had told him most the Shen lived in teeming cities on the far coast. Complex folk who loved intrigue, the Shen nobility shunned the open country, deeming it the realm of peasant, outlaw, and beast. Tam was grateful for that much.

They followed the road for most of that day, then Seek bid them cut across country again.

"So where are these mines?" Tam asked, riding alongside his friend and Shel.

"Not far." Stogi pointed to the horizon where low hills frowned down through the dismal rain. "The other side of those hills. Broon says there's a long ridge we'll have to crest before dropping down into the mining region."

"Do you trust Broon?" Tam asked him "He seems shifty to me."

"Broon doesn't like Seek any more than we do," Stogi said. "But, no—I don't trust him. I don't trust anyone."

An hour's continued riding saw them ranging through a gap in the hills and reaching the long ridge Stogi had mentioned. It was hard to see clearly, but looking down Tam could make out large buildings and strange structures comprising metal towers with wheels and pulleys, much like the ferry house but far bigger, and there were many. They dwindled randomly as far as the eye could see through a narrow knife-cut of a valley with steep slopes, the surface bare and shining, save the odd pile of gray-black slag.

A grim place in a dour, hard country. Tam hardened his resolve. Why were they here? The valley hung with smoke from a dozen chimneys. Miners? Sword loose in scabbard, Tam rode behind Stogi as they carefully guided their horses down the rough, steep slope and entered the valley, the rain lashing their faces.

"This weather might kill us if the enemy doesn't," Tam said, wishing he had a stash he could smoke, or else a hot toddy to warm his chilled bones. They reached the nearest buildings, huge metal hangars, the likes Tam had never seen.

"Store houses," Stogi said, dismounting with the others. Their way ahead was a mess of twisted tracks, broken cart wheels, and clutter, buildings and fences surrounding them in random fashion. "We'll not lead our horses through that."

Hulda, Shel, and the others stayed with the horses, sheltering inside one of the hangars after checking it for occupants. Seek hissed Broon and Stogi follow him, Tam as well. The fewer the better for this task, he insisted.

They crisscrossed over tracks and vaulted fences, staying close to walls and buildings until the nearest wheelhouse loomed close: a great tower of stone, with a tall broken chimney belching smoke that battled up through the heavy drizzle.

The stone was the darkest gray, merging well with the lowering rain clouds above and the scree-dark valley slopes on either side. Tam spat and shivered. Never had he encountered such a dreary place. Seek signaled them to wait as he removed his hat and slipped inside the wheelhouse. Moments later, Seek emerged and hopped and skipped over to another building half-hidden in the gloom. The flapping coat made him resemble a large crow jumping eagerly from grub to grub in a freshly-plowed field.

Tam heard a shrill whistle, and next moment they were sprinting toward that other building, which revealed itself as a gatehouse. The entrance led directly down to a wagon of sorts, with metal sleds instead of wheels. On closer inspection, Tam saw seats and a set of ropes and pulleys leading down into a yawning black hole, nothing visible beyond.

"Get in," Seek said. "Broon, you work the pulley."

"What the fuck?" Tam looked askance at Stogi as they clambered on board the wagon and, after Broon released the lever controlling the pulley system, the contraption commenced grinding and scraping at alarming speed down into the gaping hole, scarcely larger than the wagon itself.

Tam closed his eyes as the hole swallowed them and blackness followed. He blinked, saw nothing but dark and cursed Seek once again. Beside him Stogi clutched the sides, his knuckles white as the wagon picked up speed and careered down into gloom, rattling, crashing, rolling, and bucking this way and that.

They plunged down at breakneck speed for long minutes, the blackness swallowing them and the damp stuffy air choking their breath. Tam kept his eyes shut tight and gripped the sides expecting the worst at any moment.

I'm so fucking tired of this.

The noise was unbelievable and Tam couldn't hear his own shouts when suddenly the cart crashed like thunder onto level ground and almost threw its unfortunate passengers out.

"You're a crap driver," Stogi told Broon as he leaped free of the wreckage. "How the fuck are we supposed to get back up to daylight?" Broon just scowled at him.

Seek grinned. "That was fun," he said, leaping out with coat flapping, and grabbing a lit torch conveniently placed in a rack by the wagon's bottom pulley. "This way."

"How does he know where he's going?" Tam asked Stogi.

"Probably dreamed it," Stogi said, ducking as the ceiling of the mine shrank in front. "For all I know we're stuck down here."

A maze of tunnels led down, steep and twisting until Tam had lost all sense of direction. Seek, holding his torch aloft, crossed through that labyrinth of tunnels without any hint of uncertainty. That awarded some small comfort. Tam didn't care whether the shaman had dreamed it, or else was using some weird internal radar device. Seek knew where he was going. *You have to hang on to any positive thread you can in this life.* At least it was warmer down here, and though damp it wasn't raining.

After what seemed an age, they started hearing distant sounds of hammers and steel striking rock. Tam wondered what they were mining; he'd never thought to ask the shaman.

"Somebody here," Tam whispered in Stogi's ear. "I was thinking maybe these mines were deserted or dried up."

"Me too."

"What are they digging for? Gold? Minerals?"

"Crystal."

Tam fell silent, remembering another trip to crystal mines in distant Permio. That seemed like a lifetime ago.

I was a different man back then—a better man.

He shut out the memory and the pain it contained. Crystal. The High King's crown had come from those mines.

"For what purpose," Tam asked eventually. "Jewelry?"

"Buggered if I know," Stogi shrugged as they entered another tunnel. "They say the cities of Shen are magnificent like no others, their roofs and gables carved with jade and crystal."

"You are a font of wisdom," Tam said.

"I know," Stogi said. "You're lucky I'm your friend."

"I'm not feeling lucky at the moment," Tam said.

"Me neither."

The hammers were closer now, and some large blowing device sent a draft that lifted Tam's hair and smarted his eyes. He blinked, seeing a distant yellow light. Lanterns?

"Nearly there," Seek said, turning another corner and vanishing in the gloom. Tam and the other two hurried to keep up.

The draft was stronger here, and a sucking sound like a giant bellows pumped and sighed with constant rhythm. There was another sound too. It came from somewhere far off in the mines and didn't belong there. An eerie sound that sent a shiver up Tam's spine. Pipe music, shrill and haunting.

"Do you hear that?" Tam asked his friend.

"I cannot hear anything through that racket," Stogi complained.

"A piper," Tam said. "I heard pipes playing—just for a few seconds."

"Happy for you," Stogi grunted at him, and Tam wished he hadn't mentioned it. The light flickered and swelled ahead and then suddenly the tunnel's walls fell away, revealing a wide-open area lit with sconces that flickered and shuddered in time with the bellows, their yellow glare casting dancing shadows along the walls.

"Steady, now—there's no railings and it's a long drop," Tam heard Seek whisper before stopping just in time and looking down.

"Shit!" Stogi crashed into Tam's back. "That was close." Below was a pit, hard to tell how large. But when Tam's eyes adjusted to the lantern light he discerned tiny figures at work down there.

"Ah . . . our people," Stogi said. "Slaves to the Shen. So how do we get down, Shaman?"

"The usual way, unless you're planning on flying," Seek said, walking along the edge and then vanishing from sight, like a scarecrow hit by sudden storm.

"I really don't like him," Stogi said, as he and Tam and the grimly silent Broon followed, and soon discovered stone stairs leading down into the pit. They were glistening with water and very steep, the wooden treads split and broken in places, some even missing entirely.

Twenty minutes and they were down. Tam grinned in relief as his feet found level ground. It was colder down here, and Tam realized this pit was much bigger than first he'd thought. They stood in a great underground cavern, its edges veined with gleaming rock that shone like polished glass in the torchlight. Again, thoughts of distant Permio pricked his memory. This was far less impressive, yet similar in some ways.

"Crystal—you were right," Tam said. "These mines must be very old, built by the Aralais like Seek said."

"Who cares?" Stogi said. "Let's concentrate on our task, shall we?"

They walked for several minutes, at last reaching the nearest wall. Here miners could be seen working from scaffolding high above. There were dozens of shabbily clad workers toiling up there. Tam was surprised to see both men and women working, grimy and bow-backed, their faces filthy and eyes dull with fatigue. None took any notice of the strangers approaching.

But someone else did. A Shen warrior in green robes stood at the foot of the nearest scaffold; a long pole with a twisted blade, the steel over two-foot long, was gripped in his gloved hands. The guard shouted a challenge, swung his weapon, and strode towards them, but pitched forward with a yell as Seek's knife pierced his throat. Tam could see other guards posted further away.

"Should we kill those too?" Tam asked Seek, worried they'd be spotted at any minute.

"No need. Let the creature in the mines deal with them," the shaman replied, waving an arm.

Tam looked at Stogi, who shrugged. "You didn't expect a sensible answer, did you?"

Tam thought of the mystery pipes and kept his lips together. The Jynn at the crossroads. Seek. Two sides of the same coin? Unlikely but there must be a connection. Too many coincidences. But how? And why would the Piper haunt this place? Evidently there was more to these mines than crystal and workers.

"What's he doing now?" Stogi said, watching as Seek vaulted up the nearest scaffold like a gibbon, all arms and swaying legs, the coat catching and tearing. "There's a bloody ladder over there."

"Guess he's in a hurry." Tam sprinted, caught hold of the nearest bamboo strut, and heaved himself up.

"You're too keen—that's your problem," Stogi said as he swung up alongside.

"Got my reasons," Tam said. "I don't want to let that bastard out of my sight." Tam saw three men and a woman laboring with huge sacks, their backs bent under the weight.

"Drop those!" Seek said, as they turned and gaped at him. They looked scared, as though they were seeing an apparition. And maybe they were, thought Tam. The shaman was no common sight, with his high hat and drooping coat tails, and their eyes dimmed by time spent down here were most likes struggling to focus.

The woman dropped her sack first. Tam marveled at how strong she must be, the tight woven cloth was brimming with glass chips—shards of priceless crystal, no doubt.

"You won't need to carry that again," Seek said. "I only want the one sack."

"What's he talking about?" Tam asked Stogi, standing beside him halfway up the scaffold.

"He's up to something," Stogi said.

"Think perhaps his plan was not as transparent as we thought," Tam said.

"You think?" Stogi said, the sarcasm weighing his tone.

"Doesn't matter," Tam said, watching the men drop their sacks and back away from Seek. The woman stood her ground, appearing tougher than her companions. She was small and slender, and the sack she carried almost as big as she was. She looked wiry though—tough.

Tam studied the woman's hard features. She didn't look like a

Tseole, with her pale skin and flinty dark eyes, and a thin white scar cutting through her left brow. Her clothes were half rotted away, but she stood poised like a dancer, despite the crook in her back.

"Who the fuck are you?" the woman said, staring at Seek, his three companions circling behind.

"It's a good question," Stogi said to Tam. "Often asked it myself."

"I'm Seek, a shaman of Dunnehine. I need some of that crystal from one of those sacks. Just a few pieces will suffice. Reason why I'm here—oh, and you can escape if you want. I'm not stopping you."

"You lied to us!" Tam leaped toward Seek, his hand on pommel.

"No, I didn't," Seek said. "I twisted the truth a little, so what?"

"These aren't our people, they're Shen!" Broon who had been brooding in silence rose up to confront Seek. The Tseole leader's face was red with fury. "I see some Laregozans and a couple of other strange folk—but no fucking Tseole." Broon's sword was in his hand. "You're a deceitful turd."

"How was I to know that?" Seek flicked an acid stare at Broon which had the leader backing off again. "I thought there would be some Tseole here," he said. "Made sense, and I daresay there are if you want to look about. As for me—I've got what I needed."

Seek scooped up the sack the woman had abandoned, spilled out most the contents, and then slung it over his shoulders. "I'll be away now," he said. Broon followed behind without further word and Tam wondered what strange hold Seek had over the Tseole leader. Tam shook his head and gazed down at the tiny fragments of crystal, trying to guess their worth.

"We'd best follow him if we want to escape here," Stogi said. "Then once we're free I'm going to cut his fucking gizzards out."

"Good idea," said Tam. "I'll watch, after I've pricked some answers from him." He turned to the woman, on closer look scarce more than a girl. "You coming? You others too?"

"Seems like a good suggestion," the young woman nodded. "I'm weary of this place."

"How long you been working here?" Tam asked her, offering a hand as they started climbing down the scaffold. She glared at his hand as though it were a snake.

"Working here?" The girl shrugged. "Stupid question." She vaulted the rail and began climbing down, hand over hand. "I'm a slave," she yelled back up at Tam as he tried to keep close behind. "I don't work—I exist."

"You have a name?" Tam said, surprised at her manner. He'd expected gratitude, relief, and maybe even a smile. Instead the woman had scolded him.

"Tai Pei—recently of House Zayn but now a slave." There was no bitterness in her tone, just reflection.

"House Zayn?" Stogi looked excited as he jumped down alongside Tam. Behind, the other miners were on their way down too. "You've noble blood? The Zayn are the highest family in Shen."

"What?" Tam braced his feet as he landed on dirt. "She's a what?" he wondered how Stogi knew all this. For a mangy goat-stealer, his friend was a wide storehouse of information.

"We were," Tai Pei said. Her sharp eyes were on the guards, Tam noticed. "But my parents and retainers were murdered by assassins from House Xuile. Those like myself who survived were sold into slavery, and most of them are dead."

"Yet you live," Stogi murmured at her.

"I haven't made plans for dying yet," Tai Pei said.

Tam pushed Stogi's shoulder. "Never mind her—which way did he go?"

"Down there," Stogi said, pointing to the far end of the cavern, half-concealed by gloom. "And no need to shove me."

The ground was slippery and uneven, and they negotiated as best they could without a torch to light the way. Once they'd got past those guards they could run for it. Stogi led the way, Tam following close behind, and Tai Pei, the Shen girl, behind him. Judging by the shuffle of feet, the others were following close behind. Good idea, thought Tam, if they wanted to survive.

He glimpsed Seek reaching the far end of the scaffold and tossing the sack over his shoulder again before sliding down the pole ladder. Took a different route. Despite his anger at the shaman Tam had to admire his agility; Seek was losing them again, even with the sack slung over his shoulders.

"He's getting away," Tam said watching Seek jump to the floor in front of them, then turned, hearing a shout from behind. Torches and a flash of steel. Guards alerted to trouble up there on the scaffold. They'd seen Seek and started running, pushing terrified workers out the way, some falling to their death as they were shoved. Tam shielded his eyes. *Six guards.* The closest was shouting and pointing down at Tam and the others. All carried whips, and a few had heavy, curved swords. Fortunately, none seemed to possess bows. Tam assumed they'd not expected this kind of trouble in the mines.

The guards started racing toward the far end of the scaffold, meaning to cut them off. The nearest had cleared the top and was stepping off, when Tai Pei sprinted past Stogi and Tam, vaulted back up the scaffold, and neatly kicked the guard square in the face, knocking him back into his companion below, and causing them both tumble from the ladder to the stony ground below, barely feet away from where Tam and Stogi gawped.

"Well done!" Stogi said; the woman just looked down at him. The other guards were closing fast, and Tam heard shouts of more joining the chase from behind. They left scaffold and pits behind and reached a long slab of congealed crystal, the surface treacherously slippery and

345

glowing, like dragon eyes in the gloom

"Can we walk on that?" Tam asked Stogi and then winced as Tai Pei vaulted onto the crystal, skidded sideways, found her feet, and started sprinting again.

"Looking like it," Stogi said, wiping snot from his nose. "Come on."

They negotiated the glittering slab with relative ease and from this half-clambered and half-slid to a lower level, where Seek's departing shadow could be seen in the distance. More guards had appeared from another entrance and some were racing to cut them off, the others jumping down from the scaffold above.

"Going to get busy," Stogi said.

Tam heard screams and turned. The miners running behind Tai Pei were not so quick as she, and the guards had killed two already. Tam saw the rest cut down by those vicious pikes.

"Passage—Seek and Broon must have fled down there!" Stogi pointed to a distant crack of black in the farthest end of the cavern, a few sconces marking the way. "Suggest we follow."

"Good idea." Tai Pei raised a brow. "Lead on bold heroes."

"What's her problem?" Tam said, as he sprinted alongside his friend.

"She's Shen, from an important house," Stogi said. "They can be a bit uppity."

"Interesting attitude for a slave," Tam hissed, catching the girl's eye.

They sped. A guard with a curved sword ran to cut them off. Tam ducked beneath his swipe and rammed his pommel up into the guard's jaw, snapping it. Stogi jumped on the man's belly and stamped hard down on his neck. The guard slumped silent.

"Clumsy, if efficient," Tai Pei said, sprinting over the dead guard's body.

"Thanks," Tam and Stogi responded in unison.

They reached the passage and were plunged into utter darkness again, not helped by the nearest sconce choosing that precise moment to expire. Seek had vanished somewhere ahead, the pursuing guards were yelling close behind, aside that they heard only the sound of their own breath and patter of their running feet.

"What the—? Whoa . . ." Tam slid sideways crashing into Stogi. The passage descended at an alarming rate, and the two men struggled to balance their descent. The girl seemed to float past them, her dark eyes hinting amusement.

"You're all arms and legs," Tai Pei said to Stogi. "I've seen more grace in a three-legged ox."

"Thanks again," Stogi responded breathless. "Kind of you to comment, girl. What now?" He asked Tam.

"You're asking me?"

They slowed as the descent proved more and more treacherous, causing Tam and Stogi to trip several times. Tai Pei glided over any obstacles with irritating ease.

"She's very graceful," Stogi remarked once after scraping himself back off the floor.

At last the passage leveled out and they picked up their pace again. "For all we know we're descending into the pits of Yffarn," Stogi said.

"What goes in must come out," Tai Pei said. Tam ignore them both and slowed to a walk, seeing a strange light ahead.

Another cavern? More shafts? Didn't look like it.

"You seeing what I'm seeing?" Tam said.

"Lights," Tai Pei said, without breaking her pace. "But not torches."

"Wait . . . stop!" Tam hissed at the girl as Stogi leaned down to get his breath back. "That glow doesn't look right to me."

"So?" The girl didn't look back. Tam and Stogi stared at each other and shrugged.

"After you," Stogi said. The light shimmered and throbbed brighter as they approached, as if welcoming them forward.

"Are you thinking what I'm thinking?" Tam asked Stogi, screwing his eyes up to see ahead.

"Aye—a portal, some kind of door."

"To another dimension," Tam nodded. "The Piper at work again." The light filled the passage ahead like a living entity, its colors changing constantly, shifting from deep pulsating blue, through green and yellow, into crimson, then back through to throbbing blue again. The atmosphere around it shimmered and the air gave off an alien heat.

"Have you seen this before?" Tam shouted at Tai Pei still paces ahead of them.

"No," she said, stopping at last and allowing them catch up.

"Were you just going to walk on through it without a second's thought?" Tam studied the young woman's pale features.

"Of course—why hesitate?" Tai Pei said.

"You don't know what it leads to—could be bad," Stogi said.

"Probably," Tam said.

"Like being boiled alive slowly in a vat of oil?" Tai Pei said. "That's what they do to runaway slaves in Shen."

"That's just spiteful," Stogi said. "Hopefully this won't be that bad."

"We shall see," Tai Pei flashed them a feral grin and turned toward the shimmering light. Within seconds she had vanished, swallowed up in its glare.

"I like that girl," Stogi said, then pushed Tam hard so they both fell to the floor. The spear just missed Tam's head. "Looks like company," Stogi said. Shadows and shouts—the guards had found the passage and were coming their way.

Decision time.

Tam leaped to his feet and together with his friend started running at pelt toward the pulsating weirdness ahead. There was no sign of Tai Pei. Tam assumed the ex-slave had already gone through the doorway, or whatever it was.

They reached the light, the sound of shouts, boots on stone, and clashing steel getting closer. A shadow blocked Tam's way. A man stood there, small and neat, dressed in deep blue jacket and trousers, a wide smile smearing his round face and a small reedy pipe gripped between fleshy fingers.

The Jynn!

"There isn't much time," the Piper said. "This portal will close any second."

"Where will it take us?" Tam asked the Piper as he shoved past, aware of the guards closing the gap behind them.

"Back to Graywash Hall," the Piper said. "From there you can find a way through to the Castle of Lights. Ask Cille—she knows." The Piper vanished, and the light strobed outwards, sending tendrils that surrounded the two, cocooned them, and then pulled them in to the source.

"Who's Cheelee?" Stogi said, as he fell through the light and disappeared.

"A witch—I'll explain later!"

Tam yelled as he dived headfirst into the light, the mine guards jumping after him.

Shit.

Tam cursed as the stabbing light stung his eyes and he was squeezed down through a narrow gap like a rat sucked from a pipe in a flood. Tam emerged out the other end like wet bolt shot from crossbow, then pitched forward into nothingness, the sounds of whispering voices and shadows all around him.

Here we go again.

Chapter 29 | Corridors

Tam plummeted through cold bright air. He saw clouds rushing up to greet him; they sucked at him with damp fingers as he dropped within but couldn't hold him, and he fell right through them, his body blazing like a comet, opening out again on a clear blue sky.

Far below were green fields ringed by stone walls, buildings, the odd cluster of trees, beyond them the gray churning of a cold winter sea. Tam felt his body glide, shift, and angle sideways along that fringe of coastline. He saw dunes, a blaze high on a hill. The river.

And there it was. Graywash Hall. Swelling in size as he plunged toward it. A congealed inky mass of chaotic rock, with spikes and spires twisting and jerking out at every angle. Like a giant stone sea urchin, it appeared from that height. Tam tumbled toward those crooked towers, the wind rushing through his hair and eyes smarting with its cold sting. Voices whispered his name, calling up and beckoning him inside. A stone tossed down a well, Tam's speed increased, and the Hall swelled in size as it rushed up to meet him. He closed his eyes.

This is going to hurt.

Seconds passed with no impact. Tam wondered if he were already dead and these last few days just dreams, fragments of thought clinging to whatever essence still remained of him. But the air was cold, and his body felt numb, except his ears. They hurt and were filled with the rush of icy breeze. Tam hoped the pain would be over quickly. For a second time that trickster Jynn had sent him to his death. Why? It made no sense.

Seconds passed, became minutes, and those dwindled too. The wind fell away and was replaced by silence. Something fluttered past his face. Tam opened his eyes. He stood in a hall filled with steam and in the distance could just make out the shape of someone watching him.

I am alive.

"That word has no meaning here," Cille said, emerging through the steam, her lean limbs clinging to the dripping red gown she wore. Tam could see her nipples and the dark patch between her thighs. Tam felt a flush of excitement mixed with fear.

Wasn't expecting this.

Cille took his hand in hers and Tam started at the iciness of that touch. Her green-gold eyes were cold as an owl's and she smiled at him. "Glad you came back," she said. "I missed you these last few hours. You're more interesting than the other one, though he's doubtless a better man. You I could enjoy." She rubbed a leg alongside his and kissed his mouth. "Ah . . . that brings back sweet memories," Cille smiled. "The taste of a mortal." Then with sudden coolness Cille pushed him away. "Regrettably, you need to leave right away," she said. "Time has no meaning in this room but is passing quickly elsewhere."

"It's been days since I was here," Tam said wiping his mouth, his head buzzing and mind racing with a thousand questions. "A lot has happened since then, though I'm none the wiser."

"You must leave now Tamersane, while you still can," Cille said. "The others have gone but will return soon. Even I cannot protect us here as the world fabric is crumbling. Soon they will penetrate my walls."

"Who?" Time felt groggy, almost drugged in that heavy atmosphere. "Stogi? The slave woman?"

"Go," Cille said, pushing him again, this time toward a door which had emerged through the steam. Tam saw a dull green light lining the edges.

"The Piper was right," she said. "The portals are closing, and you must stop my sister; in doing so you will save the one you love."

"I don't understand," Tam said.

"You will in time."

Cille and the steamy room had disappeared. Instead, Tam was looking down a length of endless corridor, lit on either wall by flickering sconces, the flames dancing on the surface of mirrors alongside.

"Cille?"

"Take the third door on the left," her voice sounded far away. "Don't hesitate—time is limited as we approach the nexus. That door will lead you to the Castle of Lights. Once there you must—"

"Cille!"

"Ahh, they are back," Cille's distant voice faded and was replaced by a heavy scraping sound, followed by a long wail that trailed off into a scream of agony.

Cille?

Silence. Torches flickering, mirrors reflecting their flame, and a cold tunnel breeze lifting his hair. Tam wondered if he were back in the mines and this just another an illusion. Or else Seek had him tripping on rogue weed.

He paced the corridor at speed, focusing on the torches far ahead, and ignoring those he passed. Each sconce and bracket resembled the arms of some hideous beast. They creaked into life as Tam brushed past, reaching out and singeing his hair and shoulders with their brands. Another illusion. Shut it out. Tam started to trot, and glancing back, saw the sconces join together into one great flame and rush behind him.

He ran, forcing back panic. The corridor resonated menace, a feeling that he was not alone, that some cruel entity or malicious spirit was stalking him. Tam tried not to look, but occasionally his eyes were drawn to the mirrors lining both sides of the passage. There were faces in there, staring back out at him. Cold, cruel faces. They watched him pass with hungry eyes. Burn, those eyes said. *Burn.* Behind and closing, the lone sconce flame crackled and leaped.

A door appeared on the left, from it a pale hand reached out and beckoned him inside. Tam tripped as the hand grabbed his jacket. He shoved it aside, gasping at the coldness of that touch. Unlike Cille's, that touch felt like death. Tam staggered to his feet. Ran on.

A second door loomed on his right, high-arched and archaic, the stone lintel crumbling. A man stood there. A giant encased in steel, his head hidden by a barrel helmet, hollow slits hinting where the eyes should be.

"I'm waiting for you," the metal giant said as Tam skirted past. "You cannot escape me." Tam left giant and door behind.

Ignore everything. Third door on left. I've got this.

Tam passed two more doors, both on his right. Guardians stood there but Tam ignored them, refusing to accept their existence. A second door emerged on his left, more like a crack in the wall. A woman's voice called out to him.

"Lord Tam—love me; it's been so long."

He glanced inside briefly as he passed. A woman stood there, naked save a robe she had draped across her shoulders. In horror Tam saw her long finger nails were dripping blood, and crimson pooled the dirt beneath her feet.

"I need flesh!" the woman shrieked as Tam rushed by, dreading what the third door would reveal. The corridor turned, twisted, and if he'd had any sense of direction he'd have lost it by now. It was hotter here and the air cloying as though he were inside the belly of some huge serpent. The walls pressed in on him and those mirrors clinked and split asunder as Tam sped past.

A wall loomed ahead. The corridor dead ended! Cille had lied to him.

No way out. Tam saw a long mirror hanging from that wall. As he approached, he glimpsed his reflection, and something else—another figure, much larger, looming over him. Tam turned, sword slicing. Nothing there.

Trapped!

He looked back down the corridor reflected by its own mirrors, the torches flickering faster as the gathering flame swelled large toward him, the mirrors exploding as it rushed past. Tam heard the sound of crunching feet and saw the metal giant emerge through that flame, a huge mace swinging in his steel fists. The giant's mass filled the corridor, and the flames caressed and licked that armor, as his steel-shod feet crunched closer, the metal mace scraping the floor and filling Tam with terror.

This isn't real. Hold it together—there's a door here somewhere. Has to be!

The giant was closing fast, his metal head sparking off the corridor ceiling as he stooped. Tam looked around, the panic tearing him open. No door, and no alternative except going back, and that meant facing that giant.

"Do something!" Tam heard his voice echo down the corridor.

Something . . . something . . . something . . .

You are close—don't fail now. The voice was Cille's and came from the mirror on his left. Tam saw a man's image within. A man he knew, but hadn't seen in years. A creature from his past. A cruel man, and in his hand a bloodied knife.

Who are you stalking, Sulo?

But Tam knew the answer and cried out in pain when he saw Teret standing alone in a hall of glass, her face stricken with terror. She hadn't seen Sulo creeping up behind her, the knife raised high.

"Teret!" Tam's fist struck the glass of the mirror and it exploded into a thousand shards, blinding him in the glare and cutting open his face. Tam blinked through blood and tears. The giant rose over him, the mace already falling.

Tam leapt forward into the gap where the mirror had hung. That had vanished, replaced by a gaping hole. *The third door on the left.*

Tam had found it at last, but was he too late? He jumped through as the mace swung wide over his head, and flames soared behind it.

A rough hand grabbed Tam and pulled him out into cold salty air. "Got him!" A familiar voice said. Tam blinked; the air crackled behind him. He turned, saw a fissure of light closing like a clam at returning tide. Within it Tam glimpsed the corridor and flames shrinking and dwindling, and then disappearing. He heard a chuckle, staggered to his feet and someone punched him lightly. Tam swayed, tried not to spew as he steadied himself. He opened his eyes, saw the sea crashing to his left and heard the cry of gulls overhead. "Where?"

"Don't ask," Stogi said leaning over his friend.

Tam blinked up at him, seeing the Shen woman, Tai Pei, standing behind, her expression slightly curious. "We're out of time," Tam said, taking quick stock of this new situation. He stood on a beach, the sea just yards ahead, and huge breakers crashing upon pebble, sand, and rock. It was warm and sunny.

"Am I outside the Hall?" Tam's face hurt, and his eyes stung, and he could see nothing but sand, sea, and sun for miles and miles, broken occasionally by the triangular lumps of rocks spilled from the hills crumbling away into distance. A seashore unlike any he'd seen.

"Where . . .?"

"No idea," Stogi said, staring at the ocean as though it were a nest of serpents. "We just arrived here." Stogi looked confused and edgy. "Been walking this . . . beach for hours with that . . .water . . . trying to soak us every step."

"He's scared of the ocean," Tai Pei said, curling her lower lip.

"This isn't the sea that surrounds Graywash Hall," Tam muttered to himself. "That's a cold sea—a gray desolate region. This is different."

"What's he talking about?" Tai Pei said.

"He does this," Stogi said. "Smoked too much weed for too long, distorted his mind somewhat. Always off on trips."

"That would do it."

"Shut up and tell me where we are," Tam said.

"What makes you think we know where we are?" Stogi said. "I've just told you we arrived here from that . . . doorway? Whatever it was in the mines."

"A portal, bridging space and dimensions," Tai Pei said. "Such phenomena are commonplace at a time like this."

"A time like what?" Both the Tam and Stogi stared at the girl.

"A conjunction," she curled a lip. "The nine planets in a line—makes it easier for things to cross. Astrology versus cosmology. When you study the stars for long enough, a pattern unfolds—like a road map. Common sense," she said.

"Well, I'm impressed," Stogi told her, receiving a slap for his trouble.

Tam heard a soft chuckle and looked up. He wasn't overly surprised seeing Jynn the Piper standing behind Stogi. Tai Pei saw him too and lashed out with a clawed hand. The Piper laughed and deftly jumped back out of reach.

"She's quick that one," Jynn said. "And bright. Schooled in lore—

a Shen thing. A keeper I'd say." He winked at Stogi who was staring at him with an expression blending anger, amazement, and distrust.

"Where the fuck did you come from?" the Tseole said.

Tam pushed Stogi aside. "Where's Teret?" Tam squared on the small man who smiled up at him, the pipes stowed neatly in his belt.

"You're close," the Piper said. "But you need to hurry—she is in grave danger."

"Sulo, I know," Tam said. "I saw him with a knife. He was—"

"Yes, your enemy is there too." Jynn waved a dismissive hand. "And others, more dangerous than him."

"Is Teret—?"

"She lives, for the moment, but the minutes are counting."

"Where is she?" Tam reached forward to grab the Piper by the throat, but he'd vanished from sight, and instead Tam stared at empty sky and beach.

"How did he do that?" Stogi asked.

"A magician," Tai Pei said, matter-of-factly.

"Oh, you think?" Stogi said. Then Tam saw his friend had turned to look at something behind him. "That wasn't there a minute ago," Stogi said scratching his head. Tam and Tai Pei turned to look at what Stogi had seen.

A lone tower stood like an accusing finger on a remote rock about a mile ahead of where they were, a paved road leading up to was flanked by iron lanterns lining the way, their silvery lights piercing bright, despite the midday sun surrounding them. The tower gleamed like a wet luminous shell. The sight dazzled Tam as he tried to focus.

"The Castle of Lights," Tam said, blinking at the apparition.

Teret's in there.

"I've heard tell of it." Tai Pei looked impressed for the first time since Tam had been acquainted with her. "But never believed in its existence."

"Rundali," Stogi said. "Excellent. We're where you wanted to be then? Tam—?"

Tam ignored his friend as he started running for the road that led into that distant floodlit tower.

***

For Teret the vision was different. What lay ahead was a castle unlike anything she had imagined. A huge cluster of sparkling towers, thrusting up like brittle needles into a deep viridian sky, their color ranging from rose-pink, through ultra-marine, to deep violet blue, the bright sun dazzling off the polished surface of its multifaceted walls.

The sky surrounding the castle was a vivid green, the water below sparkling like summer with tints of turquoise. She saw beasts sliding through those waves, and exotic birds circled high above the lofty pinnacles, swooping specks of orange, blue, and gold, their shrill cries reaching her as she walked beside Carlo Sarfe, a cautious smile finding her lips.

It was three days since they'd left the left the forest. A walk through fertile warm lands, filled with beasts and wonders during day, the nights noisy with their cries as predator stalked victim. Teret's first sight of the Castle of Lights had been at dawn, it emerging as a shimmering beacon surrounded by waves. Throughout that day they'd hastened their steps, both eager to discover what awaited them there.

Teret was nervous, her mind caught in a cage of fear that pressed down on her, hurting her head. But she was excited too. She would see Tam soon, and somehow be able to save him. *The point of all this.* But she was sorrowful too. The days with Carlo had had their own magic. The warmth of his companionship, that sunny smile. Carlo

Sarfe was a good man and easy company. She would miss his support.

But Carlo had his own destiny to pursue, a country to find, and a family to save. Teret wished him luck with that, but her heart sagged at the thought of never seeing him again. Theirs had been a brief joining of lost souls in a wide and empty wilderness.

But Teret loved Tam and missed him, despite the last troublesome months when the drugs and drink had worked wickedly upon him. Tamersane was still the best of men; he had only to look inside himself and reclaim the warrior he'd once been before that terrible day in the dungeons below Wynais Castle. The day he'd killed his brother and changed forever. And changed Teret's life too.

The road led down onto a beach, forked left and ran parallel with the sea for a couple of miles, the gleaming castle dominating the horizon ahead. As they got nearer Teret saw banners and gonfalons trailing from those pinnacles. A huge fortress—she hoped an army didn't wait for them inside.

"Wonder what we'll find there," Carlo said gripping her hand briefly, his brown eyes warm and probing her reactions.

"We'll know soon enough," Teret smiled back at him. "I shall miss you Carlo Sarfe." She squeezed his hand quickly then pulled hers away.

"Ha," he laughed bitterly. "'Tis ironic. We both desperately seek something that will prize us apart forever. Part of me hopes we will fail, and I get to spend out my days moping along this empty beach with you."

"I'd have to knife you then, to save you from yourself," Teret said, a tiny smile tracing her lips.

"Maybe not my best idea then," Carlo said, looking hurt for the briefest moment before his easy smile returned. "You are a hard woman, Teret of the Rorshai."

"Reason why I'm here." They were getting close, and the castle rose like a wall of glass ahead, its bulk sprawled square on a large plateau of rock. A long ridge of stone separated that from the cliffs ranging out behind. "I daresay you'll forget me soon enough once you're homebound."

"Certainly shan't," Carlo said, giving her a frank stare. "I've never met a woman like you before. It breaks my heart we'll be parting soon."

"That's if we survive what awaits us in there," Teret said, pointing at the glittering walls filling the skyline above.

"Good point."

"Elerim will help us," Teret said.

"Wish I had your confidence in that witch."

"Just a hunch," Teret said. "And I wish you'd stop calling her that. She's our ally."

"For now . . ."

Teret ignored that as she picked up her pace. "What a magnificent sight," she said. "I've never seen such vivid colors—it's like the castle is alive and breathing."

"And maybe it is," Carlo's voice hinted irony behind her. Again, Teret ignored him.

Almost there. The Castle of Lights rose up before them, a glistening wall winking down upon two tiny figures, impostors approaching its gates along the sea road.

"So, what do we do?" Carlo said. "Just walk on up and bang on the doors?"

"First we have to find the doors," Teret said. "Can't see anything in this dazzle." As Teret shielded her eyes she followed the road up towards the base of the castle, but the light was so intense she couldn't see where it led. "Must be a tunnel or barbican leading inside."

"And guards," Carlo said.

"No doubt."

But as they approached all they saw was a vast opaque wall of glass that hurt the eyes and distorted vision. The road angled up then disappeared inside a shimmering fusion of light. A tunnel? Hard to tell.

"What do we do now?" Teret saw Carlo screw up his eyes as he tried to make sense of the distortion of lights ahead.

"Walk on through," Teret said. "We haven't come this far to fail at the first challenge."

"I'm with you," Carlo said. "Just asking the question." He thrust out his hand. "Come, let's embrace our destiny, Teret of the Rorshai."

"I'm ready," she said, grasping his hand, and together the pair stepped up into the light.

Chapter 30 | Reflections

Garland made his way along a stone bridge high above crashing waters. A narrow twisting causeway washed by flat featureless sea, and far away the sound of a woman's voice calling out at him, beckoning him forward.

Find Tamersane, bring me the bow . . .

Cille's voice drumming through his head. So many questions and so few answers. The Bruhan? His men? *What has happened to them?* Again, Garland saw Kargon's dead face staring up at him from that pit. Were they all dead? Was it just him alone in this desolate place, a victim of sorcery and deception?

No matter, he'd a task to do and moping would not see it done. *Got this far, so no holding back now.* Ahead, the Castle frowned down at Garland, a gray stack of stone piled on stone, flanked by churning waves on one side and pebbled beach on the other. Garland wondered whether this was just another part of Graywash Hall—a side he hadn't seen. A mirror within the mirror, or perhaps a trick of the light? But the atmosphere was different here, warmer, and his instinct hinted a return to Ansu. Garland clung to that small seed of comfort, hoping it would grow.

He walked, sword slung over shoulder, negotiating the long stone path leading from the bridge over to huge iron gates. Garland saw no guards, which struck him as odd. *Focus on the positive—one less barrier to cross.* He stopped before the gates and looked around. Stone and sea, crashing waves, and not a soul in sight.

Someone's inside . . .

Garland felt a draft along his neck. Not caused by the weather. Something waited for him in that castle. Expected him. He might be alone, but company would find him soon enough. Again—the silent voice warning him make ready.

So be it. Garland chewed his lip. Time to resolve this business and then return home if he could.

Here we go.

Once inside, Garland saw a courtyard of stone flagged by slate, the walls dripping water from somewhere high above.

"Anyone home!?" Garland called out, convinced he was being watched so might as well announce his presence. "I'm Captain Garland from distant Kelwyn. A soldier and honorable man, so kindly announce yourself. I know you're watching."

No answer.

Garland crossed the courtyard quickly, seeing a stairway at the far end. He ducked beneath an arch and took the stone steps two at a time, puffing at the steep ascent. The stairway spiraled up, eventually opening on an expansive hallway with high arching windows awarding wide views of ocean and sky outside.

Garland saw an empty table and a lone crystal candelabra with three lit candles casting shadows on the walls. Green, red, and blue. Garland stared at the candles for a moment, knowing those colors had meaning.

Those witches . . . He suspected the three sisters were here, or their essence lurking somewhere inside this place. Ysaren's candle was blue, Cille's red. The third sister's the green one.

A creak on the floor. The cold draft returning informing him he wasn't alone. Garland slid his blade free of its scabbard and turned very slowly, both hands gripping hilt.

"Who's there?" Garland said.

The blow came from nowhere and sent him spinning across the floor, his sword knocked from his grasp. Garland clenched his teeth against the pain. He rolled, found his knees, only to be kicked in the face by a huge steel boot. That took a tooth. Garland spat it out. He looked up, his mouth streaming blood, and saw a giant clad in steel leaning over him, face hidden behind a massive helmet, two slits showing where the eyes were hidden behind.

Not good.

The giant hefted a huge mace the size of a small tree stump. Garland tried to move but found no muscles to assist him. The giant stood over him, iron legs braced, the mace swinging down.

Garland rolled, kicked up at the monster, and broke a toe. Cussing, he rolled again, and the mace shattered the stone inches from his head and stuck fast. The giant tugged at it, but the stone turned to liquid and sucked the mace deeper into the floor.

What the . . . ?

Garland felt a sudden rush of wind lift his body and push him like strong hands hard across the floor. As he was thrust back, Garland could see the giant sinking through the marble floor, arms flailing. The floor sucked him down, swallowing legs, chest, and finally that metal helm. The giant vanished, and the floor shimmered where he had been, leaving a faint whiff of dust that trailed up and crept out through a gap in a window.

Invisible hands pushed him again, this time more of a nudge. Garland heard whispers, then silence. Alone again. Shivering and shaking, his body hurting and his face a bloody mess. At least that metal brute had gone.

The chill breeze fell away and the hall vanished with it. Garland blinked twice. He stood in a passageway filled with a glow so bright he had to cover his eyes. A green dazzling glare. Garland shielded has eyes with an arm, glimpsed his sword propped against a wall as though he'd just rested it there.

He wiped blood from his mouth with a sleeve, staggered forward, and retrieved it, hoping the giant wouldn't return as he couldn't see two paces ahead. Garland heard voices close by. Different voices—human. One voice laughed, another screamed—a long shrill cry of terror and pain; it resonated all around him.

Keep walking; ignore everything.

The green light faded slowly, and Garland saw long shadows retreating down side passages. He stopped, reaching more stairs. These led down into blackness—a hole deep and cloying. Pass on that one.

Garland turned, blinked, saw movement. Heard the sound of heavy feet. The giant had found him and was coming his way. Garland bit his lip and took to the stairs and blackness below. As he jumped down those treads the void swallowed him whole, and a sense of dread left a sheen of sweat running down his face to mingle with the streams of blood.

***

As Teret entered, the swirling gas pulsed and tickled her face with wet invisible fingers. A cold, clammy, probing touch. She saw faces in that mist. Hints of cruel eyes mocking her. A woman called out to her, another whispered something obscene in her ear.

Teret heard Carlo shouting, a clash of steel on steel. The sound dwindled, and she heard him call her name from far away. The swirling gas thickened in intensity then vaporized to nothing. Teret fell forward, felt a thud, and realized the sound was her head hitting the stone floor. She shook her head, glanced about, and rolled to her knees. Surrounding her was a highly polished stone floor; upon it was a crowd of people gathered eagerly around her.

Carys stood there, and the others from the fishing village in Gwelan. Carlo too, and Teret saw the copper sky shimmering down on them from high above. Close by, flames blazed a trail through woods. She was back in Gwelan. Her heart skipped a beat.

This cannot be—I don't accept this!

But the fires dwindled, and light faded in the sky, the deep copper clouds melting like ceiling wax, replaced by a high vaulted ceiling, a huge crystal chandelier hanging from it thirty feet above her head.

Carys? Carlo?

Teret tried to speak but discovered her lips were stuck together. There was no sign of her friends. Had she imagined them? Or had it been some cruel jest of whomever haunted this castle? Maybe a sorcerer had tapped into her thoughts? Teret shut down that part of her mind, no need to go there lest she lose her sanity.

She gazed up at the ceiling, seeing shadows creeping down the far corners where pillars of alabaster stood like great beasts' hind legs. Whispers rushed at her then disappeared. Teret circled slowly, saw no-one. Then she heard a loud scraping sound and jumped.

"Carlo?"

"I'm here," Teret felt a flood of relief rushing through her veins hearing his voice.

"Thank the Gods, but I thought I'd lost you," A shadow took form before her and Teret saw him standing there, face wild and hand on sword.

"I don't think the Gods care overmuch," a voice said from somewhere beyond where Carlo stood. The Piper emerged, clad in blue and yellow chequers. "They have more pressing concerns."

"Might have expected you to show up," Teret said, and saw Carlo leveling his sword at the little man. "Past time you told us what's happening here."

Teret felt a warm touch and turned to see Carys smiling at her. "So, I didn't imagine you," Teret said smiling. "What happened to you all? It seems like a distant dream, how is it you are here?"

"I don't know," Carys said. "We were lost in Elerim's wood, and then that . . .. man. The Jynn he calls himself. Him with the pipes—he sent us here. Told us we had to be here, we'd be needed." Teret saw the old man and the other survivors from the village hovering behind Carys.

"Glad you're alive," Teret nodded at them. "For a moment I thought we were all back in Gwelan."

"Perhaps you are," the Piper said, walking towards her smiling, and ignoring Carlo's leveled sword. "You stand at the gateway between worlds, Teret of the Rorshai. The hub of the wheel around which everything spins: Gwelan, Ansu, the outer dark, the Aralais, their ancient foe, the three enchantresses, the shaman, Seek and his villainous schemes—everything and nothing, fused together at this precise moment for maximum impact."

The Piper's face seemed to shimmer and shift, and Teret felt suddenly giddy as confusion, worry, and rising panic sought to engulf her. *I don't understand what is happening here.* She shoved back those thoughts and instead, focused on the only thing that mattered.

"And what of Tamersane—is he here?" Teret felt a new thread of excitement mix with the confusion and dread.

"Oh yes," Jynn the Piper said, the smile splitting his face. "You have only to find him. But beware of the traps!" He vanished as the room exploded with light, and Teret cursed as a flash of sparks blinded her and sent her spinning through air.

"Carlo!"

Nothing. Teret fell, tumbled down stone stairs, her body screaming in pain as she banged her arms, shoulders, and head and collided with a wall. She stood shaking and tried to recover her bearings.

"What's happening?"

"I'm happening—bitch!" Sulo appeared out of a wall and stabbed at her with his knife. Teret jerked her body sideways and twisted free of his lunge. The light flickered, green to gold, and Sulo vanished as quickly as he had appeared.

Teret checked her body for scrapes and bruises. She was in good shape, though shocked and worried, especially having seen Sulo. Had he been real? Or just another illusion?

Eyes wary, Teret prowled catlike through a room comprised of soft candlelight and welcoming fire on hearth, the flames from both a deep rose pink. Those flames licked higher as she rushed past.

She walked on, head straight, heard voices, a clash of steel, yells and roar. Teret ignored them and picked up her pace until a far wall appeared in the distance. The end of this hall or another part of the world—impossible to tell. Voices rose and fell like wind through storm shutters. Teret saw tiny figures fighting. Carlo was there, and men she didn't know. They were surrounded by a sea of foes pressing in. Their situation seemed hopeless.

Carlo.

Then the room parted like folding curtains, opening on a deep wide stairway with green velvet carpet descending into a shimmering silver glow. She saw Elerim's face for the briefest instant, and glimpsed her long fingers beckoning her down. Teret took heed and ran.

She yelled out in alarm seeing the stairs folding beneath her, and the ground softening to hot bubbling mud, sucking greedily at her feet like a lover's hot caress.

"Hurry!" a voice said, "You will drown if you linger!" A man's voice, gruff, urgent. Teret cursed as she pulled her boots free of the goo, struggling forward slowly, the hot, wax-like ground sucking harder at her boots, the sole of the left one already half rotted through. It was though tiny steel fingers were pulling her down through the floor. A hidden menace. A sentient malice that desired her essence and would grind her bones to powder.

Teret ripped free, reached the end of the stairs, and jumped, just as the stairway turned to water and flooded the room behind her.

A strong hand gripped her arm and pulled her up to a balcony looking out over a valley lit with tiny green lights. They winked wisely up at her as though knowing her thoughts. Teret saw a face loom close, kind and strong, and almost familiar.

I know you . . .

"Lady Teret—I'm seeking your husband," Garland said.

"As am I," Teret said. Then the Grogan crashed upon them.

***

"More bloody mirrors," Tam said, finding himself in yet another corridor, radiating with silver light which reflected off the multi-faceted glass and sent their reflections winking in a thousand directions. "Looks like we're back in Graywash Hall."

Stogi and the Shen woman Tai Pei were pressed close to his back as the three wedged their way through the tightest corridor yet.

"I think we're going to be swallowed alive," Stogi said.

"There are worse deaths," Tai Pei said, though Tam couldn't think of any at present.

They'd entered the castle a half hour ago and found a maze of passages leading inside. If there were occupants, then they were keeping to themselves. Tam even wondered if the Castle of Lights was a living entity and they were inside its stomach, being digested slowly.

I hope this is just one big, nasty dream.

But it was real enough. A pale hand emerged from the nearest mirror and pulled Tam inside.

"Fuck!"

The corridor vanished and so had his friends. *Here we go again.* Instead, Tam stood in a wide hall filled with strange green light, dully throbbing like heartbeats in the middle distance. He turned slowly, sensing he wasn't alone, and saw two women standing on a dais of solid emerald crystal; a third woman was seated in an emerald chair.

Behold the Sisters three.

The one in the chair had coiling black hair, the others gold. The faces were the same, except one of the golden-haired women looked older and more haggard. All three stared at Tam with tense, eager faces as he walked toward them, his sword free in hand.

"What's happening here, Cille?" Tam said, addressing the dark-haired woman seated in emerald chair.

"Lord Tamersane," Cille smiled, and the women beside her nodded. "These are my beloved sisters, Lady Elerim and the Lady Ysaren. We three have been waiting for you."

"This is the one?" the older-looking sister said.

"A wretch hardly worthy of the woman who loves him," Elerim said. "Teret is too good for you, boy."

"Is she here?" Tam's eyes flicked toward the golden-haired beauty, who looked younger than the other two.

"Everyone is here," Cille said. "But not everyone can win today." Tam approached the dais and stared up at the three. They looked down at him with cold dispassionate eyes.

"So—I'm still in Graywash Hall after all? Thought so." Tam carved a circle in the air with his sword. "Let me climb up there and murder the three of you—I'm so tired of you witches and your silly games. I thought you hated each other."

"Retrieve the bow, shoot the arrow, and save the day." The three sisters spoke the words in unison, and Tam was spun around by fast invisible hands. "The time is upon us!" Their voices crawled inside his head, boring deep, and sending shooting pains through his skull. Faster and faster Tam spun, until his stomach threatened to empty itself. Yet he could see the sisters looking at him, their beautiful faces intent.

The spinning stopped, and Tam dropped to his knees, gripping the stone floor with hands greasy with sweat. He looked up and saw Cille rise and walk toward him like a queen addressing a wretched beggar at court, her red gown slipping like melting wax from her leanly sculpted body. Naked, Cille kneeled alongside Tam and ran a probing finger up his leg. Tam gasped, both at that icy touch and the knots twisting in his belly.

"Love me," Cille breathed, her narrow fingers questing up his leg. "Whilst there is still time. Soon everything will change. I need your earth energy, your mortal essence inside me. Free me from them!" Cille's free hand pointed back at her sisters, both approaching slowly. Tam choked back vomit and tried not to yell out.

"Those ladies would destroy me, Tamersane." Cille leaned forward and kissed him with her hot wet mouth. He pulled away, despite the eagerness he felt below. "Only your love can free my bonds." Tam saw the other two witches were walking towards him, both naked now, and their faces caught in eager need.

"Ignore her; she would have you all to herself," the sister with the green fingernails said. "I am Elerim; love me first, and you will live forever." Elerim smiled slyly as she slid in beside her sister, pushing her aside, and Ysaren, the third sister crept up behind her. Cille's fingers clawed at Elerim's neck, but the younger sister ignored her and kissed Tam's lips with vicious hunger, biting hard. "We are out of time," Elerim gasped. "We have only this one moment—we three." Tam swallowed blood, and then shuddered as Ysaren's probing fingers clawed in beneath his trousers.

Cille rose up before him. She turned and kissed Elerim briefly and then the pair fell upon him, with Ysaren close behind. "Come, siblings dear," Cille said, hugging Ysaren close and kissing Elerim again hungrily, as they tore at Tam's worn garments. "Let us drain his life-force while there's still time."

"Stop!"

Tam fell to the floor as though struck by a hammer. *What now?* He shook and rolled, rose to his knees, vision blurred and head spinning. The three witches had vanished, leaving him both very relieved and oddly disappointed. Bruised and battered, the ground spinning beneath him. "He is not your plaything," the voice said, and Tam could hear shrill shrieks responding somewhere far away. On the walls were faint streaks of red, blue, and green; like misty fingers they crawled toward him. "Begone!" The streaks vanished, and a rush of icy wind stole through the airy room, rattling the doors at the far end. Strong hands pulled Tam to his feet, and he found himself looking into the chubby freckled face of Jynn the Piper.

"I thought Cille was my friend." Tam shuddered and rose to his feet. "Thanks . . ."

"This way," the Piper said, without offering explanation. "The bow awaits—your destiny, Lord Tam." Tam looked about but the hall was empty.

"Where did they go?"

"Not far," Jynn said. "The stakes are too high for them to quit now."

"Where am I? Graywash Hall; this Castle of Lights—they feel like the same place."

"For good reason," Jynn laughed. "Both are different manifestations of the island of Laras Lassladden, where all things are possible and everything both an answer and a question."

"Thanks—but that hasn't really helped." Tam had heard that name before. A mythic island rumored to be birthplace to the dead Gods.

"You haven't much time, Lord Tam," said the Piper. "We have reached the nexus. The point when all angles intertwine and every outcome is possible. You had best retrieve that bow and set about your task."

"About which I know nothing," Tam said. His body was recovering and accompanying it came rising anger. "You and those witches and your stupid fucking games. Where's my Teret?"

"Down there," Jynn pointed to where a door had emerged, revealing a long corridor, a dull green light glowing within. The door was open just enough to see the woman standing behind it. Her face was bloody, those lovely eyes stricken with horror like deer trapped in torchlight. But she was alive and in reach, and that was all that mattered.

Teret!

Tam raced down the corridor towards that distant door; he could still see her standing there, but the faster he ran the further away she looked. "Teret!"

She turned as though hearing his voice, but her stare was blank, the terror still showing in her eyes. "I'm coming!" Tam yelled, willing his feet move faster as his heart thudded like hammers inside his chest.

She was shrinking before him, fading, her body no bigger than a doll's. "No!" Tam felt the corridor close in on him as before, and his shoulders brushed against rough glass—yet more mirrors on either side. "Teret, it's me, Tamersane—I'm back." Tiny, in the distance, Teret looked up and for the briefest moment recognized her husband. Then a hand covered her mouth and pulled her out of sight.

"Teret!" Tam squeezed his body through the shrinking corridor, but the door vanished ahead. Teret was lost to him again. Instead, Tam almost wept as the frustration and rage tore up from inside. He was back in the hall with the dais, the Piper standing with feet braced apart and that smug smile splitting his face.

"You need to be quicker than that," Jynn said.

"What have you done with her?" Tam swung out with his sword, but the Piper vanished. Tam arced the sword through air and stepped sideways, repeating the motion until he saw the Jynn smiling at him again.

"You're a shifty little bastard," Tam said.

"Needs must, I assure you," the Piper said. "You're wasting precious moments here."

"What have you done with my wife?"

"What have *I* done with her?" Jynn's expression hardened like quick-lime drying in midday sun. "I have no part in this business, though I'm trying to decipher the deceptions surrounding it." Jynn's round face relaxed. "I'm sorry—been a long millennium. But you must realize that you cannot save Teret without the bow, Lord Tamersane," he said. "Everyone seeks Kerasheva. The witches need it for their devious schemes, the Grogan creature to return to his home, the villagers from Gwelan, the same, the Bruhan and his men to help defeat the enemy. Captain Garland—"

"Who—what are you talking about?" Tam was looking everywhere for a way out of this hall but saw nothing but gleaming, featureless walls. "And I thought time didn't matter here."

"Normally that's so," Jynn acknowledged. "But this is the conjunction, the one instance when all worlds collide and everything is possible, especially here in the Castle of Lights."

Tam let his sword point rest on the stone. He felt shattered and defeated. "What must I do?"

"Try again," the Piper said. "Don't lose heart. See, look—over there." He pointed off to the distance over to Tam's right. "The corridor; it's re-appeared again. Take it, have faith—it will show you the way," Jynn waved him go quickly. "Heed not any diversions. This time keep your head. Hold Teret's image in your thoughts and focus on how much you love her. Love is the greatest gift you humans have—use it! Now go!"

"But I saw Teret there," Tam said, hesitating as the door hovered like mist in the distance. "Someone had her by the throat."

"You saw both what you desired and most feared seeing," the Piper said. "An easy error to make, tripped by their crafty illusions— but a deadly one. You were lucky you escaped the trap. This time, keep your mind neutral, hold the memory of the first time you met her, and that will give you strength to survive what's down there."

"And what is down there?"

"Your mortal death, Lord Tam," the Piper smiled. "Just another doorway."

***

The mace swept high over Garland's head as he dived to the ground, side-sweeping with his sword and catching the giant's inside leg. That blow dented armor but brought no reaction. The eye-slits turned his way as that huge helmet loomed over him, the mace swinging back like a pendulum arcing down towards Garland's head. Again, the swing went wide, but Garland knew he couldn't keep this up. His body was tiring fast, whereas the monster in metal showed no signs of fatigue.

Garland, breath bursting from his chest, rolled free as the Grogan kicked out at him with an anvil-sized boot. He could hear the woman Teret yelling at someone approaching, but daren't risk a glance to see who was coming to help.

The giant lashed out with his steel boot again. This time he got lucky and caught Garland's shoulder, sending him sliding across the polished marble floor and crashing into a wall, the plaster and splinters exploding in his face. Garland cursed at the pain and feared his elbow must be broken.

The giant loomed above him, the huge mace gripped in his massive iron-clad paws. He swung down, hard and fast. Garland closed his eyes and waited for the explosion in his head.

It never came. Instead Garland heard a woman's voice yelling something obscene. He opened an eye, blinked back blood, and saw the woman Teret, her skinny brown arms and feet wrapped around the metal giant's iron neck as she stabbed down with a thin dagger and a rage he'd seldom witnessed. Teret screamed as she stabbed, so many times the knife's tip buckled on the gorget protecting his neck. The giant hardly noticed her assault, but the distraction gave Garland just enough time to find his feet, stagger over, and collect his sword with his good hand, scraping it up from the floor.

"Thanks, my lady," Garland said, walking slowly and carefully to where Teret sat, broken knife in hand, her arm bleeding badly. "But let me deal with this overgrown rust-heap."

The giant pushed Teret aside as though he'd just realized she was there. Garland watched her body slide along the floor. "I've got this!" he told her, turning back to face the Grogan.

A metallic chuckle resonated from inside that barrel helm, like grinding steel wheels in bad need of oil rubbing together. "Keep laughing, shithead." Garland gripped the sword in his good hand and started to swing, his eye on the mace rising up from the ground. But the giant paused as though puzzled.

Garland heard a thud, and saw that something hard had impacted the giant's back. The Grogan turned, the mace gripped in both steel hands. Garland saw a man standing behind the creature, armed with a rock—a solid lump of green crystal.

"Got your attention, have I?" The stranger threw the rock at the giant's head and it bounced off his helmet.

"Teret, jump!" the newcomer yelled, and hurled himself like a missile at the metal giant. The creature raised its mace again and turned toward this new attacker. Garland, after regaining his breath with gasping gulps, seized his chance, spotting a crack in the armor just behind the knee.

He braced his feet, sword gripped tight in good hand. *One chance—make it count.* The other man held the giant's attention. Garland stole forward, leveled his blade, and then stabbed hard and fast. And very accurately. The broadsword's tip bit deep into the sinew and muscles hidden beneath the leather straps supporting the giant's heavy iron greaves.

With a hollow metallic roar, the metal giant sank to his knees, dark blood streaming down his metal flanks and pooling on the stone. The man with the rock had produced a sword. He sliced up under the monster's helmet, then jumped up, prizing it back until a thin sliver of gray flesh was exposed.

"Kill it!" Teret's yell came from behind him as Garland staggered to aid the stranger. No need. The newcomer's blade sawed down deep into that neck crack, squirting black gore across the room.

The Grogan lashed out, kicking and spewing blood from neck and hamstring, as Garland and his helper stabbed and stabbed wherever they saw gaps in the armor. The Grogan staggered and tumbled like slag sliding from a mountain. Garland and his accomplice, and now Teret too, jumped on the metal back and finished the grisly work until at last the Grogan shuddered and lay still.

Garland lay panting for several long moments before clambering back to his feet. The man was standing behind him, a wry grin on his handsome face.

"Thanks," the newcomer said. "That was one big ugly metal bastard. I'm Carlo Sarfe, by the way."

"Very happy to meet you," Garland said, his voice hoarse with exhaustion. "I'm a—"

"Captain in the Bear Regiment, as I recall." Teret had freed herself from the mess surrounding the giant's carcass and was wiping her hands and smiling at Garland. "I remember seeing you at Queen Ariane's court."

"I wasn't there often," Garland said.

"Me neither." She turned to the man standing beside her. Watching their faces, had Garland not known better, he would have thought them lovers. "Carlo," Teret said, "this is a countryman of mine. A hero of the old wars. I—" A hand silenced her mouth, and before Garland or Carlo could move, had pulled Teret's wriggling body through a side door.

"Get the bow—save my husband!" Teret yelled at them before disappearing from sight. They gave chase, crashing through the doorway, but Garland saw no sign of Teret or the man who'd stolen upon her.

***

Sulo pushed Teret against a wall and then punched her hard in the face. Teret slumped, half unconscious.

"You've caused me some trouble, little bitch." Sulo spat in her eye. "But it's over now. I'm going to cut your belly open and let you bleed slowly. Let the flies settle and creep inside. You'll wish you had been a slave like I planned. Then I'll find your husband," Sulo smiled, "I know he's here somewhere, the witches told me."

"Fuck you," Teret coughed blood. She struck out at Sulo, but he slapped her face with the back of his hand, and she slid to the ground. She noticed that the man from Gwelan, the coward Boal, stood hesitating behind him, then stepped up and shook Sulo's tunic with an urgent fist.

"What is it?" Sulo said, without taking his eyes off Teret.

"The Grogan," Boal said, leaning closer, and Teret saw the Grogan's former slaves shuffling behind.

"What about him?" Sulo turned and glared at the men.

"He's dead—they killed him!" Boal was shaking.

"What are you talking about?" Sulo, distracted, rounded on Boal, his killer face flushed red with rage, and his concentration lost for just a moment.

All Teret needed. She slid the tiny knife free of her secret sheath up her left arm, a gift from Carlo, and stabbed up hard between Sulo's legs, catching him inside his left thigh.

Sulo yelled and twisted in rage, leaning down and tugging the blade free. He kicked out at Teret with his good leg but missed. She found her feet again, spat in his face, and then shoulder-charged him into the wall, the man Boal and his companions watching like ghouls from behind.

"Cunt," Sulo snarled, and made to strike her again, but Teret jumped clear. She turned, and raw with emotion, sped full pelt down the hall, leaving Sulo and the Grogan's men staring after her. Teret turned once before exiting the hall, saw Sulo kneeling, his hands pressing hard as he tried to halt the red stream seeping from his leg.

"Hope it hurts, you bastard!" Teret left the hall behind.

The instant she closed the door behind her and turned, Teret slipped and noticed in horror that her feet were balanced precariously on a ledge. A fall of several hundred feet dropped sheer to rocks and ocean below. She spread her hands flat against the wall and reached for the door again. But there was no door there now. Instead, a sheer wall of granite stretched out on either side allowing no purchase.

"Climb down; you need to climb down here!" Carlo's voice came from somewhere below her. Teret glanced down but saw no purchasing holds anywhere.

"I can't!" she said. "It's sheer; I'm stuck on this ledge." Even as she spoke, Teret's knees wobbled and her feet slipped again. She pressed herself against the rock wall but couldn't stop her feet from sliding. "I'm slipping!" Teret yelled, as she slid and then fell from the ledge, arms flailing and heart racing, the rocky ground racing up to meet her.

Teret closed her eyes and braced for impact. After all she'd been through, a swift death awaited her—if she was lucky. Her body breaking on rocks, or else drowning beneath those blue churning waves surrounding the castle. Teret closed her eyes. At least she'd tried . . .

Tam.

"I've got you!" Strong arms gripped Teret and pulled her close, and when Teret opened her eyes she found herself staring at her husband for the first time in weeks, or months, or maybe longer. He stood by the sea, a man and woman she didn't know standing close behind him, their faces mildly curious, as if examining wild flowers on some country stroll on a lazy summer's afternoon.

"Tam—I"

"Live," he said grinning and pulling her close. "We caught you, my love! Stogi, my ruffian friend, and I."

The man with the tattoos smiled and then looked at the pale-skinned woman beside him who shrugged indifference.

"But I was falling so fast." Teret looked about her, seeing sand and sea, feeling the warm sun on her face. "The rocks—where are they? The castle." She felt dazed, unsure if this was real, and refused to close her eyes in case she lost the dream she witnessed.

"You were floating actually," the woman spoke, her accent strange. "Like a leaf drifting down in autumn breeze. All these two fat idle lumps had to do was hold out their hands and pull you in. Simple, it was."

"Another illusion," Stogi said, his gold earrings jingling. This one looked half savage, but his smile was genuine and his eyes filled with ironic humor. Teret liked him at once. "We're still inside that bloody castle," he said. "Someone is playing with our cocks, I feel."

"I don't have a cock," the woman said.

"It's just an expression," Stogi said, looking at the woman. Teret hardly noticed the pair as she stared at her husband, stroking his face to make sure he was real.

"I think I'm dead," she said. "Or else dreaming. You, these others—all part of an illusion. That said, I'm past happy to see you." She kissed him then, and Tam responded, holding her close, as tears streamed down his face.

"I know," Tam said between kisses. "Nothing is real. Since I lost you, everything has become a tangle of mystery and weirdness."

"Thanks," said Stogi wryly from somewhere behind.

"You look good," Teret stared hard at Tam, still struggling to believe he was right there before her. "Tired but sharp. Strong—more self-assured."

"This is lovely," the woman said, with a weariness to her tone. "But shouldn't we be doing something? I mean, before another illusion, or giant metal monster, or perhaps warlock, witch, whatever—attacks us, and slices us all into neat little pieces?"

"Fair point," Stogi said. Teret saw him smiling at the woman who then cuffed him across the ear. *Odd couple.*

"You saw the metal giant?" Teret suddenly thought of Carlo and her countryman Garland. The worry returned. "My friends killed it," she said lamely, not wanting to mention Carlo's name, and feeling awkward at how she missed him.

"What friends are these?" Tam said. Teret made to reply and then glanced down in surprise as water soaked her foot.

"Tide's coming in fast." The woman pointed languidly across to where the sea was rising up before them like a steel tower, the waves combing and frothing white in churning coils.

"I hate this." Stogi stepped backwards. He looked terrified of the water.

"Best we brace ourselves," Tam said, clutching her arm tighter. "No time to run from that wash!" The wave rose higher like a congealed column of green-blue ice, solid, frozen, and gleaming. The water at her feet was sucked back, and Teret stared in fascinated horror as the towering wave exploded, and a million tons of water crashed upon them.

"Tam!"

Teret felt her body wrenched from her husband's grip. She heard him shout, and then the torrent tore her away and Teret was flushed through narrow holes and squirted out onto a highly polished stone surface. The water had half-drowned her, but it disappeared as soon as it had come, leaving Teret breathless and gasping like a stranded whale at tide's low ebb.

She heard voices close by. She opened her eyes and discovered herself sprawled akimbo in a huge cavern, a deep green light resonating from the middle distance.

"Time we all got acquainted." A woman's voice, deep and solemn.

Elerim?

Teret rose to her feet, shook herself off, and saw Tam standing just yards away among others, including the wild-haired Stogi and his strange looking girlfriend. Teret made to walk across to them but discovered her feet glued to the ground. She tugged at them to no avail; the boot soles were stuck fast.

"I need your attention too, Teret." Like a shimmer of heat haze, the owner of the voice emerged before her, a slight smile on her stunning but ancient face.

"Elerim?"

The woman's eyes hardened to narrow slits and she lashed out, hitting Teret across the face with the back of her hand. "You little trollop! I'm nothing like my sister!"

"No, Ysaren," another female voice spoke, coming from behind, sultrier and subtler. "She at least retains her beauty. Not a dry crusty stick like you, Sister."

"Keep out of this, Cille," Ysaren said, rounding on the woman behind her. "It's none of your damned business! This is between Elerim and myself."

"Oh—think you?" The husky voice was rich with sarcasm. "You two cannot tie your bootlaces without consulting me first."

"You're an interfering cow," Ysaren said, turning to glare at a vague red shape drifting past her. Teret glimpsed a flash of red, long silky black hair, and a sharp glance rendered her way.

"Pretty—if a little rural," Cille said, with clipped precise tones. Teret tried to see her but couldn't move her legs. She threw up her hands up in a futile gesture, catching Tam's eye. He winked reassurance at her.

It will be all right.

"This is all leading somewhere," Tam called across to her. "Hold strong, my love. Guess we'll find out soon enough when these harridans stop bitching at each other."

Teret's lips froze before she could respond. Another shape was emerging like jade-colored smoke and gliding toward them from the far side of the cavern, the green light deepening behind her.

Teret saw a woman, tall and slender, walking with grace, and carrying something in her outstretched arms. Teret recognized

Elerim, and then wondered how she had mistaken the other woman for her. Ysaren was indeed a dry stick by comparison—thinner and appearing older, though they were similar in some ways, sharing the same feline grace and elfin features. Ysaren was chiseled and harsh, whereas Elerim simmered with cat-cream charm and lofty elegance. She glided towards them, the hem of her long green dress brushing the floor, and her smile serene as ever.

"About time you arrived," Ysaren said, turning to see her other sister's approach. "Always late—nothing changes with you, Elerim."

"I didn't realize it was a race, sister." Elerim stopped thirty feet away and held out her arms, palms open and upward, the thin needle-like object she carried lying across them. Teret saw what it was for the first time.

An arrow—long and slender, its triangular tip and feathered fletch deep green in color, the wooden shaft a paler green. Elerim flashed Teret a grin and thrust the arrow point down into the polished floor. It quivered then stilled. "And so, it starts," she said, looking pleased with herself.

"One of three." Elerim was still smiling at Teret, or at least it seemed to her that the enchantress was staring directly at her. "Only fair, as there are three of us."

"Then we need three champions to our cause," Ysaren said, walking across to where her sister stood. "Every queen deserves a hero," Ysaren said, "and there are none queenlier than us." From her shimmering blue gown, she produced a second arrow. "I've kept this for some time," she purred.

"Always you were a hoarder." Elerim greeted her sister with a kiss and hug. Ysaren broke free after a moment and wiped her mouth.

"You're too sentimental, Elerim," Ysaren said, glaring at her sister for a moment. Then she smiled viciously and stuck her arrow in the stone floor alongside Elerim's. The force left it quivering slightly

"Think you can patch things up at this late hour?" Elerim ignored her.

"Your turn, Cille," the sisters said. "We know you have the last one." Teret heard the soft sound of someone walking past her quietly. A shimmering sheen of red.

Fingers lightly brushed her shoulder, and Teret shivered, suddenly aware of breath like stale flowers abandoned at graveyard. A husky voice whispered in her ear.

"Thought you'd be prettier, the way he mopes about you." Teret craned her neck, saw the third sister leaning over her, willowy and tall, her eyes the same green-gold of her siblings, but her hair dark like thick smoke over charcoal. *Eyes sharper than flint.* She had both Elerim's grace and Ysaren's anger, and much more besides. Teret guessed this sister to be the most perilous of the three.

Cille.

"Where is your arrow, sister?" Ysaren sounded peeved, as though Cille was spoiling their clever game. "We're all waiting here: these kind people, your sweet sisters, the other ones—lurking like grubs in the shadows out there."

"Oh, do shut up, Ysaren—already I tire of your nonsense." Cille rounded on her sister. "Easy to see why Elerim stuck you in that prison by the lake."

"That was you!" Elerim said, her face suddenly angry. "It was her, Ysaren, she's lying as usual."

"You're both lying," Ysaren spat at her sisters, as Cille glided across to greet them, a slight quiver of a smile smearing her deep red lips.

"Well, here we are." Cille turned to face the watchers and ignored her sisters, and Teret could see the fury and confusion on their faces. They yelled at her but she ignored any protestations. Instead, Cille addressed those standing in the hall, most of whom Teret couldn't see.

"Thank you for coming, everybody," Cille said, clasping her long pale hands together and smiling at some private joke. "We three appreciate your company and support in this pressing business. My sisters can be grouchy and have their differences, but they are not entirely wicked, but rather victims of their own machinations. Artful spiders trapped by their own complex threads."

Teret noticed how Ysaren and Elerim stared at Cille with loathing, and more than a hint of fear in their eyes. Ysaren looked ready to stab her but did nothing, and Teret wondered what power Cille had over the other two.

"So," Cille said, dropping her hands. "To business. Any questions before we start?" No one responded. Teret tugged at her feet but they remained put. Tam was smiling at her. "How is everyone feeling? At this very special moment."

As though released from spells, a rush of voices echoed around the hall. Teret heard Tam shout, and Stogi too, and then to her relief she heard Carlo Sarfe's warm laughter somewhere behind her.

He lives.

"Happy to be here," Carlo said, and Teret found herself smiling at the ridiculous situation she was in. Husband and comrade entertained by three witchy sisters in a castle of illusions, while a mad-dog murderer prowled around in the background. She'd no doubt Sulo was still alive and part of this crazy jigsaw.

"Just explain what you want from us so we can be about our day," she heard Carlo say, his voice barely audible above others.

"Very well, since you've been so patient," Cille said without a hint of irony. She raised a white hand.

"It is time!" The other two sisters screamed as though they knew what Cille was up to. Teret didn't. All she saw was the jet of green steam coming her way; she felt its searing heat burning her face.

"You might want to move, Teret of the Rorshai," Cille said, winking at her.

"I'm stuck here, you witch!"

Teret sighed in relief as her feet sprang free from the floor. Just as well—the blast nearly scorched her to ashes. Teret dived low as the vent of hot green steam whistled over her head. "Time I introduced myself," Cille said, her voice seeming to come from walls, ceiling, and floor. The cavern was flushed with emerald light. "Behold sisters! And you others! Your Emerald Queen is back!" Cille's image shimmered and her face fell to ashes as the green steam ripped into her skin. The other two sisters screamed, seeing their sibling destroyed. But another woman had replaced her. A tall, stately, beautiful figure, gowned in green glass. Serenely beautiful, wise and ancient.

Teret heard Tam's gasp from nearby. "The Goddess is back— Elanion lives!" Then the ground shook beneath Teret and she fell into darkness.

Chapter 31 | Destiny

Garland gulped at the green jet of air spurting toward him. He jumped, sliding across the floor, his damaged arm screaming at him, and Carlo Sarfe crashing on top of him as the searing heat whistled above them, disappearing with a long fading sigh like a kettle freed of steam.

Carlo rolled free allowing Garland to sit up, clutching his bleeding arm.

"You all right?" Carlo Sarfe asked, and Garland nodded.

"I think so." He tried to take in what was happening, or what had just happened—hard to define which. A cavern filled with noise like groaning thunder, sickly green light reflected from glass, and sporadic blasts of green fumes spurting up from holes appearing in the floor. A lot to take in.

"We stand at the vortex," Garland heard one of the witches say, but couldn't tell who, the voice sounding different than before and coming from some distance away. "Only Kerasheva can set the dimensions back in their correct place."

"I need to see that bow," Carlo said, finding his feet and staggering away from where Garland sat. "My ticket back to the past!"

"Wait!" Garland leaned on his sword and pulled himself up,

grimacing at the pain, the cavern floor shaking and stones falling from the roof all around. People were running in all directions. Garland glimpsed Tam and Teret arm in arm fleeing into a far corner. "It's my task to find that bow—I made a promise."

"It will see me home!" Carlo turned and yelled at him, then a blast of green smoke erupted between them. Garland heard Carlo cry out, and then had to dive low again as stones, dust, and jade crystal shards shot his way.

Carlo?

An explosion ripped through the cavern and shook its roots. Dazzled, Garland could hear the woman's voice again, rising up with somber resonance, her clear tones like a bell tolling, and accompanied by the soft lilting of far-off pipe music. Garland shut out the sounds, clung to his sword with one hand and gripped the floor as best he could with another. He closed his eyes and felt the nausea of pain and giddiness pulling him down.

Hold on—got to get through this.

Count to three. Garland opened his eyes, and again peered through the glare. The cavern had ceased rocking, the stones settled, and spurting jets of green air dissolved. He gazed about saw no sign of life or movement. Emptiness and silence surrounded Garland like some unanswered question. A final scene played out on the stage and he'd missed it. *Too late.* The curtains were already drawn. Or else he'd been sickly for months and woken to find his world had moved on. And perhaps it had. Useless to dwell on these things.

I have a task to complete—why I'm here.

Garland willed the pain and nausea into the background. He clambered to his feet again, dusted off his coat and trousers and, broadsword slung across shoulder, started pacing toward the far end of the cavern.

***

Tam found Teret's hand in his just before that last explosion ripped through the cavern, the Goddess's voice booming over their heads. Together they sped across the cavern, finding a niche at the far side, a crack of sorts leading into a maze of tunnels. They ran, hand in hand, too stunned and weary for words. No time to process what had happened. Just relieved that they lived and had found each other again.

Seconds became minutes, drifted into hours. Tam and Teret saw no one and heard nothing save the drip of water somewhere close as their journey through the passages led them deep into the roots beneath the Castle of Lights.

"I think we're on the road to Yffarn," Tam muttered as they slowed to a stop, both exhausted and unable to walk further without resting.

"There has to be a way out," Teret said, resting her back against a rock and sliding down. "Gods, but I'm exhausted," she said.

"Gods?" Tam smiled at her and wiped sweat from his face. "Try Goddess—she was there, Teret. *Elanion.* Did you see her face?"

Teret shook her head. "I don't know what I saw."

"Doesn't matter—nothing seems real here," Tam said. "All that matters is you're alive. I can't believe I've found you again, my love." Teret looked at him but said nothing.

"Nothing has made any sense since last I saw you," Tam said. "I've felt lost and lonely; the fool on the hill." She looked at him, her eyes moist. Tam took her hand and kissed it. "All I know is I love you, Teret, and I hope you can forgive the hurt I've caused you."

"Is that my husband I hear speaking?" Teret smiled wryly.

"It is," Tam said, nodding his head passionately. "I'm back, Teret. Been a long dark road but I'm free of the past. It's taken this jolt to shake sense back into my thick head. Now I'm just sorry and ashamed of how I've been." Tam looked up, hearing a distant boom from high above. The sound brought them both back to the present.

"I wonder what is happening up there?" Teret said.

Tam shuffled up beside her and Teret placed a sweaty arm around his waist. "I don't care and would rather not go see," he said. "Let's rest and get our strength back while we can." Tam kissed her softly and she responded, and next he knew they were locked together, arms entwined, rolling on the ground, their weariness, pain, and fear extinguished by the joy of finding their love again.

"What now?" Tam said after they'd made love on the hard stone, the sound of dripping water their only witness. "What do you think happened back there?"

"The witches," Teret said. "I don't know—a quarrel? Cille . . . she changed."

"Into Elanion," Tam nodded. "It's about time's passage and shifting dimensions," Tam said, sitting up and leaning against the wall. "And the alignment of the planets."

"What are you talking about?" Teret smiled up at him.

"Hints I heard from a shaman a few days back."

"A what?"

"A wizard of sorts," Tam said. "I thought him full of shit but now I'm not so sure." Tam sighed. "The world's turned on its head, Teret. But in the middle of this mess something incredible has happened. I can't really believe it, but that was Elanion we saw—right?"

"I told you I wasn't sure."

"The Goddess lives, so the others must too," Tam said, standing up, banging his head on the cave ceiling, and gesticulating like a frenzied zealot. "Whatever happened seven years ago wasn't the end. If they've survived, then hope can too." Teret laughed and bid him sit lest he knock himself out. Tam slunk down beside her, his face flushed with passion.

"The three witches are part of it," Tam said. "The Piper too. A new dance. Everyone we've encountered, caught in some cosmic rupture, itself an event brought on by the last war of the Gods—I thought they were dead, Teret. Gone. That knowledge killed part of me. But it was a lie. Elanion lives!"

"Those witches became the Goddess?" Teret looked worried, and he placed a hand on her shoulder. "Cille duped her sisters, but what of herself?"

"It's a puzzle, but the pieces are falling into place." Tam leaped to his feet again, lost balance, and crashed into the wall of rock to his right. "The Emerald Queen is back." He giggled uncontrollably and noticed Teret's puzzled expression.

"I thought the Emerald Queen was bad," Teret said.

"The Goddess?" Tam gaped at his wife. "She's the guardian of this world, Teret. Ansu—the life and essence of everything in it. I have to reach Ariane; my cousin needs to know." Tam started giggling again and struck his hand hard against the wall.

"Tamersane?" Teret frowned at him.

"I'm not stoned," Tam said, waving her relax. "Haven't been for weeks—don't even miss that shit."

Teret shook her head. "I wasn't implying you were. It's just—"

"Have you heard tell of Laras Lassladden?" Tam said suddenly, his eyes oddly bright as though he'd solved some impossible riddle.

"Of course," Teret said. "Who hasn't? The legendary island where the High King found the sword Callanak. Everyone knows that story."

"And where my ancestor Erun Cade became the warrior Kell. The mystery realm that shifts through time," Tam said. "Slowly, or like quicksand, its substance and form ever changing."

"What are you saying husband?" Teret's blue eyes studied his face.

"Are we trapped in Laras Lassladden?"

"That's exactly what I'm saying," Tam grinned at her. His smile fell away when Tam heard the soft sounds of hands clapping close by. They turned slowly, and Tam almost laughed seeing Jynn the Piper sitting on a ledge close by, his instrument neatly laid across chubby knees.

"You've traveled far," the Piper said. "But there is still one task left." He raised his pipe and placed it to his lips, but no notes followed. A shadow brushed past Tam. He saw a glint of steel and witnessed Sulo's knife cut deep into the little man's back. It happened so quickly. The Piper vanished, and Tam turned to see Sulo lunging for Teret, knife in hand.

"No!"

Too late Tam got there, the knife cutting deep, and his wife slipping to the floor. Sulo lunged at him too, but in the second he forgot her, Teret pulled her knife free with her teeth, dropped it into her hand, and stabbed up, hard and fast. Deep into Sulo's groin.

Sulo screamed and shuddered. He dropped to his knees trying to stop the blood coursing down his legs.

"That's for my kin, you bastard," Teret said. She pulled the knife free and stabbed him again.

Tam—hands trembling with rage—freed his sword, stood over the weeping Sulo and sliced down, shearing his neck, sending his head spinning through the air.

"And that's for hurting my wife!"

The Piper reappeared before him as Tam knelt beside his wife, his hot hands trying to stem the blood oozing from her belly.

"There's still time," Jynn said, his eyes sad. "But you need to find the Emerald Bow. Only that can save Teret."

"Which way?" Tam said, staring wildly at the Piper like a man witnessing a ghost rising from the grave at midnight.

"Follow me!" the Jynn said.

***

Carlo was thrown yards by the blast, his ears deafened, and a painful ringing battering his head. He landed badly and lay still, nursing his aching body. He'd heard voices, whispers in the dark. The sound of mountains crashing into the sea. He saw a great fire and a shadowy creature within. He saw his father's face, and heard his mother calling out his name.

Save us, Carlo.

The vision passed like memory of nightmare, replaced by silence and the thudding of his heart. Carlo took stock as best he could. He was unhurt, though badly shaken. Finally satisfied his mind was still intact, Carlo found his feet and looked about.

The cavern was gone. He stood by the sea again, waves crashing all around him, and looking out, Carlo saw a ship moored close by. Not just any ship. His ship. *The Arabella,* her sails neatly trimmed and timbers freshly painted.

"It's yours to sail again, but I need that bow first." Elerim appeared and stood beside him, her serene smile unchanged. Carlo knew this to be another illusion, so he refused to be baited. Instead, he turned and awarded the sorceress a keen stare. "Are you Elerim or someone else?"

"I'm whomever you want me to be."

"What happened back there?" Carlo said, gazing at his ship like a marooned sailor trapped and watching his life vanish with the tide. So close. So far. All trickery, but for what purpose? "Your sister duped you?"

"Not Cille's doing, though I'm sure she'll take the credit."

"Then whose?"

"We actually want the same thing," Elerim responded smoothly as though she hadn't heard his last question. "My sisters and I. Ysaren's bitter, and Cille believes she knows more—and maybe she does, the arrogant bitch. But we all need that bow, and you, Carlo Sarfe, are the best man to get it for us. You have to save us from the Emerald Queen."

"Why don't you get it yourself?"

"Can't," Elerim chewed her lip. "Not permitted."

"Says who?"

"Says I." Carlo turned and saw a man dressed in shimmering silver, his face hidden by a floppy black hat, and in his chubby hands a slender pipe carved with runes and shining like wet alabaster.

"I've seen you before," Carlo said, eyeing the harp suspiciously. He'd also heard pipes recently but couldn't remember where. "In some similar guise. You're another conniver." Beside him, Elerim hissed in alarm like a snake releasing venom.

"Ahh—She is in me again." Elerim shook and stumbled, and it seemed to Carlo that he was looking at someone else, a different woman, with Elerim trapped inside.

"You cannot stop us this time, Father." The voice wasn't Elerim's but came from her lips. "Ansu is My planet," the strange voice said. "You gave it to Me."

"You think I forget that folly—trusting in my first-born?" The faceless man folded his chubby arms and leaned back against the rock. He appeared amused, something Carlo sensed even though he couldn't see a face. "You have forfeited the right, as have your kin," the Piper said.

"You thought us dead!" The woman with Elerim's face rose up, towering over the faceless man. "But we've fooled you, Father. What you created cannot be unmade!" A shimmer and whirl of light. Carlo saw sparks like fireflies shooting into the air, accompanied by a flurry of pipes. He turned, saw Elerim crouched weeping beside him.

"You have only yourself to blame for that," the faceless man said. "You three deceivers were deceived. But *she* cannot escape me forever."

"It wasn't my fault!" Elerim's tears streamed down her face. "Cille . . . she caused this to happen." The enchantress sounded like a chided child whining about some unfair punishment she'd received.

"You are all to blame," the faceless man said. "Hence our recent arrangement." He dipped his hat to Carlo. "Sorceresses," he said. "Can't trust them. But there's always someone cleverer than yourself, heh, Elerim. By the by, Carlo Sarfe—you are needed elsewhere."

"What about my ship?" Carlo said, cursing as both Elerim and the faceless man shrank before him like melting wax dripping from candles, as did his surroundings, replaced by darkness and a distant hollow echo.

Carlo folded his arms and waited.

I'll pay their price if it gets me home.

He sensed he wasn't alone and that whatever was happening would play out soon. "Ready when you are," Carlo said, straining his eyes through the dark. "Don't rush on my account."

A distant sound resonating across. A bell? Carlo could hear tolling, slowly at first. It sounded far away but each toll was louder than the one before, and after a dozen chimes, the noise was battering his ears.

Light appeared a long way off. Like the tolling of the bell it grew in resonance. A green vivid glow, deepening from pale jade to dazzling emerald, swelling until it filled every horizon, and Carlo realized he could see for miles.

He walked toward the source of the light. Carlo saw shadows walking with him on either side. He ignored them, focusing solely on the light source far ahead. A green glowing circle rising from nothing, like dawn in a distant world. Time passed, and Carlo had no idea how long he'd been walking, but suddenly he noticed a long green tower silhouetted against the rising sphere behind it. A spike of pure emerald shimmering and throbbing with light.

The source.

An emerald needle perhaps thirty feet high, so bright it hurt his eyes to glance at it. But Carlo would not be deterred. That source held the keys to his passage home. He was close, and he had only to face whatever waited and do as he was bidden.

As Carlo approached the thin green tower, he saw a basilisk curled prone at its base. Wrapped within its jade coils was a bow of simple wood, corded with strips of glowing green.

The Emerald Bow of Kerasheva.

"Take it now before the serpent wakes!" Carlo heard Elerim's voice somewhere close. She sounded desperate. Carlo bit his lip and knew he had no choice but to obey her wishes. He took a step forward and then cursed as someone knocked him aside, and Carlo saw the shadow of a man rushing toward the obelisk.

"Garland?"

***

The cavern had fallen away on either side as Garland had walked, alone, afraid, yet determined. Then he'd seen it—the obelisk. A thin column of emerald, throbbing and pulsing, sending jets of vivid green in every direction. Garland saw people standing all around it. Tiny figures, almost impossible to define. He slid his broadsword free of its scabbard and walked closer. Unnoticed and unbidden.

The green tower rose before him like an accusing finger. Garland stopped when he saw the basilisk lying coiled at its base. Huge and motionless, a great reptilian monster. Its lids were closed in deep slumber. Then Garland noticed the bow lying half-buried amongst those foot-thick coils.

Bring that to me.

A voice that resembled Ysaren's whispered in his ear.

Do that and I'll repay you dividends, Sir Garland.

"I'm not doing this for you," Garland said, shouldering through a crowd of people he discovered blocking his way. Someone called out his name, but Garland ignored the warning. He strode towards the sleeping serpent his sword held level. The creature opened its eyes, and Garland swung.

***

"No!" Tam yelled as he saw Garland hacking at the flesh of the basilisk. The creature was stirring in anger and rearing up at the captain. "I need that bow!" Tam wriggled past the people watching in frozen silence. Once free, he ran toward the basilisk and vaulted onto its mass of coils. barely balancing, Tam reached down and grabbed the bow Kerasheva in both hands, wrestling it free from the serpent's coils as the monster writhed and rose around Garland, whose wild hacks were proving useless.

Tam fought free and raced away to where Teret lay dying, the faceless man standing behind her, having delivered them to this place. Tam placed the bow in Teret's hands. He glanced up at the Piper.

"Give it a moment," Jynn said.

"Teret . . . You cannot leave me!" Tam cried, the tears streaming down he face. "I cannot bear to lose you a second time." Then her eyes opened.

"Next task." The Piper handed Tam his instrument. The pipe became an arrow the instant he touched it. A long green shaft; Tam ran his fingers along it dreamily as he gazed down at Teret. Alive— but for how long?

"What must I do to keep her alive?" Tam said, quelling the panic as he saw Teret's eyes were half closed.

"Kill that creature," Jynn said.

Tam nodded. "As you wish," he fumbled with the bow but stopped when a soft hand caught his arm. She stood beside him, pale as linen sheets left out to dry. Teret.

"You need rest," Tam said.

"There'll be time soon enough," Teret said. Her eyes were glazed and she looked drugged. "I'm the archer remember," she said, a faint smile creasing her lips. "I have just enough strength left in me."

"I cannot let you do this!" Tam stared wild-eyed at Jynn, who shrugged.

"It doesn't matter who kills the serpent," Jynn said.

"She isn't herself!" Tam said dropping the arrow.

"Oh yes, I am," Teret said. "Never been better." She nocked arrow to bow, waited as the serpent reared high over Captain Garland, and then loosed.

**

The arrow came from nowhere, cutting deep into the serpent's green skin and causing it to writhe and shudder. Garland collapsed under the weight of angry green coils whipping and lashing his body and squeezing the breath from his lungs.

I'm dying.

Garland choked and pushed at the scaly bulk crushing him. The pain was horrible.

Ariane—I found them, and my task is done.

Garland closed his eyes and let the pain and blackness consume him. It passed like storms over ocean. The weight shifted, slid from his body, and a strong hand pulled Garland free of the serpent wreckage.

Garland coughed and spewed muck, and it was some time before he knew what was happening. He was alive, and for the moment that was enough.

"That, my friend, was perhaps the stupidest and bravest thing I've ever witnessed," Carlo Sarfe said, passing Garland's badly dented broadsword across.

Garland grasped the weapon with shaking hands and just stared at it. "I don't know what came over me," he said.

"I was about to do the same thing, but you shoved me aside," Carlo said.

"Sorry about that—I can't remember."

"Someone fired an arrow killing this snake. Aside that, I'm as confused as you are," Carlo said.

"What now?" Garland gripped his sword with both hands and staggered to his feet. Everywhere, green light pulsed, and he heard voices shouting and a great movement of feet.

"We play this game out," Carlo smiled at him.

***

"I thought you said it would save her?" Tam crouched beside Teret, the tears coursing down his face and blurring his vision.

"It's all right my love—I feel nothing, no pain." Teret lay in his arms, her face pale and breath shaky.

"That's because you are fading," the Piper said. "The gateways are opening for you. You're a very lucky girl to get to use the express route. And for you, Lord Tamersane, should you wish to accompany your wife it can be done. I don't normally allow this, but I'm fond of you two children."

"I know who you are," Teret smiled. "I can see you clearly now." Tam noticed how her eyes were glazing over. "The Weaver of this tangled thread . . ."

"Teret, you cannot die—I love you!" Tam kissed her face, eyes, and lips, and held her tight as he could. "The bow was meant to heal you. You said it would!" He rounded on the Piper who stood with arms folded neatly, his face hidden by the light.

"And so it has," Jynn said. "Bow and arrow fired. Teret is free from pain and sorrow. You can be too Tamersane—your choice as to whether to accept this gift. I'll repeat. Not something I do for anyone. Choose quickly, even I cannot hold the doors open for long. I made them too strong."

Tam hardly heard the words; he was looking at Teret's eyes. They seemed so far away. "Always I loved you," Tam said, the tears streaming down his face. "Even when I was acting the goat, I never stopped loving you. You're my rock, Teret—you always have been. How can I possibly survive without you? This world means nothing to me anymore."

"Then leave it behind," Jynn said. He grabbed Tam's arm getting his attention. Tam looked up but still couldn't see a face. "Make your choice, Tamersane. I cannot hold the portals open much longer. Order has to be retained less Chaos and His minions creep back in."

"Then I choose death, happily." Tam wiped his eyes. "So, I can cross over with her?"

"There is no such thing as death," the faceless man said. "Only gateways leading to different paths. Everything is but a beginning and an ending. Time—the cords that bind it together. But even time is an illusion, albeit a necessary one. Everything *is* nothing, Lord Tam. Go you can. But you need to act now."

"I am ready." Tam gripped his wife's hand tight and smiled down at her. He closed his eyes, felt a warm rush of air, and it seemed to him that his body was lifted, a leaf in the wind, drifting, floating out, rising and falling . . .

A new journey had begun.

Chapter 32 | A New Dance

And now for the next part . . . Jynn smiled as the tapestry was laid bare at last. He saw the game in full and marveled at the cleverness of His eldest daughter's deception. Cille—the perfect disguise. She'd hidden from Him, escaped His wrath as had the other one—her husband, and brother. The man called Seek.

Jynn folded His arms and watched as Cille walked calmly toward the dead basilisk and tugged the arrow free from its scales. She turned to her sisters smiling. "We each have an arrow," Cille said. "But mine has serpent poison on the tip, thus is more potent than ever."

Jynn smiled again as Elerim and Ysaren joined their sibling at the base of the column, its emerald fading to dull gray, and a landscape slowly revealing itself all around. There were people there, beasts, towns and cities, farms and homesteads surrounding green fields, landscapes, oceans. It was though the three sisters stood on a towering precipice overlooking all of mankind's machinations.

Jynn took a moment to survey the scene, smiling at *His* work: every mountain, every river, each breath steaming the air—all were a part of *Him*. Satisfied, Jynn returned His gaze to the witches.

"Ansu is beautiful, is it not," Cille said, licking the poison from the arrow tip and then wiping her red mouth. "My Queendom. A thing to be cherished." Jynn stole silently up behind her and Cille turned, her eyes wary seeing Him standing there. Jynn hopped closer on the ledge. He'd swopped his attire to a long white coat with sleeves flaring at tips. He wore sandals and concealed his features beneath a deep hood. He twirled the pipe between his fingers. *This is going to be interesting.*

"You . . ." Cille's face turned sour, and the other two looked askance. "What do you want?"

"Just thought I'd drop by." Jynn dipped his hat.

"This is My realm," Cille stared directly at Him, much like a child refused a bedtime story.

"And yet you almost destroyed it," Jynn said.

"Unfair," Cille said, turning and looming over the Piper, her shape willowy and tall. "You changed the parameters, Father. Took our favorite toys away. What were We supposed to do—your first-born—lie down and die?"

"Move on, like most your brothers did," the Piper said, rising to meet her gaze. "They are content with their existence on other worlds. They haven't given me much trouble lately."

"Give them time," Cille said. "Come sisters, join me again. We must finish what I started earlier. Father needs to know how powerful I've become." She showed him her back.

Both Elerim and Ysaren shrank back in horror. Elerim spoke first and Ysaren nodded as her sister pointed her long fingers at Cille. "You conspired without our knowledge," Elerim said. "You offered yourself to her. Sacrificed your soul."

"Someone had to do something," Cille said. "Take a risk. You two were squabbling like stray cats in an alley. I, at least, have been proactive. Even though that cost me, I am part of something bigger now."

"By drawing that artful Piper's attention to us," Ysaren said, pointing to Jynn.

"Quite so. I deemed our situation intolerable and decided to address that to Him," Cille flicked her green gaze at the Piper. Jynn watched without responding. *She doesn't know I'm on to her.*

"Divide and rule, Father—that was your plan, wasn't it?" Cille pointed a narrow finger at the Piper again. "Drive a wedge between us and then push us aside, much like splinters blown off fresh-planed wood."

"He's not our Father!" Elerim raged.

"I'm not talking to you!" Cille's retort stung Elerim to silence. "You and Ysaren are mistaking this Piper for someone else." She turned and flashed Him a grin, almost smug. "They think you're Arollas the Golden, Father. They've become quite senile, poor dears."

"I am everything and I am nothing." *It is time.* Jynn placed the pipe on his lips and sent chords sailing up into the air. "And *you* were banished daughter."

"This is *My* realm," Cille insisted.

"You were custodian, with your husband," Jynn said. "A task you both neglected, allowing Old Night to return. And resulting in Myself having to deal with Him once and for all, and then clear up your mess."

"That wasn't My fault," Cille said. "I've always loved this world, whereas You, Father, abandoned it. I didn't deserve Your harsh judgement."

"You brought that upon yourself," the Piper said. "You and those arrogant siblings rebelled against the Natural Order. Not once, but three times. Your vain brother was mostly to blame, but you never consulted Me, Elanion, though you must have suspected his return. Never asked for My aid. That hurt, daughter. I'd have treated you more kindly if you hadn't fled battle with your husband. Skulking in forests and hiding your body inside those brittle witchy shells."

"What's she talking about, sister?" Jynn glanced across, seeing how Ysaren's pale features were anxious and taut. "I thought it was Arallos the Golden who tore us apart."

"And so it was," Cille answered her sister. "Arallos fooled the sorceresses, Elerim, Ysaren and Cille—but like him, these women perished seven years ago. I took over their forms to hide from the Weaver and prepare my case against His cruel accusations. To do that I needed Kerasheva, made for Me by your Aralais kin long ago. Cille became the mind of the Goddess, Elerim the heart, and you, frail Ysaren, the eternal ache She carries within."

"And you succeeded in hiding from Me for a time, cunning as you are," the Piper said.

"You made us that way, Father. Elerim, there, housed my beauty, wisdom, and mystery. In her Forest of Dreams where my power has always been prime. Ysaren contained my anger and resentment, her guardian a mirage of her fragile imagination. I needed Ysaren grounded. And Cille . . . was the only truly wicked one of the sisters, so I took her soul. You two are manikins, shades, and fragments. Nothing more."

"So, you *are* the Emerald Queen," Elerim said. "You've come for us at last."

"Yes, Cille said. "Now we sisters must join together and drive our Father out."

Jynn stowed His pipe and folded those chubby arms. *Good luck trying . . .*

"No," Elerim's face was pale. "You cannot do this!"

"Join the arrows," Cille said. "The Aralais sorcery locked inside will shut Him out. I'm right, aren't I Father? *Ansu* is My world. You have no place here," Cille said. "You gave Ansu to my husband, but he wasn't worthy. I have always been true."

"I created this world and gave it to you, ungrateful bitch," Jynn said, surprised at the flash of anger He felt. "This is how you repay

Me?"

"Enough." Cille held forth her arrow and the other sisters did the same, despite straining against it. Like manikins on a thread they had to obey.

"Now!" Cille said thrusting her arrow forward to touch the green tips of the other two. Upon that contact the tips merged into one. "Come sisters, embrace!" Cille's face cracked open, her body shattered and crumbled into a hundred pieces. Elerim screamed and green vapor tore inside her and melted her form. Ysaren tried to flee but her brittle body snapped and broke apart at the word of the woman who had risen from the wreckage of her sisters. The Emerald Queen gazed down at the mess. The three witches had served their purpose.

The Goddess stood on the edge of her world. A towering figure; Jynn felt tiny beside her.

"Impressive, Elanion," Jynn said. "But before you get excited, know this. Mankind hasn't done too badly without your help. You weren't missed."

"You think?" The Goddess loomed over the tiny shape of the Piper as if she meant to crush him. He spoke a word, and his shape altered again, expanding and becoming level with her own "You let us fight, Father," Elanion said. "Goaded us on, and then abandoned us—my brothers and myself. And all because our eldest has always let you down."

"All of you children have let me down," Jynn said. "He just let me down more. But Old Night is history—three strikes and gone to Yffarn. He won't be coming back this time, not even I can change that. I might have created this world and spawned the life within, but the codicils I made are bigger than I."

"That's because you deserted this quiet corner of the galaxy," Elanion said. "We did our best as custodians. But it was hard without your guidance. You never listened, Father, and then came back to destroy us."

So, it's all My fault . . .

Jynn chuckled wryly. "You almost destroyed yourself, daughter," He said. "My wrath against you should be greater than it is." *My weakness has always been love, the Giver who cannot take back.* "The evil your brother spawned is out the bag, Elanion. What's done cannot be undone. That is why the universe is corrupt. You, His siblings, could have halted the spread, were you not cat-fighting and posturing. You and your husband as bad as the rest."

"I don't talk to him," Elanion said, her beautiful face darkening with anger. "Besides, he's gone. Lost, out there in the ether—and good riddance!"

"Oroonin is closer than you think," Jynn said. "My craftiest son has a perennial talent for survival."

"So . . . what now?" Elanion said, looking bored with the subject.

"You have the bow Kerasheva and your island, Laras Lassladden," Jynn said. "I'll not take those from you."

"I meant *Ansu*—it's My planet," Elanion said.

You haven't changed daughter. Jynn almost expected her to stamp her feet. *Four thousand years old but still a child.*

"That is why I alone refused to leave," she said, "even though you promised oblivion for any God that stayed. You've always been hard on your firstborn."

Not hard enough. "My firstborn and my first disappointment," Jynn said. "And you weren't the only one that stayed. I know where your brother/husband lurks. Oroonin is hiding somewhere close. I can feel his cunning venting through the walls. But he is too late this time." *Are you listening, Seek?*

As Jynn spoke, he braced his legs wide. A loud crunch and a fissure erupted at his feet, cracking open the high ledge where they were standing, breaking it away from the rest of the world, falling far below. The rock soared up into space, the Goddess Elanion trapped upon it. His favorite daughter launched into orbit again. *I hope she'll learn one day.*

"You disobeyed me, Elanion." Jynn's voice was everywhere. "Dividing Your divine self and hiding inside three ancient witches. *Fragile shells.* Thinking You could exist in those broken forms until My attention was focused on the other side of the universe. You lack your husband's guile, my dear. My attention is everywhere and always. Constant as light over darkness. I miss nothing daughter . . . I am EVERYTHING . . ."

That should do it.

Jynn cast down his pipe, smashing it at his feet. The Weaver became a white hawk and lifted wing-fast, a diamond spark diving out into whirring space, leaving the spinning emerald rock and its furious Goddess tenant far behind, until Laras Lassladden dwindled and vanished into void.

Hawk-Jynn swooped back down. *One task still awaits Me.*

Are you listening, Seek . . .?

The shaman sat bolt upright. That voice boomed like a gong in his head. *He's on to me.* Seek almost screamed at the severity of the vision. *Father . . .?*

The emerald tower, the guardian slain, the three witches—so clever of his wife to hide from him there. Almost he was impressed. "But I'm sharper than you Elanion—harder to track," Seek said quietly to himself. *Why they called me the Wanderer.* Like the Emerald Queen, Seek had disobeyed His father's instructions. On pain of annihilation, He had opted to stay here on Ansu. The planet He was gifted before His wife stole it from Him. But that was eons ago, and Seek didn't hold to grudges.

Get what you need and move on. Father makes things. She nurtures them. I bend them to My purpose—it was ever thus.

Seek witnessed the bow clutched in the dying woman's hands, saw Tamersane and the Tseole pup Stogi close by. The emerald tower was broken and the Castle of Lights no more. That didn't matter. The Nexus had occurred, and He could breathe again. Return to His own form using those stolen remnants of crystal to bend time back towards the past. There were things that needed changing. Why be immortal if you can't learn from lessons past—and then go back and revamp?

Father was too highbrow. The Maker makes—a simple job, and overrated. Oroonin had the tools now. And more imagination. It was past time for a new Dance. *His Dance.*

Seek smiled at His deception. He saw Laras Lassladden drifting off into void and waved at His wife. *Bless Her for a looker but not much between the ears.* Elanion had failed but Seek/Oroonin was only getting started.

He had the crystal from the mines and emerald shards from the Castle of Lights. With binding runes Oroonin would fashion them into something potent—*a mirror to hide Me from Father.*

Seek had done well for his puppet master. But the scarecrow shaman was no longer needed. A rip and tear, crunch of bone, splatter of gore—Seek's body exploding into mist. A useful soul stolen from a shaman who'd delved too deep. *Be careful what you wish for.* A shadow reached down and scooped up the tall hat, all that was left of Seek the shaman.

The God Oroonin smiled—he liked hats and would keep this one. *Time for the next phase.* The witches' power was broken. The Emerald Queen's vanity had summoned the Maker/Weaver and Father had sent the lot of them to Yffarn.

Round two.

Like smoke over water, Oroonin hovered at the shoreline, watching the waves, His body shifted and faded like smoky rain. Oroonin spread His arms wide and cast the tall hat high into the sky. It vanished in a bolt of light. Oroonin became a bird and took to the water, a white swan alighting softly on the ocean and gliding over toward the distant ship, the word *Arabella* painted on her prow. He had set the seeds for discord; time now to raise the stakes. That meant returning to the start. The next Dance had begun. The swan's sharp eyes saw a shadow swoop overhead. Oroonin recognized His Father and heard that voice calling out.

I'm not done with you yet, Wanderer.

The hawk vanished, but the swan felt the echo of His anger. Undeterred, He approached the ship. It was time to return to Gol and shake things up again. *You are no match for me now Father.*

***

Stogi stood at the docks, watching in fascination as the waves lapped lazily against the hull of the great ship. His keen eyes caught a glint of light, saw a white bird glide down through that clear blue sky, a hawk or an osprey perhaps. Then Stogi spied another, much larger bird gliding toward the ship they were about to board. Pale as lily the swan approached. The sight made Stogi shiver.

"You sure you want to do this?" Stogi's new friend Carlo Sarfe asked, standing beside him and admiring his ship, returned from wreckage in mint condition. Another result of the craziness they'd endured. "You told me you hate the sea."

"I lied," Stogi said, watching the swan glide out into open water until lost from view. "How can you hate something you've never seen? But it scares me shitless, truth be told. All that water—it's not natural."

"Hah—it is to me." Carlo grinned and rubbed his hands together.

"It spells home." His warm eyes were smiling at Stogi. "It's her—isn't it?" Carlo said. "You've gone soft in the head. Tai Pei wants to come, so you're coming too?"

"I'm fond of the girl," Stogi admitted. They both watched as Tai Pei vaulted up the rigging and grinned down at them.

"You haven't known her long," Carlo said, admiring how the girl had taken to his vessel in minutes.

"You didn't know Teret long and yet you would have died for her." Stogi saw the white hawk settle on a post and preen its feathers, its sharp black eyes watching them.

Carlo sighed. "You're right. And I miss her."

"As I miss Lord Tam and his sad long face," Stogi said. "Will we ever see them again, do you think?"

"I doubt it," Carlo said. "The Piper said they'd moved on to other dimensions, just like Garland the soldier. A man I would have liked to have known better."

"Me too," Stogi said. "Strange choice that fellow made. I thought he was returning to his queen in the west."

"He'd done his duty," Carlo said. "Old soldier, not ready to settle. You never know what people want in this life."

"But to choose to go through that vapor knowing death—or worse—could wait on the other side," Stogi said, shaking his head. "Strikes me as a tad reckless."

"I think Captain Garland knew where he was going," Carlo said. "Seemed like a man with a purpose. Come on, time to find your sea legs, Master Stogi—we've a long voyage to make. I doubt you'll prove as graceful as that one." They glanced up again, seeing Tai Pei stretched out on a yard, some thirty feet above their heads. She looked beautiful, Stogi thought, her pale bare legs dangling in the sunshine. He sighed. *The things I do . . .*

"So where are we going?" Stogi asked his new friend.

"A journey through time and across strange oceans," Carlo said.

"Oh—good, I almost expected a sensible response. You are as bad as Lord Tam. Just tell me you have ample liquor on that tub," Stogi said, eyeing the ship as a man studies a dangerous beast that's broken free of its chains.

"Enough for a long voyage," Carlo assured him, and turned away, crossing the quay and returning to his ship after long weeks away.

Stogi shrugged and followed, his knees wobbly as he strode over the creaking gang plank. "Strange life," the Tseole said. "But compared to what?"

***

Shel watched Hulda emerge from her tent and yawn. "Another day in paradise," she said, and Shel smiled, enjoying the warm sunlight on her freckled face.

Three months had passed since Stogi and Lord Tam had left. Seek had vanished soon after. Shel didn't miss the shaman, but she wished Stogi would return. And Lord Tam—Shel had liked Lord Tam. The Tseole survived the result of Seek's antics by journeying far north and crossing the Shen River near its sources. Seek had left them there, vanishing one night. Shel had found his hat abandoned by the fire. Together with a dead, headless hawk. A creepy discovery that had left her skin crawling for days.

Since then, they'd fared deeper into Tseola, keeping watch on the roads and witnessing ever greater traffic between Shen and Ptarni. Seek had failed in his plans to disrupt the two nations. The alliance seemed stronger than ever, and Shel knew it was only a matter of time before those great countries united and bled her world dry. The Tseole would survive. They always had.

***

413

"Your people can live in Largos," the kindly Bruhan Dahali had told her. "The city's expanding; they can find work and lodging easily enough."

Since then, Carys had settled into life in that hot dusty city. The memories of Elerim's forest and Carys's country Gwelan faded as years passed and she married and gave birth to three healthy children. The Bruhan had become governor of Largos after the Rana disappeared in mysterious circumstances several years back.

Life was good, though the war in the north touched them almost every day. But word was Shen was crumbling from within, and Ptarni stretched like butter over too much bread, as the mad emperor gathered his forces to invade the west. His relationship with Shen had dwindled due to countless trade disruptions and goods lost from an unprecedented number of raids from bandits roaming the wilds of Tseola. They said a scarecrow on an eight-legged horse was stirring things up in that country. And she'd heard rumors of a ghostly rider in the night sky. Doubtless such tales were exaggerated.

Carys cared little about these grand affairs. They seldom touched her busy little world. But it seemed to her the odds were turning against Ptarni. That country was breaking inwards. She might yet live out her life in peace, in Largos—a place she'd come to love, her children knowing nothing of the horror Carys had seen. She often thought of brave Teret and handsome Carlo and wondered how they fared. Those two wonderful people who had saved Carys that terrible distant day.

***

Tam smiled as he watched the white hawk swoop past, the gulls crying out at this bold intruder. He could feel the cold sting of salt air on his face and the warmth of her small hand inside his. A perfect day, thought Tam as he smiled at the angry gulls weaving high above.

"I was born in that town," he told Teret, pointing down to where gray-thatched houses clustered around a wave-locked harbor. "Grew up there, before my mother remarried a nobleman and moved us to court in Wynais. My brother and I," Tam sighed for a moment. "A secret always—we were lowly born but attended schooling in the city. King Nogel took us in as his own, and I grew up alongside Princess Ariane. We were fond of each other."

"So much so that she sent Captain Garland to find you," Teret said. "Poor man–what a trial he had." Teret squeezed Tam's hand. "Come husband—we cannot linger here," she said. "We two have no substance in this place—our souls are tugged to and fro at the whim of this chilly sea breeze."

She turned and walked away, her shape fading and vanishing above the dewy grasses of the downs. Tam's smile saddened.

"So many things I would change," he said, looking down at Port Wind a final time. "But a man can only do his best with the life he is given."

Tam turned and followed his wife's shifting passage. Both figures soon faded from view as the white hawk sped high, the gulls crying His name out, and evening falling soft and golden upon that dwindling summer's day.

Marei wiped her tired eyes and scraped clean the fireplace. The inn had been strangely busy lately, and Dafyd had returned as often as he could to help out. Hard for him, now he had a wife and child in the village.

At least Graywash Hall had left them alone. Something had happened there; recent travelers had remarked on a change. The beacon fires no longer burned, and Marei suspected some of the tenants of the Hall had moved on. That happened now and then.

She kept busy; it helped keep the loneliness at bay.

A soft sound at the threshold behind her. Rough boots scraping, and a quiet, polite cough. The shadow of a man stood there. Marei cursed quietly, not ready for business yet.

"We're not open until tonight," Marei said. "Unless it's lodging you want, then I'll be with you as soon as I can."

"I was hoping for something more than that."

"What?"

Marei wiped grime from her face, dusted her sleeves and turned. The man blocking her doorway had the evening sun behind him. A silhouette, it was hard to see his face, but she knew that voice well enough.

Marei laughed, "Sir Garland—you came back!"

"Had nowhere else to go." Garland smiled as he strode into Torrigan's Tavern and threw his strong arms around the laughing girl. "It's been several years, but I'm a man of my word, Marei."

"Several years?" Marei laughed as he held her close. "You must be drunk, man. 'Twas only six months you left here, Sir Garland."

***

"The Queen will see you now." The courtier inclined his head and ushered him in. Doyle's eyes were dazzled as he entered the wide, glittering courtroom, glimpsing the dozen or so people standing around the throne, the young woman seated upon it.

A man stood close to her, his sandy hair thinner than it had been. Consort Raule smiled at Doyle as he limped over to the throne.

"Here is a man with a story to tell," Lord Calprissa said, and bid Doyle approach the Queen. The resplendent nobles parted to let him through. The woman seated on the throne turned her head towards him, and Doyle bowed low as he looked into the keen dark eyes of Queen Ariane of Kelwyn.

"Where is my Captain, and the rest of his men?" The Queen's

sharp gaze studied him. Doyle was aware of many other eyes on him. He glanced at the silver drapes, the arched windows, Lake Wynais, and the city sparkling far below—anything rather than gaze at those sharp eyes.

"My Queen."

"No need," Ariane's strong face softened with a wise smile. "It's good to see you, Captain Doyle."

"Your Highness, I'm only a lieutenant," Doyle shuffled his feet and noticed Lord Calprissa winking at him.

"You look exhausted," the Queen said. "Have you eaten yet?"

"I came here at once," Doyle told her. "There is much to tell."

"Sleep first," Ariane said, motioning retainers go prepare a room. "Rest and eat, then we'll talk this evening, you and I."

Dismissed, Doyle took much needed rest, returning to the throne room that evening to discover the Queen alone with her peruse. She stood by a table, a pot of tea and two cups arranged on a deep green tablecloth.

The Queen bid Doyle take seat and then took chair opposite.

"We won't be disturbed," Queen Ariane told him. "So?"

"Where to start." Doyle sipped his tea and winced at a sensitive tooth.

"The hazards of drinking hot tea," Queen Ariane smiled, then gazed at the windows and her city beyond. "I dreamed of Tamersane last night," she said. "He was smiling and laughing and walking arm in arm with his lady Teret. Did you ever meet her?"

"Your Highness—I."

"Good woman—strong. Don't think she liked me," Ariane said. "But she was good for that boy. Agh—I miss him so. Well, Captain. You had best tell me everything."

This Wolf Bites! Introducing Corin an Fol.

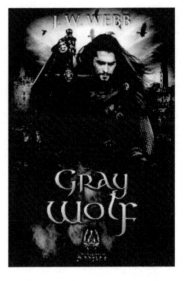

If you enjoyed The Emerald Queen then you will love this first adventure in the Legends of Ansu series. Gray Wolf features Corin the mercenary, a man trying hard to forget his past.

Read the first few pages here. You can get the eBook free if you join our fun newsletter the J.W.Webb VIP Lounge. Don't miss out. Subscribe and pick up Gray Wolf to discover this exciting series today.

www.jwwebbauthor.com

Enjoy this book?
You can make a big difference

Reviews are the most powerful tools in my arsenal when it comes to getting attention for my books. Much as I'd like to, I don't have the financial muscle of a New York publisher. I can't take out full page ads in the newspaper or put posters on the subway.

(Not yet, anyway).

But I do have something much more powerful and effective than that, and it's something that those publishers would kill to get their hands on

A committed and loyal bunch of readers.

Honest reviews of my books help bring them to the attention of other readers.

If you have enjoyed this book I would be grateful if you could spend just five minutes leaving a review, (it can be as short as you like) on the book's page.

Thank you very much.

Gray Wolf

Chapter 1 | Raiders

They came at dawn, and it was Corin who saw them first. Three ships emerging as sleek gray shadows piercing the mist, their oars dipping and raising in measured silence. These were no fisher craft; their narrow hulls and brightly colored sails gave them away. Crenise Pirate ships. Corin had often heard his father speak of these vessels while trying to hide the loathing in his voice. He watched as excitement, anger, and fear fought to control him. Raiders had come!

Corin froze, his hands at his side, witnessing the three vessels beach the strand and shaggy figures wade ashore. He could hear their laughing and curses as they slung shields across their backs and made for the nearest houses of Finnehalle, his village. He'd been out early this morning before his kin were up. Corin usually slept as late as he could, but this morning he was restless, so he'd risen early to stroll the town and watch the sunrise from the harbor. Corin was a scarce hundred yards from his cottage when the ships emerged through the mist.

He stood, hovering and fretting until at last the fear won, and Corin sped up the hill to where the warning bell hung above the well, at the corner of the square. He tugged the rope, and the bell clanged and tolled until Corin's arms shook. The raiders were yelling, rushing toward where he stood pulling on the bell cord. There were perhaps twenty or thirty—it was hard to tell as the mist still clung to their ring-mail and furs. They carried shields across their backs, and in their hands were axes and curved swords.

Corin felt terror churning inside him. His stomach griped, but he was determined not to let his fear show. Out at sea the mist had cleared, and Corin could see other ships far across the water. He tugged the bell cord a final time and then turned for home.

Corin ran, picking up speed as the panic rose again in his belly. He heard shouts and the sound of breaking timber. Horrified, Corin turned and witnessed two bearded raiders crashing through the doors of his neighbor's house below. Shortly after, he heard screams from within. Shaking with rage, Corin turned away and sped up the hill. His long legs brought him level with his own front door, just as it burst open to reveal his father, Tollan, standing with bloodshot eyes and rusty blade in hands.

"Boy, get inside!" Tollan growled at his youngest son.

"I'll fight beside you, Father!" Corin felt angry and proud despite his fear. He wanted his father to know he was brave.

"Get in—idiot boy!" The burley fisherman yanked Corin by the hair and shoved him into the house. Corin's three brothers were in there, and his eldest sister, Ceilyn. His mother, Alize, stood by the hearth, her brown eyes wide with horror and her arms wrapped around the sobbing Daliene, Corin's little sister. Corin watched as his father strode out into the street and closed the door behind him. "Bar that door!" he told Corin, who complied swiftly, lifting the heavy metal rod and dropping it into place.

Inside the cottage, his brothers looked at Corin, their faces frozen in the misery of uncertainty and terror. They weren't like Corin. They were fisherfolk, as were their father and mother, and sisters too. Corin was different. A fire burned within him—always had. He couldn't stand here and let Father face them on his own. Corin stared at the door, the rage and terror conflicting inside him.

"Who are they, Corin?" Ceilyn's eyes were wide with terror as he turned and gazed at his sister.

"Crenise Pirates." Corin almost spat the words out as his hatred soared inside.

Noise and shouts filled the morning. The screaming was the worst. Corin heard babes crying, their yells silenced by steel. Dogs howled, snapped, and scampered, and a woman screamed somewhere close by.

Corin pushed past his horror-stricken brothers and stared out their only window, his kin too terrified to watch. Down there near the harbor, he could see the raiders had already put torch to the first two houses, and Corin could hear the screams of those trapped inside. Daliene cried out, and their mother held her tighter than before, her own tears mixing with her child's.

Corin gripped Ceilyn's hand in his own. "It will be alright," he told his favorite sister. They both knew his words were forlorn hopes, but Ceilyn nodded bravely and bit her lip until it bled. Corin could stand it no longer. Mind made up, he approached the door and lifted the heavy bar. "Stay here!" Corin yelled at his family. "I've got to help Father. Bolt the door behind me!"

"We're coming too!" Gordellen, his eldest brother, shook himself from his trance.

"No." Corin bid Gordellen to stay inside. "You three protect Mother and the girls!' Corin turned the latch, pushed the door wide open, and ventured out into the street. The raiders were closer now.

A shout turned his head. Three raiders were running toward where this father stood with the old sword gripped tight with sweaty hands. They slowed their advance when they saw his blade. The closet and biggest laughed.

"Looks like this one wants to fight." He grinned, and the two with him grinned back. Corin was dimly aware that his brothers had ignored his command and now joined him, while his mother and the two girls were fleeing up the hill toward the woods. Corin could see men already giving chase. He wanted to follow, but the raiders were circling his father now.

The three Crenise stood laughing at Corin's father. "Gut him, Brokka." The middle one revealed rotten teeth as he urged the biggest to attack Corin's father first.

"Be glad to." Brokka laughed and tossed his blade through the air, deftly catching it, his eyes never leaving Corin's father.

His father, hiding his fear well, swung hard, his sword slicing air as the raider, Brokka, jumped clear, laughing again. He was still laughing when he slid his curved blade between Corin's father's ribs. Corin watched in horror as his father dropped the sword, his big hands cupping the rent in his chest.

Corin screamed as a second blow severed his father's neck and his head rolled back into the empty house. Corin could hear his mother scream as she witnessed her husband's death from the edge of the village. He glanced up briefly, seeing her ragged face before she turned and fled out the gates. Corin turned as one dreaming. He looked up at the savage men now gazing upon him

Time froze. Corin's senses twitched as though he were primed by lightning, and a deep slow rage, like bubbling magna, filled his veins. He was dimly aware of his brothers' yells as they fled with the two other raiders hard on their tails. Corin focused on his father's killer, who stood with feet braced apart, his broad face clearly amused as he surveyed a skinny lad glaring up at him with hate-filled eyes.

"You're a fiery little shit." Brokka's eyes were bloodshot and his voice raspy, as though he smoked too much. Like his comrades, he wore chain mail and leather and stank of tobacco and stale sweat. A salt-and-pepper beard framed his heavy face, and he carried a round shield slung casually across his back. But in his right hand was the short sword that he'd used to kill Corin's father. Corin glared as Brokka pointed the seax at his chest and grinned. "Time to join your old man in Yffarn!"

Brokka swung hard at Corin's neck, but Corin was quicker. He dived low and rolled across to where his father's sword lay abandoned in the dusty grime.

Corin seized the hilt with both hands, then rolled again as Brokka hacked down hard upon him. Corin lashed out with a kick and—by sheer luck—caught Brokka between his legs. Brokka stumbled, allowing Corin the seconds he needed to find his feet and plunge his father's sword deep into Brokka's side.

"We gotta go!" one of the marauders said. Corin saw Brokka's companions looking out to sea. "Torval said to waste no time!"

"What about Brokka? We cannot leave him here."

Corin saw that the other raider had turned away and was running toward the gate.

"Yffarn take Brokka and that boy— it's the women we want. You coming?"

Corin was dimly aware of them leaving.

He watched Brokka twitch in agony beneath him. Corin savagely twisted the blade, and his father's murderer screamed. He pulled the rusty blade free with a savage tug of his palms, then he stabbed down again. And Again. And five more times, until a blow sent him reeling in the dirt, and Corin an Fol knew no more.

Glossary

Kelwyn

Queen Ariane.

Lord Raule Calprissa, her consort formerly known as Tarello.

Captain Garland.

Lieutenant Doyle.

Garland's Troop:

Pash.

Coife.

Taylon.

Mullen.

Kargon.

Tol.

Ptarni

King Akamates, recently deceased.

Callanz, his son. Self-styled god-emperor.

Tam, a former warrior now fugitive.

Teret, his wife.

Sulo, a renegade from Rorshai.

Rol Sharn, a merchant.

Red, a tavern owner.

Ysaren, the Seeress at the Lake of Stones.

Tseola

Stogi, a cattle rustler.
Broon, Stogi's former leader.
Stogi's family:
Hanadin.
Rholf.
Hulda.
Shel.
Seek, a shaman from Dunnehine.

Laregoza

The Rana, ruler of Largos.
Topaiz, her seneschal.
Bruhan Dahali, an officer from Talimi Garrison.
Callicastez, a soldier.

Rundali

Jynn the Piper, guardian of the crossroads.
Elerim, an enchantress in Rundal Woods.
Solace, custodian of the Manor in the Woods.

Shen

The Magister, an important official.
Tai Pei, a slave, formerly of House Zayn.

Gwelan

Carlo Sarfe, a shipwrecked sailor from Gol.
Boal, a zealot.
Carys, a young woman.
The Grogan, a steel-clad giant.

Venland

Marei, a widow. Proprietress of Torrigan's Tavern.

Dafyd, her son.

Rosey, his sweetheart.

Gray Wash Hall

The Chamberlain, himself.

Cille, a sorceress, sister to Ysaren and Elerim.

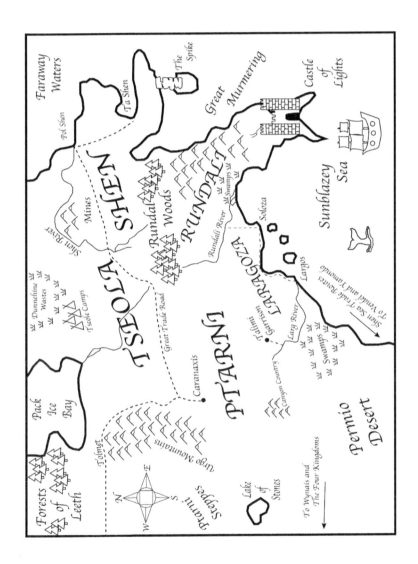